I0772729

the RISE

the RISE

CHRISTOPHER COSMOS

This is a story for all those
who never stopped searching for it.

A Note to the Reader

I'M HERE TO TELL YOU A STORY.

It's a story of how it all began, and of how everything came to be, in the beginning. Yes, that beginning, the one all the way back, the one we don't talk about anymore and dismiss as easily as all of the too many untruths that have been told and spread and believed since it happened, the ones we've tried to pass off as myth and explain away with things like science and law, and all else we've come now to call fact, or perhaps more boldly, "accepted narrative," but that's why I'm here, because me . . .

I'm here to tell you the truth.

I've heard they call Phosphorus other things now—Lucifer, Satan, or the Devil himself, even—and I've heard them claim that in our first hours she came from him, from a tiny, small piece under his arm, and that she was given so he wouldn't be lonely, as if anything was given just for one and not both, as if that type of judgment could come from God. And when I first heard all these things, I wondered how many more lies there were, and why they had been told, and for whose benefit, but there were so many I couldn't keep track.

And so that's why I'm here.

I'm here to tell you what really happened, all the way back, when everything began. How could I possibly know all this, you might be wondering, or why should you believe my story instead of all the others?

It's simple actually.

I know, because I was there.

I saw all that I'm about to describe, I was a part of it, and I fought, too, and more than the fighting, or the seeing, and more than anything else that happened at the beginning . . .

I also felt.

And that's important.

I know it might not be clear right now who I am, and the part I played in all I'm about to tell, but it will be by the end if you follow closely, and if you trust me. If you look inside, and if you find what's hidden there, then you will know me, I promise, you will always know me, from now until the end, and you'll also realize that you always have.

Are you ready?

Because if you are . . .

I'm here to tell you a story.

Prologue

*H*IGH ABOVE ALL that would soon be, Michael sat by himself and wept, because he knew the Kingdom of Heaven was broken. It was all he'd ever known, and now it would be gone in a blink, in an instant, in the exact length of time in which most momentous change occurs and it would never be able to return or come back as it once had been, not with what must happen, he knew, and with what must now come, and that was why he wept.

It was failure, he knew, and it was irrevocable.

And it was also a failure he felt acutely as his own.

The kingdom had been his responsibility to guard and protect, and he'd been given both strength and truth to do so, and so why had he failed? He let himself think back and wonder when it had happened, when it had gone wrong, and if there was anything he could have done to prevent it. As those thoughts all came to him, flooding with waves of pain and guilt, they settled for a moment, but then after they settled they shifted, changed, then came from a different place: they came from somewhere deeper, somewhere much deeper, and the guilt and pain that had been there before began to slowly, slowly, slowly get swept away until all that was left was truth, and not thoughts of the past anymore . . . but a vision of the future.

Tragedy and change occurs, he knew.

But with it could also be brought opportunity.

And that's what he then saw.

He saw what everything would lead to, what would soon be made, and he also saw the great and profound addition of that which was still yet to come and the effect it would have on this Creation and all else, too. He was grateful for this new vision that he was sure had come from God, and he was also grateful for the hope it brought with it, and so with some semblance of peace then inside him, he slowly wiped the tears from his cheek.

He looked around, near where he'd been sitting.

He looked at the palace, next to him, and the high walls.

He knew that all the others were gathered inside and waiting for him there—gathered and waiting for his judgment—and before he left to give it to them, he took a moment to pause, and he looked inward again.

This was now the moment, he knew.

This was now the moment when everything would change, for one way or the other, and a collective future would be born and begin to take shape and that future would grow and spread and expand into something brave and bold and new. And while this future was something he'd just seen glimpses of, only glimpses, in that collective future he'd seen, he also saw eternity.

He saw eternity both for him, and for all else that there was, and would be.

And it was time for that eternity now, he knew, and it couldn't wait any longer.

So, he finally stood . . .

And then he began to walk.

HE WALKED TOWARDS the high walls of the palace that were there at the edge of Heaven and then he went under them and into the great and wide courtyard where they were all gathered in a large circle. They were all there and already waiting for him, the entirety of the host of

Heaven, all wearing bright, shining breast-plates and polished armor, with swords strapped at their sides and strung across their backs, all of these gathered angels who were dressed as warriors.

And there was another that was there, in their midst.

He was larger and older than the others, and he seemed to shine brighter than all the rest, too, and he stood with his head bowed in the center of their circle and when the other angels saw Michael approaching, the circle parted and Michael walked inside of it to face the one that was there waiting. They were both still for a moment, both these two angels of the same size and age and brilliance, as Michael stood in front of him.

Then the angel with the bowed head spoke.

"I know that you've seen it, too," he said very quietly, without looking up. "I know that you've seen it, Michael, and felt it, what is to come, the same as I have."

Michael hesitated, paused.

He hadn't realized that the vision he'd just been given hadn't been given only to him, but rather it had been shared with another, too, and though he didn't yet know why it had been shared, and this new information took him by surprise, Michael was an angel of truth, and so truth is what he spoke.

"Yes," he said, nodding, acknowledging. "I've seen it."

"And you'll just accept his judgment?" the bright angel with the bowed head asked. "You'll just accept that all we were born for was to serve?"

"We were born through his will," Michael answered. "And so it's his will that we answer to."

"Then why would we be made to feel what we feel?" the angel asked, then finally raised his head and as he looked up his beautiful eyes flashed as they met Michael's, and they stayed there. They were irrevocably linked, Michael knew, as they were the two angels of all the entire host of Heaven who had been given this vision of what was to come: Michael, the angel of strength and truth, and Phosphorus, his friend, and the angel of light.

"We've been given exactly what we've been given," Michael spoke, his voice pitched lower, "and it's for reasons that are his own, as it always is and will be."

"So join me then," Phosphorus' eyes flashed again. "Give in to what you feel, to what we know is inside of us, *both* of us, and we'll rule together."

"You know that I won't."

Phosphorus paused then and looked back at Michael across from him, his bright and unwavering eyes filled with purpose and conviction, and he recognized again the gift of his friend. "He may have given you strength, Michael," Phosphorus finally responded, his lips slowly turning up into a small smile now. "But he gave me something, too. Something besides just light."

"And what's that?"

"I daresay you'll soon find out."

Michael stood a little bit taller and put his hand on the hilt of the sword he wore at his hip as all the other angels watched closely what would happen. "You've made your heart known, Phosphorus," Michael said. "So now it's time for you to face your judgment."

Then there was an even longer pause between them with all the other angels waiting to see what the bright one would do, knowing he wasn't as strong as his friend across from him. Phosphorus' lips were still turned up into a very small smile, and they stayed that way—they didn't move, or change, not at all—as he spoke for the last time as an angel of God:

"If it's judgment that I deserve," he said, very quietly, "I suppose it's judgment that will come."

Then Michael and Phosphorus each drew their swords.

There were bright flashes of light on steel as metal scraped against metal and wings quickly exploded from where they'd been tucked behind their backs.

They looked at each other there, in the courtyard, everyone gathered around them waiting, watching, for just one more moment.

Then they flew across the distance between them.

They covered the ground in less than the blink of an eye, each with sword raised, powerful wings pumping and outstretched, and they swung.

Metal crashed against metal for the first time and that loud and terrifying thunder of betrayal echoed through every known and unknown corner of Heaven as in front of the gathered angels the great battle began.

Phosphorus flew high into the air.

Michael rose quickly, after him.

Their duel was a dizzying dance as they ascended into the white and clouded sky, Phosphorus using his agility as they fought, and Michael using his strength.

The angels below watched as their two oldest and strongest were pitted against each other, more thunder echoing as their swords *clang, clang, clanged* again, the blows between them becoming even stronger, then Michael unleashed a great haymaker which left his own midsection vulnerable and he was cut across the torso by a blow from Phosphorus' sword, but as the blow came it brought Phosphorus closer to him—*too close*—and even through the pain from his wound, Michael grabbed the other angel and used all his strength to hurl him down through the air and crashing into the ground.

The stone beneath Phosphorus cracked and broke.

Michael descended after him in a flash, as Phosphorus painfully stood, but Michael was already there and grabbed him again and threw him against a nearby pillar, which also shattered, and Phosphorus' sword fell from his hand.

The gathered host watched as Phosphorus stood, once more, for the last time.

He reached for his sword, but Michael was there first, and he kicked it away.

"Kneel," Michael said with steel in his voice as he looked down at the unarmed and defeated angel in front of him and seemed to grow in stature as he did.

"No," Phosphorus shook his head. "Not ever again."

"He gave you everything," Michael whispered softly.

"Not everything," Phosphorus smiled.

"Why did it have to be you?" Michael asked, and the pain of this betrayal was in his eyes then, too, and in his voice, as the two angels came to what they both knew was going to be the end. "You were his favorite," he continued. "You were the Light-Bringer, the Morning Star, the Shining One . . ."

"I am only as he made me," Phosphorus responded, very slowly, but with a truth in his words that Michael recognized. "So what I felt, and what I still feel . . . if all indeed does come from him, as you say, then that must be from him, too, right? And you know as well as I do, Michael, what that means . . . because it means I'm not the only one to feel it, not the only one to which it was given."

Michael paused at those words because he again recognized truth, but he firmly shook his head and put it from his mind because he knew what he had to do, what came next. The two angels stood and looked at each other, each bleeding from their wounds, Michael's eyes filling with his strength and purpose, and Phosphorus' with his own belief, too, and something else, something that Michael wasn't quite able to place, or understand, as it was something he'd only heard spoken about.

But Michael wouldn't focus on that now.

He'd only focus on what needed to be done.

"Do you have any last words for him, before it ends?" Michael asked instead.

"He knows what's in my heart," Phosphorus answered. "So I have no need of words."

"Then I pray that's enough," Michael said, and he nodded to his friend, one last time. He took a step back and closed his eyes and as he did his body began to glow with a bright cobalt blue aura, starting and originating from inside him—deep inside his very essence and being— then growing, expanding, and the light that came from it was blinding, even there amongst the light of the heavens and Michael himself even seemed to grow, breathing deeply, powerfully, and his final word was given: "Phosphorus, Light-Bringer, Morningstar, once-proud angel of God and friend to all who stand before you now in judgment, you are hereby banished from Heaven and this Kingdom and all of God's dominion, to spend the rest of eternity in darkness, and for him that was once light, there will now be no more."

Phosphorus opened his mouth, one last time, for one last response, but just before it came—

The cobalt blue aura exploded, in a great shower of light.

It enveloped him and lifted him from his feet and threw him from the palace, out into the heavens, past stars and planets, through space and time and on towards the vast darkness that was away and beyond.

Then when he was gone, it was quiet in the palace again, and all of Heaven.

Michael closed his eyes and a tear slipped down his cheek, as all the gathered angels started to slowly disperse and leave.

But two of them stayed, and came forward.

"Let me look at it," Raphael said, the first, an angel of both wisdom and healing, as he gestured towards the wound that was on Michael's torso, but Michael shook his head.

"No," he said, still not opening his eyes because the wound to his flesh wasn't what he was feeling and wasn't why he wept.

"What was the Light-Bringer talking about?" the second angel asked in a low, deep voice; Gabriel was an angel of strength, larger than all the others, and he was also the leader of God's armies.

"When?" Michael answered him.

"The vision that he saw," Raphael spoke softly. "The one he said you *both* saw."

There was a long moment as he thought about the question, then Michael finally wiped the tears from his cheek before he opened his eyes and turned to look at the worried faces of the two angels next to him and when he saw their eyes, he knew then why Phosphorus had said what he'd said: Michael recognized the doubt that Phosphorus had wanted to create and spread, and what his purpose was in creating it, what he was trying to sow, even in his final moments of covenant. "God is going to create a new world," Michael finally answered, giving truth to the others, always giving truth, what they needed. "And this new world is going to be his gift."

"His gift for who?" Raphael raised his eyebrows.

"New beings, that he'll shape and create in his own image, but that will have their own choice and will." And as Michael spoke, he saw bits and pieces again of what he'd already seen and a smile finally came to his lips then, too, through the sadness, but there was still uncertainty in the eyes of the other angels as they stood there with Michael, the three of them, together, in the shadows of the tall and un-breached walls of Heaven.

"Do you think that wise, to allow them that?" Gabriel finally asked. "Phosphorus was given the same gift, and we've seen what he chose to do with it."

"It's his word, Gabriel."

And then Michael was silent again, for a moment, and the other angels were silent, too, as they all turned inward together and they each thought of everything that had happened and perhaps everything they knew then would before Michael spoke again, his final words, or perhaps his first, and he also knew they were the only ones they would need, from that moment until the very end of the eternity he'd already seen . . .

"It's God's word," Michael said. "And so it will be."

BEFORE

1

SHE OPENED HER EYES.

If she had known how important this moment was or would be she would have perhaps done it slower, or with more ceremony, but instead she just quickly opened them and then inhaled sharply at her first experience of sight.

It was a deep, purposeful breath.

The first breath of life.

Then with her lungs filled she blinked against the bright sun that was shining directly in her eyes, and as she did, and her eyes closed again, then opened, she looked around: the first thing she saw was the great mountains that were in the distance in front of her, and then she saw the waterfall that rushed and tumbled off the edge of them and plunged down to crash against the rocks below. And then she looked further and saw that the water that crashed against the rocks formed a large pool, which turned into a river that flowed away from the mountains, and her eyes followed the river as it wound and twisted and came closer towards where she was sitting. Then her eyes moved again and she saw the field she was in, that was surrounding her, full of dandelions and thousands of other wild flowers, and the dense forest that was beyond the field, in the opposite direction of the mountains and the waterfall. And after she took all that in—everything she could see, and all the details that went along with it—she waited for another moment, took another deep breath, then slowly stood.

She didn't know her name, or where she was at.

She didn't know who she was, or even what.

But she knew beauty, because she'd just seen it.

She looked down at her hands, next to her side, and her legs, and her feet.

She wasn't sure what she was supposed to do with them, so she let her mind ask for guidance and as soon as she did, she then felt something, that came from deep inside of her, deep in what she didn't yet know was called her stomach, and she listened to what she felt.

It told her to go to the river that was flowing from the distance.

She could hear the pleasant sound the river created, the sound of water rushing over the smooth and polished stones that were there on the river bed, and she didn't know why it was so pleasant, only that it was.

So, she began to walk.

She found her legs were wobbly and weak at first, but then with every step they seemed to get stronger. She walked slowly, going through the wide field of ankle-length grass in which she'd woken up, past the dandelions and wild flowers, touching them with her hand as she went, smelling the refreshing and beautiful scents, more and more confidence and strength coming with each step, then she was to the water.

She bent down next to it.

She didn't yet know what it was called, that which was there in front of her, but just that she was thirsty and it was water she needed. So she put her hands into the cool stream and cupped them together in the current and brought what was there in her palms up to her lips to drink. She drank, then drank again. When she was full, she looked back down at the stream once more, and as she did, she paused, because that's when she saw her reflection for the very first time and she thought she would have been more startled at its sight, but she found that she wasn't.

She stared back at herself.

Then she used the image she saw in the reflection to reach up with her hand and touch her nose, mouth, cheek, jaw, feeling the contours, the subtleties, the shape, her first glimpses of herself and the miracles that were possible in Creation. She continued to feel and touch then finally ended on looking back at her deep, brown-colored eyes, and though she didn't yet know the word for soul she somehow knew she'd just seen it.

The feeling inside her came again, the one that came from her stomach, and she listened.

That's me, it told her.

And so she knew that it was.

She stood from the stream and looked into the distance.

She could see where the river and the water went and the direction in which it continued to flow, but she couldn't see where it ended, and she wondered about that. And as she let herself wonder, enjoying how wonder felt, she then heard again the voice that was inside her: she heard what it said, and that it was time, it told her, to keep walking. It was time to keep following the river onwards towards where it bent and rolled into the distance, into the unknown, towards where she couldn't see, always towards where she couldn't see.

Once again, she listened to what came from inside . . .

And so she began to walk.

SHE DIDN'T KNOW how long she walked, or why she stopped.

She had followed the river for some time: she'd gone through a large forest, then far enough to where when she looked behind her, the mountains that were there when she'd woken had become much more distant. She could barely see them, rising above the tops of the trees, and she found she could no longer hear the sound of the great waterfall that came from them and crashed down against rock below, either, and as she was thinking about that sound, she found she was thirsty again so she went to the bank of the river and bent down and cupped her hands in the water like she'd done before, and she drank.

Then she stood again.

She turned and was about to keep walking, to continue down the river towards wherever else it might lead, and that's when she heard the voice coming from behind her, and she was startled.

"Thank goodness," the voice said. "I was so afraid."

And she realized something about the voice, as she first heard it . . .

She realized it didn't sound like her own, that she heard inside herself.

Then she quickly turned and saw the man that was there in the distance, coming from the depths of the forest and towards her, and even though she had just heard that his voice was strange—lower, and pitched different than her own—and she could see he looked different, as well, she also could see he was the same as she was, too.

She didn't know how she knew . . .

But she did.

"Who are you?" she asked him.

"I don't know," he answered, staring back at her.

"What were you afraid of?" she wondered, looking back at his face, too, at his eyes, then hearing her own words and voice spoken aloud for the first time and realizing that she was right, after all, and that her voice didn't sound the same as his.

"What?" he asked.

"You said that you were afraid."

He hesitated for a moment, almost as if he regretted what he'd just said, and he waited so long she thought he wasn't going to answer.

But then he did.

"I was afraid I was alone," he finally said.

And they stood there for a moment, looking at each other, and she felt for the first time something that even if she'd lived a million more years she wouldn't be able to describe, at least not the strength and depth of that first time she felt it, in those woods, and next to that river. She wondered about that feeling, and then he spoke again:

"Where were you going?" he asked her.

"I saw this river," she nodded towards it, "and so I decided to follow it."

"Follow it to where?"

"I don't know . . . to wherever it led, I suppose."

He looked back at her, and opened his mouth, about to speak again, but then seemed to change what he was going to say and instead settled on something different.

"Is it alright if I go with you?" he asked instead.

And as soon as he'd asked, she saw his lips begin to turn up into a smile as he looked at her, and even if neither of them yet knew that's what it was called, they both knew it was good, so she let her lips turn up, too, and she smiled at him in return, then she nodded.

"Of course," she told him.

And so they began to walk.

They went in silence for some time, and she looked over at him as they walked together. She had already heard his voice, and how it was different than her own, and she took in other differences then, too: she saw how he was taller than her, and how his chest was shaped differently than her own, as well as his face, the lines of bone in his cheek, his jaw, and the definition of the muscles in his arms and back. And as they went, she saw him looking at her, too, and knew he was seeing the same things, the differences in her own body, where her own muscle was gathered more in her thighs and legs, and how her face was formed differently than his own.

They kept going, then soon came to a clearing.

It was near a bend in the river, and they saw that in this clearing there were just two trees and because somehow these trees felt more important than all the other trees they'd passed, they paused, and looked at them, taking each of them in. One of the trees was very large, they saw, and towered above all the others that they'd passed in the forest, and the other one was smaller, much smaller, closer to the ground and with more gnarled branches coming from the limbs. These trees were surely different than all the others they'd seen, they each thought, and though they didn't yet know why they thought that, they did, and they were sure.

"What do you think they are?" he finally asked.

"I don't know," she answered, still looking at them, feeling their presence as much as seeing it, as they stood there in front of them.

And then they received their answer.

"The smaller one is the Tree of Life," a strong, truthful voice said from behind them. "And the larger one, next to it . . . that's the Tree of Knowledge."

They both quickly turned and she saw Michael walking towards them, coming from the forest in the same way the man had before, and Michael was no longer dressed in his bright and polished armor, but rather a simple, white tunic, with his wings folded and hidden underneath it, and he carried no weapon, either. She thought of the voice she'd just heard, and she realized that it wasn't like his, the man that was next to her, and it wasn't like hers, either, it was somewhere between them in tone and tenor. She studied him closely for a moment, taking all this in, turning it over in her mind, deliberating, analyzing, and then she asked him:

"Who are you?"

"A messenger," Michael answered.

"A messenger from whom?" the man narrowed his eyes, stepping forward.

"From God," Michael smiled, reassuring him. "Who made you both in his own image, and brought you here to his Creation."

"His . . . Creation?" she wondered at the word, but she also heard the truth that was in Michael's voice, so she knew that it was.

"Yes," he told her.

"To do what?" she asked him.

She looked back at Michael as he let this question linger there between them. And as he did, she then turned to look at the man next to Michael, the man she'd travelled down the river with and who had been quiet during most of this exchange, and it was almost as if by seeing him there it was answering her question for her, though she didn't yet know it. Their eyes were together then, the two humans. The man finally began to relax in Michael's presence, and as he did, she could see in his eyes the same questions that were in her own—perhaps not the answers, but definitely the questions—as well as many other things, too, and she knew they were each then wondering the exact same things:

Who are we?

Why are we here?

And what's our purpose?

They were each then wondering for the first time all those questions that are meant to be asked and perhaps not ever meant to be known or answered—just asked—which Michael also saw as he kept smiling back at them both, there at the beginning, at the first steps being taken.

"What you do here . . ." Michael finally said. "That will be up to you."

"That's your message?" she asked him.

"Yes."

"So what comes next?"

"That will be your decision to make."

"Who was created first?" the man asked abruptly, breaking his silence and interrupting the conversation and she saw Michael frown as he heard the question. She turned and looked at him next to her, and she wondered where the question had come from—if it had come from deep inside him, from his own voice that perhaps spoke to him in the same way that hers spoke to her—and she also wondered why it needed to be asked, and what answer he was hoping to hear.

There was a long silence.

And then the angel spoke again.

"What do you mean?" Michael finally said. "You're both here. You've both been made."

"I was in the forest," the man explained. "I heard the water, when I first woke up, so I decided to walk towards it and when I finally reached it, she was already there waiting."

Michael was silent again, for a moment, as he took the man in, and his words.

Then Michael stood straighter, taller, some inches above the height in which the humans before him stood. "You were both created at the same time, from the same things, and in the exact same way," Michael finally answered. "That was his will."

"How do you know?"

"Because God has spoken to me, and I've felt him, and if you give yourself to him as I have then you will feel him, too, and hear, and then you'll know as I know."

She had been looking between them and then watched as the man received this information, and she saw the change that came to him when he did. She wondered why he'd asked what he'd asked and why it seemed so important to him because somehow she knew that it was, and it was her own voice, that thing deep inside her that she'd already learned to listen to that told her it was, even if she didn't yet know why.

Then she felt something else, something that also came from her stomach.

Hunger.

"What are we to do here to sustain ourselves?" she asked Michael instead, thinking about this new feeling that she was experiencing.

The angel smiled again, and the moment that had come before was gone.

"That's a very good question," Michael answered. "I'll show you, and you'll learn. You have everything here that you need to survive."

She had asked the question in innocence, because she had just felt hunger, and she didn't yet know anything about life, and seeds, and the tilling of the soil, and the growing of plants and fruits and nuts that would be picked and consumed and would nourish their bodies. And she also didn't yet know anything of shelter, and community, and home, and family, and all the other things that are built and would also soon come as life began together there in that clearing that would soon be made their own, deep in the heart of this new Creation that had been made just for them and all else that was there. Neither of them could see glimpses of the future, as Michael had, so neither of them could yet know how their life would expand, and grow, and change, the same as everything else around them, and that they too would be no exception to those rules, and that they would be part of all that they saw, as well.

She didn't yet know any of those things, and neither did he.

But Michael did.

And so he would show them.

$$2$$

$\mathcal{D}$EEP IN THE DARKNESS, in the place that had no name, he lay on the ground.

He was covered by a pile of rubble from where he'd burst through the ancient ceiling made of carved and ageless rock and had fallen down to land on the cold, dusty stone floor, in the dark and forgotten place where he'd been driven to, out of his home and across space and time by Michael's strength and judgment.

He thought he was dead, or gone beyond . . .

But he wasn't.

For a moment he wished that he was, but then the moment passed.

He slowly lifted his head and pushed himself further up and then saw where he'd fallen. He saw how the ceiling above him was cracked and broken from where he'd plunged through it, then he looked around at the walls on each side of him, carved from dark stone, and the state of disrepair it'd all been allowed to fall into, this place where he'd landed that had clearly been a once-great palace, and then as he continued to look around, he saw something else:

He saw a throne.

It was on the far side of the room, and made of polished, carved obsidian.

And the sight of the throne seemed to change him as he began to slowly push the rocks off himself that had broken and fallen from the ceiling, when he'd crashed through, and then he painfully stood. He brushed the rest of the dust away and then began to walk towards the throne. When he'd finally crossed the chamber and reached it, he bent down and felt the eternal stone—cool under his touch—and just as he felt it there was something important he then knew, that came to him in a flash, in an instant. It was something important and something he'd thought he'd known and felt before, deep inside himself, and now he had his confirmation.

It was true, just as he'd told Michael.

He wasn't the first.

Because there was the evidence, right in front of him, there in the darkness.

Another small smile came to his lips as he realized this, the very same as the small smile that had come during his last moments in Heaven—because if he wasn't the first, then he was correct, and he wouldn't be the last or the only, either—and then he saw in the reflection of the obsidian his own once-bright eyes that had been turned completely dark, the solemn color of ash. It shocked him when he first saw it, but then he realized it didn't matter because there in that throne and in that darkness and in that ruined but once-great palace was his validation, his validation for all that he felt inside, the way he always *knew* he'd been made, just as he'd told Michael. Because he knew then that was truth, too. And with all of those feelings swirling inside of him, he turned and walked away from the throne, because he also knew it wasn't time yet, and there'd be time for that later, time for it when it had been truly earned so he left the throne behind and went towards a door that was there on the far wall, then he went through the door, and outside.

As soon as he set foot outside, he coughed violently.

The air was thick and humid, full of swirling dust, and he wasn't used to a place like that, a place without light. He finally gathered himself, clearing his lungs, holding a hand over his nose and throat.

Then he looked up.

He looked up to see that he stood underneath a sky full of black ash and dark clouds, and the dirt that was being picked up by the wind and swirled in front of him was the same black color. He watched as more of it was picked up and blown across the dry, cracked earth, then he squinted his eyes and further out and away from the palace he saw there was a large lake made of flaming, bright fire.

Phosphorus took in all of this.

He took in this kingdom.

For he knew then that it was indeed a kingdom, because if there was a palace and a throne, then that meant there had been a king there, one that came before him, one that he didn't know.

Did Michael know him, though?

And did God?

He thought of this and the great darkness rose again inside of him as he thought of all that had been kept from him and then as he continued to look out on all that was there before him, he wasn't surprised when he saw a solitary dot on the horizon, cutting down from above and through the dark clouds, over the lake of fire and heading towards the palace that had been built many eternities before and as the angel flew, Phosphorus recognized him.

The angel landed, and then came closer.

"What are you doing here, Báal?" Phosphorus asked.

Báal coughed, too, as he turned and looked behind them at the lake of fire for a moment, and the cracked earth around it, then he turned to look at the high palace walls under which they stood together—the walls that were not so very different than the walls of Heaven, which they both knew so well—before he finally turned even further and met Phosphorus' once-bright eyes with his own.

"I've come here to serve," he finally said, through his dust-filled lungs.

"You've come here to serve who?" Phosphorus asked.

"We weren't all made of light and strength, the way that Michael was, and the way I once thought you were," Báal answered him. "And you gave voice to that, to all those who were made differently, and who have felt what you've felt, too . . . something that Michael will never know, or the rest of them, the rest of his host who are strong and brave and truthful and only wish to use that for one reason, and one reason alone."

"No, you're right, he hasn't known that which you speak of yet, Báal, but I know him better than anyone," Phosphorus answered. "He hasn't known darkness, or the other, that which dwells and burns deep within us . . . but it's in him, too, whether he'll admit it or not. I've seen it, and felt it there. And so he still might."

"I heard him speak of the vision," Báal continued. "The one that you both saw, the vision of eternity."

"And?"

"It's begun. God's made his new world, and in it he's created a woman, and a man, too."

"He's created what?" Phosphorus frowned, not yet familiar with the words.

"New beings, shaped in his own image. Humans, they're called."

Phosphorus paused at that as he looked back at Báal, studying the angel's eyes with his own as he took in this new information and realized the name of that which he'd already seen, and he processed it all, and what it might mean for them, for all of them. "If he created these humans," Phosphorus spoke, very slowly, "then they will serve him."

"No," Báal shook his head. "He may have created them, even in his own image, but they know nothing of God yet. They've learned nothing of him, or his ways."

Phosphorus took that in.

And then it struck him.

Like a bolt of lightning it came, and just as powerfully and quickly, just like a new person in a new land opening their new eyes for the very first time. And when it came, it serviced that same feeling that Phosphorus had felt all his life, the one that had been there since before he could remember and made him different than Michael, he knew, and different than all the other angels who served him and it was the same feeling that had led him there to this dark kingdom, and what would soon be his dark throne.

He didn't know anything about humans, at least not yet . . .

But he knew about nature, and that which can burn within.

And he also knew the strength in which that nature can burn.

"If they know nothing of him or his ways, then perhaps they should learn something else instead," he spoke very softly.

Hearing those words, Báal nodded . . .

And he knew that he'd come to the right place.

Phosphorus began to walk away from the palace and the walls.

He began to walk out towards the lake of fire that was there in front of them, and as he went, Báal watched, then called after him.

"Where are you going?" he asked.

"To see these new humans for myself," Phosphorus answered, without turning around. "I want to see them myself, so that we can know them, and discern their weaknesses."

"And what of me?"

"Fly to every corner of the kingdom. Find all those who share our dissent and pride and making, all those born of God and Heaven, the same as we were, but desirous of something more. Find all those souls, Báal, and bring them here to me."

"Yes, my Lord."

"No," Phosphorus said, and he paused. "Not yet."

"If not yet," Báal asked, "then when?"

Phosphorus took in the angel's words as he thought again of the dark throne of obsidian that was there inside the ancient and ruined palace from which he'd just come. He thought again of that throne, and who else had sat there, and who else would, then he finally turned back to Báal, very slowly, and as he did there was a new smile that was on his lips, one just for him, and for all that he knew then would be.

"Soon, my friend," he said. "Very soon."

Then Phosphorus spread his great wings.

And he exploded into the ash-dark sky.

PHOSPHORUS CAME silently to the forest.

When he had been cast out from above, as soon as he'd been defeated and Michael's aura had begun to grow, and change, he'd lost his power. He'd felt it leave from inside of him, as clearly as he'd ever felt anything, but when he'd fallen into the darkness below, he'd also felt it return again, little by little. And while it had returned while he was there in darkness he wasn't surprised to feel that it had begun to fade once more as soon as he'd left, and with every moment he'd gone further from the darkness it became less and less, until he'd landed in God's new creation and could barely feel any of it at all anymore, the same as above.

Phosphorus knew what that meant.

It meant he was vulnerable in this new world, the same as in Heaven.

And he also knew he needed to find out how that vulnerability could be overcome.

It was all information that he stored, and he knew he would come back to in the near future, but instead he would focus on the moment, on the present, on the task at hand as he made his way through the many trees that were there in front of him, on his way to the clearing which the humans would soon make their home. He walked amongst the trees, stopping in any darkness and shadow he could find, to make sure he wasn't seen. Then, the trees began to part, as he kept walking, and he saw Michael. He was standing there in the clearing, in front of him, and it was the first time that Phosphorus had seen him since he'd been cast out from above and unmade, and emotions swirled within him, and not all of them were dark. He kept looking, past Michael, and he then saw the two new creatures Michael was speaking to—the humans that Báal had told him about, the ones that had been made in God's image—and when Phosphorus turned his eyes from Michael and looked upon their faces for the first time, he inhaled sharply in the darkness where he hid because he was surprised to see in them so much of the same that he knew was in his own.

He froze for a moment, which he hadn't done in recent memory, or perhaps ever at all.

He froze, because he was shocked.

That hadn't been what he'd expected.

Then he felt uncertainty, and that was a new feeling for him, too.

But then he knew he needed to put this discovery about the humans from his mind so he tucked it away for later thought and deliberation; he tucked it far away along with the other discoveries he'd already made about strength and power since he'd left light and darkness, because none of those were the reasons he was there in Creation and in that moment, those weren't the thoughts he needed. And besides, it wasn't doubt he'd asked and searched and fallen for—it wasn't doubt at all—so he shook his head and listened to their conversation from afar.

He listened as Michael took fruit from a tree, and showed it to them.

He told them how it could be eaten and that it was sweet when it was bitten into. Then he showed them the seeds that were there hidden inside the flesh, and how the earth could be moved and the seeds placed in it and covered again and where the seeds were placed, more fruit would grow, and the garden would expand.

"This seed will soon become a tree," Phosphorus heard Michael say. "It will grow into a great tree, like all the others you see around you, and the flowers and fruit that hang from the branches will provide you with your nourishment."

"Nourishment?" Phosphorus heard the woman ask.

"Food," Michael answered. "To sustain life."

Phosphorus watched as she took that in, her hand moving to her stomach, then Michael shifted his attention to the man who was standing there and watching both her and Michael. It was hard for Phosphorus to read what the humans were thinking in that moment, what was hidden there behind her eyes, her hand still on her stomach, and in his eyes, too, as he watched her, as they watched each other. It would be difficult for him to read exactly, he knew, and it would take all his skill to try to understand these new beings who were both different and the same . . .

But he would try.

"And then what do we do?" Phosphorus heard her ask again, turning back to Michael. "What do we do when the garden's grown and we have our nourishment? How do we fill our days then?"

"That will be up to you," Michael told her.

Phosphorus watched as each of the humans heard that and processed it.

And he saw them each process it differently, and he took note of that, too.

That was something, he thought, that difference he saw, and the fact that though they were the same, he knew they were also not the same, at least not in that regard.

And in how many other ways was that also true, he wondered?

He knew that could be one of the keys to discord.

And since he then knew that, he kept watching, and listening.

He saw how the man turned and looked at her, then how she in turn looked at all that was around them, seeing in the great and wide clearing everything it could be and already feeling the pleasure that would come from the work that would be done to make it so.

That's the purpose and future that she saw.

Then she turned, and looked at him, next to her, deep into his eyes . . .

And Phosphorus could tell she saw purpose and future there, too.

"There's only one rule," Michael said, breaking the moment they'd just shared as they both then turned back to look at him. "You shall only eat your own fruit, and that which you grow, and you shall not eat the fruit of the Tree of Knowledge, for if you do then it will be the end of everything—the end of all of this—and your time here. Do you understand?"

She kept looking at the angel . . .

Then she nodded.

"I understand," she said.

And he waited for a moment, just for a moment.

Then he nodded, too, after she did.

"I understand," he said as well.

"Good," Michael smiled at both of them, then he turned to leave.

"Where are you going?" she asked, confused to see him start to leave so soon after he'd just arrived, and told them all of the new and wonderful things she was so glad to know and have learned.

"This is your world now," Michael said very simply, "and as such, it's time for me to go back to mine."

Then they watched together as with nothing further, Michael continued into the forest, in the opposite direction from where Phosphorus waited, hidden in the shadows. They watched as he left, then the woman and man were alone again. They stood there and waited for another moment, each looking at the place where Michael had disappeared, then they turned to the other again, to look at each other one more time, and when she looked at him she took in the differences between them once more: the physical differences, or at least the differences between the way she'd seen herself in the river and the way she saw him in front of her.

"What do you see?" he asked softly.

She waited for a moment.

Then she answered.

"I see you," she told him.

And Phosphorus saw and heard all this, too, from the place where he hid, and even though she didn't yet know it herself—what it was called, and what was happening between them—Phosphorus already did because it was something he'd once felt, too. It was something he'd once felt and still did so he knew how powerful it was, and how it could be used, manipulated, divided, because even then, an eternity and an entire world later, he could still feel it in him as if it was just as fresh as when it had first come. He smiled then, because he knew what he'd been given and that he was now armed with, exactly what he'd come searching for, and even more, besides, so he then walked away from the clearing and away from the forest. He walked back through the trees, in the exact way he'd come, then when he was far enough to not be seen he once again spread his great wings, rose high above Creation, and flew back towards darkness and dust.

"SO IT'S DONE THEN?"

"Yes."

"And now what?"

"Now we wait."

Back at the palace in Heaven, Gabriel and Raphael had seen when Michael had returned, and they had gone to him. Michael had landed just outside the great walls and tucked his wings back close to his body then Raphael had come and asked again about Michael's wound, the one from his battle with Phosphorus, and this time Michael didn't protest when Raphael told him he wanted to treat it. Gabriel watched as Raphael sewed the flesh back together and though the flesh itself could be sewed and mended, they all knew it was a wound that would never fully heal, because of the way it had come, and what it represented. They also knew that perhaps Michael didn't want it to heal, either.

"Do you think that wise?" Gabriel finally asked him.

"Do I think what wise?" Michael asked, frowning as Raphael finished his work, then they both stood.

"Do you think it wise to make that decision," Gabriel answered. "To allow them all the freedom they've been given?"

"It was his word," Michael told them. "You know that."

"But are you sure, though?" Gabriel asked. "Because if they're given will, and if they're given choice, even if it is his word, then they're also given the choice to fall, as the Light-Bringer did."

"Yes, I'm sure. And yes, that's true."

"Then why, Michael? Help us understand. We won't be able to help them if we don't understand."

Michael looked back at Gabriel, the strongest of all their host, then at Raphael, too, their wisest, and he thought back to his time with the new humans in Creation and the information he'd given them. He thought back to how she'd taken it in, and what he'd seen when she did, then he thought back to the last thing he'd said to them, the last thing before he left, before he'd walked a few paces then turned and watched them from the forest and saw the way she looked at him. He saw the way he looked at her, too, and the beginning that was there, as they moved closer, the spark that was in their eyes and the promise of the bright and happy and shared future they could have together.

"Because without their will being free, Gabriel, and without the gift of choice . . ." Michael spoke softly, the vision of all he'd seen still there and dancing in his eyes, " . . . without those things, then they would never be capable of real love."

"Is that so important?"

"It's more than important," he said.

Then he turned back and looked at his friends, standing with him at their place in the light, and Michael's lips finally begin to turn—up, up, up, they went—and he smiled.

He smiled all the way to his eyes.

"It's everything," he finally said.

Then they understood, and the other angels smiled, too.

3

SHE RAN THROUGH the field of dandelions near where she'd
first woken up.

Her legs were more muscled and had become even darker from her
time in the sun, and her lungs had also expanded from what they'd
been before and she found she could run for as long as she wished
without needing to stop. Each day she'd been in Creation she'd gone
progressively further from the clearing, where they'd decided to stay
and make their home, carrying in her hand a woven basket she'd made
in a technique she'd discovered after Michael had left. And while she'd
found a great many things on her first journeys from the clearing, the
discovery she'd made on that particular day made her stomach growl
with hunger and anticipation, which is why she ran, because she couldn't
wait to make it back to show him what it was she'd found, and then,
also, where she'd found it.

She left the field and went through the forest.

She dodged between the trees and branches hanging overhead.

Then the forest started to thin, and she finally came back close to
the clearing, where she began to slow, and in front of her, as the trees
parted, she saw he was still working on the structure they'd created

together, the one which they'd decided to build and call their home. It was a structure that was supported by wide poles that were pushed into the earth, deep down into the soft brown soil in much the same way Michael had shown them how to bury seeds to help them grow. But the poles were only pushed part of the way into the ground; the rest of them rose high into the air to where they supported a roof on top, creating a very tall ceiling and open area below for the wind to pass through and cool them as they slept underneath. At first, when Michael had left, after he'd told them about shelter and the importance of it, they'd decided to work on it together. But then after the poles had been raised, and the roof completed, and it was far enough along for them to sleep under it, that's when she started to venture further out on her own, to explore and search for new foods and things they hadn't yet discovered. And while she did that, he stayed behind in the clearing to keep working on and finishing the structure, as well as tilling the earth around it, in the new garden they'd planted in the way Michael had showed them.

"Look what I found," she said to him, catching her breath.

He was outside their home and in the middle of working on building a flat, raised surface that came up to about their waists. He was sweating as he worked under the hot sun, and when he heard her voice he turned, wiping the moisture from his brow and hair and saw the excitement that was in her eyes as she came out of the forest, and he smiled.

"Let me see," he said.

And then she smiled, too.

She opened the lid to her woven basket and showed him what she carried inside, which was all of the many different new fruits she'd found and brought back: there were pomegranate, oranges, apples, cherries, pears . . . nearly every type of fruit that could be imagined.

"There's so many," he said, looking down into the basket.

"What do you think they taste like?" she asked.

"You haven't tried them?"

"No, I wanted to wait for you."

He turned and looked at her then, deep into her eyes once more, like they'd done so many times already, as he wiped sweat from his brow again.

"I'm excited to find out," he told her.

"So am I."

"So let's try them."

"It's not time for dinner yet."

"It's just us here."

"So?"

"So that means it can be time for dinner, if we want it to be."

She looked back at him, at the glint of perhaps mischief that had come to his eyes—the look of pride that was there, at the power they had over their own fate—then she smiled with him, too, and nodded. She watched as he picked up the four-legged structure he'd been building and carried it inside with them, through the doorway and past the two small beds they'd created to sleep on when the sun went down, and he went towards an empty area of space where there wasn't anything yet: it was a space they hadn't decided how to use, or what to put there, and he set the structure down in the middle of the area. Then he brought two stools he'd also carved from wood and set them around what he'd created, and she understood then what he'd done, how he'd created a place for them to be able to sit and eat together, and talk about their day and anything else that had happened.

She thought about the questions she'd had about him.

She thought about the questions that had come after she'd heard what he'd asked Michael, in those very first moments they'd met.

But then in that moment, looking at what he'd just built and understanding why he'd built it, all those questions washed away as she stared at this simple thing he'd done. She smiled wider than she'd yet smiled in Creation as she put the basket with the fruit on the smooth and flat surface, then they both slowly sat and looked at each other across the freshly carved wood that was more than just wood then, because it was theirs, together.

She looked at his eyes, deep into them.

Then they each took a piece of fruit and they ate.

And as they ate, they set aside all the seeds they found within the sweet flesh.

"It's delicious," he said, licking pomegranate juices from his fingers as he finished the piece he was eating then reached for more. "Where did you find them?"

"There's a field near where I first woke up," she told him, remembering why she'd run back so quickly in the first place. "It's a field full of dandelions and thousands of other wild flowers, then beyond the field there's the mountains, and a waterfall coming off them and leading down to the river, and to where I first saw you."

"And that's where the fruit was?"

"Yes," she nodded. "It's by the same river, only further up, beneath the waterfall. And just think . . . the seeds that are left from them can be planted in our own fields, then the same fruit will grow into an orchard here, too." They ate in silence for another moment as they thought of this, then she looked at him, still licking his fingers, and they each reached for one more piece. "It's beautiful," she continued. "The field of dandelions, and the mountains, and the waterfall. I'd like to show it to you."

"I'd like to see it."

"Tomorrow then."

"I have to continue my work tomorrow."

"It's just us here."

"So?"

"So it can be a day that we go to the waterfall, if we want it to be."

She saw him pause when he heard her words, which were really his words that she'd kept inside and just said back to him, and he stopped eating the fruit for a moment as he looked back at her, at the very serious look she knew was on her face. Then she allowed her lips to turn up and part into a small smile and she saw him realize the game she was playing, then he smiled again, too.

"Then that's what it will be," he said. "We'll go tomorrow."

As they finished the fruit, the sun began to set outside, moving lower and lower in the sky and then behind the tops of the peaks in the distance, the peaks she would show him the next day. So she stood from where they sat and started to gather all the seeds they'd set aside as he then stood, too, and went back outside to find his tools and put them away until they'd be used again: the day after the next one, perhaps . . . the day after they went to the waterfall.

She saw that the sun had almost fully disappeared, behind the mountains.

And with it so too disappeared the light.

She thought back to everything that had just happened, and how she felt. She thought back to sitting there at the table with him, talking about what they'd each done, finding something she wanted to show to him, and how they'd joked about it, and made their plans for the next day. It was something so simple but also so special, she realized. And it was something she knew she always wanted to remember: how such simple things could bring such great pleasures. Thinking back through all of it once more, she also realized that because of it she'd begun to feel closer to him, and more comfortable in his presence, when they were together. It felt good to her then, in a way it hadn't felt before. She thought about that, also, then she thought about what she had seen in his eyes, and the way he'd looked back at her, across the table he'd built, as they ate together and shared their meal, and from what she'd seen she then thought that perhaps maybe he felt that way, too.

These were the last moments of the day.

She watched as he picked up his tools, straining as he carried them, and just as she'd noticed the muscles in her legs had become leaner and more firm, from her running, she also noticed the muscles in his back and arms had done the same thing, too, from his work, and she kept watching as he carried the tools, putting them each away, back into their place until the next day they'd be used.

What's our future, she let herself think.

What's our future here, together.

Then she felt the answer come, from deep inside her again, something she hadn't felt in some days.

The future will be when it's supposed to, the voice said.

She heard and felt the answer to the question she'd asked, and so she would listen and she would also know that what she'd heard wasn't false, but was truth: it was the same as when she'd listened and followed the river which had brought her to him, and then Michael, and the clearing in which they'd made their home and where they were happy.

The sun had completely disappeared behind the mountains, she saw.

And so without any more light, they both then went back inside their house, because then with only darkness left they knew it was time to close their eyes and rest.

He slowly went to his bed, on one side of the room.

She went to hers, on the other.

They looked at each other, one last time, then they turned.

She went to lay down, and he did the same, and as soon as she did and her head touched the pillow she'd made, she cried out in pain. She didn't know what the pain was, or what was happening, or where it had come from; she only knew there was a sharp stinging in her skull just behind her eyes and for a moment it was sharper and more painful than anything she'd ever felt before.

"What is it?" he asked, as he jumped from his bed and rushed over.

She waited for a moment then it started to back away and everything began to go back to normal as she breathed deeply in and out, and when the pain finally left altogether, she realized it left behind one thing, a feeling she'd never felt before: it was a feeling of deep uneasiness, that didn't come from the same place as the other voice in the pit of her stomach, though she felt it *near* the same place, but this feeling was from somewhere else. She thought about it and couldn't make sense of it the way she was able to with the other feelings that had come since she'd woken in Creation. She saw him still there and watching her, with concern in his eyes, and she knew she needed to answer his question.

"I don't know what it was," she finally said.

"What happened?" he asked again, looking at her with his concerned eyes, his eyes that hadn't changed.

And she thought about that.

She thought about how she could possibly explain to him what she'd felt, and then what he would think when he heard it, and she decided she didn't want to; she decided she didn't want him to share in that feeling with her—she would bear it for the both of them, she decided—so instead she just shook her head and told him, quite simply, which was also the truth:

"It's gone now."

"Are you sure?"

She met his eyes again.

He still looked worried.

"I'm sure," she said, then nodded.

He waited next to her for another moment and she watched as he searched her features, perhaps looking for something she wasn't telling him, that she wasn't sharing, before he finally accepted her words and what she'd said then slowly went back to his own bed, looking over his shoulder as they both lay back down again. There was silence in their house once more, but before they each closed their eyes for the second time, they lay on their beds and looked at each other in the darkness—*through* the darkness, across the distance and space between them, in the house they'd built and would continue building—and she let herself wonder again about the pain she'd just felt, and what it might mean. She let herself wonder, just for a moment, but she also knew it was no use wondering too much about it because just the same as had happened with everything else in Creation, it would be made clear to her in time, she knew, and was sure, and so she would accept that.

Then her thoughts returned to the present and she smiled because in the present, she looked forward to the next day, and what it would bring. She looked forward to going to the waterfall and showing him all that she'd found. And with that as her last thought, she closed her eyes, then he did, too, and she closed hers first because she knew as soon she opened them again it would be the next day, and it would be their day . . . and it would once again be beautiful.

HIGH ABOVE IN HIS KINGDOM, at the exact same time she'd cried out in pain, Michael's eyes had snapped open because he too felt the very same pain, deep in his skull, and just behind his eyes. He'd been sitting outside of the tall walls with his eyes closed in thought and prayer and meditation and he'd been focusing on the light, searching for it, reaching for it, as he always did when he prayed, but then change came and the light he saw became clouded by great darkness. It was a darkness that had begun to close in on him and overwhelm him and cast shadow across all he could see, and as soon as it had, that's when he'd felt the pain. He sat there with his eyes open and wondered what it meant, what he'd just seen, and felt, then he heard a voice and knew his answer wasn't going to be very far away.

"Michael!" the voice cried out.

And then Michael turned.

He saw Gabriel hurrying towards him again, leaving the palace and going past the walls.

"What is it, Gabriel?" he asked.

"They're gone," Gabriel said. "They've left."

"Who?"

"Báal, and others with him."

Michael paused, as Gabriel reached him and he took in this information.

And as he did Michael then saw more images and with these new images he felt again the same pain he'd just felt, and the pictures that came to him did so in great bursts, in quick and bright flashes in his mind, and this is what he saw:

A lake of fire.

Black, cracked earth.

A dark palace, and a throne carved from obsidian.

And in the middle of it all, he saw one who had once shone, one who was once a morningstar, a light-bringer, and he saw others that were gathered there with him in darkness: he saw all those that had left Heaven and God's dominion and traveled the same path as the Light-Bringer had travelled, away from that which had made them . . . and down towards that which was clouded and dark and below.

Michael saw all this, and then he knew.

He sighed, with the burden of this vision etched on every line of his face now, and weighing down his strong and broad shoulders.

Raphael had seen Gabriel and Michael together, and he came over then, too, and stood with them.

"What is it?" Raphael asked, studying Michael's face. "What have you seen?"

"They've followed him to darkness," Michael whispered, very quietly.

"Traitors!" Gabriel shouted in his loud and thunderous voice, as others around them and in the distance stopped and looked.

"No, not traitors," Michael shook his head. "Just . . . deceived perhaps."

"So what do we do?" Gabriel asked, his hand moving to the sword that was at his waist. "How do we punish them?"

Michael thought about that for a moment.

He went back through all the images and pictures that had just flashed in his mind, knowing why Phosphorus and the others had gathered below and in darkness, and also knowing what they would want to do when the light was weakened or when it was gone, and so Michael knew what the angels had to do, too, both him and all those that remained by his side, the angels that were still of light.

"The only thing that we must do," he finally said, "is we must protect God's Creation, as we swore we would. We must protect it with all the strength and power that we have."

"How?" Raphael wondered.

Michael turned, and looked directly at both of them:

"Take another with you, Gabriel, and go there," Michael told him.

"Do not enter Creation or disturb the humans, in any way, but we must make sure it's never left unwatched or unguarded again."

"Where would you have us watch them from?" Gabriel asked.

"Aetlas," Michael told him. "The mountain peaks, there at the northern and western edge, far enough away from where they live that they won't see or feel you, but close enough to watch and respond quickly in case he comes."

Gabriel heard Michael's words, and their truth . . .

So he bowed his head.

"It will be as you say," Gabriel answered.

Then he turned to walk away and went a few paces to where he touched another that watched them on the shoulder and whispered in his ear, a young and strong angel named Muriel. They then went a few paces more before they spread their great wings wide and exploded into the sky, on their first journey out and towards that which they had not yet seen, to the new kingdom that God had created, and to protect those that had been made to live there.

Michael looked up, towards the clouds, watching until they disappeared.

And then he watched even after that, after they were gone, still deep and lost in his thoughts.

"And what of me?" Raphael asked him, very softly.

Michael was silent for another moment, then he turned to Raphael.

"I need you here," he told him. "Go and tell the others what's happened, and what I've seen. Make sure they're all ready for what is to come, too."

Raphael heard Michael's words, and then there were none further, and he knew there wouldn't be. So instead of saying anything else, Raphael just put his hand on his friend's shoulder because he knew then what Michael knew, and he felt what Michael felt and even though he knew what the pain he felt was and why it was so deep, it was also a pain that Raphael didn't understand, not fully, and he wouldn't try. So instead they just stood there, together, for a few more moments, before it all began to pass and Michael finally turned to slowly start walking back towards the bright palace and the tall walls; he began to walk back, with Raphael by his side, both angels together as they returned to the light that was still there and had remained.

DEEP IN THE DARKNESS, Phosphorus stood in front of his own ancient walls.

Báal had done as Phosphorus had commanded and gone to every place he'd known to go and he'd spread his message far and he'd spread his message wide. He'd found all those he could find that shared what he and Phosphorus felt, deep inside, and he'd brought them there, to the dark palace with the great and high walls and the wide, long lake brimming with fire in the distance, alongside the scorched and cracked earth. And all those that he'd found and brought, those were the lost souls, the ones that didn't care if they plunged into darkness and exile and other, as long as it fed what was inside of them, that thing that was there and they'd long denied existed. And it was now Phosphorus—the one amongst them who had once shone the brightest—it was him who now allowed them to see and acknowledge and not feel shame about what they knew and felt, and that was why they were there.

They were there for ambition, power, glory.

They were there for all the same reasons the one who was once called Light-Bringer was, because they were the ones who would betray for all that they felt.

And that was also why they would serve him.

"Tell me," Phosphorus asked of them, as he stood in front of the now-gathered host and looked out at each in turn, meeting their eyes with his own from where he stood in front of his tall and dark walls. "Tell me why you're here . . ."

There was silence, for a moment, amongst them, then a voice.

"You know why we're here," one of the larger and older angels named Mamanos answered, stepping forward.

"Of course I do," Phosphorus told him. "But I want to hear you say it."

They all looked at each other for another moment, then at Báal, where he stood next to Phosphorus, in front of the walls, and they met his eyes, too, and Mamanos spoke then, for all of them: "We heard your words, Light-Bringer," he said. "And like you, we also don't wish to spend our lives and eternity serving and bending the knee to another, as Michael would have us do."

"And what makes you think the darkness will be any different than what Michael offers, or any different than what you were given in Heaven?"

"I don't understand," Mamanos frowned.

"There's a throne here, and a palace, and there will be a lord soon, too," Phosphorus looked back at each of them, meeting their eyes again in turn, and with all he counted and recognized he estimated a third of Michael's host had left, and that was a betrayal that would cut deep, he knew.

But it wasn't enough.

Not yet.

"You heard my words, Mamanos," Phosphorus told him, continuing. "You were there, and you heard them, exactly as I spoke them to Michael . . . but you didn't understand."

"What didn't we understand?"

"It's not bending the knee that ruins us: it's being given nothing in return for that service."

Mamanos took that in as Báal stepped forward then, his fingers wrapped around the hilt of the sword that was strapped to his waist. "We have the strength now," Báal said to Phosphorus. "We have the strength to go back and take Michael's kingdom and make it our own, and then there will be enough for all of us, enough to feed all our desires."

"No, not yet," Phosphorus spoke slowly in response, measured and calm. "Michael and his host are still strong, and they still have the strength that comes with Heaven and with light, the strength that we've lost. If we fought them now, we would lose. But there are still other ways."

"What ways?" Báal asked.

"If we want to strike a blow against God," Phosphorus continued, "if we want to strike a greater blow than any we could strike through battle with Michael and his host, then there are other things we can do to hurt him, other things that will hurt much more."

"What things?" Mamanos asked.

"We go after his heart," Phosphorus answered, and he was silent again for a moment.

Then he closed his eyes, and continued, and told them all he'd seen.

"God's built a new world," he said, "and in this new world he's created humans, who he's shaped and molded in his own image. If we want to destroy God, if we want to bring him to his knees . . . then that's how we do it, and where we strike, deep into the heart of his newest and most delicate creations."

Then Phosphorus opened his eyes again, and they all saw them.

They all saw how his eyes were then startlingly bright again with purpose, desire, strength, and if there had ever been any doubt before, there was then none left as to why the one in front of them had once been called Light-Bringer, Shining One, Morningstar.

They cowed in front of his strength, and his power.

They bowed their heads before him, and then Mamanos spoke again.

"Teach us," he whispered.

"We're ready to fight for you," Báal also said, very softly.

"I know," Phosphorus responded. "And the time will soon come, for both those things, but now, right now . . . right now there's something else that still needs to come first."

"What's that?" Báal asked.

Then Phosphorus paused, for another moment, one last time.

He paused for both desire and affect, then he looked out past his walls, past the cracked and dark earth and towards the gathered host of lost souls and dark angels and the lake of fire around which they were gathered, underneath an ash-gray sky that seemed to stretch on and on, forever and ever.

"Sin," he finally said.

And his eyes shone even brighter.

$$4$$

$\mathscr{T}$HE NEXT DAY, both the humans woke before the light.

They rose from their beds and she put hers back the same way it was before they'd slept. She turned and saw he was about to go outside and leave his as it was, unmade, but then he saw what she'd done and she watched as he then stopped and came back to do the same to his, then they went outside together.

She led him away from the clearing, and he followed after her.

She showed him the way she'd walked up the river, towards where they'd first met, in the forest, near the soft bend, then they went past the bend, and further on.

She took him to the place where she'd drank after she woke up and saw herself, her reflection, and she took him past that, too, and to the field of dandelions and wild flowers where she watched as he bent down and plucked one and handed it to her. And she was happy . . . she was happy to be there with him, surrounded by the colors and scents and the wide field of flowers, and she was especially happy about the one that was in her hand that he'd given her.

She pressed the flower flat and tucked it away.

Then she turned and showed him the mountains.

She watched as he took them in, rising high in the distance, his first close glimpses of their towering height, their majesty, their immensity and vast beauty. She let him stare at them for another moment, taking them in with awe, as she continued to look at them, too.

They kept walking.

She showed him the base of the mountains near where the water from the waterfall crashed against rock and turned into river, and she showed him where she'd found the new fruit they'd eaten the previous night and would plant the seeds near their own garden in what they would call an orchard so that the seeds would grow into similar trees and produce more fruit, flowers, blossoms, and sweet scents, and then after she showed him all that, she took his hand and began to lead him up, and higher.

She took him past the waterfall and towards the rocks.

"Where are we going?" he asked.

"This way," she said.

And as the terrain got steeper, they began to climb.

She showed him the way up the steep and sheer faces of cliff and rock next to the tumbling spray of water that crashed down and past them. She watched as he looked down and followed the tumbling water to where he saw it explode against the boulders below, then gently flow from the pool where it collected into the river they both knew so well— the river that went from the northern mountains where they were and wound its way through Creation and back towards the clearing that was their clearing—and when he opened his mouth again, looking at all this from a height and vantage he'd not yet been or seen, she knew he was nervous about the height so she reassured him with a look and touch of her hand to his shoulder.

"It's just up here," she told him.

She could see he trusted her, and so he nodded.

Then, again, they kept going.

She led the way as they continued their climb and soon came to the top of the great waterfall where they walked out onto a smooth piece of stone and from there they were at a height from where they could truly see everything that was in front of them, everything that there was.

They saw the waterfall that was now directly beneath them.

They saw the river they knew, that came from it, and the field, too.

And then after that, they saw the large forest that was beyond the field, and further in the distance she pointed to where they could both just barely make out their clearing and the tops of the two trees that were there—the largest, the one that they'd been warned about, the Tree of Knowledge, and the smaller one, too, the Tree of Life—and they saw the distant outline of the roof they'd built to be their shelter, their house, their home, there amongst the rest of the tall canopy and growth around it.

"It's beautiful, isn't it?" she asked him, her eyes not leaving what was in front of them as she then turned back to look at him and she was glad he was there, and that she was sharing this with him.

"It seems like it goes on forever," he answered, looking even further into the distance.

"I think it does," she said.

And they both looked together, past their house and past their clearing.

They followed the river with their eyes towards where it *flowed, flowed, flowed,* winding through more of the great forest and then bending around other mountains, on and on, through all of Creation, never-ending.

"There's so much," he breathed. "And it's ours. All of it."

"Unless there are others that are here," she said with a frown, turning back to him again.

"If there were," he said, "then we would definitely know by now."

"But if it's as endless as it looks, then there could be others out there in places we don't yet know about. Anything could be out there: more of us, more of them, from above, like the one who came and taught us, or even something else entirely."

"Maybe," he responded, still staring into the endless distance.

Then he nodded and repeated the same word again, softer the second time.

"Maybe . . ."

She watched as he looked out at everything, and she thought about that, his answer, his word, and what she then thought she saw in his eyes. She tried to make sense of what he'd said, and where it was coming from, but she didn't really know what he meant or what the look was that she saw in his eyes but she also didn't want to ruin the day by pressing further, and asking him. She wanted to do what she'd brought them there to do so she put her doubts and worry from her mind as she walked further out onto the piece of stone they were standing on, further out towards the edge and near where the water flowed from the rock and plummeted *down, down, down* in a dizzying drop towards the boulders, and pool, and the start of the river.

"Are you ready?" she asked, turning back to look at him.

"Ready for what?" he responded, finally tearing his own eyes from the distance, from all that lay in front of them, to look at her now, there next to him.

"To trust me," she said.

"I do trust you," he answered, frowning.

"I know."

"So what do you want me to do?"

"Come here."

He hesitated for a moment, as she watched him.

Then he finally walked towards her, out towards the place where she was standing while being very careful not to lose his balance or look down, but then he did, and looked over the edge, the same as she'd done, and he saw what she'd already seen: the sheer drop over two hundred feet and the water crashing against the rocks and emptying into the small pool.

He kept looking, then moved back, away from the edge.

"I don't understand," he said as he shook his head.

He turned back to look at her.

She waited for a moment, one great, long moment.

Then she smiled.

"Follow me," she told him, happy he was there with her and happy for all she knew was about to come. "Follow me, and then perhaps you will."

She backed up.

She went further along the long piece of stone they were standing on, then when she was far enough, and to the spot she remembered, she stopped.

She stood there, gathering herself, as he watched her curiously.

Then she began to quickly run.

She used the strengthened muscles in her legs and she picked up more and more pace with every stride of tanned and powerful limbs, and she saw him watching her, so many questions in his eyes, and his mouth open, until soon she was going as fast as she could go, sprinting across the rock, past him and hurtling towards the edge.

"What are you doing?" he yelled.

And there was panic in his voice as he tried to reach and grab her, tried to reach and save her, but she ignored him and dodged his outstretched hands.

She gained even more speed, more momentum.

She kept running towards the very end of the stone they were standing on, every stride bringing her closer then she launched herself off it, making a great leap from the precipice and out into the air and she was suspended there for a moment, suspended there in nothing, weightless, timeless . . .

"No!" he yelled again.

And then she began to drop.

She held her breath as she quickly plummeted down towards the ground at an astonishingly fast rate, through the waterfall which sprayed mist in her face and she'd pushed herself far enough out she knew she'd miss the boulders that were there and as she fell, she looked below her feet to see the pool, and how it was racing to meet her—or maybe she it, she wasn't sure—and she pointed her toes sharply, took a deep breath, as it got closer, closer, then—

. . .

. . .

. . .

She tore through the surface with a loud noise that sounded like a great thunderclap and the force of the impact pushed the breath she'd just held from her lungs as water came flooding into her nose and mouth. The water was cool and pleasant, though, and she didn't panic while she was submerged, she just smiled again—just once, for herself this time, underwater—then her feet found the rock on the bottom of the pool and she bent her knees and used the leverage to push herself back up to where she broke the surface again, then wiped water from her face and eyes as she turned to look above.

She saw him standing there, staring down with fear in his eyes.

Then when he saw her re-emerge . . .

Relief.

"What are you doing?" he yelled down to her.

She kept smiling at him but then remembered his greatest fear—the one he'd first said, that he'd first told her, his fear of being alone—and she realized perhaps she shouldn't play with that fear. She shouldn't play with his fear, she realized, in case anyone discovered her own and did the same, so she swore to herself that she never would again.

"Come on down," she yelled back to him instead, now that it had been done and couldn't be undone. "The water's wonderful!"

She saw him look around, with the worry still there in his eyes.

It was more fear that she still saw, the dislike of heights.

"How far is it?" he asked, his voice a bit smaller than it had been before.

"Just come on!" she yelled again.

He hesitated for another moment until he finally backed up, the same as he'd seen her do, then got his running start, also in the same way, and went barreling towards the edge of the stone where he then launched himself out and into the sky until gravity came for him, too, and he also began to plummet, the same as she had, *down, down, down,* until—

. . .

. . .

. . .

SPLASH!

His body broke the surface of the pool and he plunged deep into the water until his feet also touched rock, and he bent his knees and pushed himself and shot back to the surface where he joined her, spitting water from his mouth as she waited for him. And then when he saw her there, waiting, she also saw his eyes slowly begin to change, and his fear fade a little until there was something else that was there . . .

Joy.

Happiness.

The pleasure of a shared experience, and a new secret that was just their own.

Then he almost smiled, too, just as she first had, though she also saw he tried very hard not to, and quickly hid it.

All these feelings had come to him at once, the same as they had to her.

They swam there, next to each other, together.

"Why didn't you tell me you'd done it before?" he asked her, realizing what had happened as they came closer to each other, treading water in the small pool with their faces inches apart, their hair wet and eyes together as they each breathed deeply, purposefully, in and out, chests rising and falling in unison, synchronicity, a pattern, together, the same.

"I did," she told him, very softly.

"How?"

"I told you that you could trust me."

"I already knew I could trust you. We didn't have to jump off a cliff for you to show me that."

"Maybe."

"Maybe what?"

"What else do you know?"

"What do you mean?"

She was thinking of the look she saw in his eyes, his words, his questions.

"What else do you have inside you, that we haven't yet spoken of?"

He opened his mouth, about to answer, but then he hesitated.

"When you jumped . . ." he said, then swallowed. "When you jumped, I thought I wouldn't know what to do here if I'd lost you. If I'd lost you for good."

She watched as he stared back at her for a moment, after he spoke, and it was in that moment she first saw his soul, just for a flash, just for an instant.

"What's the matter?" he asked her.

"Nothing," she told him, and shook her head.

And she meant it. She truly meant it.

She was still thinking of his soul and what she'd seen and how she was so glad of that moment, that glimpse, then she came back to herself and they were there, together, in the pool, close to each other, so very close.

Then he leaned closer still, his face next to her own.

She didn't know what was going to happen next . . .

But she searched herself, her feelings, and she knew she wanted it to.

She waited as he reached up to touch her cheek then tuck her wet hair behind her ear, and he closed his eyes and she realized she didn't like that part—she didn't like when she couldn't see the depths of them, and in them see him, in the way she desired, the only real way she knew how—but then he moved forward, even further, and his lips moved forward, too, until soon they were pressed against her lips and all the feelings she'd had before suddenly changed and washed away and became something she hadn't yet felt. It was something that up until that moment she never knew she *could* feel, or that was inside her, and she let herself enjoy feeling it as she experienced what he tasted of for the first time, what he smelt of, because it was different than her, and in this new closeness she also realized she felt more connected to him than she ever had before, since the beginning of their time together in Creation, which scared her, but in a new way and in a way she found that she perhaps liked to be scared.

The kiss ended, then he moved away, and opened his eyes.

When he did, she saw the confusion that was in them, the confusion where once not many moments ago there had been fear and she also saw something else in them, something she recognized as longing, and a question, wondering about what had just happened between them, and why. She knew why he was feeling all those things because she felt them, too, how the very fabric of who they each were or thought they were had just been torn wide open—there on a perfect day, in a perfect pool, underneath a beautiful waterfall—and she knew and felt that where that fabric had been torn, it would then be mended, and made whole again, and it would be beautiful because even though they didn't yet know it, the way it would be mended and made whole was with pieces of each other.

"What am I feeling?" he finally asked.

"I don't know," she breathed, very softly. "But I think I'm feeling it, too."

There was one more moment between them in the pool then she saw him smile again as he finally let himself feel all that she already had. She smiled, too, and made a decision as she leaned in herself this time and tilted her head up so her lips reached his and kissed him one more time. She kissed him deeply, in a different way than he'd kissed her, and it was all they each thought about as they tread water there in the pool that was now their pool, with the waterfall crashing behind them against worn and smooth rocks and the mountains climbing high into the sky beyond. They kissed again, then once more after that, and as they did and were there together, there was nothing else, they forgot everything, completely, even what their arms and legs were doing and that became a problem as they both started to sink, but they didn't care, and they went under the water together.

And even there, under the water, they still kissed.

They finally began to run out of oxygen so they came back to the surface and then they were laughing, together, a new type of brightness in their eyes and voices that neither had yet known because it was the type of brightness that comes when something is shared, which makes it even brighter. It was also the type of brightness that comes with losing the essence of oneself then finding it again changed, shaped and re-formed, in the union with another, which makes it both brighter and better.

She didn't know all this then.

She only knew what she felt, and that it was good.

But behind them the sun was beginning to sink, and it was getting late, so she gave him one more look there in their pool then she started to swim back towards the shore and he followed after her. He followed her towards the rocks that were there at the edge near where the river began, and where they would climb out, together, and start to head back towards the field, towards the forest, towards the river, both of them ready to again follow the path that would lead them back to the place they called home.

THEY WALKED IN SILENCE, and as they did, she looked down at her hand.

It was by her side, and also next to his hand, which was bouncing back and forth as they went. Every time they took a step, a stride, his hand was moving just a little bit then coming to rest in a slightly different position, and she watched the pattern in which it moved as she weighed a small internal battle. Then she used the timing she'd been studying, the movement, and as he took another step and his hand went forward, then back again towards hers, she reached and took it in her own as it was swinging. Holding his hand was something she'd done before, like when they were climbing the mountain to the top of the waterfall and it had been for a very specific reason then—she'd done it to lead him, to show him the way, the path she'd already found, and to bring him comfort, the feeling of safety—but now she felt it was different, now she felt it was all different.

Because now, this time, she did it for another reason.

This time she took his hand simply because she wanted to.

And there was freedom and pleasure in that, too, as she felt the calloused skin of his palm against the smoother surface of her own palm. His skin was warm and sticky from his perspiration, but even through the moisture and heat, there was a type of energy that was there, a charge that came from him and went through her. It was a feeling unlike anything she'd yet felt in Creation, and that voice inside her—the one she always now listened for when things came she wasn't familiar with, or she was unsure about—she asked the question of it again, and the voice told her this was also good, and so she knew that it was, and that it would be.

She turned and looked at him.

He stayed staring straight ahead as they walked and she wondered if he'd felt it, too, if it had been a current and energy that had gone both ways.

Then she smiled, because the answer to that question also came from inside.

The answer came, and she knew that he had.

She also knew that it was her that had made it happen.

And that . . . that made her smile, too.

THEY KEPT WALKING, and they soon came back to the clearing and house they'd built, and everything there was as it usually was at that time of day. She was still holding his hand just as the last of the light from the sun was finally about to disappear behind the mountains behind them, and they paused and watched it together. They watched as one moment the sun was still a circular and complete orb, then as it moved behind the mountains, it became just a piece of a circle –a sliver of what it had been—then it kept moving and was finally gone altogether and they were left with nothing but a soft orange glow that washed over them and everything else around them for as far as they could see.

They looked at where the sun had been, for one more moment, then they turned and looked at each other.

They both knew things had changed.

But they didn't yet know how much, or the complete extent.

"Let's go inside," she said.

"Yes," he answered, nodding.

Then he followed after her.

He followed her as they went back towards their house then underneath the high roof, their hands still together as one, for just another moment more, then they slowly parted as he went towards his bed then reached it, and layed down, and she stayed standing there and looking at the thing he'd constructed, the place where they'd sat together and ate. She looked at the place where he'd sat, then she looked at the place where she'd sat, across from him, and she looked at the two other sides to the square construction that were between those two places and she wondered why he'd made it that way, or if he even had a reason why.

Then she heard a voice, the one that came from inside.

"Table," she said, repeating the word she'd heard.

"What?" he asked, wrinkling his nose.

"That's what it's called," she told him, then saw him nod, slowly, and so they knew it was.

She wanted the moment that had just happened to last even longer, but even in the short time she'd been in Creation she knew it wasn't always possible for that to happen, so instead she went to her bed on the opposite side of the room as his, and she layed down, too. They did this every night, and it had become their ritual: they each went to their beds, layed down on them, then closed their eyes and went to sleep.

But this time they didn't.

This time they kept looking at each other, there in the darkness, across the room. She saw him rubbing and feeling his hand, where she'd held it, remembering the feeling, just as she did, and she thought perhaps that meant he was longing for it again, the same as she was, too. She knew something had changed between them when they were in the pool, because she'd felt it. And when they were there and he'd opened his eyes again and she was able to look into them once more, into that bright window to where she knew now she could see his soul, she could then see that he'd felt it, too, even though she didn't yet know exactly what it was, or where it would lead them, or how long it would last, or anything else. It was all those thoughts and more that came rushing and tumbling in a great cascade through her consciousness as she lay there on her bed, the same as the waterfall crashing over rocks and down into the river but the orange glow outside was gone now, and in its place there was only shadow and darkness, and there in the darkness she then thought of something else . . .

She thought of the first thing he'd asked, when they'd met the angel who had come.

Who was created first?

She found herself wondering about this now as she looked into his eyes, across the room, through the darkness, as he still felt the hand she'd touched with his other hand, and she found herself again wondering why he'd said it, and also why it was important to him.

Was it something he felt deeply?

Was it something he held within himself, and that he believed?

She thought of all those things, and scenarios, then she thought again of the pool.

She thought of their day together, and how she'd felt.

She thought of the energy that had come when she'd taken his hand and her skin had touched his skin, that energy she knew was good and she knew he was thinking of that feeling, too, that energy he'd also felt, because of the way she could see him still rubbing his hand with the other, and despite all the previous thoughts she'd had—some of which could of course be construed as doubts, about so much of what had happened, and the change that had come so quickly—despite all that, all she could think of was that she wanted to touch his skin one more time, and feel her own pressed against it. She wanted to feel that energy again, once more, before she went to sleep, that energy she hadn't ever felt before that day, but now she had . . . she realized it had changed everything, all she'd thought she knew.

She wondered if it had for him, too.

She hoped it had, or that it would.

Then almost as if in response to her thoughts, he stood from his bed and started to walk across the dark room towards her and when he got close to where she lay, he gently started to lower himself down and into the bed next to her, their bodies near each other again, fitting perfectly together, lines and curves that complimented and matched, and once he was there next to her the energy that had been between them before returned and at least in that instant, and that moment, there was now one thing she *did* know for sure, and that was this: that whatever other differences they might have, their thoughts, on that night, and in that moment, were wholly and unequivocally the same.

"Is this alright?" he asked, very softly, and she could feel his breath warm and gentle on her shoulder.

"Yes," she whispered.

He nodded, slowly, and breathed in.

Then he moved closer.

When she shifted her weight to make more room for him, she felt and noticed again the way their bodies fit, so perfect and flawlessly complimentary, and she realized how she felt with him in the bed next to her was something that had been missing up until that moment and she never wanted to sleep without him there again. His hand reached out and found hers where it rested in front of her stomach and their fingers laced together, her smaller palm inside his larger and calloused one, then she put all the doubts she had previously had from her mind— she put them as far from her mind as she possibly could—and there in the darkness they both smiled, together, as one, because of what they'd just discovered and found in each other, and because it was good.

5

THERE HAD BEEN a bird with all its feathers a deep shade of black that had been perched on the highest branches of a tree next to the pool at the head of the river. Neither of the two humans had noticed the bird while they were there, swimming in the pool and beneath the great, tumbling waterfall, and neither of them had noticed the bird when they'd swam to the shore and got out or when they'd left and started to walk back towards the clearing and place they called home.

The bird watched as they walked together along the riverbank.

Then it left its place on the branch and flew into the sky to watch from its vantage overhead as they kept going. It watched as she'd hesitated, at first, but then finally reached out and took his hand in hers, and it watched as the look in her eyes changed then so did the look in his eyes, too. It watched as they walked through the field of dandelions and wild flowers. It watched as they went through the forest, and came to the clearing, and stood there together for a moment in the soft orange glow left by the setting sun and it watched as they both went back inside their house together, and it still watched as the last of the soft orange light began to disappear, in the distance, sinking even further behind the mountains.

Then, the light was gone.

And darkness slowly came.

The bird sat there on a branch at the edge of the clearing, for a long time, waiting, even after the darkness had settled. Then when the bird judged that the moment was finally right it flapped its wings and flew towards the ground and as it did, it began to shift, change, morph, elongate, then it reached the ground and that's where it finally returned to its original form, becoming Phosphorus again, standing in the forest at the edge of the clearing. And when his change was complete, Phosphorus then quietly left the cover of the trees and went across the clearing and towards the structure he'd heard the humans call home. He waited for a moment, standing there on the threshold of the structure, wondering what might happen when and if he took his next step, and he also knew there was only one way he could find out.

So, very quietly, he took a single step forward.

Nothing happened, so he took another, past the poles that were plunged down into earth and rose into the sky above until he was underneath the roof. He waited there for a moment, too, but still nothing happened to him. He was surprised that Michael didn't protect it somehow, but it seemed he hadn't, so Phosphorus looked around. He looked at all that was before him and saw the great and wide space inside the structure that had been created, then he saw the table the man had made, where he'd sat with her and ate their fruit, and he wondered about it. He shook his head and put it from his mind as his eyes continued and he finally saw them together in the bed. He watched them as they still held each other there, breathing together, chests rising and falling in synchronized rhythm, inhaling, exhaling, a hypnotizing and peaceful pattern to their rest.

He looked at them, for another moment, then he frowned.

And he frowned because this wasn't what he was expecting to find, and it caused him to hesitate. Standing there and looking down at them made him feel something deep inside himself, deep in the depths of his own soul that he'd thought he'd guarded himself against, and would never have to feel again, but there it was, and it had caught him unawares.

He shook his head.

He tried to push what he was feeling as far from him as he could.

He tried to push it away because he had something important to do there in the darkness and shadows, something that couldn't wait, and that was why he was in Creation, for that reason and no other.

So he silently moved closer to the bed, careful not to wake them.

Then when he was there, he inched even closer still.

When he was finally near enough to where they slept, he leaned in even further, directly over them, and began to softly whisper into her ear. He whispered into *her* ear, not his, and this was a choice he'd made because of all he'd already seen: both during the first time he'd come to the clearing, and watched them together with Michael, then what he'd just witnessed, at the waterfall, and on their way back to their home as they'd walked alongside the river and through the field and the forest.

It was her, he knew, from all that he saw . . .

It was her that he wanted.

So he leaned even closer still and began to whisper very softly and let words drip from his mouth into her ear. At first she didn't move, didn't stir, didn't do anything and his soft, beautiful voice kept coming like sweet honey—deep and persuasive and beautiful—then he moved his hands until they hovered over her exposed throat as he kept speaking, kept whispering in the darkness, all of his quiet and twisted words, then all of a sudden—

HER EYES SNAPPED OPEN.

There was terror in them at first as she left the unknown of her dreams and the darkness of sleep and came rushing back to the known and her home. Her eyes quickly darted around because of the fear that was there in her chest, clenched in a tight knot just behind her sternum, but she saw nothing new or out of the ordinary—there was only the house, just as they'd left it before they'd gone to sleep, and as it was supposed to be—then she looked down and saw him in the bed, in the new spot where he was sleeping next to her. His chest was gently rising and falling in the synchronized rhythm of sleep that had just moments ago been hers, too.

She swallowed as she looked at him, and when she did, she noticed her throat was dry, and she was thirsty.

So she quietly stood from where they'd slept.

She made sure not to wake him as she left the bed, then the house, too.

She went past the threshold and on through the damp grass on her way towards the river where she knelt on the bank and cupped her hands and brought some of the cool water up to her lips. As she did, the chilled night breeze picked up and rustled the grass on the far side of the river, and she paused, hesitated, because the feeling had come back again, the same one she'd woken with, the feeling of dread and fear gathered in a small, tight knot behind her sternum.

And the fear told her something.

It told her there was someone else that was there, and that she was being watched.

The rustling on the other side of the river continued and she followed it with quick darting eyes to where she thought it was, then as the cool wind picked up even more and even stronger, the noise and movement seemed to disappear altogether, and there wasn't any more rustling at all.

There was just quiet, and darkness.

And that's then when she heard another noise, and it was closer.

She quickly spun on her heel, holding her breath, because the new sound was coming from directly behind her. She still held her breath as she searched the other side of the clearing now, not finding anything, and then the noise came again and it was even closer this time, and that's when she finally saw it, where the noise seemed to be coming from, as if it was the only thing that was there, in startlingly clear and immediate focus:

The Tree of Knowledge.

It was standing tall and unmistakable, right in front of her and illuminated by the bright light of the moon, and it was the only thing that seemed to be illuminated at all, at least on this surreal night.

She looked at it for a moment.

Then she began to slowly walk towards it.

She felt herself drawn to it even though she didn't yet know why, and she was drawn to it in a way she hadn't ever been drawn before. After she took a few more steps, she soon stood there in front of it and looked up at the great and gnarled trunk and the many crooked branches that were coming from it. She looked at the fruit that was there on the branches, which was fruit she realized she hadn't tasted yet.

And that fruit was knowledge, right?

Isn't that what the angel had told her, the angel that had come?

She thought again about all the deep and important questions she'd had since she'd opened her eyes in Creation, especially the ones that had come in the last few days, and all the many things she'd been wondering and answers she'd been searching for.

Could this tree hold those answers, she wondered, the answers to all those questions?

Could this tree hold the answers to *everything*?

She was mesmerized by the thought and idea of what it could be, and what the fruit might taste like—the unknown of it, the brightness, the mystery and truth it contained—but then she paused and wondered where these intrusive thoughts were coming from because they were thoughts she'd never had before. She thought back and then finally shook her head and put the temptation and thoughts aside because she remembered again all of what Michael had come and told her, and all that she'd promised in return: that she must not touch the fruit, that of all the things in this clearing, that was the one thing she must not eat, so she wouldn't. Those were the thoughts that were going through her mind as she stood for a moment longer in the shadow of the great and gnarled branches, then she heard a low, attractive voice that came from directly behind her.

"It is beautiful though, isn't it?" the voice said.

And as soon as she heard the voice, she spun around again, back towards the river, to see someone standing there. She'd never seen this person before so she didn't yet know his name, or who he was, or why his voice sounded familiar. She didn't yet know that this was Phosphorus, who had once been called Shining One, Light-Bringer, Morningstar, as well as many other things, and she also didn't yet know this was his most beautiful form, and one that he'd been working on, just for her, just for this very moment. She didn't yet know any of those things, she just knew he was a stranger, and she was startled to see someone else there in the clearing, the first new person she'd seen since Michael had left. Though this visitor wasn't the same as Michael, she realized, because when she was in the presence of this visitor, she felt very different than how she felt when she'd been in the presence of the previous one.

"Who are you?" she finally asked him, whispering in the darkness.

But he ignored her question and instead just started to walk.

He did so slowly, and with long, deliberate strides, getting closer to her.

He came nearer and nearer, until finally he was standing directly in front of her and she looked up at him: she saw he was much taller than she was, and she could also feel the intoxicating nature of his presence.

"What a beautiful clearing," he said, with a wide smile on his lips as he gestured around them. "A beautiful clearing, in a beautiful garden, with a very beautiful woman in it, and just think . . . this could all be yours, all of it, everything here that you see."

"It's not mine," she answered, looking back at him.

"If it's not yours, then whose is it?"

She thought of that for a moment, frowning, realizing she'd heard those words before. Then it came to her. It was the same as the words the man had spoken, when they stood together at the top of the waterfall and looked out on all of Creation. She made note of that, as she narrowed her eyes.

"It's *ours*," she told the visitor.

"Well, some of it, maybe," he said, then turned from looking at the clearing to meet her eyes with his own that were bright and shining in a million different and splendid ways, all of them equal forms of his deception. "But not everything, right?"

"What do you mean?"

"All the questions you've had, and all that you still don't understand," he said as he kept smiling. "Here are the answers, right here, right in front of you . . . just waiting for you to reach out and take them."

She opened her mouth to speak again but she found no words came, and there was one more moment as he stood there in front of her, their eyes together, then the moment passed and he turned and looked at the tree that was there next to them and the fruit that was on its branches. He turned to look at it first, then so did she, in the same way, and an overwhelming sensation came to her, something she could feel in every part of her body and especially in her mouth and it was almost as if she could taste the fruit now, a great explosion of flavor and texture and newness. The imagined taste that came was sweeter and better than anything she'd ever yet tasted in Creation, and after that feeling came there was then another feeling, too, and one that told her this taste was all she'd ever wanted, all she'd ever desired and ever would. She thought about that feeling, that desire, how strong it was and where it came from inside her, and she realized it didn't seem to come from the same place as the other feelings she'd had before, the ones that had come during the light of the day and that she'd asked for and listened to, and the voice that she had inside which she knew was good, and was truth.

Something was different about this feeling and this voice she could now feel.

And something was different about this night, and this darkness, too.

So she'd listen to what she knew, and she resolutely set her jaw as she stared back at the stranger across from her.

"No," she finally told him.

"No?" he asked. "Why would you say such a thing? Aren't you at least the tiniest bit curious?"

"I know what you would have me do, but we were warned against it. We were forbidden to eat the fruit."

"But why?" he asked again. "If it wasn't meant to be yours, then why would it be here, in your clearing? And if it's knowledge that's truly what's there in the fruit, then what type of person would wish to deny that from you? Surely not one whose intentions are goodness, right? Because knowledge is knowledge, it's eternal, and it's essential . . . and it should belong to everyone."

She paused as she considered his words and looked back at him one more time. She didn't know why she still hesitated, because she didn't yet know his voice and words were music—his own special brand of divine persuasion—and she also didn't yet realize that was one of his many gifts. But she was strong, as he knew, too, so as she weighed what he'd said and what he was offering, she did the only thing she could think to do, which was to listen to her own voice she had within, deep within—not yet knowing this voice was *her* gift—and she heard it, and listened, and shook her head.

"No," she said again, and firmly.

"I don't understand," he frowned.

"Just because it's here doesn't mean it's mine," she continued. "And it's not my garden."

"But if it's not your garden, then whose is it?"

"All of ours. Any who come, and wish to share in it."

She watched as he paused for a moment, his eyes turning down, and he stayed like that, looking at the ground . . . then the moment he'd created passed, and he slowly looked up again.

"And what about the knowledge?" he finally asked her.

"You're right," she said. "It is essential, and eternal. But I'll find out what I'm meant to, when I'm meant to."

She watched as he heard her words, and she watched as he just stared back at her. There was perhaps a little bit of surprise in his features, she saw, because he knew what his gifts were and the power they had, but what he hadn't known or calculated was that she too might have similar gifts and power of her own: he hadn't calculated that until that very moment, there in the clearing and under the moonlight and beside the river and great tree where she'd now shown them to him, all of that which *she* had inside.

"Of course," he finally answered, realizing, and then the smile returned to his lips as he changed the course of his questions. "But there are still things you want to know, aren't there?" he asked her. "There are changes you've felt, that have now come, and that you've wondered about."

"No," she answered, as she swallowed.

"Yes," he breathed. "Changes between you, between both of you, together. Changes that you could understand, with just a small taste, just one little bite . . ."

She heard his new words and realized what he'd done.

He wasn't speaking to her mind anymore, he wasn't speaking to her mind at all . . .

He was speaking to her heart now.

Her heart, and her soul.

She waited as his words echoed and lingered all around her then he reached up and took one of the pieces of fruit from a low branch where it hung. He looked down at the fruit for a moment, in his hand, considering it—the size, shape, color, all of it perfect—then he finally turned back and slowly extended his arm, and she watched as he held it out to her.

"Here," he whispered. "Everything you've ever wondered about could be yours . . . all the questions that are there and that you have could be answered."

"No," she breathed again, thinking of the taste that had come earlier, the overwhelming sensation.

What it tasted like . . .

And what it might lead to.

"Just one bite," he continued. "Just one bite and all the feelings you've now felt and doubts and questions that have come with them, the doubts about him, and your future, and what comes next, what this leads to, and how it all ends . . . all that knowledge is here," he smiled even wider. "It just takes one bite, one small piece of the flesh, between your teeth . . . and it's so sweet."

He moved closer to her still, using all the power of his voice and his presence, and it was even more overwhelming as he held the apple out and she looked at it and realized she *did* want to know all he'd said and offered; she did want to know all she knew she would if she tasted it. But she'd made a promise. She'd made a promise to the one that had come and helped them, the one she knew was good and who had come in light and in truth, and so she would keep that promise.

She shook her head, one last time, as firmly as she could.

"No," she said, with even more strength.

But then before she realized what had happened, and that he'd moved, he was even closer, right next to her. He breathed down on her as he ignored her words and held the apple out even further, and as he did, she found that she couldn't move. In a single instant all her limbs had seemed to become completely paralyzed and frozen, but she saw his weren't, and he was so close now that their chests were nearly touching and she could feel his warm breath on her. She looked at him with dread in her eyes as he moved the apple towards her mouth.

Closer, closer, closer . . .

It was almost there, almost to her skin, the flesh just nearly touching her lips, and there was panic in her eyes now.

"*No, no, no . . .*" she whispered, softly at first.

But he ignored her as she kept saying the word, over and over, then she said it louder, stronger.

"*No, no!*" she started yelling.

Her words didn't do anything to stop the stranger or what was happening, though, then her lips began to open—once again involuntarily, and against her will—and the apple started to move between them, towards her teeth. It didn't yet touch her, but was just millimeters away, almost to her, almost reaching, the moment now upon her then just before it happened, just before she came into contact with the flesh she inhaled deeply, a rush of breath and cold night air filling her lungs, and then—

Her eyes snapped open.

She looked around and saw the man next to her, not the stranger, and he was shaking her.

There was no more clearing, or river, or Tree of Knowledge in front of her, rising tall and ominous in the moonlight and there was no more fruit being picked and offered by a stranger who spoke with a voice that was music and words that were honey.

"Where am I?" she finally asked.

"You're here," he said, still holding her, in their bed. "You're here, with me. You're home."

The dream and what had happened still felt like it was all around her and she could still feel the dark, cold air that she'd breathed swirling in her lungs and she could still feel the fear lodged in the small, tight knot just behind her sternum. She quickly blinked her eyes and looked around at the walls of her home again and the newly-built table across from them in the open space, and she realized he was right: that all of this was again real, and that she was back in her bed, and back with him.

But she also felt and knew that the other had been real, too.

She felt that the darkness and temptation had been more than real.

"What happened?" he asked, still looking at her with concern in his eyes.

"I don't know," she finally answered, as she sat up and her eyes turned towards the threshold. She saw that it was still night, and she found herself wishing the darkness that was there outside would leave and the morning would soon come.

The morning, and the light.

"You were saying *'no, no, no,'* over and over again, and it woke me up," he told her, from his place by her side.

"I'm sorry," she said.

But he brushed that off.

"What did you see?" he asked again, looking into her eyes now. "What were you telling to stop?"

She waited for another moment, still looking outside at the darkness, then she saw the first and faintest glimmers of the light that would soon be there, the light that would soon come and rise and once again shine all around them and when it came on this particular morning she'd wait as it built, she knew, and let it surround her, blind her, penetrate into every piece and corner of who she was, because she knew that she needed it.

"I don't know what I saw," she finally told him. "And I don't know what it was that happened."

"Are you alright?" he asked. "You're cold."

She turned and looked at him again, deep into his still-worried eyes.

"I am," she said. "So hold me."

When she met his eyes with her own, she still saw there was fear and confusion in them, but he wrapped his arms around her as she'd asked and held her close and she could feel his warmth. They sat there together like that and as they did, she thought back again to her just-spoken words and she knew it was truth that she'd said, what she'd told him: she didn't yet know what she'd seen, or why, or what had just happened to her, but there was also something else, too. There was something she was sure that she *did* know, which was that she knew how real it all had felt, how real it all *was*—both the fear that had been there, and everything else she'd seen, and heard, and had happen to her—so she knew one other thing, too, and she knew it as surely as she knew anything else. She knew it as surely as she knew the voice deep within her was light and truth and soul, and as surely as she knew how the man who now held her made her feel when they were together, and she wondered what it would all mean, and what it would then bring, and how it would change the future that was there for both of them, together, the future that they'd been given.

Because she knew then that they weren't in Creation alone.

6

THE NEXT DAY she rose before dawn and walked in the direction of the sun.

After her dream, the one of fear and temptation in the clearing, she hadn't been able to go back to sleep, so instead she went outside, with him by her side, and they sat together and watched the sun rise. When it was finally high enough that their skin had warmed and she'd started to return to herself and there was less concern in his eyes, he went to begin with the work they'd planned for the day. They'd decided on an area next to their home where they would plant the seeds they'd saved from the fruit she'd gathered and they'd eaten, and that was where he worked. The place was next to the field they'd already planted with Michael, and though they knew it would take the trees and bushes some time to grow, it would be their orchard. He'd created a tool that was made from two pieces of wood they'd gathered with a stone inverted on the bottom and tied to the handles with the same weaving and materials she'd used to make her basket, in the way she'd learned after Michael had left, to make the work of plowing and planting easier. And as he pushed the tool he'd made through the field and it turned up dirt, she followed behind with the seeds they'd gathered and put them into the exposed earth then gently covered them with soil again, patting it down until it was level.

She watched as he worked in front of her and she looked at his body again, studying it. She noticed he'd changed even more, too, the same as she had, and the muscles in his arms, legs, back were further shifting, growing, expanding. She had seen that hers were, as well, but they were growing in a different way than his because of the different types of work they did, she thought, and she found herself still looking at him and deep in thought when he turned back around.

"Are you alright?" he asked.

There was a moment, then she nodded.

"Yes," she told him.

He looked at her for a little bit longer, then seemed to accept her answer, and the concern left his eyes again as he went back to his plowing in the field.

His body had changed, that much was clear, she knew, as she turned back inwards to her thoughts.

And if his body had changed, what else had changed, too?

Do our hearts change, and in the same way?

Do our minds?

Our souls?

Soon after she had these thoughts, the sky opened and rain came.

They both hurried back inside as the rain started, soft at first, then more and heavier until it was cascading off the roof of the shelter and forming large puddles in the grass outside.

"Well, it's perfect timing and it'll be good for what we've already planted," he said, as they both sat under the roof and watched as the rain steadily came down.

"Yes," she answered absently.

She knew he could tell again that her thoughts were elsewhere.

They continued to watch the rain together until the light started to fade, then it was dark, so they both went to the bed they now shared and got into it together; her first, and then him. She was glad he was there with her, and that he'd sleep there, too, next to her, but it was different this time, the second time they'd sleep next to each other. The energy that had been there after their time in the pool, it wasn't there again, or at least not in the same way. Instead, there was just a nice and simple comfort in their proximity, in the feeling of being close to each other and flesh touching flesh, skin touching skin, and they layed there together and tried to get as comfortable as they possibly could as they listened to the soft and beautiful sounds of the rain falling on the roof.

He soon drifted to sleep . . .

But she stayed awake.

The bed was really only made for one person, so every time he moved or stirred it kept her awake, but that didn't really matter because she found that she'd lost control of her mind, there in the darkness, and she couldn't shake the previous night from her thoughts.

How real it'd felt.

And how it was still with her.

She stayed in the bed for most of the night, even though sleep never came, as she stared blankly up at the ceiling, lost in her thoughts.

Then just before dawn, she rose.

She was careful not to wake him as she got up, gently extricating her limbs from where they were between his own, and she quietly walked towards the threshold. When she got there, she paused for a moment before she left and turned and looked back at him. He was sleeping so peacefully, in their bed, by himself now, chest rising and falling. She breathed it in, breathing him in, the dawn, the moment, the feeling, all of it, knowing it was something that needed and deserved to be remembered . . .

Then she turned and kept walking, outside, and into the morning.

THE GRASS WAS STILL WET as she walked through it, and it clung to her ankles.

She passed through the forest and the trees where there was moisture still gathered on the leaves and branches, too, just as the sun was beginning to come up in the distance. As the sun slowly rose, the light it brought reflected off the drops of water and as she walked she caught brilliant glimpses of the entire spectrum of colors reflected in each of the drops. She took it all in as she went through the soft mist that was settled between the trees, slowly rising then burning away, and as she did it struck her that there was something inordinately special about that part of the day, about the part when it was only just beginning and when she found her thoughts were most clear. She looked at all the mist and forest and colors and also the promise of more light that was soon about to come from over the peaks of the faraway mountains, and the only reason she wouldn't be able to tell someone why this time of day and what she was feeling was so true and special was because she didn't yet know the word for magic.

What she did know, however, was that she needed to think.

She knew she needed a quiet moment, alone with her thoughts, after all that had happened, so that's why she had begun to walk. It was aimless at first, and without direction, but then as she kept going and the trees in front of her started to part and she saw the large and familiar field of dandelions and wild flowers, she knew where her feet had been taking her, and it was back to the place where she'd began.

She went and sat in the middle of the wet field, not minding the dew that was still there, too, and she was surrounded by the grass and dandelions and the beautifully scented flowers as she sat and watched the sun rise in front of her.

It climbed higher, above the mountains.

As it did, more light came, then along with the light, she saw something else in the distance, too . . .

A rainbow.

It arched high over the tall mountains and reflected through and across the great waterfall.

She looked at the rainbow and all the colors that were there with great awe as she sat and took in another of the new and miraculous wonders of Creation she'd just found, then the rainbow slowly began to fade and disappear, and as it did, she felt her mind and thoughts begin to wander again, as well.

She'd seen and felt darkness now, of that she was sure.

But what of God, and what of light?

She'd been told of God by Michael, but who was he?

She'd heard him spoken of, but what did she really know of him, and why did he not speak to her?

Why did he not speak to her, in the same way the angel had?

She kept looking into the distance, and she thought about it all even further.

There had been a voice inside her, from the beginning, a voice that spoke to her, and still did.

Was that God?

She didn't know.

Then she thought of the questions that had come when they'd first met Michael and asked him about all those things: who are we, why are we here, and what truly is our purpose?

Perhaps, the same as those questions, these questions that she now asked, too, were only meant to be asked, not answered, just asked, and as often as possible.

And then, at the right time . . . perhaps the answers might come.

But what about him?

What about the other one that was there in Creation with her, the man she'd left that morning in her bed and that she'd begun to care so deeply about and every single day felt herself growing closer to? She knew from the feeling deep inside her that temptation would come and intrude upon them again, but what she didn't know was what form it would take.

And would they be ready?

That's what she now wondered.

When they'd stood together on the rock above the waterfall, he'd looked out over everything and wanted it all to be his, which is something she couldn't understand, because it wasn't something she felt.

Should that worry her?

Was that a weakness, and perhaps something the darkness could exploit?

She thought about the dark angel that had come to the garden in her dream that was more than a dream and she thought about how he'd looked like the man to her, or at least he'd looked more like him than like her, she thought, and she realized how what he'd said had been similar to what the man had also said, though the man had said it in innocence and without darkness. But even without the darkness, both their words had been so similar, she realized, both laced with the ideas of possession and worship of strength, and there was also something she thought she could see in the eyes of both of them, something she saw when the dark one offered her the fruit and the same thing that she saw when the man stood and looked out at the horizon, taking in all he thought could be his, and wanting to claim it as such.

She had a voice, inside her, that spoke to her, and she had wondered about this before, and now she did again.

Maybe he had a voice, too, she thought.

And maybe those were the things his voice had told him.

She thought about his body again, and what she had seen of how it had begun to change, and she thought about her own body, too, and how it had also changed, but in a different way.

That was it, she thought, that might be the key to it, to all of it.

That might be the key to her questions, and what she'd been wondering.

She'd begun to feel closer to him with each passing day they'd been in Creation together, and she wanted that to continue—she wanted that to always continue—so there was only one thing now she knew she must do: she'd tell him about everything she was feeling, and ask him about everything he'd felt, then there would never again be any more secrets or questions or anything else but truth between them.

She smiled as she thought about it, and she felt warmth.

Then after one more moment, alone in the sun, she stood and began to walk back towards the clearing.

7

WHEN SHE CAME BACK to the clearing, she saw the tool he'd used the previous day to turn dirt was still sitting in the field, unused, and as she saw that, she frowned. She waited for a moment, thinking about and wondering where he might have gone, since he clearly wasn't in the field doing what she thought he would have been doing at that time, so she walked past the orchard and through the field and to their house. When she went inside, she didn't see him there, either, so she then looked to the table he'd carved and where they shared their meals, then she looked past it. There was something missing, something she couldn't quite put her finger on, then she did, and realized what it was.

The two beds that were normally there were gone.

She walked towards the space where the bed that had been hers had previously been and saw the faint outline of dust around where it had once sat, where its legs had once rested. Then she looked further, towards the then-exposed wood of the floor they'd made and she saw a slight hole in it, a crease, a small space that had been created. Her hand involuntarily went to her side and she felt what she'd carried with her there for the past two days in the tunic she'd woven to keep herself dry and warm. She hesitated for just a moment, with her hand still resting there, then finally reached all the way into her pocket and took what was there out and looked down at the flower he'd picked and given to her in the field. She stared at it in her hands and didn't know why she did what she did next, but she raised the flower to her lips and kissed it before gently pressing it flat and then bent down and carefully put it in the small hole that had been exposed.

She waited for another moment, looking down at the flower that was now hidden there, in the crease, underneath the place where they usually slept . . .

Then she heard something.

It was loud, and unfamiliar.

She waited for another moment then realized it was the sound of work that she heard, of wood being ground and sanded, and it was the same sound that had been made when he'd created the table where they sat and ate their meals. She listened to it as she stood there, realizing where it was coming from, then went further on through their house—towards the other side of it, and towards the noise—and she walked outside, and when she did . . .

That's where she found him.

He had both the structures they'd used as their beds with him, both of the things she'd noticed that were missing from inside the house, and she watched for a moment as he worked: he'd taken the interior sides off each of the beds then pushed them next to each other so it made one larger bed, and he'd started securing each of them together in that way so it seemed as natural and crafted as the singular version that each of them had previously been on their own. She kept watching him, and as soon as she saw what it was he was doing, she of course knew why, and she thought about it, and him, and couldn't help it as she smiled, very widely, as widely as she could remember.

Then after a moment, he turned and saw her there, too.

When he did, he smiled, also.

They looked at each other for a moment, then she spoke.

"I thought you'd have been in the field," she said.

"You were gone when I woke this morning," he told her, then shrugged as he looked back at her. "I thought maybe the reason you left was because you couldn't sleep, that maybe there wasn't enough room in the bed for both of us. But I liked how it felt to sleep with you next to me, to close my eyes knowing you'd be there when I opened them again, and feel you breathe next to me when I breathed . . . so I thought I'd try to do this before you returned."

"I did leave because I couldn't sleep," she told him. "But it wasn't because of the bed, or because of you next to me."

"Then what was it?"

She thought about that, for a moment.

Then she walked closer to where he was and bent down to admire what he'd created and the craft and care he'd put into his work. As she reached out and felt the wood, running her hand along it, it was almost as if she could feel within the material the strength of intention and purpose he'd made it with. She could feel the goodness that had flowed from his heart and through his arms and down into his hands and then finally to the structure itself and the wood it was made from and that would hold them as they slept together.

"Did you have another dream?" he asked, watching her very carefully, studying her.

And as soon as he spoke, she felt a cloud pass overhead and turn what had once been a very bright moment into something much darker, with long and jagged shadows all around them now, and there was also a chill that came on the breeze.

She turned and looked up at the cloud, above them.

She looked at how the cloud had come and completely covered the sun and it was the only one, the only cloud that was around or in the sky as far as she could see.

"It wasn't another dream," she finally said to him, very slowly, still looking up at the sky. "And I'm not sure if the first one that came really was either."

"If it wasn't a dream . . . then what do you think it was?"

"A test," she said.

The words came quickly, so quickly and unfamiliarly that she wondered if they were even hers, but that didn't matter because she knew they were truth.

He waited for a moment, taking that in, a frown coming to his face.

"Tell me," he finally said to her. "Tell me what you're feeling, and what you saw, in whatever it was."

She was still looking up, above them, at the sky and cloud that had come and covered the sun, and she waited for a moment, just one more moment, then she finally looked away from the cloud, and sun, and back to him.

"Alright," she said, then nodded.

She knew that he needed truth, too.

So she took his hand in her own, very gently, and began to lead him away from the clearing—away from the shadows and darkness that had come—and back towards the river.

THEY SAT ON THE BANK of the river with their feet in the water and that's where she told him everything. She began by telling him she only wanted there to be truth between them, as she watched their toes move gently back and forth in the current, with the sun above them again, and she asked him about that day on the rock, on top of the waterfall, when they looked out at all of Creation. She asked him about what he'd felt, then what he'd said, and what he'd told her.

He waited for a moment, taking in her question.

He knew that truth is what she wanted, and what she deserved, so truth is then what came.

He told her that when he stood there and looked out at all that there was, all that they could see, he'd heard a voice, too. It was one that came from deep within him, and it told him to stand there and take it in, everything, all that he could see in front of him . . . and then go and make it all his.

That caused her to pause, when she heard it, both because of his candor, and because of his nature.

It wasn't what she'd expected.

But should she have?

She knew they were different, but also the same.

And she knew for sure then, too, that he had a voice, also, but it didn't tell him the same things her voice told her.

But that was as it should be, she thought.

It was all as it should be, because it came from inside, and what comes from inside must also come from God, right?

She turned and looked at him next to her.

She looked at his eyes, that were looking back at her own.

Then she layed down there on the bank of the river and let her head rest against his chest; she let it rest there, very softly, and she liked how that felt. He leaned back and propped himself on his elbows so that her head could rest even more comfortably, and she liked that, too, she found. She liked how her head rose and fell with the movements of his chest, up and down, and she liked how she could feel him breathe: the rhythms of his nature, of his body, the proximity of his heart, and of his soul.

"Now it's your turn to tell me," he finally said, as he gently stroked her hair, pulling it back from her eyes and tucking it around her ear. "Now it's your turn to tell me what you saw in your dream that wasn't a dream."

She waited for a moment, gathering herself as she lay there.

Then she took a deep breath, and she told him.

She told him how in her dream she'd risen from their bed because she was thirsty, and she'd left the house and walked down to the river, right next to where they were now sitting, and when she was there, that's when she'd heard the rustling, and felt like she was being watched.

And then she saw him.

The angel, the dark angel.

"How did you know what he was?" he asked her. "How did you know he was different than the other that came, and that he was one of darkness?"

She heard his question, then she told him.

She told him that it was a feeling that had come and washed over her when she was there in his presence, and she also told him that as she'd thought about it all further, she realized that just as there was an angel of light, the one that had come and that they'd seen together, then surely that must mean there was one who was of darkness, too, right?

He took that in, thinking of the shadow and the cloud.

And then he nodded.

He'd heard her words, and he heard the wisdom in them.

"And then what did he do?" he asked, her head still on his chest.

She felt him breathe again, chest rising and falling . . .

Then after another moment, she told him.

"He brought me to the tree," she said very quietly.

"Which tree?"

"The larger one. The Tree of Knowledge."

"And it was just the two of you there?"

"Yes."

He paused at that, and frowned.

Then she saw as he turned his eyes down and looked at her.

"What did he look like?" he asked.

"He was beautiful," she told him, honestly.

She felt him tense at those words, and she knew why, too.

"And then what happened?" he asked quickly, his voice lower now.

"He told me to eat the fruit, and I told him I wouldn't," she said, slowly, and kept thinking back to the moment as she looked at the water flowing and swirling around their ankles, then she thought back to what had happened next, too, what had happened after she'd told him. "But then, there was an instant, just after he spoke . . ." she continued. "And in that moment, something happened I can't explain and I seemed to lose all control of my body. I couldn't move my arms, my hands, my legs. I couldn't move anything at all. And that's when he kept coming: closer, closer, closer."

"Did he hurt you?" he asked sharply.

His eyes blazed as they searched her own for any signs of pain, injury, trauma, and when she looked back at him there above her, she saw this fire that was now in his eyes and it was there in a way she'd never seen before.

She could feel it, too, and not just see it, emanating from him.

It was part of his strength, she realized; it was a great part of his strength that was different than her own strength.

"No," she finally told him, shaking her head. "He didn't hurt me."

"Are you sure?"

"He took one of the pieces of fruit from the branch and offered it to me," she told him. "I tried to say no, but I wasn't able to. My lips didn't work either, and no words came. He kept bringing the fruit closer and closer, and it was almost to my lips, almost to my teeth, almost touching them, and that's when I woke up."

He still looked down at her and she could see the realization come to his eyes.

She could also see some of the anger fade, too, and some of the fear.

"That's why you were saying 'no' before you woke up," he said softly. "That's who you were telling to stop."

"Yes," she nodded.

"But you didn't eat it, right? Not even in the dream?"

"No."

He took that in, and then nodded, too.

"So it was just a dream," he said. "And even in the dream you didn't eat the fruit, so what's the matter? What's still wrong?"

So she told him.

She told him about all the questions she'd had and all she'd wondered from the first moment she'd opened her eyes. She told him of the questions she'd wondered about Creation itself, and also about him, and their purpose, and the questions she'd wondered about what he'd asked of Michael—the first time they saw him, about who was created first—and then the questions he'd asked again when they stood above the waterfall and looked out at Creation.

She told him all that, and he looked back at her, shaking his head.

"What does that have to do with your dream?" he asked.

"Don't you understand?" she said, looking back at him. "It was knowledge that I sought, ever since I opened my eyes in Creation . . . and so it was knowledge he tempted me with."

He sat back then, as he heard her words, and she could see he understood now. She could see they both then knew he would return, the dark one, the dark angel, there was no doubt about that, and she could also see he realized now why she'd told him all she'd just told him, and why it was so important.

"You think he'll come to tempt me, too," he said, very softly, and they both knew it wasn't a question.

"Yes," she nodded. "I do."

"What do you think it will be?" he asked her. "What form do you think he'll take to seduce me, or what do you think he'll offer?"

"I don't know."

"But if you had to guess?"

"Power," she said quickly, too quickly.

Then as soon as she'd said the word, she paused, because once again she didn't know where the word she'd just spoken had come from. She'd spoken it, and it had come from her lips, but she didn't know what had made her say it, or who.

She thought about that, trying to calculate.

Next to her she saw his eyes as they began to blaze again, too, brightly and defiantly this time, and with all the strength he thought he felt inside.

He sat a little bit taller, there on the riverbank, and moved closer to her again, and held her. "Whatever it is, and whenever he comes again . . ." he said. "I'll be ready. I promise you that."

She moved closer to him, too.

She sat up and rested her head against his shoulder now, in the place that was between there and his chin, with his arm across her chest, and she liked that.

"I hope so," she said, and she knew this time where her words came from.

"I'll be ready," he said again, nodding now, and she could feel his voice, too, vibrating deep in his chest as he spoke. "I'll be ready for him, and I won't give in. Not to whatever he says, whatever he does, whatever he offers."

He thought about that further, then he was silent.

She kept looking back at him, next to her, as they sat.

She kept looking at his now-blazing eyes that were next to her own and as she did, she also looked at the fire that was still there in them. She kept looking at him and his eyes and as she did, she let herself hope; she let herself hope with everything she had inside and everything that was there between them that the words he'd just spoken were truth, and that they would be. She let herself hope, for just one more moment, then when that faded, too, and there was nothing else left, they finally stood and slowly turned to start on their way back towards the clearing, on the way back up and towards the home they shared, both of them hoping together that the shadows and darkness were finally gone, and the light had once again returned.

8

"WHAT DO YOU THINK his plan will be?"

"It's impossible to know, so all we can do is be prepared. But for what . . . I don't know yet."

"And what about the humans, in Creation? Do you think they know about it?"

Michael paused as he walked with Raphael, through the courtyard of the palace and underneath the high walls, then he turned to him: he was connected to the humans and to Creation, so he had felt it, too, when she'd woken from her dream of darkness and temptation. He'd felt the disturbance of it, but not the details or anything specific; just the emotion, the fear she'd felt, the uncertainty.

"I think they do know there's darkness that's come, yes," Michael finally said, nodding.

"Have they done anything about it?"

"I don't know."

"How do you not know?" Raphael frowned, as he looked back at Michael. "Haven't you been watching them? Haven't you been going back?"

"Not since I first visited," he answered. "Not since they were first made."

Raphael took that in as both he and Michael then turned towards the courtyard and all the other angels that were already there: they all had weapons, swords buckled at their hips and across their backs and in their hands, and they were practicing against each other in combat. Since the other angels had left and gone to darkness, the ones who'd remained were preparing for what inevitably would now come, they knew, either sooner or later, when those angels returned from darkness and came back in strength and force to either Creation or Heaven.

The weapons they practiced with, though, were new to them.

They'd brought them out at Phosphorus' trial, when the Light-Bringer had been cast out by Michael, but that was the first time in many thousands of years there had been swords or armor worn amongst the host of Heaven. There had been a revolt before, they knew, back at the beginning of time and all things, but there weren't any memories of it left amongst those that were still there in Heaven; there were just stories, passed down, and some even too hard to believe. But the stories were also truth, Michael knew, and there had been one who had come before them, one who had previously been in Heaven and had been cast out and fallen into darkness. Michael also knew that after the one who came before had been cast out, he then soon tried to return, and the great battle that ensued had shaped everything that now was and everything they now knew, which is why Michael had told them to sharpen their blades and begin to practice against each other.

"You asked Gabriel to watch over Creation," Raphael spoke slowly. "But you also asked him not to enter."

"Yes."

"Why? Why wouldn't you tell him to help them, if they needed it?"

"Because they haven't asked yet. And we must not interfere in their affairs unless they ask."

Gabriel took that in as he recognized Michael's words for what they were—truth, and also the words of God—and he thought about it further, and what it meant. He thought about the commitment to will and freedom that defined both Michael and God, the commitment to will and freedom for right or for wrong, for better or for worse, for everything, and that commitment would define both Creation and the humans who lived there, too, Gabriel realized. He thought about all this, then he finally nodded, in agreement, and understanding.

"So it shall be," he said.

Then he turned and he met Michael's eyes.

They stood there together for one more moment, then they clasped arms and Gabriel stayed by the walls while Michael kept walking on his own. Michael went through the courtyard near all the angels who were training. He walked by without looking at any of them in particular, then he was through them and on to the other side, but just before he left the courtyard, he did notice one who caught his eye, and he didn't know why. He looked younger and was more beautiful than the others, with features that were both soft and gentle, and hard and defined, all at the same time. He was sparring against another angel, and the metal of the blades they swung in great arcs clanged as they struck each other, and Michael watched them. He watched the young angel's natural ability, the seamlessness of his movements and precision of his blows, then when the angel finally got past his sparring partner's guard for what must have been the hundredth time that day, he struck a blow to his chest that would have won a real battle, and they stopped their match. They both sheathed their weapons and looked at each other and laughed, with friendship in their eyes, companionship, warmth, and a great deal of love, too. Michael kept watching as he listened to them talk, and as he did, his thoughts began to wander.

He wasn't expecting it, not there, not in Heaven, not in the light . . .

But a moment of darkness had returned and clouded his soul.

And it was a darkness, he realized, that was brought by regret, and longing, and something important that had been lost. Watching the two angels together, the beautiful and bright one's arm around the shoulder of the other, as they relived each moment of the mock-battle they'd just fought, Michael again felt something he hadn't felt in a very long time.

He wanted it to be good, but the truth was, while it once had been good, and it once had been beauty, it was now only pain for him.

And he felt that pain again.

As he did, and bowed his head, to try to hide it . . .

"Are you alright?"

He heard the voice next to him and he waited for a moment—he was gathering himself, and his strength—then the moment and pain finally started to pass as he looked up and saw the young, bright angel watching him, the one that had caught his attention, the one with the beautiful features and Michael saw the angel's partner was next to him watching, too.

Michael stood there and looked at them, one more time.

He studied the bright angel's face, his eyes, then Michael finally spoke.

"What's your name?" Michael asked him.

"Anael," the second angel responded first, and when Michael turned and saw Anael's eyes, too, the younger of the two of them, he also saw the younger angel's eyes were distinct in their own way as the color of them was a much deeper and more luminous shade of green than he'd ever seen before.

Michael took that in, curiously, making note of it.

"It's good to meet you, Anael," he said, then turned back to the first angel. "And you?" Michael asked. "What's your name?"

There was one more moment, as they looked at each other, and the bright angel finally answered.

"Selaphiel," he said.

Michael heard this name and as he did, he looked back at Selaphiel and studied him further. He looked at the fineness of his features and the strong lines of his jaw. He looked at the way his face was shaped and also the way his features seemed to carry in them so much youth and hope and promise for the future, and it brought him back to the memory of another bright angel who had youth and hope and light in his features, too, just like the one in front of him did, and an angel who had once been Michael's friend.

"Is there anything we can do for you?" Selaphiel asked him, his eyes not leaving Michael's, searching them for any wisdom and knowledge the older angel might have and wish to give, and also wondering why Michael had stopped to speak with them.

Michael looked back at Selaphiel and Anael, waiting for a moment. But then he just shook his head.

He didn't need to burden them and their youth with what he was thinking, and what he was feeling, and all that was now swirling inside him and threatening to spill out.

They didn't need that, they didn't need it at all.

So Michael just shook his head, as he looked back at them, then nodded.

"Keep practicing," was all he said instead. "Keep practicing, every day, for I fear that one day soon it won't be practice any longer."

Selaphiel understood what he meant and slowly nodded.

Then so did Anael.

Michael looked at them each for another moment, then he turned and kept walking.

As he went and was a few paces away, he could hear the loud clanging of their blades again as they resumed another round of combat, and as he heard that sound, he glanced over his shoulder: he looked back behind him and at them each one more time because it was something he realized he couldn't escape. It was because he saw himself in them. He saw himself and the one who had once been his friend, and more than that, too. Not once been . . . he still was, Michael knew. Michael knew he still was or at least could be as he looked back at the angels and saw his own youth and happiness from that time, from that time in his life that he'd felt the most and had been the happiest. In an instant it all flooded over him and he relived the joy of it, and also the pain. He thought about it, all of it. He thought about the only other angel he knew with such strength and beauty, the only other angel with such bright and luminous eyes, and were they still bright?

Or had they changed?

Had they, too, turned to darkness and ash, like everything else?

Michael thought about it all, and he wondered where Phosphorus was and what plans he now made, in darkness. He wondered if his friend still remembered, like Michael did, all the thousands of moments and afternoons they'd spent together like the one Michael had just seen play out in front of him, with Selaphiel and Anael.

Those were moments Michael had treasured, and still did.

Did Phosphorus still treasure them, too?

Or had those been moments, Michael wondered, and were those memories that had also been swallowed by darkness, like the part of Phosphorus' soul which made him do what he'd done. Michael kept watching the two angels in front him but his thoughts were somewhere else then because his thoughts stayed with Phosphorus and he wondered a great many things more. He wondered again about who they'd been together, and what had happened between them, and perhaps more than anything else—more than all the other things together—Michael wondered how Phosphorus still thought of him, and as he continued to watch Selaphiel and Anael, he felt pain; it was a great pain that came and settled in a cloud over his heart, and it did so because it was the worst type of pain, the type that was born of thoughts of all that once was, all that once could have been, but was no longer.

THE LIGHT THAT CAME from the fire danced across his handsome face.

Phosphorus stood near the blazing lake and watched as his own army of angels trained, too, not knowing that above him and in Heaven, Michael had been doing the exact same thing at the exact same moment. Phosphorus breathed heavily, in short, labored bursts, his body still not used to the humid and dust-filled air that was Below. He wasn't yet used to a great many things about his new life and kingdom and his place in it, with the air and darkness perhaps first among them, and as he watched the angels sparring against each other in the darkness, getting ready for all that would of course soon come, his thoughts turned to his previous life, too. The long and sharp shadows created by the flames from the lake flickered across his features as he thought again of Michael, and light, and Heaven. He thought again about who they'd been, and what he'd felt, and the choice Michael had made. Because that had been what it was, right? It was a choice, he told himself, and that choice is what had changed everything.

Phosphorus thought of all that, then he thought of something else.

He thought of Creation.

And he thought of the humans that were there, too.

When he'd first gone to Creation he'd seen his glimpses of them, as they stood in their clearing, with Michael, and looked together at the space that would soon be their home and the fields and orchard that would surround it. There had been the beginnings of it, in their eyes, he'd seen, the beginnings of it there in the way they'd looked at each other. He felt pain when he first saw it, deep inside, but the pain he felt there in Creation, the first time he'd gone, was nothing compared to the pain he'd then felt when he returned. When he'd gone back and disguised himself and then gone into their home while they were sleeping and had seen them there, together, in the same bed, holding each other, holding each other so close as they slept, it was as if a great blow had been struck in the pit of his stomach. That's why he'd froze as he stood and looked down at them, and why he'd inhaled so sharply: it was because he hadn't been ready to see, right there, in front of him, everything he'd always wanted and that he had with Michael. He'd had a very specific vision for his life and what he wanted it to be, ever since he could remember, ever since he'd been very young but in an instant that all had been taken and shattered and it had been taken and shattered by the one he'd trusted and loved most.

And so then, after it had been shattered, what then would matter to him?

Certainly not God, or light, or any of the rest of it.

Because he knew what he felt, the depths of it, and where was God in that?

Where was the light and goodness in what had come and what he knew then would be his eternal pain?

He shook his head to try to clear his thoughts, but he couldn't.

He hadn't meant to move against Michael and God so soon, but what he'd seen had stirred something in him, something he couldn't shake. He no longer had any power at all in Heaven, he knew, and he had less in Creation than he did in the darkness, that he'd discovered, also, and less than Michael and his angels of light. But there was still a way victory over his enemies might be achievable, because there was still a place where he had more power than they did, a place where Michael had never been or ventured before, and where his own power that came from light would weaken and fade, because it was a place where there was no light.

He looked around him.

He looked at the lake in front of him, and the fire coming from the surface, then the palace with the cracked stone and high walls behind him and he thought of the forgotten throne that was inside.

Then he turned and looked again at all the gathered angels, the ones who had once been bright, but had now turned to darkness.

He watched as they kept training and kept on with their exercises as they grew stronger and stronger by the day, the further they stayed away from the light, and the longer they were there, with him, in darkness. That was good, he knew, their gathering and expanding strength. He'd first gone and tried to test the woman with his temptation—temptation to eat the fruit, and all it would bring with it, all she desired, he knew— but she'd resisted, and he'd seen the strength that was in her soul, so he'd have to then test them in a different way.

He'd tested her soul, so now he'd have to test her heart.

Were his angels ready for that, and what would come with it?

Were they ready for the inevitable battle, and that which would shape all that would come after?

He didn't know yet.

He walked towards the palace then stood in front of the high walls.

In front of him all the angels stopped their training, then their collected eyes and attention turned to his, and he waited for a moment, the humid and ash-filled air lingering between them.

Then he cleared his voice and he spoke.

"You've trained, as I've asked you," he told them. "And you've all grown stronger."

"Is it time?" Báal asked, stepping forward from amongst the others.

Phosphorus turned to see his eager eyes, and he waited another moment, then finally nodded.

"Yes," he said. "It's time."

He watched as a murmur ran and spread through all the gathered host at this news, and he smiled a very small smile when he saw their reaction.

Then he raised his arms again, and they quieted, waiting for more words.

"You all know what's now happened," he told them. "You know that God's made a new place in the World he's called Creation, and in Creation he's made new beings, that he's called humans."

"Is that where we're going?" Mamanos asked, from his place next to Báal.

"They say that God's Creation marks the beginning of a new world, and the dawn of a new time," Phosphorus continued, still looking out at all of them. "I've seen these humans, these new beings he's made in his image, and while they might have been made in his image, they don't have all his strength, or Michael's, and yes, Mamanos, that's where we go. We'll go to Creation together. That's the blow we'll strike against him, and against Michael, because while he and Michael might think with this new world that's been made, so too has been made the future. But they're wrong. They're both so very wrong."

"How?" Báal asked.

"Because they didn't account for us. And just as there's no light without darkness, there's no future without all those who stand here today, so after that moment that will come—after our victory over God, and Michael, and over everything and everyone else that stands above us in judgment of who we are and how we've been made—we'll claim Creation as our own, and the humans that are there will serve us. And it will be our dominion, all of it, above and below, both, to rule over and do with as we will," Phosphorus told them, then paused in the middle of his sentence. He paused and looked around, at all those gathered. He met all the collected eyes that were there, then he smiled again, at what he saw, at all that was in front of him and his smile was wider this time, much wider, reaching all the way to his eyes. "Because after all that, and all that's going to now come," he finally told them, finishing, "that's then when a new world will truly begin."

9

$\mathcal{T}$HE NEXT MORNING, the night after her dream and the first night they spent together in their new bed, she slept straight through to morning, without waking, then she rose. After she'd risen, he felt her get up, so then he did, too, and they went to the table together where they each sat in their specific chairs and ate the remainder of the fruit she'd brought from the place near the waterfall. They ate together, as the sun rose, then when they finished, she carefully gathered all the seeds they'd set aside as they picked them from the flesh and their teeth, and after she'd gathered them, she gave them to him to plant in the field. They'd begun to see the very first bits of growth from the seeds they'd previously planted, together, but it would be a little while longer until they grew enough and matured enough to bear fruit of their own, she knew, so while he worked to plant even more crops that would grow, she would go back to the place by the waterfall and anywhere else she could to forage more food to sustain them until that which they'd planted became ready.

They left the house together, and as they did, he kissed her once, on the lips.

He went to the field, and she watched for a moment, as he began his work.

Then she left, too, to go about her own.

THE SUN WAS HIGH, and it was hot that day, so that's why she walked, instead of running. She carried her woven basket as she went through the forest—around the great trees, and underneath the branches that hung overhead—but her thoughts were still in the clearing and at their home. Her thoughts were still with him, and the river, and the cloud and shadow that had come and passed overhead and the moment they'd shared. Her thoughts were with him, and his chest, and her head resting there, rising and falling, and her thoughts were also with what would come next, both for them and for Creation.

As she continued to walk, the trees began to thin.

She was almost to the wide field of dandelions and wild flowers, the field where she'd first woken up, and that's then when she heard it.

It was a noise, coming from the trees.

She turned to where she thought it had come from, but there was nothing there. She was about to continue on, to leave the forest and head into the field, but then she heard it again, and this time she recognized it.

That's the sound a bird makes, she thought.

But there wasn't a bird in sight, not anywhere she could see.

She turned and turned, but there was still nothing she could find, then she heard it once more, and closer, and she whipped her head to try to find it but before she could, she heard it again, from a different place, more menacing, louder, and more near.

This didn't feel right to her, or good; it felt like darkness.

So she gave up trying to find it and started to run.

She wanted to make it to the field where there was more space, and more light, and the trees in front of her started to thin as she ran and was almost there when she finally saw it, the bird she kept hearing.

It was sitting on a branch, right in front of her.

She skidded to a halt before she reached it because she felt something deep inside her and recognized it as the same feeling she'd felt during her dream, when the angel had come to offer her the fruit and tempt her with its knowledge.

She skidded to a halt.

Then she spun the other way.

She was about to run back towards the clearing and her home, and the way she'd just come, but she stopped before she went any further because just as she was about to begin to run again, she saw he was already there.

The dark angel.

He just stood there, blocking her path home, not speaking.

And there was a smile on his face: a small, secretive smile that was spread wide across his features, and she breathed in fear now as she looked back at him.

They stood there in silence, taking each other in.

Then she found her voice.

"Who are you?" she finally asked him.

"I believe you've already asked me that," Phosphorus said as he kept smiling back at her, and she looked at his eyes now, his once-bright but now ash-grey eyes.

"So you're real, then?" she asked. "Or is this another dream?"

"No, it's not a dream," the angel told her. "But even then, even in your dream . . . I was real then, too."

"What are you doing here? What do you want from me?"

"But you already know that, don't you?"

"No."

"I want you to eat the fruit."

She looked back at him, trying to gauge his intention, and what might happen next.

Then she shook her head.

"No," she said again, and started to slowly back away.

"It's alright," Phosphorus breathed as he came forward, his strides longer than hers, bringing him closer. "It's just you and me here. It's just us now."

She watched as he reached his hand out.

He opened it, and in his palm, she looked down and saw the bright color of the fruit he'd taken from the Tree of Knowledge and brought along with him.

He'd offered it to her once before.

And now he offered it to her again.

"It's a gift," he told her. "It's a gift you should take, and that you should eat."

"I can't."

"Yes, you can."

She tried to look over his shoulder.

She tried to look past him towards the forest and the trees, and towards their clearing, where she knew he was working, plowing the field, planting the seeds they'd saved from the fruit they'd eaten.

But even if she could call to him, and get his attention . . .

Could he help her?

She didn't know.

Phosphorus saw her eyes, and knew her thoughts, what she was thinking.

He just smiled wider.

"He's not coming," Phosphorus told her. "He's still busy in his field, with his tool, turning the dirt and planting your seeds. And even if you call, he won't hear you here, where we are," he said as he came forward again, offering the fruit one more time, bringing it even closer. "Just one bite," he breathed. "Just one single bite, and there's no one here to see you do it."

"Yes, there is."

"Who? It's just us, and I won't tell."

"I'm here."

He paused at that, and cocked his head to the side.

It was almost as if it was a foreign thought to him, one that had never occurred, that we can be our own judge and hold ourselves accountable to what we should be and should do, even if the world doesn't, even if the world can't.

He wasn't human, she knew, of course he wasn't.

But as he stared back at her curiously and thought of her words, she realized he'd just perhaps seen his first real and true glimpse of this new type of creature she was, and just exactly what it might mean to *be* human.

She watched all this, as it passed across his face, then she watched as his face changed, and darkened.

"You can either eat the fruit of your own will," he told her, "or I can force you to eat it. This isn't a dream. This time it isn't something you can wake from. This is your future, and there's no one here to save you from it, no one else here to help."

She heard his words, and as she did, it sparked something inside her.

Especially the last two things he'd said.

There's no one here to save you from it.

And then, the other part.

There's no one here to help.

She'd heard his words, but were they true?

She turned inside and asked herself for guidance—this moment being one she knew she needed it more than any other, more than any other moment that had yet come in Creation—and that's when she once again heard the voice that was there, inside, and that she carried with her.

She heard the voice as loudly and clearly as she ever had before, and she did as it told her.

She closed her eyes.

Then she began to whisper, a silent prayer.

"*Please, God . . .*" she began. "*Lend me your strength now, here amongst your trees, in your forest, in your Creation; lend me your strength to help deliver me from this darkness that's come.*"

She spoke the words that had come to her, then she was quiet, and she didn't know the effect these words would have.

She didn't know that this silent, whispered prayer would be heard and cause Michael's eyes to snap open in fear from where he sat in Heaven, in deep meditation, and she didn't know that in an instant after hearing her prayer and call for help that he would gather all the host of Heaven to him and he'd also send word to Gabriel, where he waited on the peaks of Aetlas, there on the far northern and western edge of Creation. Michael's word would come in an instant through the divine connection they shared, and as soon as it did, Gabriel would spread his great wings and rise into the air with his companion Muriel next to him, then start to fly.

She didn't know any of this.

All she knew is what she felt she should do—what she'd been told to—and so she had.

In front of her, Phosphorus still stood there, and she could feel the anger emanating from him now.

"You shouldn't have done that," he told her, his voice pitched lower.

"What else would you have me do?" she asked him, meeting his eyes with her own.

"I'm not your enemy. On the contrary, I'm the only one who's offered you what you truly want, aren't I? Perhaps you should think about that because I'm the only one who's offered to give you the knowledge that you seek, and that you deserve. Why wouldn't Michael give it to you, or God? If knowledge is truth, then why should that be kept from you? Why should it be kept from any of us?"

She wanted to respond to him, with steel in her voice.

She wanted to respond to him with strength and fire and light.

But when she opened her mouth, she found no words came, and she knew the reason why, too. She heard his words, and what he'd spoken, and didn't it seem to make sense to her? She'd promised not to eat the fruit, but if it was truly knowledge the fruit held, should that really be something denied to her?

And how long would it be denied?

Forever?

For all their time in Creation?

For all the length of humanity?

Her mouth was still open and she thought of all this as she looked back at him, across from her, then just as her words were about to come the entirety of the earth was shook to its very core as Gabriel descended from the sky in a great flash of feathers and light and shining armor and slammed to the ground between them, herself on one side of him, and Phosphorus on the other.

She looked at him, and studied this new angel.

She hadn't seen him before: she'd only seen Michael, and the dark one.

And as she looked at him and compared the two of them, the first thing she noticed was he was bigger, physically larger, and with wings that would spread wider than either Michael's or the dark angel's in front of her, she thought. He also radiated the same goodness that Michael did, she felt; he was surrounded by the same light.

She took all this in as then another came and landed next to him, the angel that was called Muriel, who was smaller than Gabriel, and Michael, and the dark one.

"Back away from her," she heard Gabriel say, with strength in his words.

Phosphorus waited for a moment, looking back at Gabriel, across from him, and then she saw it . . .

His smile.

His small, dangerous smile.

"Why should I do that, Gabriel?" he asked.

"Because you were banished."

"I may have been banished from Heaven, and above . . . but there was nothing spoken of Creation."

"You're not to be here or anywhere else where there's light," Gabriel said, his hands then moving towards the two swords which she saw he wore across his back. "And you well know that."

"Yet, despite all I might know, here I am," Phosphorus said as he kept looking back at him, the smile still on his lips. "So tell me, what happens now?"

And in response to Phosphorus' question, Gabriel drew his swords, sunlight glinting bright off the polished steel.

Then next to him, Muriel did the same.

Phosphorus saw them, but he had no eyes for them anymore.

Instead, he looked past them, behind them, and she watched as he looked straight at her.

"It's time for a choice," he told her in his softest, most beautiful voice. "Come with me, and this will all be over, and come with me now because it's the last time I'll offer."

She paused and looked back and forth between them, between the light and the dark; she waited for Gabriel and Muriel to do something, or to say something . . . but then she realized they wouldn't.

She realized they were waiting for her.

They were truly letting her choose, as Michael had told them to do.

And in that moment, she discovered more about Creation and her place in it than she had in all the other moments she'd been there, up until that one.

It was darkness, that was offered, and it was light.

It was knowledge, that was offered, and it was belief, and she could only have one of them, she knew.

So she also knew what she must do.

"No," she said, finally, and with strength in her voice.

There was a short moment as they all waited, and that single word of denial and devotion echoed amongst them, and between all the trees around them, and there was still that smile, that small and dangerous smile that was there on the dark angel's lips, never moving, never wavering, then he spoke again, and his voice was different:

"As you wish," he told her, very softly.

Then it all began.

His wings exploded from beneath his tunic, the wings he'd kept hidden and she hadn't yet seen, and he quickly drew a sword, too, from where it had been strapped and held to his back.

His wings pumped and he flew across the distance in an instant.

Gabriel raised his blade and it met Phosphorus'.

She heard the deafening noise that came from the crashing of swords, the deafening sound that was now thunder echoing between the trees and all around them, and she covered her ears.

In front of her, the three angels rose into the sky.

They fought, great metal blades striking against great metal blades, and Phosphorus tried to get past Gabriel, tried to get past him and come towards her, but Muriel joined with Gabriel and they stopped him.

Or at least they stopped him for the moment.

Their blades kept spinning and striking against each other as they fought and fought and the thunder that came and continued to come was loud enough she was sure it would reach all the way to the clearing, and when it did, she knew what would happen.

He would hear it, coming from the forest, as he plowed the fields, then he'd stop and he'd wonder, and he'd be afraid.

Then he would come.

He'd come racing through the trees, looking for her, desperation and fear in his eyes—the two things she'd already seen there before, at the thought of losing her, at the thought of being alone—then they would watch the terrifying battle that was in the sky above them, together, and at least if they died at the end of it, or during it, then at least that would be together, too, right?

She thought of all that, then her eyes turned back above her.

She could still see the angels as they fought, and she heard Gabriel yell in his loud and deep voice:

"Go back below!" he shouted to the dark angel.

But Phosphorus remained calm and he just smiled.

"I rather like it here," she heard him say in response.

And then there was another flurry of mighty blows.

Phosphorus swung his sword quickly and Gabriel parried all the attacks, then Phosphorus whipped back around to Muriel while Gabriel was still recovering and Phosphorus swung again with Muriel bringing his sword in time to block the blow, but as she watched, she saw it knocked the younger angel off-balance and left him vulnerable and that's when Phosphorus took his opportunity and quickly flew forward and grabbed Muriel and threw him through the air and into the distance.

Then he turned back to Gabriel.

The two of them faced each other, and they were alone.

The angels looked at each other, as they flew, with Gabriel breathing heavily, slowly, gathering both himself and his strength.

"You forsook your time here, when you betrayed God," he told Phosphorus, and felt the conviction of his words deep in his heart and his soul. "You forsook everything with your betrayal and what you did."

Phosphorus heard his words and he just kept smiling.

"Perhaps you're right, Gabriel," he said, speaking slowly, calmly, measured. "Or perhaps when he cast me out, it was the end of his time, and the beginning of another."

"What other time?" Gabriel asked.

"*Mine*," Phosphorus answered.

Then his eyes flashed.

He flew forward in a great rush of air and power and he swung his sword.

It happened too quickly for Gabriel to defend himself and the blow caught him across the mid-section and sliced into his skin as Gabriel grunted in pain, then blood came. He was weakened, but even weakened he was still strong, and he brought his blade back around to parry the next strike from Phosphorus, and that was the one.

That was the one in which Phosphorus used all of his power, all his strength, and Gabriel realized as he defended himself that all the blows that had come before had only been made to pave the way for this great one, the one in which Phosphorus used everything he had and while Gabriel had been able to bring his sword around to defend himself—to parry the blow, once again—the strength of it knocked him backwards and he spun through the air, falling, falling, falling . . .

. . .

. . .

. . .

Until—

He slammed painfully into the ground with a great crash and shower of dirt, and it was right in front of her, right in front of where she stood, right there at her feet.

He looked up.

His face was covered in dirt and blood now, she saw, and as he looked up, she met his eyes, and could see the fear that was there in them and it wasn't something she'd ever seen in the eyes of an angel before, either light or dark, and it was terrifying.

"*Run*," he whispered.

She hesitated, just for a moment.

Then he told her again, stronger this time, louder.

"Run," he shouted. "Now!"

So she did.

She began to go in a zig-zag pattern though the trees as above her the dark angel flew and flew and he gained ground, getting closer to her. He had to dodge the branches of the forest as he went—the branches that were above her—making sure they didn't hit or puncture his wings as he flew, and she tried to push herself as hard and fast as she could, straining all the muscles she'd recently built in her legs and from her time running those very same paths, but soon there was an opening in the branches and he was almost to her, about to swoop down and stop her, when—

She heard blades crash again, above her.

She dared another glance upwards as she kept running and that's when she saw that Muriel had returned: the angel had almost caught Phosphorus unawares, because Phosphorus had forgotten about him, but he turned his head just in time and parried the blow that came.

Then Muriel yelled at him.

"Stay away from her!" he said.

But Phosphorus just shook his head, as he raised his sword again.

"You chose the wrong side, Muriel," Phosphorus responded, and when she heard his words, she heard the familiarity in them and realized for the first time just how well these angels must know each other, which meant the wound of the dark one's betrayal must be very fresh, that the time since he'd been cast out from above hadn't been very long.

Then she watched as Muriel unleashed another blow, but Phosphorus easily blocked it.

She saw as above her they rose further into the air, together, high above the trees now, once again locked in a deadly dance but unlike Gabriel, this angel was no match for Phosphorus' strength.

Their swords spun and twisted in the air.

They struck great blows against each other as they flew.

But then soon Muriel's strength began to wane as he was overwhelmed by Phosphorus' power and skill, and he was pushed further and further down and towards the ground, with Phosphorus above him, pushing him even further, lower, then Phosphorus flicked his sword in a neat, tight arc, and it cut Muriel across the left wing, slicing it in half.

Muriel yelled.

He screamed in pain as steel cut through feather and bone.

Then she saw as Muriel spun in the air, changing trajectory in mid-flight before gravity came and without the angel's wing intact to fly, he began to quickly plummet towards the ground, still spinning, spinning, then finally hit the grass and dirt and he used his arms to brace himself against impact and as he did, she saw one of his wrists bend back and break. He yelled in pain again, just as Phosphorus descended, and landed next to Muriel, on top of him, his foot pressed down onto Muriel's throat, choking him, holding him in place.

Muriel struggled, but it was no use.

Not with a broken body, and not against the dark one's strength.

"You chose the wrong side, Muriel," she heard Phosphorus tell him again, and she wondered at that, at the same choice of words. "You know that, in your heart."

"I honored my oath," Muriel said, struggling to get the words past his lips.

Then she stopped running and watched what would happen, from her place in the forest, with horror in her eyes as she saw Muriel swallow then spit blood.

"No," Phosphorus told the angel, shaking his head. "You chose chains, which is no choice at all."

"There are no chains on these wings."

"I know that's what you think, and that's also why you now have to go."

There was one more moment.

There was one more moment, when they just stood there, all three of them, then in one quick motion Phosphorus raised his blade, and—

He stabbed it down.

He used all his great strength and the sharpened edges of the weapon plunged through Muriel's breastplate and deep into his body and as it did, the angel's eyes went wide—they went very wide—and for a moment everything was calm, and completely still.

She knew there was nothing she could do now, nothing she could do to help him, so she turned and began to run again and as she did, she didn't see what happened behind her, and how Muriel's body started to change.

Light came, from inside, from deep inside . . .

And it caused Muriel's body to begin to glow.

Energy emanated from it, leaking from the pores of the skin and spilling out in fractured beams of great, arcing light that reached up, up, up, back up towards all that was above, back up towards Heaven.

The light kept growing, expanding.

It kept growing and it became stronger, brighter, more powerful, until all of a sudden the moment happened and Muriel's body exploded in a great shower of light that scattered all around, between the trees and up into the sky, and the force of it knocked her from her feet as she ran and she fell back to where she landed heavily on the ground again.

She was stunned.

She lay there for a moment as she paused and tried to regain her bearings again through the ringing that was now in her ears from the great explosion.

She painfully tried to stand, and that's when she saw him.

Phosphorus was now right there again, standing in her way, blocking her path through the forest and back towards the clearing and her home.

She got the rest of the way to her feet.

She stood and faced him again.

"Stay away from me," she told him.

But he ignored her words and started to walk forward.

He kept coming and coming, and she found she was frozen in place again: she was frozen in place as he came towards her, in the same way she had been in her dream, and she couldn't move her arms, or her legs, or her mouth anymore, she found, then he was about to reach her and even if she could have moved, it was pointless then, she knew; it was pointless when he could fly, and she could only run.

Then he was there.

He was to her, close enough to where he could reach out and his hand would touch her own hand, and he could put in it the fruit she saw he carried again, and she knew that's what he would do and she wouldn't be able to stop him. She was about to close her eyes, not wanting to witness it, not wanting to witness her end and betrayal, but then the ground shook again: more dirt and earth was displaced as she shielded her eyes, then when it settled, and she was able to look once more, she saw a familiar sight.

It was Michael.

Then she saw more of them, all of them, coming from above, coming from Heaven. She watched as they all came and landed next to their leader and then Gabriel came, too, from the distance, and they all looked back at Phosphorus there across from them as the dark angel now faced in front of him an entire army.

It was an Army of Light.

But Phosphorus didn't look worried.

He just watched very calmly as Michael slowly turned his eyes to the place where moments before Muriel's body had rested, but was now gone, and all that was left was the charred grass that had been bent and burnt from the fire and light that had exploded from within him.

"You've gone too far," Michael said, and his voice was just a whisper, because it was shaking. "You've gone too far now."

Then he turned and met Phosphorus' eyes.

"I think I've heard you tell me that before," Phosphorus said as he looked impassively back at him, without blinking.

Michael shook his head, clearing his thoughts, clearing his mind.

Then he drew his sword from where he carried it at his hip.

"It's over," he said. "We have the numbers, and we have me."

"No," Phosphorus told him. "It's not over because how could it be when it's so clearly only just begun?"

She heard Phosphorus' words, from where she stood, and she heard the way he spoke them, and as soon she did, she knew; she knew in an instant this was the exact moment he'd planned for, ever since he'd fallen into darkness.

He'd wanted all this to happen, she realized.

And now it had.

A cloud passed over the sun, and shadows came.

She looked up and thought it was just a cloud, the same as had come and blocked the light before, when everything had gone dark, but then when she looked she quickly realized it was a cloud, but it was also something else, too, and her heart sunk deep in her chest when she saw.

It was more of them.

It was more dark angels that had now come to the forest—that had come up from their place below—and they'd flown there to Creation while its borders had been left unguarded, then they began to come down from the sky. They flew quickly, dark wings guiding their path until they came to land next to their leader. There were then two armies that faced each other, across a narrow distance that was spread between them, two great and powerful hosts.

One made of light.

One made of darkness.

Michael sized them up, those that were across from him.

Then he slowly shook his head again.

"You've made a mistake," he said loudly, addressing all of them.

"How could it be a mistake if it's what's in our hearts?" Phosphorus answered evenly, and for all those who stood next to him.

And that was it, she could see, those would be the only words spoken, and that's then when it really began.

Great wings spread from the angels on both sides and from both gatherings, then they all rose into the air, two great hosts moving as one, rising above Creation . . .

They each drew their swords.

Then she watched as wings pumped and there was a rush of wind that blew her hair back and nearly pushed her to the ground as the angels exploded into motion and the space that was between them disappeared in an instant—in perhaps even less than that, she thought—and angels from each side crashed into each other and the trees and ground and very earth itself shook as some of the angels were knocked from the sky and fell to the grass a few paces from where she stood, only to quickly rise again and fly to rejoin the fight.

She covered her ears from the great noise, and she looked up.

She looked up from her place on the forest floor and through all the pandemonium—through all the winged-bodies that flew and fought and dueled—and in the middle of it all, in the very center of the battle, that's where she saw Michael and Phosphorus.

They each fought through many adversaries.

Then they engaged each other, again, one more time.

Their strikes were lightning and their blows were more than thunder.

She was mesmerized by it, watching their beautiful and deadly dance that had been practiced and rehearsed so many times in their youth and had led to this single moment of familiar combat.

Then she heard something else, over the noise of battle.

It was a voice, a human voice, and it was calling to her.

She turned, and when she did, she saw it was him, and that he was running towards her, just like she knew he would after he heard the noise of the battle.

The first thing he did was look at her, across the space between them.

When he saw she was alive, she saw the relief that came to his eyes.

Then she watched as his eyes turned, and he looked above them, in complete awe at the scene that was unfolding in the sky above Creation.

There were angels everywhere.

There were blades, and wings, and feathers, and blood, and some of the angels had begun to fall all around them as she yelled to him across the distance.

"Stay there!" she called.

But he didn't listen to her.

Instead, he began to run towards where she stood.

He ran underneath where the battle continued above and more angels fell from the sky to the ground. He dodged the bodies as they crashed into earth, then the angels that fell pumped their wings to rise back to the sky, and she watched all this, too.

She watched as Michael and Phosphorus continued their great battle.

And she watched more than that, as well.

She watched as Raphael fought against Baal, and Mamanos swung his sword to meet Gabriel's.

And closer to her, away from those great battles near the center, she watched as the young angel Selaphiel fought against three of the dark ones by himself, with Anael at his side, fighting another that came. She saw Selaphiel hold his ground, even against the overmatched numbers, but next to him Anael wasn't as strong, and he soon became overwhelmed. She watched as a blow from the angel that Anael was fighting got past his guard, and it sliced him across the wing.

It caused him to spin in the air.

Then the dark angel came closer.

The dark angel kicked him in the chest and pumped his black wings with great strength, as he kept his feet there on Anael's chest and forced him down, down, until they crashed into the ground, right next to where she stood.

The dark angel was on top of Anael, pinning him to the earth.

She took all this in, then in a split second without stopping to think of anything else or further, she rushed forward to help, and the man who still ran towards her called to her, telling her to stop, and so did Selaphiel, still battling against the darkness above.

"No!" they both yelled.

But she didn't listen.

She hit the dark angel with her clenched fist, to push him off Anael, but when she punched him . . .

He didn't move.

Instead, he slowly turned to see her standing there, behind him, then he swung a great back-hand that caught her squarely on the jaw and sent her flying through the forest.

She landed heavily.

The man saw this, and kept running, then he was to her.

"Are you hurt?" he asked.

She was still dazed, catching her breath, the wind knocked from her, but she shook her head

"I'm fine," she breathed.

She stood with him helping her to her feet, and looked next to them, to where she saw the dark angel still on top of Anael and pinning him to the ground, his sword raised now, his sword raised and ready.

"Don't . . ." she whispered, very softly.

But the dark angel just smiled as he looked back at her then he brought the sword down in the blow that would take Anael's life just as a blur sped from the sky faster than eyes could move and tackled him to the ground and when the shower of dirt that came with the impact cleared, she saw Selaphiel was on top of the dark angel and she saw his bright sword as it ran clean through the breast of his enemy, then he pulled it back out, and turned to her.

"Go," he said. "Quickly now."

There was one moment, between them, their eyes together, all of them.

Then she nodded.

She took the man by the hand and they began to run together.

Behind them, Selaphiel helped Anael to his feet before they both spread their wings and flew back above to rejoin the battle as the body of the angel they left began to glow, emanating darkness from inside of it, rather than light. She didn't see this, though, because she was running with him at her side, holding his hand, and as they did more bodies fell from the sky and they dodged them as they fell all around, until one fell right in front of them, and they skidded to a stop, just as—

The body of the angel behind exploded in a great burst of darkness.

The force of the explosion threw them from their feet and forward through the air and they landed heavily.

They both quickly tried to sit up, dazed from hitting their heads, then they slowly stood again, together, regaining their bearings.

Once they did, they saw one of the dark angels had fallen during the explosion, too; he'd fallen from his place in the battle and in the sky and fought fiercely with another angel of light who was wounded, there on the ground—both locked in combat together—then the dark one got the upper-hand and ran his sword through the breastplate of his enemy.

The angel of light fell to the ground and lay still.

The dark one stood over the body.

Then he bent down and picked up the body, just as it began to emanate light from inside and he used all his strength to throw it to the other side of the forest so that when it exploded and burst into light and the soul departed, it would be away from them and where they were, then the dark angel spread his great wings and was about to go back to the battle until he saw the humans, where they stood, and he paused.

He looked at them, his head cocked to the side.

Then he began to walk.

He came straight towards them.

She saw this, frozen in the middle of the forest with him by her side, and the battle still waging above them, all around them. Then the man went forward and she watched as he went to stand between her and the dark angel that was coming, and nearly to the place where they were.

"Don't come any closer," she heard the man say.

The dark angel smiled.

"Brave," he said. "But also misguided."

"Leave us alone."

"Why should I?"

"This isn't your dominion."

"It might not be, but who's going to stop me. You?"

She looked around them, desperate to try to find some sort of escape, but there was none.

Michael was engaged above, as were all the others.

The dark angel could fly faster than they could run, she knew, and so did he, then she watched as the man saw something.

A sword.

When the dark angel had thrown the body of the angel of light across the forest, the angel had been holding his sword which had spun from his grip as his fingers loosened and slacked while his life departed, and the man went forward now and bent down next to where the blade lay in the grass. He looked at it for a moment, then slowly wrapped his fingers around the handle of the celestial weapon, and stood again.

He went back to his place in front of her, his place between her and the darkness.

He faced the dark angel, with the weapon now in his hand.

"No . . ." she whispered, and tried to move forward, knowing what would come next.

But he wouldn't listen to her.

"It's the only way," he said.

And she knew he was right.

She knew there was nothing else they could do.

"Surely you can't think this will change anything?" the dark angel asked, with a smirk now on his lips.

The humans just looked back at him, neither answering.

So the dark angel shrugged.

"Very well," he said.

Then he came forward and swung his blade, with the man bringing his own around to meet it, and their weapons struck.

Dark steel clashed against light.

And the battle between them began.

The dark angel quickly brought his sword back around in a great blow that the man parried, and she watched as he did, and saw his muscles strain and flex under the force of the blow, the muscles she'd watched grow as he worked in the field and orchard.

Then she turned and saw something else.

She saw the look in the dark angel's eyes.

It surprised her because the angel seemed to be surprised, too, and she knew it was because of the strength he saw come from this human. Then she peeled her eyes from the duel and looked around: she wanted to find another sword or anything else she could that might help. There was a lull in the battle in front of her—the man and the dark angel circling each other—then the man saw her as she searched, and knew what she was doing.

But he shook his head.

"No," he told her.

"I can help," she said.

"Just stay back."

She could hear the confidence in his voice.

It was a note and tenor she hadn't yet heard before.

She opened her own mouth to respond, but then paused, because the look she saw in his eyes now she recognized because it was the same as the look that had been there on top of the waterfall, as he'd stared out and surveyed all of Creation. It was a look of conquest; a look of strength. Her mouth was open, but then before any of the words came, the dark angel rushed forward and their duel began again and there was a great flurry of blows which he parried—every single one of them in neat, strong, confident movements—and the dark angel kept pushing forward, attacking every opening he saw, trying to exploit every weakness he could find but in doing so, he left his own guard open, only for a moment, only for a split second but she watched as the man saw it, too, then brought his own sword back around in an arc and flash of blinding metal and natural, intrinsic instinct, that surprised perhaps even him, and ran the dark angel through his chest.

His sword pierced straight through the breast-plate, and it stayed there.

The dark angel looked down at the wound with surprise in his eyes.

He opened his mouth, but then death began, and no words came though just before the angel departed, there was something else she saw in the angel's eyes, too, and it was a realization, perhaps; a realization of the strength and fortitude with which his opponent had been made, something he hadn't expected to find in these new creatures, these humans he'd been told about and that he'd now discovered.

He stood there, and watched all of this, too, then she spoke, breaking the moment.

"*Let go*," she whispered quietly.

"What?" he answered.

"Let go of it," she said, louder now.

He frowned as he turned to her, then followed her eyes and looked down: he hadn't realized he was still holding the handle of the blade which had begun to turn red-hot and glow and burn his skin, which he could now smell and feel, and when he heard her words, and understood what she was telling him, he quickly let go of the sword.

It fell to the ground where it slowly began to melt.

Then the dark angel fell, too, down to the grass in front of them.

She saw this then looked up to the battle still raging above them, the forces of light just beginning to push back the forces of darkness, and then turned back in front of them: the body of the dark angel he'd just killed began to glow, then more bodies fell from the sky, and they began to glow, too.

She knew what would happen, what was about to come.

"Run," she said to him.

"What?" he answered, his ears still ringing from the thunder above.

"Come on!" she yelled.

Then she grabbed his hand, and they began to run, together.

They ran through the forest and back in the direction he'd just come, towards their clearing, as more and more bodies fell around them, some getting up to rejoin the fight, some laying still, the life leaving them, and then beginning to glow. As they ran, she risked one more glance above them, and when she looked up, she saw Michael and Phosphorus still locked together in combat, at the center of everything, at the center of the fighting, then she saw Michael unleash a great blow that knocked Phosphorus back and away from him.

Phosphorus was knocked off-balance, she saw, then he regained his bearings and looked around.

She watched as he took in what was happening, that everywhere he turned the dark angels were losing, being overcome by light, and she watched as he then opened his mouth wide and yelled to his angels:

"Higher!" he called to them.

She heard Phosphorus shout, as she ran, and so did he.

The dark angels that followed also heard, and they listened.

They all disengaged from their opponents and began to fly up, up, higher and higher, towards where Phosphorus had disengaged himself from Michael and was waiting for them.

Then when they were there, they all turned as one.

They looked at their enemies, all the angels of light, arrayed against them in Creation—where the darkness had less power—then the dark angels all spread their wings again, and there was a loud noise as they exploded into the sky, on their way back to Below, and from where they came.

She saw Michael rally his angels to him, too.

He called for all his angels to join, and follow him, and there was another noise as they spread their wings and gave chase, another loud and thunderous sound.

Then there were no more angels in the sky.

Still, though, she kept running, with him next to her, and she went even faster now, trying to urge him to keep up because behind them on the forest floor she knew the bodies of the angels that were all there and had fallen were beginning to glow even more, even brighter—emanating both light and darkness—and the moment was almost upon them, the moment she knew was about to come.

"Hurry!" she yelled.

And they tried to go faster.

They pushed themselves, as much as they possibly could, and she led the way with her strong and well-muscled legs, pulling him behind her, and they ducked under branches, dodged between trees, until finally—

KA-BOOM!

They staggered at the first explosion, and almost fell, then—

KA-BOOM!

KA-BOOM!

KA-BOOM!

Even more explosions rocked the forest as the bodies behind them all exploded in great mixtures of darkness and light and the release of such energy and power brought with it a force that leveled all the trees around them and lifted both humans well off their feet.

They flew wildly, through the air.

And then they began to fall and landed heavily on the ground, next to each other, and they lay there for a moment.

Then once again, they slowly stood.

They checked each other for injuries, and dusted themselves off.

"Are you alright?" he asked, as he looked her up and down.

"I think so," she told him. "Are you?"

"I think so, too."

They each looked at the other for one more moment, and they were each whole, it seemed.

The angels above them were gone, they saw again.

And they had survived.

They kept looking at each other as they took that in, then slowly turned and looked behind them at the destruction that had come to the forest, and the great crater that was now there in the ground: the massive hole that had been blown into the dirt from the force of the exploding bodies and departing souls.

Then she turned to him, next to her.

He was still staring at the bent and splintered trees, and the great crater in the earth.

"What was that?" he finally asked.

"That's what happens when they die," she told him.

"Why?" he asked.

She shrugged.

"I don't know," she said.

They stood there together and surveyed the destruction for one more moment, then she saw as his eyes turned back down to his hand—the one that had held the blade that had glowed and melted—and she saw it was shaking as he rubbed it with his other hand.

"Does it hurt?" she asked.

"No," he answered.

She knew he was lying.

Then he spoke again.

"What do we do now?" he wondered.

"I guess we go home," she said.

He stopped and looked back at her.

She met his eyes and recognized the look that was there in them because it was the one she'd now come to know so well—the look of pride, and of strength—but then she saw something else, too, something she didn't quite recognize and she wondered about it, but then quickly received her answer.

You're my home, his eyes said.

She once again saw truth, so she knew that it was, and they turned to leave, together, to head back to the clearing.

ON THE OTHER SIDE of space and time, Michael and all the rest of the angels of light soon came to the dark kingdom that was Below.

They descended down through cloud, dust, and ash.

As they did, they began to choke on the hot and unfamiliar humid air.

It caught in their lungs, and they coughed as they flew.

Then they burst through the cover of clouds and as soon as they did, they saw Phosphorus and the others in front of them. They were there waiting, near the lake of bright, burning fire, and as soon as Michael saw them, he also heard Phosphorus yell.

"Now!" Phosphorus shouted.

The word echoed through the humid air.

It echoed across the craggy, dark landscape.

Then Phosphorus and all the dark angels that flew with him reached down into the lake and grabbed handfuls of the water which they threw and as the water spun and twisted through the air, it turned into great balls of flame.

Michael saw this, and what was happening, and as he saw it, he shouted, too, a warning.

"Protection!" he yelled.

Then he raised his sword, and his strong and armored fists.

So did the all the others around him, just as the wall of fire crashed into Michael and his angels with a great explosion and it knocked them backwards, scalding and burning their bodies and their feathers and wings, then they all heard Phosphorus yell again.

"Forward!" he shouted.

And the dark angels flew as one.

There was a giant wave of them, all flying in sync, at the exact same time, getting closer, closer, as Michael and his angels braced themselves, the momentum from their flight halted and stymied then Michael and his angels raised their swords in defense once more and the two lines crashed against each other and the battle resumed.

The dark angels had the advantage.

The angels of light were vulnerable, after the attack with the fire.

Michael saw all this so he cut his way through a few of his enemies, using his superior strength, then found himself engaged with Phosphorus again because this was the only way to end everything, he knew, the only way to end this rebellion of darkness.

Then he was to him, and there wasn't any more time for words.

There would just be steel between them now.

Just steel and blood.

Michael swung his blade, and Phosphorus parried.

But instead of immediately gaining the upper-hand with his superior strength, as Michael had in Heaven, and as he also had in Creation, here in the darkness, this battle was different, he could feel, because here in the darkness, he felt his strength start to ebb.

As soon as he felt that, he also felt Phosphorus' power begin to grow.

"What's happening?" he asked, speaking softly, not more than a whisper.

Then he thought more, and he knew.

It was also in that moment he understood Phosphorus' plan and why he'd attacked Creation only to lure them there, Below: he understood that all the power he had came from light, so then he also understood that Below there was no light, only darkness, and the one in front of him which it fed, the one who had once been his friend and had once been called Light-Bringer, but now was no more.

Michael looked around and saw all his angels begin to falter, too.

They began to falter, becoming overwhelmed.

"Fall back!" Michael yelled.

He yelled as loudly as he could, knowing that to continue to fight in the darkness was nothing but death for them, and all the angels of light heard him, and they tried to disengage with their opponents.

Michael surveyed what was in front of him, and next to where he flew there was an angel named Urania who fought against Báal, and she began to get overwhelmed, too.

Michael saw this and tried to fly to help her.

Phosphorus also saw, and he cut Michael off, re-engaging him in their battle and their blades swung again and struck together.

"Get out of my way!" Michael yelled to him.

But Phosphorus didn't move, and didn't respond.

He just kept fighting.

Michael knew he couldn't get past Phosphorus, not there in the darkness and without light, so all he could do was just look past him and watch as Urania fought.

Báal flew above her.

He got higher than she was and used his strength to overwhelm her.

He disarmed her with a neat flick of his sword, and her own fell from her hand and plummeted down towards the dark and ash-filled ground below them.

She was defenseless, alone.

She looked at Michael, to her side.

Then she looked at Báal, above her.

There was nothing that she could do, so . . .

She spread her arms wide, one to each side, closed her eyes and began to softly whisper a prayer.

"No!" Michael yelled.

And he yelled because he knew what came next.

He watched as Báal smiled, then flexed his muscles and ran his dark sword through Urania's heart and Michael called out again because it was as if his own heart had just been pierced, too.

He watched as she froze, there in the air.

Then her wings slowed, and stopped altogether.

She began to spiral in a fast and dizzying circle as her body fell down through the darkness, following the same path as her blade had taken moments before.

Michael watched as her body fell.

Then as he did, he saw something else.

He saw all the rest of the great battle laid out in front of him, and how badly his angels were losing. Everywhere he looked he saw light being overcome by darkness, and he wanted to help them, but Phosphorus blocked his path, and he realized this was his intention and had been his game; it had been his game from the very beginning.

But Michael couldn't take his eyes from the scene.

He couldn't peel them away from all the pain and failure and death.

Near where he flew, he saw Selaphiel and Anael fighting next to each other.

They were fighting against unwinnable odds, against a host of twenty dark angels, led by Mamanos, and they did their best, against them all, but without their strength, and light, they were soon overwhelmed, too.

Selaphiel fought against most of them and held his ground.

But next to him, Anael began to fail.

Anael fought as hard as he could, then a blow caught him under the chin which caused his head to snap back and when it did, it left his entire chest exposed.

Selaphiel saw this, and he yelled.

"No!" he called.

He tried to fight his way though the battle, to Anael's side . . .

But it was too late.

Mamanos raised his great and dark sword then quickly brought it around and ran the blade through Anael's breastplate.

Michael shuddered in pain again.

He could feel all this death; he could feel it inside himself.

He heard Selaphiel scream.

They both saw as Anael's bright and luminous eyes shifted, changed, and became clouded, no longer the startling shade of green they once had been, and they also watched as Anael then began to fall from the sky. Selaphiel tried to renew his attack, fighting with even more rage and fury now, trying to fight through to get to his friend, but Gabriel and Raphael came forward and grabbed him.

They held him.

They pulled him back.

He was trying to fight against the entire host of darkness on his own now, which would have surely ended in his death, too, but he didn't care.

And that's why he had to be saved by his friends.

Michael watched all this with pained and heartbroken eyes.

Then Phosphorus spoke, from his place across from him.

"It didn't have to be this way, Michael," Phosphorus told him, shaking his head.

Michael was silent for a moment, as the angels of light began their retreat.

Then he spoke again.

"And what would you have me do?" Michael asked. "Just give you the keys to Heaven, and have you rule there in his stead?"

"You have no idea, do you?" Phosphorus shook his head. "You have no idea what you truly are."

"Yes, I do. I'm his servant."

"You're his slave!" Phosphorus shouted. "Don't you understand that yet?"

Michael watched as his host retreated even further, back towards the light.

He watched as Gabriel and Raphael pulled Selaphiel with them towards Heaven, and the rest followed after. They all retreated, and left, and when the last of them were gone and safe, it was only Michael that was still there in darkness.

He turned back to Phosphorus again.

It was just the two of them, and when Michael spoke, he spoke very softly, with tears in his eyes now.

"I loved you," Michael whispered. "You were my brother, and you were more than that, too."

Phosphorus met his eyes.

Then he shook his head, resolutely.

"You ruined everything," Phosphorus told him. "It could have been different, it could have been so different, but you ruined everything, all that we were and all that we had together and could have been."

Michael heard these words, and they made him pause.

Then something strange happened, and even though he was surrounded by darkness—extending in front of him, in every direction—a strange warmth came to him and he saw the faintest glimmer of light on the horizon, and he knew why. He'd heard Phosphorus' words and knew that what had now come to pass had come to pass for a reason, and that even darkness has its place when one steps back and looks at the entire and great span of things, and not only a single moment.

"No," Michael breathed, almost to himself.

"What?" Phosphorus asked.

Then Michael turned back to Phosphorus and saw all the great host of darkness Phosphorus had gathered and that had come now, and Michael was the last angel of light that was there, so it was just him who stood and faced all that darkness, and the leader of the darkness. They all flew there like that for a moment, together, suspended in the heavy and humid air, wings pumping up and down, up and down, then there was the roll of a very great and deep sound and a distant flash that flicked across all their features, and when it came, Michael smiled.

"Thank you," he told them.

And he spread his great wings, as they all watched . . .

Then he exploded back towards Heaven, and the light.

THE HUMANS WALKED SLOWLY as they returned to the clearing.

Behind them in the distance, the sky still flashed, and they also heard the low and distant sounds of rumbling and it was a sound that could have been mistaken for thunder, but despite the coming storm that was on the horizon, they knew what those noises really were.

It was more angels.

It was more angels falling, and dying.

The humans didn't know anything about Below yet, but they knew the battle between light and darkness had continued after it had left their forest, and they also knew there was undoubtedly going to be a great number of casualties on each side.

They knew all this, what was surely happening Below, and they kept walking because there was nothing else they could do, nothing else that could be done.

They finally came back to their clearing.

They walked towards their home.

The storm they'd seen on the horizon had moved quickly and gotten closer, and they felt the first of the raindrops that came with it hit their skin, so they went to the structure and stood underneath the roof, just at the edge of it, and watched from the place there that was dry as the rest of the storm then came.

Soon the sound of angels dying faded.

Then there was only thunder left, real thunder, the natural kind.

They stood and kept watching the storm for a moment, as the rain picked up and started to come even harder, then he finally spoke:

"What was that?" he asked, very softly.

She was quiet for a moment.

She took it all in, everything that had just happened.

"I'm not sure," she told him.

"They came for you again."

"I know," she said. "I was wrong."

"Wrong about what?" he asked.

But she didn't answer.

She just turned and looked back at him, once more, searching his eyes.

She thought she'd understood Creation, and perhaps what they were meant to do there, and what might come, but she'd been wrong. She'd been so wrong. She'd known they weren't alone and that it wasn't always going to be just them, just the two of them, but what of all the rest, all the rest that had happened?

She'd had no idea.

Perhaps she never would, she thought.

And was that such a bad thing?

It didn't seem so then, she felt, or at least as much as it once might have seemed, and then she realized something else: she realized where all these thoughts that came were bending towards because all these thoughts she'd just had were about *knowing*, and about *future*.

But what if that wasn't what was most important?

What if that paled in comparison to *feeling*, and *now*?

She kept looking at his eyes.

She saw again what they'd told her in the forest, and that was it, she knew: that was why she was there.

That was why *they* were there.

She looked down at his hand that was next to his side—the one that had been burnt when the sword he'd held to protect them had glowed and melted—and she took that hand in her own. He'd told her it didn't hurt, but she also knew what he'd said wasn't truth, so she finally turned away from the storm and led them further into their house where she brought him to sit at the table he'd made.

"It's alright," he told her again.

"I know," she answered.

"It doesn't hurt," he said.

Then he flexed it back and forth to show her.

"It might not hurt," she told him. "But this will help."

Then she tore a long strip of cloth from her tunic.

She walked back to the edge of the house to hold it in the rain to get it wet, then came back and wrapped the cloth around the blisters that were on his hand and tied it tightly, too, so it wouldn't move. It chilled the burn that was on his palm and it helped remove the heat from the skin. It would make it feel better, she knew, but she also knew the wound would leave a scar; it would leave a scar that would eventually fade, but never really leave.

She looked down at it there, on his hand, on his palm, then she looked back up at him.

She realized how close he was.

Their faces were inches apart from each other but it wasn't that type of proximity she felt, she realized, as it had nothing to do with physical closeness, even as she could feel him next to her breathing in short, shallow bursts, as the rain pounded on the roof above which is something she'd never felt or heard from him before, him breathing in such a way.

But she also knew why.

Because she felt the same way he did, too.

"You were right," he finally whispered to her.

"About what?"

"There are others that are here."

"Yes," she told him, still looking into his eyes, and she held his eyes with her own.

This was now a moment, she knew, and it was important.

"There are others that are here," she told him. "And there will still be more that come, too. But no matter who else comes, or whatever else there is or will be, you're here, and so am I . . . and I choose you," she breathed, and she could hear the truth in her own voice. "It's you that I choose, for all eternity. It's you and no other."

She looked back at him, across from her.

She watched as he took in her words, her promise, her sacred vow.

Then after a moment, he smiled.

"I'm already yours," he told her, answering her sacred vow with his own.

They sat there and looked at each other.

What he'd told her was truth, he realized, and he also knew that truth shouldn't be hidden so he spoke the same words once more and told her again: "I'm already yours," he said. "I'm yours, and I always have been, and always will be . . . until the very end."

There was one more moment between them.

They both felt the significance of what had just happened and the promises they'd each just made to each other, both of them still breathing heavily, their faces still next to each other, the rain still pounding.

Then she felt what needed to come next.

It was intrinsic, knowledge that came from deep inside, and she listened to it.

The knowledge that came told her many things, but the first thing it told her was to slowly stand from where they sat together, so she did, and as she stood and he looked up at her, she gently took his hand in hers again.

Then when their skin touched, he knew what she wanted.

So he stood, too.

She led him away from the table and they went across the room together, and she could feel the energy that was there in their touch again. She could feel it in all the places where their skin met, and this time it was even more than what it'd been before, too, because this time, after all that had happened—all the shared experiences of danger, fear, and uncertainty—after all that which had come to Creation and to them, the energy was now amplified and ten times what it had been in the pool, and under the waterfall, and then after.

They kept walking.

She led him towards the bed he'd built, and they went slowly, together.

Then they were there and they were to it.

She gently sat down on the flat surface, and he did, too, and they went further. She reached out and took the tunic he was wearing and lifted it up and over his shoulders so he was then wearing nothing at all, and she pushed him down on the bed, underneath her.

Then she took her own tunic off, too.

When there was finally nothing else between them but skin, she gently moved so she was on top of him, and it seemed as if every single piece and surface of who they were was touching in that moment; it was all pressed together and it wasn't two anymore, it was one. What she felt as it happened was beyond anything she'd ever yet felt or even imagined in Creation, and for that moment, it also seemed her body wasn't hers anymore, but rather there was something else that had come from somewhere far beyond her and them that was now directing what they each should do, and she let it.

She let that feeling guide her, because it was something that was far greater than her, she could feel, far greater than either of them.

But perhaps, perhaps it wasn't greater than both of them, together. Because perhaps that's exactly what it was: *both of them, together.*

She listened to her body even further and bent her head down from her place on top of him then they were even closer. Her lips reached forward and gently touched his, softly at first, then they parted around them again and she could feel it as it started, the beginning of every-thing, of two souls coming together and becoming one soul.

And that's when it happened.

She felt him strain, and she felt change, and then their union began.

She was on top of him, and she controlled everything, and he let her.

She looked down and into his eyes and as she did their souls con-nected again and they each felt the love they had for each other and this was a moment, she knew; this was the moment when everything between them and in Creation itself had now changed, and a new mean-ing and word had entered into their world, the one they shared together, and into their lives, and she was so glad it had come because this new word, this new feeling . . . it was everything, she knew.

She searched for the word, and what it meant.

Then she heard it, as loudly and clearly as if it was spoken right next to her.

Love, the voice said.

She listened and she understood.

Then she looked at him below her and reached down with her hands and felt the muscles in his chest, his arms, the muscles that were now straining in passion and union and also the muscles that were so differ-ent from her own. As she felt his body, so close to her own body now, even though they were different, she also knew she'd never been closer to him than she was in that moment, and they'd never been more the same. It was intoxicating, that feeling, that closeness, that co-existence, and she wondered how she'd ever lived without it, and she also knew she never wanted to, not ever again.

Then even when it ended, it hadn't really.

They lay there on the bed as the rain kept falling on the roof above until it finally slowed, then stopped altogether, and when it stopped the moon came. It was high in the sky and bright slivers of its light peeked through the cracks and spaces between the walls and cast its light and shadows over where they lay.

She wasn't on top of him anymore.

She was next to him now and he turned onto his side and reached over and held her. She looked down at his arms as they wrapped tightly around her body, then she moved even closer to him, as close as she possibly could and she could feel his lips on her skin and his breath warm on her neck. She'd spent so much time wondering about what their purpose was, and what everything meant, but she realized again the wondering had been useless because here it was. It had been shown to her, and it had been given—and more than that, it had been given exactly when it was meant to be given—and now it was theirs, it was theirs, and it always would be, she knew. She listened as he slowly and softly began to drift to sleep, his arms still around her, holding her, always holding her now, not ever letting go, and her thoughts shifted again and she listened to what they said, to what came from inside, one more time:

This is the future, she heard the words come.

Then she heard something else, and she smiled, because she knew.

This is us, she heard, first once, and then again.

This is who we are.

AFTER

10

After the battle in the forest, the great battle that had happened between light and dark, time passed, and many things changed. Every night the two humans lay together, the same as they had that first night after the battle, and every morning they each woke early and went about their individual tasks and work. He continued in the field where the seeds they'd planted began to grow, then when the plants were close to knee-high and filled the entire field, he decided on plowing another area, near the first one, which would become a second field. He began to plant there, too, in the second field, and as he did, his work began to double as the new plants grew and soon tripled as he tended the growing crops of different ages in the two different fields.

And as he did all this in the fields, she began to leave the clearing again, also.

She hadn't at first, in the immediate days right after the battle, but then things began to settle and no more violence or war came so she started to leave again, carefully at first, then with less worry, as she had before, and she soon began to wander further and further from their home. He tried to tell her not to, that there was still clearly danger out there, which they knew because they'd seen and experienced it, but she didn't listen to him. Ever since the battle had happened, he'd been scared that those that had tried to harm them would come again, and wherever she went he wanted to always make sure he was with her. Because if they did come again, he said, then he would be ready for them. Actually, he would be more than ready, he vowed.

"What does that mean?" she'd asked him.

"I'll show you soon," he'd responded.

And then, one day, he did.

He took her by the hand and she followed as he led her around the side of their home then down towards the river. As they went, he told her a story about how he'd been walking in the river a few days previous while he was bathing and cut his foot on something that was on the bottom. He'd reached down into the water expecting to find the stone that was the culprit, and when he pulled it from the riverbed, he saw the thing that cut him wasn't a stone at all, but something else. He'd held it in his palm and studied it: the color looked different than the dull grey of most rocks he'd seen before, as this one had a distinct pink and orange hue mixed with the familiar grey color. He'd then left the river and taken this new thing he'd found and brought it back to the house while she'd been gone—she'd been out somewhere in Creation, searching for more fruit and seeds, as she did each day, he told her—and he'd decided to heat this new thing over a strong, hot fire.

"A fire?" she asked.

"Yes," he nodded.

Then he told her what happened when he'd added fire, and heat.

He told her how when this new type of stone became hot enough and had been over the heat for long enough, it began to melt. He'd waited and watched as it did, then when it was liquid, he'd taken the melted substance from the flames and let it cool. When it finally cooled, it became firm again, but not in its original shape: it became firm and hard and stayed in the new shape it had taken while it was liquid.

He'd tested it and told her it was as hard as any rock in Creation.

Perhaps harder, even.

She'd looked at him as he told her all this, then she shook her head, not quite understanding; she understood the principle of what he'd done, and what he'd explained, but not how he'd come to do it.

"How'd you know to do all that?" she'd asked him.

Then she realized, before any more words came, from either of them.

It was his feeling that had told him; it was his voice.

She had her own feeling and voice deep inside her, in her stomach, the one she listened to and heeded its guidance when she most needed it, and she knew he had his own, too. And this is what his voice had told him: this was the guidance it had given, she realized.

And he told her this, also.

He told her how he didn't know where the voice had come from, only that he'd heard it, so he'd listened.

Then he showed her more.

He showed her what else the voice had told him.

He showed her the mold he'd chiseled from real stone—not the new type he'd found with the pink and orange hue—and how he'd melted what he told her was called copper inside it, then the copper became metal. The shape he'd fashioned the mold into was long and narrow, and thin at the edges, and when she first saw it, she realized in an instant exactly what he'd done: he'd made a mold that would create weapons that were near identical to those he'd seen the angels carry and use in their great battle. She took in the copper rock and mold and the hardened metal he'd used to make these new weapons he now showed her, and as she did, she turned and looked at him next to her. When she looked at him, she saw again all the same things that were there in his eyes, in his face, in all his features; she saw all the same things she'd seen after the battle, and the great pride that was there and in every inch of him.

She was quiet for a moment and took a breath.

She gathered herself.

Then she spoke again.

"What are you making these for?" she quietly asked him.

"I'm making them so we can protect ourselves," he told her.

She heard his voice, and the strength in it, and pride, too.

It seemed the most obvious thing in the world to him, she realized.

She turned and looked again at what he'd created: she saw that one of them he'd made was very large, and it also must be very heavy, she thought, which must be the one for him to use, no doubt, then she turned to the others he'd made, too.

He'd made them in different sizes.

Some were smaller, and the smaller ones were surely lighter than the largest of them that she'd already seen, and those were the ones he gestured towards when he saw her looking at them.

"This one's for you," he said.

Then she watched as he picked up the specific blade he'd made and held it out to her, and she looked down at it.

At first, she didn't take it.

He gestured again and she finally reached her hand out and felt the cool, long blade with her finger, which she ran along the edge, the entire length, then winced in pain as she cut herself on the sharpened edge and a small drop of blood appeared in a thin line across the tip of her finger.

"Careful," he said quickly.

He pulled the blade back and set it down again.

After he was no longer holding it, he went to take her hand in his, to help her bind her wound as she'd once done for him, but she held her hand away.

"No," she told him.

"What?" he asked, and he was surprised.

But he saw she wasn't looking at him.

She was still staring down at all the swords he'd created, all the weapons he'd made and brought there, into their clearing, into their home.

He waited for her to speak again, and as he did, he watched her eyes.

He watched as they changed, hardened, deepened.

"These shouldn't be here," she finally whispered, her words being brought to his ears and then past them on the breeze that had begun to pick up around them.

"What do you mean?" he asked, frowning.

"We have no need of them."

"How could you say that after what's just happened?"

"These have no place in Creation," she said.

And she spoke firmly, as firmly as she ever had before.

He heard her words and just looked back at her.

"But then how are we supposed to protect ourselves?" he asked.

She opened her mouth, about to speak again, but then found the right words didn't come—the words she searched for, and would make him understand—and then she realized the words didn't come because perhaps there were no such words.

So there was silence.

He took the silence as an invitation, so he began to speak again.

He told her as justification that he'd made the weapons so that when those that tried to harm them returned, then they wouldn't be defenseless, as they had been before, but she told him she still couldn't see how the metal in front of them would change that. She told him she couldn't quite see how either of them would ever be any match for the great angels that had come and fought in the skies above them, and as he heard her words, she saw his eyes flash again and she could also see it was his pride that was there in them once more, as well as defiance now, too.

He'd already killed one of them, he told her.

He'd killed one of them that had threatened her, and threatened them, and so who was to say he couldn't kill another, if it came to threaten them again?

She looked back at him as she heard his words.

They'd been in Creation together for some time by then, and living together for some time, also, and she now recognized what this was and that it would be their first fight, their first real and substantial disagreement.

"The one you killed was already wounded," she said.

"I would have killed him even if he wasn't," he told her, his eyes flashing again. "I would have killed any that would have come and tried to hurt you, whether they were wounded, or together, or alone. I would have killed any of them I had to, if it meant saving you, and keeping you safe."

"How?" she asked him. "You're just one man . . . how would you possibly kill that many? And how would you possibly kill one that wasn't wounded?"

"What do you mean?"

"They're stronger than us, and they can fly."

He heard those words and he scowled.

She watched as the pride and defiance that had been in his eyes changed and then turned into something else.

Anger.

Anger, and denial.

"They're not stronger than us," he said.

And that's when he'd shaken his head, and he'd left.

He went storming from the clearing and into the forest.

She watched as he went and she didn't move; she just stood where she was and waited for him to return, to come back again, but he didn't. The sun gradually began to sink in the sky and it wasn't until nightfall finally arrived that he did come back, the last of the light just disappearing over the peaks in the distance as he returned.

He didn't say anything to her.

He just walked past her and went into their house by himself, and she watched him, looking after his retreating back.

Then she turned and went inside, too.

They didn't speak to each other that night before they went to bed, and they didn't sleep with each other, either. The night seemed longer to her than any other they'd been in Creation, then after sleep finally came, and she woke the next morning, she saw he was already up and gone from where he'd slept on the floor. She looked around and saw he wasn't anywhere else in the house, either, so she stood and went outside and was greeted by the new day and that's when she saw he'd started plowing a third field, right next to the second one, and the first.

She stood in front of their home.

She watched him as he went about his work with sweat pouring from his forehead and drenching his tunic, even at this early hour, with the sun not yet all the way up, and she wondered how long he'd been up and working and if he'd even slept at all. She kept watching as he plowed and turned dirt with a fresh and renewed determination in his eyes and in every now-practiced movement of his hands—every straining of his back, and flexing of his arms—and even more sweat came as he kept working and she watched as he didn't even bother to wipe any of it away.

She thought about everything, for another moment, all that had happened.

She needed time, she knew, and she needed space.

So she turned and left the clearing.

If he was plowing another field for them, then they would need new things to plant in it, she knew, and not just more of the same they'd planted before, which they already had enough of, so that's what she'd go look for in Creation and as she collected the new seeds, she'd also be able to think. So she left the clearing and first went through the forest, walking next to the slow-moving river, then came back to the large and wide field with the dandelions and wild flowers, where she'd first woken, and she slowed when she saw the familiar mountains and waterfall that was then in front of her, too. It was a place she'd been so many times and it was also a place that marked as far as she'd yet been in Creation.

But she was going to change that, because this time when she came to the field . . .

This time, she kept going.

She kept walking through the field and past the wildflowers and dandelions and on towards the mountains, and when she reached the mountains, instead of going further and climbing up them, she turned and went west along the base of the great peaks, seeing if there was a way that would lead around or through them.

But she found there wasn't.

The mountains began to just wrap back around again.

The peaks were close together and they closed off any avenue or route that she could see or find where she might be able to try to climb over them, then on to the other side.

So instead, she went in another direction.

Instead of going north, she kept going further west, and it was there in the far western part of Creation where she first found more fruits and nuts and berries of a type they hadn't yet discovered. When she found them, she picked them and put them into the woven basket she carried. She kept walking through that part of Creation as she picked them, but along with the new fruit, she also found more mountains that were there in the west, too. They rose high and looked nearly the same to her as the mountains in the north, and they also did the same thing because they extended for as far as she could see into the distance and blocked her path. These mountains swung around to connect with the mountains there in the north, she knew, the ones where she'd just been, and when she took it all in and calculated, she knew there was no way through them so she decided she'd go back towards the river, the one that flowed through their clearing, and past their home.

She turned her feet and walked.

She went further south.

She'd gone some ways and was to the west of where she knew their clearing was and where he was still working in the fields, she assumed, and she kept going on and through that new part of Creation where she hadn't been before. Then once she was past the clearing, she turned east and walked until she came to the river again. She came to it at a point that was further south of the clearing, which was also another place she'd not yet been, and she followed it. She walked beside it, and followed where it went, meandering in soft and gentle curves.

Soon the forest ended.

And then, after the forest, she came to something else.

It was a long and wide area of land where not much grew and she saw it was filled with small stones and loose, brown-red dirt, along with plants of a type she hadn't yet seen, anywhere else she'd gone. She kept following the river even further, as it flowed and cut through this new and unfamiliarly dry and arid landscape.

Then she finally came to it.

She finally came to where the river continued but then there were more mountains that rose high in front of her and even though she saw the mountains in front of her that blocked her path, she kept walking, and as she did, she saw they were nearly the same as the mountains in the north, where the river began, and also the mountains in the west, but there was no waterfall here or anything else like on the northern end of Creation. Here, instead of beginning, the river neither began nor ended but just kept flowing towards the mountains until it eventually cut through them and the mountains rose into craggy and jagged peaks on either side of the water, creating a deep valley beneath the peaks. She saw that the current in the river picked up as it got closer to that opening, pounding with great force against the uneven rock as it cut between the two naturally-made walls on either side.

She came to the end of the desert and studied the river closely.

She studied how it flowed, between the mountains, in the valley it made, and she saw it was violent.

It would be too violent and dangerous to swim, she knew.

So she stood there on the bank, as close to the water as she could stand, and craned her neck to try to peer further into the narrow valley the river had made. She tried to look as far as she could into the distance and see whatever it was she might be able to discover on the other side of it, but there were too many bends and twists in the river, and instead it seemed to just go on and on. It went around a sharp curve, she saw, then back again, and as she was looking and wondering where and how far it might go, that's when her thoughts finally began to wander.

She thought about him, her husband.

Then she thought about what he'd made in their clearing.

She thought about how he'd hidden the weapons from her, and then she thought about what she'd felt, and how she'd reacted.

She thought even further back.

She thought again of the great battle in the forest and in the sky above them, and she thought again of what she'd seen in his eyes after he'd stood in front of her and then he'd joined that, too, just as all the others did, and brought his own type of death to the one that came to harm them.

She thought about her reaction.

It had been to run, or to look for help.

It had been to resolve the problem peacefully and without violence.

And then she thought about his, which had been to match his physical strength against the physical strength of the one who threatened them, even in defiance of the odds.

Or at least what she thought of as the odds.

Then she thought of something else.

She thought again of the look she'd seen on his face when he'd defeated his opponent, and she thought of the feeling that had come to her when she saw that look, because it was the same look and feeling she'd seen and felt after he'd showed her the weapons he'd created and she recognized what it was; she recognized what it was he felt, and what it was she'd seen, that had also driven him and determined his actions.

It was pride.

Pride, and love.

She thought again about his voice inside him, the one that taught him both those things and helped them build and grow and expand, and it was the same voice that had also taught him how to make the swords he'd made—tools that she knew were designed only to bring blood, death, and harm—then she thought even more and her thoughts keep turning again to those two things she'd felt and seen in his eyes.

Pride.

Pride, and love.

Is that what he was made of?

And if it was: was it a bad thing, and something that needed to be shaped, changed, and molded?

Or was it something that needed to be grown?

Was it something he needed, in order to be a man?

That was what she wanted to know.

There were so many things about his world and who he was and how he'd been made that she now realized she didn't understand, but instead of trying to mold and change which she now realized was perhaps the foundation of his very nature, maybe it was instead all as it was supposed to be?

That's what she wondered.

And then, as she wondered, the answer came to her.

They weren't the same, she heard her own voice tell her, and they also weren't meant to be, it said. That's not how they were made, or how anyone else was or would be made. She couldn't change him and who he was just the same as he couldn't change her and who she was intrinsically, and they each had been made that way so there would be symmetry between them, symmetry rather than likeness, and in the future there would be more that were made—so many more—and in an infinite number of different and beautiful and unique ways. They would each be made in exact specificity so their natures would compliment someone else, and that's what life was, wasn't it: a collection of the fragments of each of us, and together, the sum of our pieces along with the pieces of another might be able to make a whole. That's what we search for, she heard, and what we're sometimes even lucky enough to find, and it wasn't about anatomy or anything physical, it was simply about finding two pieces that fit together in whatever way they might fit and even though there might still be rough edges where the two pieces met, it was those edges she knew that were meant to be tested in the way they just had been by their fight. They were edges that were meant to be ground and ground, worn down, until soon there would be no more edges at all, there would just be them, and then . . . that's then when they would truly become one.

And that was the future, she now knew.

And more than just the future, it was also the promise they'd each made, the sacred one they'd made before their union and the one they made to each other with all Creation as their witness, and that would always remain unbroken.

She breathed in deeply as all this came to her.

Then she felt the wind as it started to pick up and she also felt it was warmer there in the south than it was by their home and in their clearing, and when the wind came, she felt something else, too; it was something that also came from deep inside her, but it wasn't the voice she heard, and that she listened to.

Instead, it felt like something had moved.

It felt like something had moved inside her.

This was something she'd never felt before and she froze right there where she stood next to the river, waiting for it to happen again, but then nothing else came. She waited even longer, but still there was nothing. The breeze picked up so it was even more brisk now, whipping her hair across her back and her face and then she saw the first hints of the sun beginning to sink in the distance to her right, over the peaks of the mountains in the west she'd just seen and explored, and the temperature around her started to drop a few degrees, too. She felt all this and knew what it meant—that Creation was giving her all its signs and signals and telling her it was time to go home—so she listened to what Creation told her, slowly turned her feet north again, then started to walk.

HE WAS SITTING THERE, alone, when she returned.

He had the larger of the swords he'd made resting on his knees and he was running a piece of rock along one side of it, making the edge that was there narrower, sharper, more deadly and more efficient for killing and taking life.

She looked at him for a moment, as he went about his work.

He hadn't noticed her yet.

Then he looked up and saw her.

Their eyes met and neither of them spoke as they just looked at each other and there was so much that was between them for the first time—so much conflict, so many unanswered questions—then she began to slowly walk and crossed the physical distance that was between them, still holding the woven basket in her hand, and reached him and sat on the ground next to where he sat.

She was still, at first, and looked at the sword in his lap.

Then she looked at his hand, the one that was holding the sword.

She saw where it rested and her eyes went to the scar that was still there, the one she'd treated after the battle, and had begun to fade. And while it had begun to fade and lessen—the red and angry skin turning white and then shrinking—it was definitely still there, without a doubt, and they both knew it always would be. It might fade more, she knew, as time passed, but it would never fully leave him, which meant it would never fully leave her, either.

He'd been silent, still looking down at the grass.

Then she reached out and took his hand in hers.

When their skin touched, and they felt each other again, that's when his eyes finally turned up and met hers and she saw there was great emotion in them and something there that had been bruised and hurt, even if he wouldn't ever admit it, and also something he wanted to tell her.

She kept watching him.

Soon he found the words.

"They're not stronger than us," he finally said, softly.

She heard what he said, the second time now that he'd said it, and she found it surprised her.

She thought back to what she'd said to him just before she'd left—*they're stronger than us, and they can fly*—and while she knew neither of them could argue that second part, it was the first part that to him had cut the deepest, and it was what he'd been left with and what he'd been thinking about since she'd left.

She thought about that and about all she thought she knew of him.

She thought of all the things she'd just felt, especially about love and pride, then she thought that maybe now and in this moment she might be able to finally understand a little bit more about him and the world in which he lived.

That was good, she thought.

It was growth for both of them.

They sat together in silence, her hand holding his, then she broke the silence that was between them.

"I found these," she said.

And as she spoke, she held out the basket she'd carried with her.

He looked at her for another moment—just her eyes, and how they met his again—then he finally looked down at the basket that was between them and saw all the new fruits, berries, and nuts she'd gathered in Creation.

A peace offering.

He waited for a moment, looking at them.

"What do they taste like?" he finally asked.

His voice was still very soft.

And then she was surprised to see him turn away as he tried to hide the tear he quickly wiped from his eye, but of course he couldn't, and she saw.

"I don't know," she told him, as gently as she could.

"Why not?" he asked.

"Because I wanted to wait for you."

She'd reached back to a different time, a simpler time between them and he appreciated that, as he remembered, too, how things had once been.

There was one more moment before he slowly nodded, and so did she, then she reached into the basket. She took a piece of fruit for herself, and she took a piece she handed to him, and they began to eat, together, in silence. In the distance, the sun sank even lower, then soon it was gone altogether which meant it was time for what they normally did when the light left so they stood and went back inside.

They walked towards the table he'd carved, and as they did, she suddenly paused.

She paused, because it looked different.

And then she saw something.

The scene was blurry, not quite in focus, and while that was true, it was also true that while it was blurry, it was also quite clear, and this is what she saw:

She saw herself at the table . . .

And she saw the table was worn.

Then she saw him, at the seat across from her.

But there was more, too.

There were two others, at each of the other seats, and they were much younger and smaller than either of them, and one of those two that was younger and smaller than them was younger and smaller than the other, also.

She wondered about it, and what it was, what she was seeing.

Then she heard a soft, beautiful voice:

"Family," it whispered.

She waited another moment, looking at this scene, as they each ate, all of them together, smiling, laughing, sharing, then—

"Ahhhhh!" she cried out in pain.

She doubled over and fell to the floor.

She clutched her stomach again, feeling the same pain she'd felt in the desert, near the southern mountains, only this time the pain was sharper, stronger, much more in every single way.

Her husband who had been near their bed rushed over.

He fell to his knees, next to her.

"What is it?" he asked urgently, studying her eyes. "What's wrong?"

She waited for a moment, gathering herself, catching her breath as the pain began to subside and she began to come back to herself, back into her body, and as she did, she asked herself the very same thing. The feeling had been just as it was before, as if there was something moving, shifting, squirming deep within her, and while she'd wondered after the last time if it had just been her mind playing tricks on her, this time the strength of it left no doubt she felt what she thought she'd felt, and that it was inside her, and it was real.

She looked up and towards the table, but it was empty now, there was no one there.

Then she thought further.

She thought back to the vision she'd just seen and which had now departed but it also hadn't, too, because even though she couldn't see it anymore she could still feel it, and what it felt like was truth. She thought of that, then she thought again of the word that had been whispered.

Family, the voice had said.

And as she heard the word again, she turned to him, to where he was still watching her with the deep and familiar concern in his eyes and she shook her head.

"Nothing's wrong," she finally told him.

"You were in pain."

"It's passed."

"Are you sure?" he asked.

"I'm sure," she nodded.

And it was truth, the words she told him, but the words also weren't all, because change was soon coming, she knew, and she also knew the change that would come was the vision she'd just seen, the vision she was sure was one of their future.

HIGH ABOVE CREATION, Michael sat alone outside his palace.

After the great battle, he'd traveled back to Heaven alone, and when he returned to the light, he'd taken in the unfamiliar sight in front of him: all the healthy angels were tending to those who'd been hurt and were bleeding, moving amongst them, bandaging wounds, and all of them were exhausted and with skin, armor, and wings stained by dirt and death and blood. And while it wasn't the first battle of its kind, it was the first time such a battle had happened since many of the angels that were there had been created, so Michael walked through them, walked through all of them, offering a hand, a touch, a comforting word, anything he could think to help, then he finally came to Selaphiel.

He was sitting alone.

He was away from the others, his spine curved and his head in his hands, his body racked with grief.

Michael came to him and put his hand on Selaphiel's shoulder, and when he did, he could feel the younger angel tense, his muscles contracting beneath Michael's touch, and at first there was nothing but silence between them.

Then Selaphiel spoke, without looking up.

"We were supposed to be eternal," he said.

His voice was soft, quiet, barely more than a whisper.

Michael took that in, looking down at him.

He weighed the younger angel's words, knowing where they were coming from, but also knowing that none of them knew the mysteries of the universe, not all of them, not completely, not fully.

"How do you know we aren't?" Michael asked him.

"Because he's gone," Selaphiel said, and his words were sharper now, and louder.

He finally turned and looked up at Michael, and Michael saw that his once-bright eyes were now broken and hollow and dead.

Michael paused for a moment.

He hadn't expected that and it took him by surprise.

Michael breathed deeply, looking back down at Selaphiel, where he sat next to him and he thought about telling him a great many things— things about divinity, and mystery, and service—but then he heard something inside him, and listened to it, and decided not to and instead just bowed his head, also.

"I'm sorry for what happened," Michael told him.

"You're sorry?" Selaphiel asked.

"Yes," Michael said gently.

There was a moment as Selaphiel paused and Michael kept looking back at him and it was then that he saw something else in the other angel's eyes, something unfamiliar he couldn't quite read as it was something that was beyond just love, grief, heartbreak, regret. It was something that was deep within him, and beginning to take hold, and it was also something Michael wasn't used to seeing there in Heaven and in the light because it wasn't the same as what he saw in the eyes of the other angels that had fought and that he'd just walked through and seen.

It was something darker.

Something much, much darker.

"Are you sorry, Michael?" Selaphiel finally asked again. "Are you really?"

Michael looked back at him and opened his mouth, but no words came, and he didn't respond.

"Well, perhaps you will be," Selaphiel told him, a threat in his voice. Then he stood and left.

Michael watched as Selaphiel went and he took another moment to gather himself, a moment to try to recover from all he'd just seen and all he'd just felt, as Selaphiel's words and their tone and intention entered and ran through him. He kept watching as Selaphiel walked into the distance, towards where all the others were still gathered and treating their wounds—tending to their own grief, trying to mend their own broken and shattered hearts—and that's when Michael finally stood, turned, and walked in the opposite direction, away from the others and towards the great walls. Then he went through a gate underneath them and outside the palace.

He wanted to feel love again.

That's why he went.

Because he knew where he could find it; he could find it if he went to see *them*, the humans that were in Creation.

So he would.

He kept going until he stood outside the high walls, then he spread his great wings—he spread them wide, and he spread them far—then they began to pump, up and down, up and down, and once more he rose into the bright, shining sky, and the clouds above, before he exploded on and into the light.

HE CAME TO THE FOREST QUIETLY.

When he landed, he tucked his wings back underneath the armor he still wore—the armor he wouldn't take off again, along with the sword strapped to his waist—which was different than how he'd come the first time he'd visited the humans in Creation, the first time he'd come after they'd just been made.

He walked through the trees.

Then the trees started to part, and he came to the clearing and saw they were already in their shelter.

He stood there for a moment, by himself.

Then there was movement.

He watched as she quietly came from their house and she was carrying a bowl she'd made, on her way down to the river to fill it with water for when they often would become thirsty in the night.

She turned towards the river, but then she paused.

She paused because she saw him.

They both stood there a moment.

There was silence between them, nothing but the sound of the wind passing between trees.

"I know you'll have many questions," he finally said to her. "About the battle, and what happened here."

She was still silent.

Then she finally nodded, and spoke.

"Yes. But you won, though, right?" she asked. "You and those who follow you?"

"No," Michael shook his head. "It may have seemed like we won, while we were here, where we have more power, but that was just the beginning, I'm afraid. And the battle was certainly no victory for us."

"Who were the ones you fought against?"

"If we're light, then that must mean they're darkness."

She took that in and as she did, her hand protectively went to her stomach, and it was a motion she wasn't conscious of making because it was purely instinct, it was purely nature.

When he saw, he smiled.

He smiled because he knew it was more than that.

He knew it was love, and he needed to feel that again, and that's why he'd come, after all.

"Can I ask you something else?" she asked him.

"Of course," he nodded.

She waited, just for a moment.

The wind kept coming, blowing past them.

"What I saw, not in the forest," she said, "but when I was here, at the table . . ."

"Yes," he nodded, letting her know he knew of what she spoke, that he knew of her vision, and what grew inside her.

"It's the future, isn't it?" she asked him.

"Yes," he nodded again. "It is."

"But why was I able to see it, before it came and happened?"

"There are layers and barriers between the worlds we live in, that separate them from each other," he told her. "But there are also moments and times when those layers and barriers can thin. It often comes when we're asleep, but not always."

"Like my dream," she said, realizing. "Like the dream when he came to me, and brought me to the tree and tempted me the first time."

"Yes," Michael answered. "Like your dream, when he came and tempted you."

She took that in, turning it over in her mind.

Then there was a noise behind them.

They both turned and saw her husband come from their house now, and she realized he must have heard their words. Michael watched as he went to her and put his arm protectively around her waist and as he did, Michael looked and saw what was at the man's own waist: it was the

sword he'd made, and it looked exactly like Michael's, he saw, and the man wore it in the same way, too, and Michael frowned when he saw it.

"You've come back," her husband said.

"Yes," Michael nodded. "I have."

"What was that?" he asked. "In the forest, between you and . . . the others."

"Our world intruded upon yours, which never should have happened," he told them, both of them now. "But it did, and I'm afraid it won't be the last time."

They were all silent, together, as they heard that.

Then she watched as her husband turned and looked at her.

Michael watched as he did, too, and he could read the look that was there in the man's eyes and what it said to his wife—*See*, his eyes said, *I told you it wasn't over*—but she wasn't looking at him, her husband, she wasn't looking at him at all: she was still staring back at the angel in front of them, and he could read the look in her eyes, too, and what she now realized.

"He was one of you once, wasn't he?" she asked softly.

She'd heard the pain that was in his voice, Michael knew; the pain that was there when he spoke of Phosphorus, and perhaps she could even *feel* that pain, too, as he could.

"Yes, he was," Michael told them, nodding. "He was once one of the greatest among us, the one who shone the very brightest, and he was my friend."

"What happened?" the man asked.

"He chose a different path," Michael spoke slowly. "He chose darkness, in the end, and not light."

"And how did that lead to what we saw in the forest? How did all the rest join him, too, then come here?"

Michael waited for a moment, studying each of them, each of the humans that stood across from him with so many questions in their young eyes.

He kept studying them, and studying himself, too.

Then he saw they were ready, and so was he, so he nodded.

"It's time you learned the history of Heaven, and Creation," he told them, as he walked closer.

"How?" she asked.

He stopped right in front of where they stood, when he heard her question, close enough to reach out and touch them.

But he didn't.

"May I show you?" he asked instead.

"You have to ask our permission?" she wondered.

"Always," he told them.

He watched as they each looked at each other again, the uncertainty there in their eyes, but also the wonder, too, of what they'd each just been promised, then they turned back to him.

"Yes," she said.

"Of course," he answered.

They both nodded, together.

Michael heard their words, and saw their nods, and he nodded, too.

He slowly reached forward and placed one of his palms on each of their foreheads, with the bottom of his strong hands covering their eyes, and as such everything would go completely dark for them, but that darkness wasn't the same as all the other, he knew.

Because then, in that darkness . . .

That's then when they would see.

11

$\mathcal{F}$OR A MOMENT there was only the darkness.

Then there within it, she saw the very first hints of light—small and soft, in the beginning—then growing, growing, larger, brighter, and as the light began to build and expand, she heard words, too, coming from above, from below, from everywhere. They were Michael's words, she recognized, and as he spoke and she listened, she began to then see images appear in front of her, and they were images that were just the same and clear as anything else she'd yet seen in Creation, and it was his words that were everywhere that told her what it was she was seeing.

"There's such beauty here now, in Creation, as you've seen," he told them. "But in the beginning, there wasn't. In the beginning, there was just God, and his word, and the promise of what was to come, and the world he would make."

And that's then what she saw.

She saw space and time, and she saw planets.

She saw them moving, taking shape, and how light was created: how it wasn't there at all, at first, then it was, as it was slowly separated from all the ubiquitous darkness.

"That's when angels were then created, too," Michael added.

And she saw that as well.

She saw how the palace was made in the light—the palace of Heaven, where Michael and the other angels lived—then she saw as Michael was born. There was just white at first, just the pure whiteness of the great and new wings covering that which soon would be, and then the new wings began to slowly move apart and beneath them she saw the outline of Michael's body, just as he began, just as he looked around and into the light for the very first time.

"What were you created for?" she asked.

And as she did, the newly born Michael turned and right there in his first moments, he looked directly into her eyes, as if she was there, too.

"We were created to serve," his voice told her. "And serve is what we did."

Then things began to change again.

"Only there was one who soon came," Michael continued, "and he was one who didn't want to continue on that path, the one for which he'd been created."

She heard Michael's words, all around her.

Then she looked further and past him.

She looked beyond the first newly-born angel that was there in front of her, and that's when she then saw another: she saw more great wings that were folded back and around each other—great wings that soon opened, and spread wide, too—and when they did, she saw who they belonged to, and who also stood there now in his first moments. She'd seen this angel before, of course, but this was the first time she'd seen him as he once was, when he was beautiful, and when he was still the one that was called Light-Bringer, Shining One, Morning Star, the one that had been God's favorite.

Michael and Phosphorus looked at each other, for the first time . . .

And she saw the look, the curiosity that was in it, and then the love, too, before the image began to fade.

There was darkness again.

"Then what happened?" she asked him.

And there in the darkness, Michael told them.

He told them how God had made more angels, then after more time had passed, he then made Creation, too, and she saw all this in front of her. She saw how the heavens had been stretched and expanded, and how more angels had come and joined Michael and Phosphorus there in the great light that shone so very brightly.

Then she saw Creation.

She saw how it was once just barren rock and vast, endless waters.

Then she saw how they were separated.

She saw as Oceans were made, and Lakes, and Rivers.

She saw as Mountains were pushed up from where before there had been none.

And she saw as Trees came, and then other Growth, too.

She saw as Forests were made, and wide Fields filled with Grass and Flowers.

She saw all this, as it was created, then she wondered . . .

What about us?

She didn't speak the words out loud, but it was as if Michael had heard them anyways, because as soon as she thought them, then she saw herself: she was in the field of dandelions and wild flowers with her arms crossed over her body and covering herself—the same way she'd seen the angels when they were first made—then she watched as her arms slowly folded back and away, and she opened her eyes, blinking against the bright sun as she witnessed the world for the first time.

She watched herself as she slowly stood.

Then as she began to walk, everything around her faded again.

The bright light that was there left, and she found she was back in the clearing, and back in the present, and reality.

She turned and looked next to her.

She saw her husband, where he stood, and in his eyes she saw he'd also seen all she'd just seen, too, then she turned and looked further at Michael across from where they were together. His arms were back by his side and not covering their foreheads or eyes anymore, but she saw his palms were still glowing with heat, with intensity, with his bright and celestial light.

She'd just seen a great many things, and a great period of time.

She'd seen things that had answered so many of the questions she'd had, and asked, since they'd come to Creation; the way they were made, and how they came to be.

But she was only thinking of one thing now.

"What happened to him?" she asked.

"What do you mean?" Michael answered.

"We saw as he was born, and he was there with you, just the two of you. But then what happened?" she asked him. "How did he go from the light to what he's now become?"

Michael paused when he heard her question.

She watched as he hesitated and looked back at her, and she saw that this was something that was painful for him.

"He was once the very best of us," Michael told her, slowly. "He was God's favorite, the Light-Bringer, the Shining One, the Morning Star, and while in the beginning you saw and for a long time thereafter, he was filled with goodness, he was also filled with pride and ego, too, which are two things that on their own can lead us to great deeds and great heights, but together, and unchecked? That's when they can consume us. That's when they can bring with them greed and corruption and betrayal," Michael swallowed, this last bit the very hardest for him. "And that's what happened to him, all of that together, and that's also how the very nature of our souls can be changed."

She heard these words and took them in, letting them fill and settle in her own soul, then she turned from Michael and looked back at her husband, next to her.

She thought of what she knew of him, and what she'd felt.

Pride.

That's what she'd seen in his eyes, wasn't it?

That's what she'd seen there, after the battle, then back at the clearing.

But with Pride, there had also been Love.

Had it been the same with Phosphorus?

"Show me," she said, very quietly.

"What?" Michael asked.

She turned away from her husband, and his eyes, and looked back to the angel.

"I want to see it," she told Michael. "I want to see how he fell."

Michael was silent for a moment, and she watched as he studied her own eyes now, and looked for purpose there, and he looked for doubt.

"It's not part of the history I came to show you," he slowly told her. "It's not part of how Creation was made."

"But he's come here now, to where we live. He's made himself a part of Creation, and thus the history of it, and us, and what comes next," she said, and she paused, out of respect for Michael, and said the next part as gently as she could. "And I would see how one that was once so beautiful has now become so dark."

She heard her own words, then knew why she'd spoken them, and so did Michael, too, and her husband, next to her, because it was clear now and it was clear between all three of them.

Because if it could happen to one that's as strong and bright as Phosphorus . . .

Then who else could it happen to?

And there was only one way for it to be prevented.

They needed to learn from what had already happened, and the one who had already fallen, and been first among them.

She watched as Michael took all this in and she watched as he looked back and forth, between them.

Then he slowly nodded.

"Very well," he finally said.

It hadn't been his plan, she knew, and as he'd told them, but he would honor what she'd asked anyways, and he came forward. He raised his arms one more time and put his hands on each of their foreheads, his great palms blocking their eyes once more, and as soon as he did this time, and their sight left, instead of everything turning to black and darkness, this time, it all became a very bright . . .

Light.

And with that light, she knew they were now above again.

They were inside the walls of Heaven.

And as the memory she was given began to become more clear, she saw the outline of the gathered host of angels, all of them standing together in a large circle, wearing their polished breastplates and bright armor, great wings spread wide or tucked underneath, then she saw the two that were standing there inside the circle they'd formed:

Michael.

Phosphorus.

She watched as they faced each other, and she saw the pride that was there in Phosphorus' eyes, and she also saw the broken heart Michael couldn't hide. She heard their words as they spoke, and she also saw the looks on the faces of the other angels that were there, those that had sided with Michael—like Gabriel, and Raphael—then she looked past the faces of those that would stay with the light and saw the others. She saw the faces of the ones she knew would be swayed by the voice and words of the Light-Bringer—Mamanos and Báal, among them—and she could see them already mesmerized by the beauty and melody and false promise in the same way she almost had been during her dream in Creation, and standing in front of the great Tree of Knowledge.

Then she saw the circle part and she saw the battle.

She saw as Heaven's two strongest rose into the sky above the great palace and were pitted against each other, and more than what she saw, she also heard.

What she heard was thunder.

She watched as they fought.

She watched as their blades clashed, and as Michael won.

Then she watched as Phosphorus stood in front of him, bloodied and defeated, and she watched as Michael proclaimed judgment and before Michael's light grew and expanded and exploded from within and sent his friend barreling from Heaven and the palace, through space and time, and out towards all the other, she also heard his next to last words:

I am only as he made me, she heard Phosphorus say.

Then the light came and grew and it was over, and when it finally was, she saw Michael's eyes after it was done.

She saw again the pain that was there, and heartbreak.

And as she kept staring at him, trying to memorize and remember every single thing she'd seen, everything around her started to distort and the memory quickly faded again, and she once more returned to Creation. When she did, she saw an older and wearier Michael in front of her. She looked back at the angel, and at the look that was in his eyes, the heaviness she saw weighing on his wings and his heart, and she finally understood more now; she finally understood about what had happened, and why, and the cost.

"So now you know," he told them. "You've seen darkness, and how it was born, and you've seen light. You've seen Creation, and you've also seen destruction."

"So where does that leave us?" she asked.

"Where it always has," Michael answered. "And that's with a choice. Because just as there is light here now, there is also still darkness, and so it will be, on and on, and for all generations to come."

"*All generations to come?*" she asked, wrinkling her nose.

Then she saw Michael smile.

She finally saw him smile again.

The darkness around them seemed to lift just a little, as this was happier business. "What you've been feeling inside you," he said to her, then looked between them, and at him, too. "That's the child you've made, that you've both made, and it's the first that will come and be born here in Creation."

She took that in, and thought back to what she'd seen at the table.

Then she thought of the word she'd heard, too, and which she now heard again, softly, from deep inside as her hand protectively went to her belly once more.

"*Family*," she whispered.

"That's right," Michael nodded.

"But where did the child come from?" her husband asked, still not fully understanding.

"It came from you," Michael told him. "And it came from her, also, and the love you have for each other."

He thought about that for a moment.

Then he opened his mouth because he had another question:

"Will the child be like me, or like her?" he asked.

There was silence in the clearing again, as she watched Michael weigh the question and words her husband had just spoken, and when Michael answered, he did so slowly, and his words were calm and measured.

"Your child will be like both of you," he told them. "And it will be beautiful."

"When?" she asked. "When will it come?"

Michael waited for a moment, then he smiled.

"There must be some mystery left in Creation," he said.

Then he turned from them, and she opened her mouth, about to ask him one more question, but he spread his great wings and with one final look over his shoulder, and one final smile, he then exploded into the sky, and when he was gone, everything was quiet again.

Their eyes were turned upwards.

Their eyes were both turned up, following after the angel, always up, towards the heavens, and while his eyes remained up and looking to the wonder of the bright stars above, even after Michael had disappeared, she turned hers back down to look at the branch of the tree that was closest to them: the tree that was still shaking after he'd rushed past, and the leaves were swaying back and forth from the gust his wings had caused, and so was the fruit that was there on the branches, too.

She looked at the fruit . . .

The fruit of the Tree of Knowledge.

She kept looking at it and thinking of all she'd seen—all she'd just learned of Phosphorus, and Michael, and of them together and light and darkness—and then her thoughts went to her own time with the dark angel, right in that very same spot where she stood again, and she thought of that which he'd offered her: the single piece of fruit that grew on the branches, and the knowledge of all there was.

Did she need it?

She wanted it, she was sure of that, because who wouldn't.

And she couldn't hide or change that, she knew, and she wasn't sure if she'd want to, even if she could, because what is a life without it, a life without the pursuit of knowledge?

She shook her head.

She thought of Mamanos and Báal, and all the others that had followed Phosphorus from light to darkness, and she knew that while she couldn't change what she felt inside, she did have a choice, she always had a choice, and she realized that was the greatest gift they'd been given. And as she realized that she also swore a quiet and solemn promise to herself, there in the moonlight, and with him at her side, still looking up and towards the bright stars, that she would always do that which was right and not choose something she might merely just want, the way Phosphorus, Mamanos, and Báal surely had. She thought of it all once more, then she swore again the path of the dark angels would not be hers, and that she would always use the gift she'd been given in the pursuit of light and truth and love.

"Are you alright?" he asked.

She turned from the tree and looked at her husband next to her.

He wasn't looking above anymore, and he wasn't looking at the stars, either; he was looking at her now, and watching her curiously, she saw.

They stood there, together, illuminated by the moonlight . . .

Then she smiled.

"Yes," she told him. "I'm alright."

He looked back at her, at her eyes, as he always did.

Then he looked further down.

He looked towards her stomach and she watched as he processed what he'd just been told by the angel, then he slowly and gently reached out and touched her belly and she could feel his calloused hands rough against her soft skin and as he touched her, she could also feel all that he was thinking, she could feel all he was feeling, and then it came again, what she had previously felt deep inside herself, the turning, the kicking.

But there was no pain this time.

There was just soft, gentle movement.

His eyes went wide as he felt the miracle of life for the first time and quickly pulled his hand back as he inhaled sharply and looked up at her. But she just smiled at him, then took his hand in her own and put it back to where it had been before, and he felt again, and she watched as he wasn't surprised this time, then he slowly smiled, too.

And the smile lasted.

She watched as he stared down at her stomach and what she carried in it, then he bent and gently kissed it, and all that had happened between them in the hours and days before was forgotten in that moment.

There was joy again.

There was happiness again, too.

Then he flexed his legs and put his arms behind her knees as he picked her up and held her and carried her back to their home, and to the bed they shared, and after they each layed down, they lay together again.

When their union ended, he went to sleep right away.

But she couldn't.

She stayed awake.

She lay there in their bed with him next to her and looked across their home at the table, and she thought again of her vision and what she'd seen. She thought of what her husband had asked Michael, the *only* thing he'd asked Michael—*will the child be like him, or like her*—and despite Michael's words, declining to give an answer, she already knew what their child would be, because she'd already seen it.

The child would be a boy, like his father.

And so would their child after him, too.

She thought of all she'd just seen of the future, then she thought of those other two things she'd seen in her husband, those two things she was so certain she'd seen:

Pride.

Pride, and Love.

Would her sons be made of the same things?

And if they were, which one of those things inside them would they give in to, and which one of them would they feed?

She closed her eyes, there in the darkness . . .

She closed her eyes, but she didn't sleep.

12

On the other side of space and time, Phosphorus sat in his palace by himself.

He was in the ruined room with the great, tall ceiling, and he stared through the darkness that was there at the empty throne across from him. He thought about all that had happened, as he stared at it, and all that had come.

Then he thought of more.

He thought again of all that had drove him from light, which meant he thought of Michael.

When he did, he thought of Creation, too.

He thought of the humans and the love between them he'd seen, and how it had grown; what it had become, and what more he knew it could still yet be.

It was something he'd yearned for, something he'd yearned for all his life, then found.

But it had been taken from him.

It was something he knew could have been perfect, with Michael, but it now could no longer be anything, he also knew, so what did all the rest matter?

What did light matter, or goodness?

What did God matter?

And if God was truly the architect of all—of everything—then it was him who had taken it, wasn't it?

Wouldn't it have been him who had taken all of it; given it, then taken it back?

Phosphorus locked his jaw.

A new and fresh cloud of darkness passed over his heart.

"My lord?"

Phosphorus heard the voice behind him and turned to see Báal standing in the doorway watching his master as he stared through darkness at the throne he'd not yet claimed, that he hadn't yet sat on.

Because he needed to earn it first.

He needed to truly earn it.

"What is it?" Phosphorus finally asked him.

"We need to know what to do, and how to serve you," Báal said as he walked forward, towards the throne, towards his master. "We're ready to fight again, and we just wait upon your word."

"No."

"What?"

"They're too strong in Heaven, and in Creation. And we're too strong here."

"So what do we do?"

"We need to be stronger."

"How?" Báal asked, not understanding. "How is that possible?"

Phosphorus was silent again, turning back inwards and into his thoughts, because there was something they could do, there was something that would make it possible.

He'd already betrayed God, and Michael, he knew.

But he also knew that which he was now thinking would be the greatest betrayal of all, one bigger than anything else that had yet happened in all of eternity because it was a betrayal that would involve the deepest of secrets, and the greatest of evils.

He turned, once more.

He looked again at the unclaimed throne.

There was only one way to truly earn it, he knew, and only one way for those that followed him to truly bow and call him lord as he sat there and ruled over them, ruled over everything, ruled over all.

"Tell the others to be ready," Phosphorus finally spoke, softly. "And tell them to wait for me."

"Where are you going?"

"We were not the first to have done what we've done and been expelled into darkness," Phosphorus told him. "There have been others before us, who like us have forsaken the light, too."

"Who?" Báal wondered.

Phosphorus looked around them.

He raised his arms and gestured to everything they saw, everything under which they stood, together.

"The same ones who built this palace, and this throne on which their lord once sat."

"What are they called?"

"Their rebellion and betrayal was a secret God kept from all but two, a secret he kept from all but Michael and myself. They were the original angels of rebellion, but now . . . now they're called titans," Phosphorus told him.

"And where are these titans?"

"They're at the furthest reaches of everything, at the edge of all that there is. That's where they were banished, by God, and sent for the rest of time."

"So that's where you'll go?"

"Yes," Phosphorus nodded, slowly. "I'll free them from their bondage and the stone in which they've been imprisoned, and with their strength, we'll be able to defeat Michael and his host, whether we fight them above, in the light, or here, in darkness."

Báal heard Phosphorus and took in his words.

Then he frowned.

"But what will these titans want in return?" he asked.

"What do you mean?" Phosphorus looked at him.

"For their service," Báal continued. "What will they ask in exchange for the strength they would bring?"

"It's the only way we can win," Phosphorus told him. "So whatever it is that they ask, does it really matter?"

There was a moment between them.

Báal looked back at Phosphorus, deep into his ash-dark eyes.

Then he finally smiled and shook his head.

"No," he said to his master, recognizing the same thing Phosphorus felt, the same darkness deep within. "No, I suppose it doesn't."

"Then so it will be."

"My Lord," Báal said, as he bowed.

Then he turned and left, and when he was gone, Phosphorus was alone, once more.

He inhaled deeply, breathing in the humid air, and the darkness.

He turned back to the throne.

With this decision he knew he would finally earn it, that he would finally be darkness, and so the throne of darkness would finally and truly be his, and he reached out and touched it, feeling the cool and smooth obsidian beneath his skin.

It would be his for all the rest of time, he knew.

And then even further beyond that, too.

All would bow to him.

All would call him Lord, even the humans, the humans that loved each other and so resembled God.

He thought about it and he felt pride.

Then he slowly lowered himself down and carefully sat on the worn and carved surface for the first time, and as he did, it felt like the most natural thing in the world to him; it felt like something he'd already done one million times, and that he would do one million more, and he knew then the choice he'd made had been the right one.

He smiled, just for himself, and for all that had been.

Then he smiled for the future, and all that would be.

"My Lord . . ." he whispered, very softly.

And he kept smiling, alone, alone, there on his throne of darkness.

HIGH ABOVE AND IN THE LIGHT, Michael returned to Heaven and the palace.

All was quiet when he returned, outside the walls, which was unusual, and as he walked towards them he saw no others around, which was also unusual. He kept walking then went past them, and when he did, that's when he saw where all the angels were gathered, there in the courtyard.

He looked around and between them.

Gabriel and Raphael were among the angels standing on one side of the gathering, and Selaphiel was with what looked to be about a third of the host that had survived the battle, and they were standing on the other side.

Michael was silent for a moment, as he looked between them, and he frowned.

"What is this?" he asked.

There wasn't an answer at first.

Then Selaphiel stepped forward and faced him.

"I don't think it's something that can be too unexpected," he said.

Michael turned to look at him amongst the others, who stood by him, and when he did, he recognized the angel next to Selaphiel as the one who used to fly with Urania, the angel who Michael tried to save but had still been overcome in the darkness below.

Michael looked at all the other faces, placing them, and as soon as he did, then he knew.

He knew what it was they felt.

"You're unhappy," he said.

"Unhappy?" Selaphiel asked. "I think it's more than that. I think it's much more."

"What do you mean?"

"You led us into darkness!" Selaphiel yelled, his voice sharp and strained with pain and grief. "You led us into darkness, where we had no strength, and look what happened to us. Look what we all now have to bear because of what you did."

"I didn't know that's what would happen."

"But you're our leader!"

"I am," Michael nodded. "And so what would you say to me?"

"I know this is your dominion," Selaphiel spoke slowly. "And I know you were charged by God to watch over all there is here."

"Yes," Michael nodded. "I was."

"Which means there will be no other ruler here, in Heaven."

"That's not true," Michael told them. "There will be what God wills."

"We've waited for God to act before, and I will not do it again. And you may rule here, Michael, you may rule here for all the rest of eternity . . . but it doesn't mean we have to stay."

"That's treason!" Gabriel shouted.

And the other angels that were with him shouted and nodded their agreement, too, and approval, but Michael just raised his hand, stopping them, asking for their silence.

"And that's what you want to do?" Michael asked Selaphiel. "You want to leave, and go away from here?"

"You let him fall," Selaphiel's eyes blazed. "You caused all of this."

"I caused *nothing*," Michael responded.

And for the first time his voice was firm, his words sharp, and unequivocal.

"You could have stopped him," Selaphiel said. "You *should* have stopped him, before it had gone too far. But you were blind."

Michael was silent for a moment.

He looked back at Selaphiel, at the heartbreak that was there in his eyes, and it was the heartbreak he saw more than anything else because it was something with which Michael was also so very familiar. "I loved him, yes," Michael finally answered. "I loved him with all my heart and all that I am. But I've never been blind."

"Would you try to stop us?" Selaphiel asked.

Michael waited for a moment.

Then he shook his head.

"No," Michael told him.

"*What?*" Raphael spoke sharply from his place across from them.

"They're free to do as they wish," Michael told all the gathered angels.

Raphael stepped forward and he spoke again.

Around him some of the angels drew their swords.

"But the darkness is growing," Raphael said. "We've already lost too many, and the fracturing of light and our host only serves to strengthen that darkness."

Gabriel stepped forward and he spoke, too.

"It doesn't matter," Gabriel said, from his place next to Raphael. "Let them leave. We'll fight whoever comes, and we'll win, with or without these cowards who no longer have the stomach for that which they were created."

"We weren't created for this, Gabriel," Selaphiel said, turning towards him.

"Then what were we created for?"

"Go," Michael told them. "Leave here and go to wherever it is you seek and look for whatever it is you're searching for . . . and do so with my blessing, and with God's."

Michael watched as Selaphiel stared back at him.

He was searching Michael's eyes, searching for a trap, for a lie.

But there was none.

There was only truth, always truth.

So with one last look, Selaphiel spread his great and beautiful wings as wide as they could be spread, and so did the others. They kept looking at Michael, and at Gabriel, and Raphael, and all the others, as they began to slowly rise into the sky, up and towards the clouds, then they all turned, following behind Selaphiel.

Michael watched as they flew, heading into the distance.

Then Gabriel and Raphael came to stand next to him, and they watched, too.

There was a moment when no one spoke.

Then Gabriel finally did, and broke the silence.

"We could still stop them," he said softly. "Just give the word and I could still go and bring them back."

"Don't," Michael said and he swallowed.

"Why?" Gabriel asked. "They've forsaken God, and Heaven, the same as the Light-Bringer did, and those that follow him."

"No, they haven't," Michael told him. "They've just forsaken me."

"It's the same thing," Raphael frowned.

"No, it's not."

"But you're God's hand and voice, here in Heaven and the World. You're the one he chose to lead us."

"I am what I am, but God is God."

"What does that mean?"

Michael heard the question and was silent for a moment as he thought of the choice he'd given the angels who had left, who had followed Selaphiel, and the choice they'd made, and he also thought of what it all might mean in the coming hours, days, years. He thought again of faith, and he also thought of will, because there it was, right there, in front of them, in front of all of them.

The birth of the eternal struggle.

Darkness and light.

Both of them, within all, within everything, never-ending.

And within that struggling eternity that was in all things, there would always be a choice that would have to be made—a choice of which thing that was inside would be fed and brought forward—and it was a choice that would have to be made in every instant, every waking moment, every last passing second between all things that had been made within God's great and vast Creation.

Michael stood there and he thought of it all.

"It means we need to be better," he finally told the other angels.

And then he turned left.

13

AFTER MICHAEL HAD LEFT the clearing, her belly began to grow. It was slow at first, barely noticeable, then suddenly it seemed to go faster.

At times it was an intrusion in how it would affect her daily life and work, but then when those thoughts came—the thoughts of how much easier things had been before—she'd feel the child inside her, squirming, moving, turning, and as she paused and felt him again, then all those thoughts would pass and she'd smile as she waited for the kicks.

She'd also started eating more as her belly grew.

The seeds they'd planted in the first field had just begun to yield fruit, nuts, and vegetables, and so while she walked through the rows of plants and harvested what she could in that field, her husband had continued his work in the second field and also the third he'd begun plowing not too long before. They were only two, just then, but they wouldn't be soon, he told her. And as such, they'd need to seed and plant all the fields because they would need extra food for when their family would soon grow.

She knew he was right, so she nodded.

But there was something else she still wondered.

After Michael had come to the clearing and shared with them the history of the world, as well as the news about their own family, the news that would change everything—and also the news that had made her husband so happy—she never saw the weapons he'd made, not ever again. She didn't think he'd destroyed them; she thought she would have known if he'd done that.

So maybe he'd taken them somewhere else?

Maybe he'd taken them somewhere out of sight, and away from their home?

She wasn't sure what he'd done, and she didn't want to ask, either, because after the night Michael had come everything returned to normal and there was peace again, and there was love, too, and she didn't want that to change. With the news of the growth of their family, their previous fight had been completely forgotten, and they began to lay together again. They lay together every night, as they had before, then every morning they woke together, too, and worked, and took their meals together in-between the work when the sun was hottest. And they worked so hard because soon it wouldn't just be her and him anymore, it would be them.

A family.

The word she'd heard so clearly and thing she'd seen so clearly, too.

So they continued on and her belly kept growing even more, and as it did, he tried to tell her not to work so much, until the child came, but she didn't listen to him. Even though her swollen belly did make certain things that had been easy before harder, it still felt good to walk, and use her legs, arms, to continue doing all the things she'd previously done before.

More time passed.

The second field grew and they finished harvesting the crops that came.

Then he spent all his time in the third field.

He used the tool he'd created to plow the field's dirt into neat and even rows, and she followed behind as he plowed and gently placed the seeds they'd collected into the dirt then covered them again.

And they were more than just the seeds they'd used in the first field.

These were seeds they'd gathered and collected from all over Creation—from all corners she'd walked and gone to, then brought back there, to their clearing—so that this field would have both a great abundance and great variety, and it would feed and sustain them.

They fell into a rhythm.

He would plow, and she would plant.

They would pray for rain, and rain would come.

The days stretched on and they were good.

They worked all day, then lay together at night, and woke and did it all again and it became a pattern, a habit.

And that's when their child finally came.

She'd been walking near the river, collecting fresh water into the bowl she used to bring it to the house for their evening meals, and as she bent to dip the bowl into the water, the pain came again, so suddenly, as if it was lightning shot straight from the sky.

She doubled over when she first felt it.

She dropped the bowl and paid no attention as it shattered against the ground, and she fell.

She lay there, in the grass, with the pain shooting all through her body.

Then just as suddenly as it had come, it left again.

There was nothing for a moment.

She breathed heavily; *in and out, in and out . . .*

Then just when she thought it had left for good, the pain came again, and this time it came with more than twice the force it had the previous time.

She doubled over on the grass, clutching her stomach.

And that's when she called for him.

She yelled as loudly as she could, through the sharp contractions, and she hoped he would hear her over the sounds of his work in the fields, that the wind would carry her voice that far, all the way to him back in their clearing.

Her voice did reach to him.

The wind did carry it that far.

There were only a few seconds between when she yelled and when she saw him running towards her and she knew he must have immediately dropped his plow and come. He skidded to a stop in the grass and knelt next to her, holding her head, asking what was wrong and what was happening.

"Are you hurt?" he asked.

His eyes searched her body, from her own eyes down her chest, all the way to her belly.

"Help me up," she told him.

And he did.

He held her under the arms and pulled her to her feet and she found she was dizzy as they stood there together, and he saw this, too, so he continued to support her.

He looked at her with concern.

"What do you feel?" he asked again. "Is it time?"

She turned and looked back at him, and her own eyes answered his question, she knew, telling him it was.

"Help me get back to our bed," she answered.

He swallowed and nodded.

And then they went.

SHE'D TRIED TO TELL HIM she could walk, but he insisted she didn't. Instead, he reached down and put his hands under her knees, the same as he did the night Michael had come and showed them both past and future, and he lifted and carried her. He brought her back to their house, her arm wrapped tightly around his neck as they went, then he laid her in their bed, and when he did, she felt the pain return, and screamed, and this time when it came it was different than the other times.

Because this time, it lasted.

It didn't contract and then recede.

And it was pain that was beyond anything she'd yet imagined or felt.

It lasted for most of the night, and then some time after it had been dark for a few hours, the moment finally happened. He held her hand through all of it, wiped her forehead, brought damp cloths and fresh water and helped her in any way he could think to help her. But in the end, this was something that was hers, she knew, this was something that was only hers, and as such, it was also something she had to do alone.

So the pain continued . . .

And so did she.

It went on, and on, and on.

Then when it finally ended and she heard the first cries there in Creation and saw the baby in his father's arms, she also saw the child was a boy, so she knew her vision had been truth. She lay back in their bed in exhaustion and watched as her husband took and held their son and began to clean him with a piece of cloth before he would hand him to her, but she told him to stop, and to put the cloth away, and to come closer.

She wanted her child exactly as it was.

He nodded and did as she told him, and handed the child to her, and she took her son in her arms.

She looked down at him, into his eyes.

She cradled him in the crook she created in her elbow and together they both bent down and looked at the life they'd just created, the life she now held. And it was in this moment she realized the magnitude of the gift she'd been given: the gift of being able to create life, which was something she'd previously thought reserved just for God. But it wasn't, because there was her child, resting in her arms, the first ever that had been born in their world. She kept looking at him and his young face and soft, delicate features as those thoughts all flooded over her, then she realized she'd been holding her breath that whole time since she'd held him, so she exhaled.

She kept looking down at him, at his eyes, her own not leaving his.

And that's when she noticed their color.

It wasn't the same as hers, and it wasn't the same as his, either; rather, it was as if a mixture of both of them had birthed a new color, making them a light and muddled hazel.

She looked further.

She looked past his eyes and at his features again.

While she'd already seen their child was born a boy, like his father, she also then saw it was her features he'd received: her high cheek-bones, her soft jaw, her thin lips, and not the sharp and defined jaw of his father. She noticed all this, as she looked down at him, then he blinked and looked back up at her.

For a moment, there was nothing, just silence.

Then he began to cry again.

It was a loud sound, and piercing.

It was also a sound that hadn't yet been heard in Creation before that night.

"What do we do?" her husband asked from his place next to them.

But instinctively she already knew what to do as she took the baby from where she'd held him in the crook in her arm and looked at him, then held him closer to her chest and rocked him back and forth. After a moment, as the baby felt his skin pressed against the skin of his mother, the crying began to soften, lessening to muffled and spasmatic bursts, then it eventually stopped altogether. She didn't know why she did what she did or why it had worked, it just felt natural to her, she realized. In fact, it felt like the most natural thing in the world: her son's little head nuzzled against her chest, then his mouth began to move— opening and closing, opening and closing—and before she realized what he was doing, his lips finally found their way under her tunic to her breast and closed around her nipple and he began to feed. She felt nourishment flow from her own body into his, and right there before her wide and opened eyes there was a new miracle that occurred and a new bond that was formed that could never be replicated, never be duplicated, never be broken, she knew, and it was one that was hers, and only hers.

Above her, her husband watched all this, as well, and he watched with all the wonder that's brought by birth and new life and the earliest moments of parenthood.

"He's so beautiful," he finally whispered.

She was silent for a moment, still watching as their son fed.

Then she smiled and she nodded.

"Yes," she answered. "Yes, he is."

They both waited as he kept eating, then soon he finished.

When he did, he moved his head closer into the space underneath her shoulder where her arm met her body, and he made himself comfortable as he closed his eyes. Then before they knew it, he began to sleep. Both his parents watched him, together. Then his father reached out and softly touched his head, gently rubbing his thumb back and forth across the small wisps of soft and new hair that were there.

"This is . . . so much," he finally said.

"So much what?" she asked him.

"So much more."

She was curious about that so she turned to look at him as he still stared in awe and wonder at his son, and what they'd created. She felt some of what she knew he was feeling, but she also knew she didn't feel all of what he felt, because of who they each were, and how they were different. And in that moment, she realized something else, too: she realized that no matter how well she might know her son, there was a chance she might not ever know him in the way his father would, because of who they each were and the way they each had been made.

Would that really be true, she wondered?

Or would there be change, there in Creation, and amongst them?

She wondered about all that, about the future of their son and their new family, then as she wondered, she turned to look at her husband again and when she did, she saw something was different. It was his eyes. They were the absolute softest she'd ever seen them, and in fact, it was the only time she could think since they'd been together in Creation that she would've described them as soft at all.

He bent down and kissed her.

In that kiss, she could feel what he wanted, that he wanted to be closer to them, so she moved over and when she did, he lowered himself into the bed next to them and he held her. She felt his strong arms around her as he held both of them, as closely as he could, as if it was a moment he didn't ever want to end and feeling he didn't ever want to live without again. She thought back to his previous words and the last thing he'd just said. She thought she knew what he meant, but she still wanted to hear him say it, she still wanted to hear his words.

"What's so much more?" she finally asked, very softly.

He was silent for a moment, looking down at their son.

Then he moved even closer to her.

He bent and kissed their sleeping child on the top of his head, one more time, right where his thumb had been amongst the whisps and tufts of new hair that would soon grow, then he turned to her. He looked down at her, also, and into her eyes, then he kissed her again, too, but his kiss was deeper this time. It was a kiss, she could feel, that was unlike so many of the others because it was one that stood by itself, alone, just a single, solitary act, and something not meant to be anything more or further than simply what it was.

"It's so much more than I ever thought I could feel," he finally whispered.

And when he did, his words were soft, and she knew what that meant.

It meant they were words that were not to be heard, not by anyone else; it meant they were words that were spoken and given just for her.

14

$\mathcal{P}$HOSPHORUS STOOD outside the great walls of his palace.

He stood there and looked at all those that were gathered in front of him, all the young and eager faces that had followed him away from light and into darkness, to stand where they now stood, in heavy and humid air and on the banks of a great lake made of fire. He watched for a moment as they all waited for his word, as all those above once did when Michael came to speak to them, and he enjoyed it, that feeling.

Then he thought of what it was they all waited for.

They waited to hear what he would do, he knew, and the knowledge he would give to them. They hadn't been able to defeat Michael and his host in Creation, and the angels of light would of course never again return to fight in the darkness—not with what they'd now learned—so all the dark angels wondered what was to come next.

So Phosphorus told them.

He told them what he knew, and of the secret God had kept from them and that only served to further strengthen their resolve, that such a thing should be made secret, that at some point God and Michael had decided they shouldn't share in that knowledge.

But Phosphorus had decided the opposite, he told them.

Phosphorus had decided they were strong, and they should know all that there was to know, and as he told them this, they all smiled back at their leader, and nodded, and Phosphorus was pleased when he saw the deep and unquestioned commitment and devotion that was growing in their eyes, and hearts, because if such a knowledge had been hidden from them, they wondered, then what else was God hiding?

And what else was Michael hiding, too?

Then Phosphorus told them more about the titans.

He told them who they were, and where they were imprisoned, and the journey to get there.

He told them about where he must now go, and how dangerous it was and how long it would take him, and they all raised their voices, in unison, as one.

"Take us with you!" they shouted. "Let us come, too!"

Phosphorus looked back at them and smiled at their enthusiasm.

But he still shook his head.

"No," he told them. "This is something I must do alone."

"Why?" one of the dark angels asked. "Why can't we help you? Why won't you let us serve you, and follow you?"

"You chose me to be your leader," Phosphorus told them. "So let me lead, and trust my judgment."

He watched them, as they heard his words, then they bowed their heads, accepting his judgment.

"Stay here and keep training," Phosphorus told them. "Protect our kingdom and that which we have already won. It won't be a short journey that I'll make, but when I return it will be with a strength that combined with the strength we already have, will make us unbeatable. It's a strength that will overwhelm Michael, and his light, and then Heaven will be ours, as well as Creation, and all else there is."

"How long will the journey take?" Mamanos asked.

"It doesn't matter how long it takes," Phosphorus told him. "We're speaking of eternity here, and the future, of everything. So are you with me?"

He looked around again, at all the faces.

Then he saw them nod, once more, eyes bright and shining at the promise of all that was to come.

"We're with you," Báal told him. "We're with you until the very end."

"Good," Phosphorus told them. "So keep training, defend our dominion here, and wait for me."

They all heard his words, his final words.

Then Phosphorus began to walk.

He went from his place near the great walls towards where they were gathered, and as he did, they began to part. They made a path for him as he walked, and as he passed by, each angel that was near reached out and touched him, to give him their strength, their blessing, their undying loyalty and allegiance, then soon he was past all of them, all his gathered angels.

And he kept going.

They watched as he did.

He kept walking and finally came to the edge of the Lake of Fire, and he stopped in front of it, on its bank.

He didn't know why he did what he did, but then he bent down and closed his eyes as he reached his fist into the flames and felt heat all around him, licking up his wrist and arm and towards his chest, and while he felt that heat, the greatness of it, the intensity, the power, it didn't burn him.

Instead, it gave him strength.

The lake and what was there began to fill his soul, not with darkness or light, but with fire, and he felt that strength now, that eternal strength, coursing through his body, the strength he would need for the journey he was about to undertake.

The journey and path that only he knew.

Only he, and one other.

He slowly stood again and spread his great wings.

He didn't look back at any of the others as he took a deep breath, then his wings began to pump, up and down, up and down, and he rose. He rose higher and higher into the ash-dark sky, his great body illuminated from within now by all he'd just consumed—illuminated in bright orange, which was in stark contrast to all the gathered darkness that was around him—and he turned towards the horizon.

There was one moment, just one more moment.

He flew there in place and his great wings kept pumping, displacing the heavy air that was above where he'd just stood, then the moment passed and with a loud crack he exploded through the sky and away from his kingdom and for one last second his body was still, a lone bright speck, there in the vast darkness, there on the forgotten horizon . . .

And then it was gone.

15

IN CREATION, time passed.

When her child was born and had come into their lives, their lives had changed, too, and everything else with it. Their once familiar and normal routine before the child was completely upended and remade, because they then had a great deal more responsibilities. They still had the same ones they'd previously had to themselves and each other, but now they also had the responsibilities that came with the new life they'd created.

So, their lives changed, in a great many ways.

And as their lives changed, the child grew.

She wished it had been different, during their son's first years, that it had been easier, but the truth was his childhood was very difficult. And it was difficult for both of them. After he'd been born, her husband made a new and special bed for the child, similar to how he'd carved the larger one for them out of wood, but the new one he'd made was smaller. It was much smaller, to fit the size of their child, and he fashioned sides to it, too, so their son didn't roll out and fall and harm himself while he was sleeping. She put this new bed next to their own so when he woke in the night they'd be right there, to take care of him, and he woke so many times. He woke and cried and needed to be taken care of, and every time he did, she woke, too, and she went to him. She cradled and rocked him, like she had in those first moments after he'd been born, and put his mouth to her breast to feed, and soon he wasn't just waking every night, but more than once per night.

"Don't," her husband finally told her one night, when they'd been woken by his crying for the third time.

"He needs me," she answered, as she began to rise from their bed, but he grabbed her wrist, stopping her.

"No," he said again, and she paused.

She looked back at him and frowned.

"What do you mean?" she asked.

"If you always go, then he's just going to cry more," he told her, and even though in her heart she knew he might be right, it went against everything she felt. "We're resilient," he continued. "We're resilient, and we're made to not always get what we want. Our son is the same. He'll be fine until the morning."

She hesitated for one more moment and thought back to when their son had been born; she thought back again to what her first thoughts had been, about her son and his father and what they might know of each other that she might not ever know, and as she thought of that, he pulled her back down towards their bed.

And as he did, she let him.

They both lay there together as their son kept crying, louder at first, then he gradually began to tire and the crying started to weaken. His cries became whimpers, first, then soon after, nothing at all, and they were all able to go back to sleep, and it was good. She would think about that for many days after. It was important somehow, she knew, what had happened, and how it had come. Because there it was again, the differences between them, and this time it had been *his* nature that was right, his intuition that had shown them the way. Would it be the same for a girl child, she wondered? Did he know what he knew of this child because it would soon be a man, like him, and not a woman, like her? And even at this still-young age, was this child already part of that world in which he lived and of which she couldn't know?

She wondered all these things . . .

And as she did, more time passed.

After the child had been born, her husband had gone back to his work in the fields, so she saw less and less of him as his work doubled, then tripled, and every morning he rose earlier and stayed later. She learned about solitude, in those first weeks; she learned about loneliness and isolation and being on her own in ways she hadn't yet learned before then. She did her part to help with their changing lives, too. She knew she needed to keep going out into Creation—discovering all the new and different parts of it—and finding fresh seeds to plant from the nuts and fruits she foraged and that they relied upon to sustain them until the crop near their house was more mature and more plentiful. But she had her child then, and couldn't go on her own anymore, and needed to adapt, she knew.

So she began to weave again.

She did it in the way she'd learned after Michael had come the first time, and the same way she'd woven the basket she used to carry all she found back to their clearing. And while the technique was the same as she'd used to make the basket, this time she wove in a different pattern. She sat in the clearing under the shadow of the great Tree of Knowledge as she did the work, with her son playing on the grass in front of her, and it took her some days to complete, but when it finally was, and she was done, she had a device she could wear and that would carry him and hold him to her chest so she could walk anywhere in Creation and still use her hands to pick and carry things and bring them back.

When her husband saw her, and what she'd made, he smiled.

He was still working in the field with the sun particularly hot on that day, and he'd paused to wipe the sweat from his hair and brow, and that's when he'd looked over. He waved to them as they sat there, under the great tree, and she waved back then raised their child's little hand to wave to his father, too, and that made him smile even wider.

Then he went back to the fields.

As he continued his work, she stood from her place beneath the tree, fastened the device she'd made around her neck and shoulders, then picked her son up and put him into it. He smiled as he looked back at her, from his place secured against her chest, where he liked to be, his skin touching her skin, his eyes looking up and at her eyes.

She tested it and found she was able to walk with him like that, and she was able to walk very easily.

So she did.

She left the clearing and went back into Creation to forage for the fruit and nuts they needed, and that soon became their routine. He woke before them and went to the fields, while she would feed their son, then fasten him to her chest, and they'd wave to him together as they passed the fields on their way out and into Creation for the day.

Each day that they went, they went a little further.

They would go to a different area or corner they hadn't yet been, and as they went and she foraged and picked, she also spoke to him. She spoke to him about everything—who she was, who his father was, the history of the Creation in which they both lived, the history which Michael had shown and given them—and she kept speaking to him wherever they went, even though he didn't yet speak back to her, he just made noises and sounds. That was their pattern: she would speak to him, and he would make his noises and sounds, and she waited for when he would be able to speak to her in return, and then one day, he did. When she heard his first words, she almost didn't believe her ears, then he spoke them again, and she hurried back to the clearing so she could share the moment with her husband. She got there and found him in the fields and told him to stop his work and he told her he couldn't, but she insisted, so he did. He came to where she'd gone to sit beneath the shade of the two great trees next to their home, and when he came, the child spoke again, and she watched as his father's eyes went wide.

"Mama," her child had said when they were in Creation.

Now they were back in the clearing and her husband had come from the fields, and their child saw his father, saw his large chest and strong arms and he smiled as he saw him.

"Papa," he said.

And she watched as her husband's eyes went wider than she'd ever yet seen them, and also as the tears came to his eyes, too. He reached down and took his son from her and held him in his arms and spoke to him; he spoke to him in the same way she always did, knowing he would understand, but this was the first time her husband had, and from that moment forward as more time passed and their child learned more and more words, their lives became easier.

The other change that came, before his words, was he began to walk.

He'd previously crawled around, or been able to go short distances while holding on to objects around him, or a hand used to support and guide, but soon his legs became strong enough and his balance adjusted well enough to be able to move without holding anything, so she didn't carry him strapped to her chest anymore. Instead, they still went into Creation together, but she walked with him next to her and holding her hand and trying to keep up with her longer strides and during this time, when he began to walk more and more, his muscles began to grow and become stronger, and he began to eat more and more, too, and grow taller. He began to walk more confidently, first, as he did, then soon after that he began to run. His legs were skinny and gangly and uncoordinated, but he ran so often soon they weren't, and instead of walking by her side he began to run ahead of her in the forest, and out of her sight, then one day came when they woke in the morning and were about to leave and head into Creation, as they always did, and he stopped her, just as they were about to leave their house and he told her he didn't want to go anymore.

"What do you mean?" she'd asked him.

"I don't want to go to the forest today," he told her.

She frowned, wondering where this was coming from.

"What do you want to do instead?" she asked and looked at his reaction, trying to gauge his thoughts and feelings, along with his words.

And that's when he told her.

He told her he wanted to stay and work in the fields, with his father, and she told him she needed his help in Creation with her foraging and gathering, but as she told him that, she kept looking at his eyes and what was in them, and seeing what was there and knowing what she knew of him, she finally nodded and agreed to what he'd asked.

He smiled, and though he tried to hide it, she saw he couldn't.

They went to the fields where her husband was already at work with his plow and their son told him what he'd asked of his mother, and what she'd agreed to. Her husband looked back and forth between them, then told his son that his mother needed help, too, and their son recognized that, so a compromise was made: some days he would go into Creation, with her, and some days he would stay in the fields with his father. He was delighted at this, and for his parents, it was when their lives began to return to some semblance of normal, or what normal had been before their child had arrived. They'd said the child would split his time between them, but more and more he chose to stay in the fields with his father, and she went into Creation alone. She recognized her son's ability in the fields, and his strength and passion for it, so she didn't fight it. He worked hard under the hot sun side-by-side with his father, and even young as he was, she watched as his muscles began to expand and grow even more than they already had. And in the evenings, he was more tired than he'd ever yet been, and began to go to sleep earlier, too, and wake later. It was during this time she and her husband began to lay together again, also, in the way they had before their son had come. Her husband had carved a new bed for their child when he began to walk and had outgrown the first one, but it was still near theirs in their home which offered little concealment, so when they were sure he was asleep and wouldn't wake until morning, they would get up and sneak out. They would leave the house and walk past the Tree of Knowledge and past the Tree of Life and towards the banks of the river where she would lay with him in the grass under the moonlight and they would make love like they used to make love. The passing of time had brought them closer, and in a way they hadn't been before, she found, when they'd been younger. They were older now, that was true, and they were parents, also, and while she found their love had changed because of it, she also found she thought it was better because of it. And she could tell he thought it was better, too.

So it became their routine.

They would wake in the morning—first them, then their son—and they would sit at the table together and have breakfast and talk about what they would do that day. Then they would each go about their work and when they returned, in the evenings, they would do the same thing after the day was over: they would sit at their table and discuss with each other all that had happened, and all they'd accomplished, or hadn't. And it was on one such normal day, when they'd risen and ate and her son had decided to stay with his father in the field and she'd left and gone into Creation by herself, it was on one such day that once again, everything in their world would change.

SHE WAS ON THE NORTHWEST SIDE of Creation when it happened.

She was walking near the base of the great mountains there and picking berries that had just ripened and putting them into her basket. That's then when it came. She ate a few of the berries as she worked, making her way amongst the plants and bushes, then the familiar pain arrived so sharply it caused her to double over and fall to the ground. Then something else happened, too, something that hadn't happened the first time . . .

She threw up.

She didn't know what it was at first, and she looked down into the grass at the splattered red stain of berries she'd just eaten, mixed with the bile from her stomach, that burned her throat, on the way back up, and she cocked her head curiously to the side, as she wondered about it, and thought of what it might mean.

Then there was no more time for that.

Because then, the pain came again, and it was almost unbearable.

It was more intense this time than it had been before, and after it came and then started to recede, just a little, she tried to crawl, and she went a short distance before she was finally able to get back to her feet. She started to walk and struggled through the forest as she slowly made her way back towards the clearing, having to stop again and again, every time the pain came. She reached and put her hands on the trees for support as she passed them, then the pain would become even more intense and she'd double over and when it left again, she'd go as far as she could, until it once again returned. She eventually made it back to the clearing, and when her husband saw her coming and supporting herself against the trees with one hand, the other cupped underneath her stomach, he ran to her, and so did their son.

She was about to fall, from the pain, and the exhaustion.

But before she did, he grabbed her.

He held her in his arms then picked her up again the same as he'd done when the pains had first come, and their son tried to help, too. He was too young, and too small, but that didn't stop him from trying and he went with his father and mother as they crossed the clearing back towards their home. He didn't understand what was happening, but his mother did, and so did her husband, because it of course wasn't the first time it had happened, it was now the second.

"What's wrong?" he asked her, his young eyes very wide.

"Nothing," she told him.

She stroked his head to try to comfort him, to try to tell him not to be scared.

"You're in pain," he said, looking at her. "You're hurting."

"I just need to rest, then it'll pass."

"Are you sure?" he asked, looking back and forth between his parents with the first hints of fear and confusion in his young eyes. "It's the middle of the day, why do you need to rest?"

She looked at her husband, next to their son.

He nodded, he agreed.

So she decided to tell her son how he came to be.

"You know how there has been three of us, together here in Creation?" she asked him.

"Yes," he frowned.

"Well, before you came, it was just me and your father, and this happened then, too, right before you were born. So now, sometime very soon, there's going to be one more that comes and joins us, just like you did."

"There's going to be . . . more?" he asked.

"That's right," she told him. "Soon there's going to be four of us."

He paused as he took that in and looked back and forth between his parents.

They smiled as they watched him think, and process it.

She knew he could see their wide smiles at this news, and the happiness and joy that had been brought because of it, and as he saw this, from his parents, she watched as joy and excitement started to come to his eyes, also. She watched as it came first to his eyes, then she watched as it passed to his lips and they started to spread and open at the thought of what he learned and then slowly, very slowly, just like his parents, she watched as their son smiled, too.

IT WASN'T LONG until she began to show.

Her stomach began to swell and expand, the same as it had the last time, and with her previous child, then she could feel the new life that was growing inside her. She let her son feel her belly, too, and his eyes went wide again at what he felt there beneath his fingers and that he then knew was soon going to come. The larger her belly got, and the more time passed, the closer she stayed to the clearing. She found a spot under the wide branches of the Tree of Knowledge where it was comfortable to sit and she could watch her husband and son as they worked together in the field, and as she did, she started to mend their clothes. They'd already made the bed that acted as a crib for their first child, so that meant they'd have it for their second, too, but the clothes were what was a problem; it seemed to her like every day her son grew taller and kept needing new tunics, so she took the time off her feet to make larger ones for him so he could continue to work even into the afternoon, when the sun disappeared behind the mountains that spread on all sides of Creation, and it became much cooler. She watched the two of them as they worked together, father and son, and her thoughts began to deepen. By this point, her son's interest in gathering and weaving was non-existent. His only interest lay in the fields, and with his father. And while when he looked at his mother, he looked at her with love, she knew, when he looked at his father, it was something else that he looked at him with.

It was respect.

Respect, and worship.

She thought of all she knew of him, all that she knew of each of them, and she wondered again who her son would be. She wondered about what parts of each of his parents he would share, and his future.

Then she felt something else, something telling her to look up, to look above.

So she did.

She looked at the branches above her head and saw the bright fruit that was there, the fruit which she knew not to eat, and that she'd told her son not to eat, as well. They'd both told him in no uncertain terms, as soon as he could understand, that he could eat any of the fruit in Creation except that which grew on the tree that was next to their house, and he'd listened to them. He didn't even seem curious about it.

At least, not in the way she was, even if she hadn't been in some time.

Then she heard something.

It was a shout, coming from the distance.

She turned her eyes back down from the branches and looked to the fields where she saw her son, first, then why he wanted her attention: he was pushing the plow on his own, for the first time, without the help of his father, and he waved to make sure she saw as he did it.

She smiled and waved back.

She saw her husband behind their son, too, helping him move the plow even though he was pretending not to help, and she smiled at him, as well, and waved, then everything she'd just been thinking faded, and all that was there and was left was happiness.

Because this was a moment, she could feel.

This was a perfect moment.

A perfect moment she would remember, for all the rest of her life.

She breathed slowly, in and out, and she kept watching them in the field as she tried to commit everything she saw and felt to memory, because it was indeed something that was perfect, she knew—something that was truly beautiful and perfect—and as such it was something that needed and deserved to be remembered and preserved and felt, again and again, on and on, forever and ever.

So that would be who she was, she realized.

And that would be what she would do.

IT WASN'T LONG from that moment until the second birth began.

She was in the bed in their home and her husband was there to help her again, though he didn't let their son come in. He sent him to the river for fresh water and several other small errands he thought of to keep him occupied, and while his birth—the first one she'd experienced—had lasted most the night, and had brought with it a great deal of struggle and pain, the second birth was much easier. It lasted only a few hours, and there wasn't as much unknown since it was the second time, for both of them, and there also wasn't as much pain. When it finally happened and was over and he'd taken their second child from her, she watched as he looked down into the baby's eyes for the first time then held him so she could see, too, and she saw their second child was also a boy. And when she looked at him, deeply into his new and beautiful eyes, she didn't see a mix of her and him this time, looking back at them . . .

This time, she just saw herself.

She kept looking into his eyes and he looked back at her with the eyes she so clearly recognized as her own, and she wondered if that meant his soul was the same as hers, too, and who he would be.

Their first-born son came back inside.

When he did, she waved for him to join them.

He came over and she told him to come even closer and he did and then he, too, looked down at his brother for the first time. She watched as he stood there and she tried to read his eyes and the look that was on his face, and she realized she couldn't. He didn't move at first, but then the new baby saw his brother and he reached up and took the middle finger on his left hand in his own small hand.

"He's so tiny," her first-born said.

She smiled when she heard his words.

"You were the same once, too," she told him.

"Can I hold him?" he asked.

"Of course."

She handed the new-born to her first-born, and as she did, and he took him in his young arms, his father was there, too, and watching.

"Make sure you support his head," she heard her husband say.

Her first-born nodded and that's what he did.

He held his brother in his arms and looked down into his new and young face, then his brother's lips started to part. They turned up into a smile, his very first smile, then after it came, he closed his eyes and began to sleep. His older brother watched as he held him and he drifted off, he watched as his new brother's little chest moved up and down, up and down, and as he did, she watched as his own lips started to part into a smile, too, and then they were a family.

THE SECOND BIRTH WAS MUCH EASIER, and she recovered from it quicker, as well, but the greatest blessing was the subsequent nights. Where their first child had kept them both up with his crying and screaming at all hours of the night, their second never woke them once.

When they went to sleep, so did he, and when they woke in the morning, he was already awake and smiling and ready for them to pick him up from his crib.

When he was first born, she stayed in the clearing with him.

But then as more days passed, and he grew, she began to bring him into Creation.

She used the same device she'd woven for their first son to strap him to her chest, so as she walked, she could carry him and still use her hands, and she brought him with her every day. She would wake, and they would go, then in the evenings they would return and when they sat around their table and discussed what they'd done, she realized something else: they had two sons now, and needed something unique to call each of them to avoid the confusion that came with who they were and having to say things like *older* and *younger* and *first* and *second*.

"So what will we call them, then?" her husband asked when she brought it up.

She thought about it because she knew names were important.

She thought about it for many days, and asked for help and guidance, and at first none came.

Then one day, it did.

She was with him in Creation when it came, on the far north-western end and near the mountains in almost the exact same place as where she'd first felt him inside her. She was picking ripened berries and putting them into her basket, with him strapped to her chest, then the wind picked up and when it did, she froze. She froze because along with the wind, she heard a voice, as surely as if someone was next to her and whispering in her ear, and along with the voice, she heard a word:

Habel, it said.

She heard the word, as it came and passed through her.

And as it did, she knew immediately what the word was.

She looked down into the face of her young son as he looked back at her from his place strapped to her chest, and she repeated it, to both of them now, and when she did, his eyes lit up as he heard her and smiled and murmured something she couldn't make out and reached his hand out for hers. She smiled as she let him wrap his tiny fingers around her own fingers, and she stood there for a moment, together with him, her son. Then the moment passed and she turned and went back towards the clearing and when she got there, she went to where her husband worked and she told him what she'd heard.

He listened to the word, which he now knew would be his second-born son's name, and he nodded.

It would be good.

But then, after he nodded, she saw him frown.

"What is it?" she asked.

"What about our first-born, though?" he wondered.

And she shook her head.

"I didn't hear anything further," she told him. "And then the wind left, and I didn't feel anything further, either."

"But we need a name for him, too."

"I know."

"So what do we do?"

"All we can do, which is wait, and know that it will be given, when it's meant to be given."

He thought about that for a moment, then nodded again, and knew it would be.

They stood there together and he smiled and reached out and took Habel from her arms then smiled even wider as he looked down into his second-born son's eyes, and repeated his name over and over—"*Habel, Habel, Habel*"—and the boy giggled as they walked towards the house. She watched them as they went, then she turned to where her first-born was taking the tools they'd used for the day to the river to clean them, and when he put them away, he went towards the house, too. She watched as he went in after his father and younger brother, then she followed after them, as well, but instead of going inside herself she paused and stood in the doorway. She looked inside from the place where she watched and saw them each take their seats: her husband at the head, their first-born son next to him, on his right, then Habel in the place across from his older brother. It was the exact scene she'd already seen in her vision, the one which had come and told her what the strange feeling in her belly was going to be, and the family they would have together in Creation. She stood there for a moment longer, in the doorway, with a smile on her face, taking in all that was in front of her and the truth of the plan and vision she'd been given, then she went to join them.

She did this same thing, for many more days after.

She didn't know why.

When she returned from Creation, she would let her family all go into the house first and sit, and she would stop and look at them from the doorway before she would then go in, too, and join them. They would sit together and talk about all that had happened during their days, and their first-born son would wave his hands and talk excitedly as he ate, telling his mother about the things his father let him do in the field while she was away, and all the things his growing and expanding body and muscles were now allowing him to accomplish. She would listen, and ask him questions, and these were the moments in the day, she realized, that she enjoyed above all others.

Then one day, while she stood in the doorway, before they ate . . .

That's then when it came.

The wind picked up again and the feeling that had come with it before returned, the one in the depths of her stomach. It told her not to go inside and join them yet, but to wait outside, so she did. She listened to the feeling and it guided her from the house and towards the great Tree of Knowledge. The sun had already sunk, and the moon was up, so the tree looked similar to the way it had so long ago, in her dream that wasn't actually a dream when the dark angel had first come and tempted her with its fruit.

She looked at the fruit again now.

She looked at all the pieces growing on the gnarled branches, and how the moonlight reflected off the color of the skin and it seemed to shine in a way she hadn't seen before. She was mesmerized by the color and the light, then the wind picked up even more, and that's when it brought another word for her, too, and as soon as she heard it, she knew. She waited for one more moment, then having received what she knew she'd waited to receive, she turned and went back inside to her family. She walked across the space and took her seat at the table and when she did, her husband turned to look at her as their oldest son played with his brother next to them.

"Is everything alright?" her husband asked.

She looked back at him, then after a moment, she nodded.

"Yes," she told him.

Then they all began to eat.

And as they did, she didn't reach for any food herself, but instead just turned to look at her son—her first-born son who sat there, next to his father, and helped cut food now into smaller pieces to feed to his younger brother—and she thought of what she'd just heard, the name she'd just been given, that had just been brought to her on the wind. She thought of it, and knew it was true, and that it would be. Then after dinner was finished and their children had gone to bed, she took her husband outside and told him what it was she'd heard, what the wind had brought them, and the name they would call their son.

"What was it?" he asked. "What did the wind say?"

She waited for a moment, just for a moment . . .

Then she told him.

Kain, the wind had whispered to her.

16

$\mathcal{B}$ACK AT THE PALACE IN HEAVEN, a great many things had changed.

Michael noticed it first with Gabriel, who seemed to retreat from his closeness with Michael after Michael had refused to let him or any of the others stop Selaphiel and those that flew with him from leaving, then Michael began to notice the same thing with Raphael, too. Gabriel and Raphael had both been his friends and staunchest supporters, but he wondered about that now; he wondered for the first time about the strength of their support and friendship, and he also wondered about his path. For the first time he truly wondered what he was meant for, and meant to do, and if he was still indeed carrying out God's will within his Kingdom and Creation, or if somehow he'd lost his way.

Michael didn't return again to Creation, but he did watch the humans.

He watched them every day.

He watched from the palace as their first son came, as he'd told them it would, then he watched as that son grew, and their next son came. He watched as the parents named their two sons and he saw the love they all shared. He saw the limitless and unquestioned love of a child for a parent, and he also saw the different type of love that came between her and him, the two parents, and how it grew deeper and changed as their family also grew and expanded. It became less physical and more endless, like the wind that had given their children their names. He watched all this and for the first time he felt envy. He thought of his own love, and as he did, he let himself wonder for the millionth time about what could have been, and even as he did, even as he wondered, he knew he would never have an answer to that question, not really, and he also knew he was destined to keep wondering one million more times, and for one million more years, then even further, too, and beyond.

What kind of an eternity was that, he thought?

What kind of a life would that be?

He normally would have turned to Gabriel or Raphael for their strength and wisdom, but so much had changed since what used to be, and they no longer spoke to him in the same way they used to, so instead he retreated to his chamber, alone, and rarely left.

Life kept going on around him, and around the palace, he knew.

Gabriel kept training the younger angels in the craft of war, and Raphael kept searching the heavens for answers and clues about Phosphorus and what his next action might be.

But all that they did, they did alone.

Michael stayed in his empty room.

And while Raphael continued to search the heavens for some sign of Phosphorus and where he might strike next, Michael did the same thing, too, only when he searched for clues about his friend, he searched within himself.

Where are you, he felt himself whispering.

Where are you, and what are you going to do.

Even though he asked, even though he whispered, there was no answer that came.

And that's when it crept up on him.

It happened on a day that felt as heavy and painful as any day he could remember, so he decided to do something he'd thought about many times, but had never done. He decided to pray and ask to hear the word of God. Always before when he'd heard God's word it had come unbidden and given information and instruction, and he in turn carried out that instruction, whatever it might have been. It was a pattern that was eternal; one that was done and followed as far back as he could remember, which was of course forever, the very beginning of time.

But he couldn't stand what he felt any longer.

So this time he decided to change it; this time he decided not to wait.

He sat in his room and closed his eyes in meditation and was completely still, completely silent, and emptied his mind entirely. Then when he was satisfied his body and mind were calm and clear enough, he lifted his words and spoke directly to God, himself, and not the other way around.

For the first time, Michael spoke of all that was in his heart.

He spoke of everything he felt, all the doubt and worry, all the pain and uncertainty.

Then after he spoke, he waited.

He waited and waited.

He waited as long as he could, he waited forever.

But he heard nothing in return.

ON THE OTHER SIDE of space and time, Phosphorus continued to fly.

He travelled through both light and darkness, and his journey took longer than even he had anticipated or imagined, and as he flew, he thought about what might be happening in Creation and just as Michael thought of Phosphorus, he thought about Michael, too, and his Kingdom, and what would be taking place there because of what he'd done. He didn't know the answer to that, because he was far enough away he couldn't feel or know—he was far enough and to a point where all things were more faint, dull, distant—but it didn't matter, he knew. None of it mattered, except what was in front of him, except the reason he made this near un-makeable journey.

He continued on his way.

As he did, he began to lose strength.

His limbs had started to grow weary with fatigue and lack of nourishment, and as he flew, his wings began to grow heavy, too. Then lightning came and crashed around him as he went through dark mist and the light refracted off shards of dust and flashed in brilliant patterns all around him. He continued to fly through it all, and just as he reached the point where he knew he couldn't carry on any further, he burst through the mist and clouds and dust he'd been inside for longer than he could remember.

And as soon as he did, everything changed.

The air got lighter and the lightning began to retreat.

He pumped his wings heavily up and down a few more times, then they gave out altogether and he began to plummet *down, down, down,* crashing towards the mountainous and rocky terrain he saw below, and he dropped quickly, the ground rising in a rush to meet him.

He landed in a painful heap and large cloud of dust, and after he did, he lay very still.

He lay there for what felt like hours.

Then he slowly began to feel his strength return.

He began to feel everything he once had start to come back to him, and he eventually stood from the spot where he'd fallen in the mountains, and raised his head, and he looked around.

And that's when he saw it.

That's when he saw what he'd made such a great journey to find.

In front of him there was an immense range of peaks that climbed high into the sky, and at the top of the tallest and greatest peak, there was an entrance to a cave, and it was just as God had described to him and Michael, all those many years ago, and it was just as Phosphorus had imagined it, too, and when he saw it, he smiled.

Then he began to walk.

His wings were still tired and he couldn't yet fly again, he knew, but he also didn't want to wait any longer, so he went forward and began to climb the slope on foot. He found an old, steep path that went up the side of the mountain, and as he started on it, he realized it was a path that hadn't been used in many thousands of years.

But it was being used again now.

It was a tough and long journey up the mountain, but Phosphorus was strong and he was driven by that which burned deep within him, the fire he'd consumed mixed with the darkness, and he soon came to the top and the entrance he'd already seen and paused outside because he knew his destiny lay inside.

He breathed deeply as he stood there; *in and out, in and out . . .*

Then he finally steadied himself and went in.

He ducked his head low as he went through the small entrance and kept his head bent as he continued on and down the narrow, dark tunnel with moisture and condensation dripping from the ceiling above. He went on like that for much longer than he thought he'd need to go on in such a small and narrow space. Then everything changed. The narrow path from the entrance with the low ceiling began to widen, and as it continued, and got to the heart of the mountain, it emptied into a gigantic open space that was as large as anything Phosphorus had ever seen. It was a room that seemed to be endless and had a ceiling that went up and up, higher than his eyes could see.

His vision adjusted to the light and scale of what was there.

And that's then when he saw them.

He almost overlooked them at first because of how large they were, chained in their places against the sides of the great walls inside the mountain. He saw the massive feet first, leading up to the powerful legs, enormous arms, mighty torsos, and the shoulders and heads that were more than three times the size of Phosphorus himself. Then alone there in the near-darkness, he allowed himself a small smile, one small smile that was just for himself and for what he'd remembered and the journey and discovery he'd just made, because he knew what he'd found, and what he saw, all around him.

Titans.

Then he heard a great booming voice that echoed and sounded like thunder in the mountain, to such a degree that Phosphorus nearly needed to cover his ears.

But he didn't.

"Who wakes us," the thundering voice said.

Phosphorus turned to look at the great titan that spoke and the place he was chained to the wall behind him, as the titan slowly blinked his ancient eyes open for the first time in many, many years. Phosphorus studied his limbs. He studied how they were bound to the cave by earth and stone, and it was a substance and bondage that was too strong even for the great titan to break, he knew, as it had been wrought and made by God himself, so many ages ago.

Phosphorus looked at the bondage, for one more moment, then up at the titan, and he finally spoke.

"You must be Okeanos," Phosphorus said to him.

"How do you know my name?" the titan sluggishly asked, his words coming in slow, measured intervals, as if he was learning again something he'd only ever once known.

"I am Phosphorus, once of Heaven, and God's Kingdom," Phosphorus told him. "But not anymore."

"So now what are you?"

Phosphorus waited for a moment.

He paused for drama and effect, as he looked back at the great titan that was across from him, the one that continued to slowly wake from his hibernation.

"Now I'm just Phosphorus," he told him. "King of the Fallen, and Lord of all that is Below."

It was the first time he'd used the title he'd created out loud, and as soon as he did, he felt a sensation run through the entire length of his body, a feeling he'd never felt before. Okeanos finally looked down at him. The titan looked from his great height, taking Phosphorus in, and the angel waited as Okeanos looked him over, from head to toe, turning what he saw over and over in his mind. Then after Okeanos had seen him and taken everything in, Phosphorus still waited, because just the same as all things that are ancient, titans do nothing in a hurry. Phosphorus waited even more, even longer than he could count, and as he did, he saw all the other titans chained to the walls of the cave begin to wake from their hibernation and blink their own eyes open, too.

"I know who you are," Okeanos finally spoke again. "You were once God's favorite, when you were in Heaven."

"Yes," Phosphorus nodded. "I was."

Okeanos waited another long moment, and Phosphorus waited, too.

All the titans around them were fully awake now and also waiting to hear what their leader would say, then he began to speak, and they listened as his words echoed and thundered through the cave that was their prison.

"We've waited a very long time for you to come," Okeanos finally told him.

"I know," Phosphorus nodded.

"So what do you offer us?"

"I offer you freedom," Phosphorus told him. "But it's freedom that comes with a price."

"What price?" Okeanos narrowed his eyes.

Phosphorus heard the titan's words and knew this was the moment; this was the moment where he could turn and leave and with enough contrition and penance there could still be forgiveness in Heaven, he knew, there could still be a way for him back to the light. He thought of light again, and knew that path was still there, he knew that in his heart. But then he thought of darkness, too. He thought of the throne he'd claimed, but which he knew he didn't yet deserve. He thought about a love he once thought had been meant to be eternal, but it hadn't been, and he thought about what it had torn within him when it had ended. Had it ended? And if it had, could it ever be mended, he wondered? Could a broken soul ever be sewn back together?

They could, he knew, souls could do that . . .

But not his.

Because he knew himself and he knew his soul, which was a restless one; it was a restless one that would never be happy without all he desired and all he so often dreamed of, so that would be his decision, he also knew, that was always going to be his decision, and the journey would now truly begin, the one from which there was no turning back.

Phosphorus breathed in, deeply, looking down at his feet.

Then he turned and looked back up to meet the eyes of the great titan.

"I will break your bondage for you," Phosphorus told him. "And I will bring you back to the world. That will be my solemn oath to you. But in return, you will serve me, once you're back in the world, and you'll serve me for all the rest of eternity."

Okeanos paused again, as he looked down at the angel, there in front of him.

Phosphorus was tiny in comparison, no taller than Okeanos' knee.

"We're titans," Okeanos finally said. "Which means that we serve no one."

"God only told two others of who you are, and where you were imprisoned," Phosphorus answered.

"So?" Okeanos asked. "What's your point, angel?"

"My point is he told us how he imprisoned you here, just me and Michael, and you know Michael will never come. So I'm your only hope. I'm your only hope to not spend another eternity chained within your dark mountain here at the end of everything, at the edge of all there is. And there's more now to return to, also, more than there was before, more even than you know."

"What do you mean . . . more than we know?" Okeanos frowned.

"*Creation*," Phosphorus said as he kept looking between them and he saw the other titans begin to watch him curiously as they stretched and flexed against the chains and earth that bound their limbs to the mountain.

"Creation?" Okeanos spoke the word and wondered about it.

"Yes," Phosphorus told him. "But it's not for you. When we defeat Michael and the host that flies with him, and God is nothing but a distant memory, I'll rule in Creation and Above, in Heaven and his

Kingdom, and you'll stay and rule Below, where you once ruled before, and where I rule now. You'll answer to me, as Michael answers to God, but you'll have your old dominion back, and your old power."

The titans paused, and as they did, they took this in.

And all those that had now woken turned to look at Okeanos.

But their leader wasn't looking at them anymore; he was staring down at Phosphorus in front of him, his great eyes narrowed. He once again tried to move his limbs, to come forward, to reach out, but the chains and earth that bound him reminded him he couldn't; he was once again reminded they were still held by the earth in the place in which they'd now lived for longer than they ever thought possible and even with their great strength they couldn't break free of that bondage. Not without help. Perhaps that was their lesson, Okeanos thought, and perhaps that was what their journey was about, and how it would end.

"You said you knew one day I would come," Phosphorus said.

"Yes, I did."

"So that means you also knew what I would ask, and what comes next," Phosphorus spoke evenly.

Okeanos heard the angel's words and he was silent again.

As he was silent, he turned inwards.

Phosphorus watched as Okeanos took him in, one more time, this angel that had travelled so far to be there in front of him, this angel that had once been an angel of light, but was now darkness. Could he be their Lord, Okeanos wondered, could he be their first Lord? The titans had never suffered to have anyone rule over them before, because there was no one they'd ever deemed worthy to do so. But Okeanos knew strength, that was what he knew, most of all, uncommon and special strength, and that's also what he now saw in front of him. Was there another way? There wasn't, he knew. So this would be it, he decided, and finally nodded. It was just once, very simply, but it was also his oath, his eternal promise, and when he spoke, his words echoed throughout the great cave.

"It will be as you say, angel," he finally said.

Then Phosphorus nodded, too, and began his dark work.

$\mathcal{S}$HE LOOKED DOWN and into her second son's young and bright eyes.

Habel had just asked her a question about the fruit and nuts they picked every day, and which of them were ready to be eaten, and which needed to wait longer until they were picked, and how to tell the difference between the two. He asked her about ripeness, and so that's when she'd looked down at him, at his eyes that were so patiently waiting for her answer and told him what she'd learned during her own time and how the color of the fruit that was ready was always brighter than the color of the fruit that wasn't, and how it would fall off the branch or bush or vine where it grew, when it was ready to come off. That's then when it could be eaten, she told him, and that's how it was with the fruit, but the nuts . . . the nuts were trickier, she explained.

She spoke to her son about that and all else she'd learned, and as she did, and heard her own words, she realized there seemed to be a larger lesson that could be taken from the way the fruit ripened and then fell when it was ready, a larger lesson about all there was, and Creation, too, and Habel seemed to take it all in and process it as he carefully felt the different berries and picked the ones that came loose at his touch, as she'd told him.

He was curious about Creation, and all that was in it, which was something that was different than his brother.

And that was something she'd recognized in him right away.

When Kain had been young and she'd brought him into Creation with her to forage and gather, he didn't ask any questions and it hadn't been long until he'd decided he wanted to stay back in the fields with his father and what he knew his father did there. He saw what that work in the fields did to his father, and how it made him bigger, stronger, more powerful, and Kain wanted the work he did to do those same things to him, too. She'd explained to him how what she did would help to build his lungs, and legs, and endurance, and other senses, also, like sight and smell, but Kain wasn't interested in any of those things. He barely heard the words, even, as she spoke them.

He knew what he desired, and who he wanted to be.

And she knew that she wouldn't stand in his way.

And while that's how it had been with Kain, with Habel, everything had been different. Everything had been so different. His childhood had been easier, and not just in the way of the sleepless nights that were there in the beginning with Kain, but in every way. He was content to go into Creation with his mother each day, and he was excited to help her and learn from her and she learned something from that, too, something she also perhaps learned the first moment she looked into his eyes, and it was this: while she knew their oldest was an equal part of each of his parents, this son, the one that came with her every day, their youngest . . .

This son, she knew, was only hers.

She thought back to what she knew of her husband, and what she'd seen in Kain, too: were those things she'd seen things that were in all men, she wondered, or just them? Were they things that were also in her sweet, youngest child, the one who spent his days with his mother in Creation; were those things that had caused her so many sleepless nights and so much temptation sitting under the great tree also lying dormant behind Habel's young and innocent eyes and questions?

She wondered all that and didn't know.

Then she heard his voice.

"Mom . . . ?" Habel said.

She broke from her thoughts as she turned to look down at him next to her, and where he watched her curiously. He'd seen her eyes and thoughts drift, she knew, and his voice had brought her back to him, and to Creation.

"What is it?" she asked.

He was silent, as he watched her, for one more moment.

Then he pointed.

She looked into the distance and saw what he was pointing at, the sun beginning to sink in the sky, down towards the mountains that bordered Creation, and as the sun crept behind the peaks, the light began to fade, she knew, and the warmth that it brought, too, and it was the point in the day that always signaled they needed to head back from wherever it was they were.

She smiled at him, happy at how much he'd learned already, even at his young age.

"Let's go see how they're doing in the fields," she said.

And she took his hand in hers, and they went.

THEY WENT THROUGH THE TREES of the forest and were almost back to the clearing they called home. They did this same routine every day now, and she knew what they would find when the trees parted in front of them and the clearing finally came into view: Kain would be working next to his father, both of them wiping sweat from their brows as they finished their tasks for the day, then they'd put away their tools before going down to the river to strip off their tunics and rinse the dirt on their skin away in the cool, gently flowing water that came to them from the mountains in the north. Kain had grown, seemingly all at once becoming taller, stronger, and bigger, and now he was nearly to his father's shoulder and it wouldn't be long, she knew, until he surpassed her height and then maybe even his father's. His strength allowed him to use all the tools in the field with ease, and his chest had expanded, too, along with his torso, which had widened at the shoulders and narrowed further down until it ended at a tapered waist, which is where his powerful legs began.

She saw all this physical transformation . . .

And she knew her oldest son was fast becoming a man.

He was fast becoming a man that was just like his father, and with each day that passed he was less and less hers, she saw, both in appearance and in other ways, too, and she'd begun to see him less and less. He worked in the fields during the day, and since he'd gotten older, he'd taken to wandering into the forest after they'd had their afternoon meal as a family. He would be gone for hours at a time after the sun went down, and she would ask him where he went and what he did, when he came back, but all he'd say was *nothing*. She knew that what he told her wasn't the truth, as he was definitely doing *something*. He just didn't want his mother to know, she realized, or his father, either.

They kept walking together, her and Habel.

Then the forest ended, and they returned to the clearing.

But what she saw when they returned wasn't what she'd expected.

This was normally the time when Kain and his father were putting their tools away and getting ready to head to the river, but this afternoon that's not what they were doing: they were still standing in the fields, tools forgotten next to them, and Kain had a bandage wrapped around his hand, a bandage that had been made from the tunic he always wore that was now stained red with dried blood.

And then, when she saw what else he was holding . . .

That's when her breath caught in her throat.

He had in his hand the smaller of the swords that his father had made from the metal created through fire and heat and molded into what his son now held. And next to her son, she saw her husband, and in his hand, he held the other sword he'd made, the larger one. The smaller one was light and he'd made it for her, he'd told her before, and she'd thought the weapon out of her life when it had disappeared after their fight, but now here it was in the hands of her son, her eldest-born son, the one who wanted to do everything his father did. Even though he'd grown, the full-sized sword would still be too heavy for him, she knew; but there, in his hand, was another that wasn't because there, put into his hand by his father standing next to him, was a sword that seemed as if it was made just for him.

She quickly crossed the distance between them.

Habel followed next to her, trying to keep up.

She was almost to them when she saw her husband glance over and see her coming, then so did Kain, too, but she had no eyes for him now.

She only had eyes for his father.

"What are you doing?" she breathed.

"He saw my hand."

"So?"

Her husband looked at her for a moment, at the anger that was there in her eyes, she knew, that was in her face, and she saw him gathering himself to face it.

He took a deep breath before he responded.

He told her how they'd been working together in the field, as they always did, and he'd let Kain use the plow that day. They were turning a new row of dirt and soil in an area of the field where they'd decided to expand and hadn't plowed before, and that's where Kain hit a rock and lost control of the plow. He'd tried to quickly grab it again, but when he did, the sharpened part of the metal cut his hand: a long thin line from the base of the thumb up across the wrist. His father had immediately ripped a piece of tunic to tie around the wound and stop the bleeding, he told her, which is the bloodied bandage she saw on Kain's hand.

The wound wasn't life threatening, but it was painful, and it would leave a scar.

"What does that have to do with these?" she asked, nodding towards the weapons, not even wanting to say their name.

"The scar led to a story," he told her.

"How?" she asked. "And what story?"

So he told her what had happened.

Kain had seen the scar that was on his father's hand, of course he had; it was something he'd seen every day since he was very little, when his father would hold him, when they took their meals, when they worked together. He asked about it as often as he could but his father never told him what it was, or where it had come from. He didn't tell him, her husband now told her, because of the promise he'd made to her when their children were born, not to tell them about the battle in the forest, not to show them the great crater that was still there, or tell them what had happened that day, so they would always feel safe, and it was a promise he intended to keep. And so, over and over, he'd dismissed Kain's questions, every time he'd asked.

But now here was the answer, right in front of him.

The metal of the plow had cut his hand in such a way that even at this early stage of the wound, Kain knew and could see that when it healed, it would heal in a nearly identical way as to how his father's hand looked. It would leave a very similar scar, albeit smaller, and less deep.

So Kain had wondered, what metal was it that had done to his father's hand what the plow had done to his own?

When Kain had asked, his father had stared back at him.

He decided he couldn't lie to him, not any longer, and not in such a direct way.

His son was nearly a man, and when the battle had occurred, her husband wasn't much older than Kain was now, at least in terms of the physical maturity of his body. In terms of his time in Creation, he'd been younger than his son, but that was because he'd been born of dirt and earth—born both fully-formed and nearly mature, at least in body—while both his sons and all the other children that would come after them had been born in a different way, because they'd been born of flesh and blood, and not of the earth.

So he told his son what had happened, before he'd been born.

The rest of their work was forgotten as he told Kain about the great battle between light and dark, and the celestial warriors that fought on either side of that battle, and the part that he'd played in it, and the part that she'd played, too. He told Kain how he'd faced one of the dark angels and defeated him in combat, but the battle with the angel left him with the scar that was on his hand, the scar his son had asked about so many times.

"What happened after the battle?" Kain then asked his father.

So his father told him.

His father told him how he'd been scared the dark angels would come back again, or perhaps any other that was out there that wished to bring them harm—any other they didn't yet know about—and he told him how he'd discovered the stones in the river that could be melted and turned into metal. Then he told him how he'd discovered that he could mold that metal when it was in its liquid form, and how in that way he was able to create a sword of his own, just like the swords the angels had carried, and used in their battles.

Kain hung rapt, on every detail, on every word his father told him; he devoured every single moment of danger and peril and heroism.

And then, of course, he asked about the swords that had been made. Were they still in Creation?

Yes, his father had told him.

He hadn't gotten rid of them, he'd just taken them from the clearing so she wouldn't see them and they wouldn't fight about it anymore, and after his father told him all that, Kain waited in the field while his father then went to retrieve them to show them to him. He handed the smaller of the two he'd made to his son, while he kept the larger and heavier one for himself, then he explained how they were used; he showed him how the angels had swung and wielded them, and how he'd destroyed the dark one that had come between him and Kain's mother. Then he told Kain how the dark angel had died, too, how he'd gone still, then started to glow, his body shaking there on the forest floor until it exploded into a great cloud of energy and darkness. She took in this story, as he told it, and wondered why it had been necessary for him to do so, to tell it to their son, then it came to her:

Pride, she thought again.

Pride, and love.

And as she thought this, she shook her head and looked at the swords again, the swords that were there and in each of their hands, and that's when it came.

It was sharp, and immediate.

And it was a vision, just like the others.

But this one was much less pleasant, and there was a piercing pain that came to her gut as images screamed and flashed in front of her:

A bloody sword.

But it was a different one.

Her son Kain, holding it, but older, his eyes darker.

The body of another, at his feet, crying out, reaching up, more blood there on the arm, the sleeve, but she couldn't see who it was . . .

Then the vision faded, and she came back to Creation, and herself.

"What is it?" her husband asked, rushing to her side again.

But she had no eyes for him anymore, her husband; she only had eyes for her son, her oldest son.

And fear.

She had fear now, too, lodged deep in her throat and it was a fear that wasn't leaving.

"What's wrong?" Kain asked, concern in his eyes, too.

"Go back to the house," she told him, her voice low, and she spoke slowly. "And bring your brother with you."

"Why?" he asked.

But instead of answering, she just gave him a look, a stern and powerful look and when he saw it, he didn't ask any more questions, he simply took Habel by the hand, as she'd asked him to do, and turned and started to walk back towards the house, but he only got a few paces away when she spoke again.

"Leave it here," she told him.

He paused and turned back to her.

He still had the sword in his hand, he realized, in the hand his little brother wasn't holding.

He looked down at it.

Then he looked up and back at her.

"Why do I have to?" he asked. "Father told me I could have it."

She heard him and saw it already happening, and shook her head.

"*Kain*," she spoke softly, in a way she never had before, fragile, shaking.

She watched as her son heard his name and the tone in which she'd said it, and he looked from her, back to his father, who nodded, once, simply, so he then looked back at her again and nodded, too, and finally let the sword slide from his hand and fall to the ground. He gave one last look, between his parents, then turned and continued on and into the distance with his brother, as she'd told him to do.

She waited, as they walked, getting closer, back towards the house, then when they were almost there, and out of earshot, that's when she turned back to her husband.

"Why?" she asked him, and the word was almost a whisper.

"I didn't want to lie to him."

"I thought you got rid of them."

"I *did* get rid of them."

"Then why are they still here!" she yelled.

And when she did, and he heard her words, he was silent for a moment.

She watched as he thought, calculating, because he knew how important the next moments were, and what he would say.

"Just because you don't want something to enter Creation, or our lives, doesn't mean it won't," he said very slowly, deliberately.

"We can control what we can control."

"But that's just the point: there are things out there that are *beyond* our control. And they've already come once, which means they can come again, whether we want them to or not. I know what I promised you, but I also made a promise to myself, too, and the promise was I'd be ready . . . that I'd never be caught unawares or unarmed again. I made a promise I'd never let ourselves or our family be vulnerable in the way we were before. That's the promise I made to myself, after they came and tried to take everything we had, and it's also a promise I intend to keep."

"But that's you," she said, her voice shaking.

"So?"

"Our son is just a boy."

"And what do boys do?" he asked, then answered his own question. "They become men."

"This is not what it means to be a man."

"And what would you know of it?" he asked her, finally losing his temper, too.

And she paused, because when she heard his words, and how he'd said them, she realized it wasn't in a way she'd heard him speak before because they were words that were meant to be cruel. It was a question that was meant to highlight the one thing she'd spent so many moments thinking about—the ever-growing divide between her and those she lived with, and loved—and it was also the one thing that had almost led her into temptation, so many times, which was also the one thing she'd sworn to herself she would never give in to.

Temptation.

Knowledge.

She thought of all that, then shook her head.

"Those weapons mean death," she told him.

"Yes," he nodded. "They do."

"Then why bring them here?"

"They were already brought here, and not by us. You told me to get rid of them, but there's no way that's possible."

"So what would you have us do, then, if they mean death? Just not try? Just give them to our children then see what happens? I thought I understood you."

"Perhaps you don't if that's what you think I've done."

She stood there.

She was silent, as she looked back at him, across from her.

"What's happened to us?" she finally asked, very quietly. "Where has our love gone, and all we used to have and be?"

"What love? You spend more time with Habel now than you do with me, or with Kain," he told her.

"What do you mean?"

"We don't do anything we used to do together. We don't even go to the river anymore."

"Yes, we do."

"When?" he asked.

Then after he asked, he stood there and waited.

She looked back at him and she thought again to the past; she thought back again to all that had happened, and how their schedule and everything else had changed when children had come, then how it had changed again and even more as they each grew older. When they just had Kain, and he was young, it was easier for them to have time together in the way they used to, just them, and their love, but then Kain grew, and Habel came and he grew, too, and with the children there was so much more responsibility, and so much less time.

"Do you remember the waterfall?" she finally asked him, very slowly.

"Of course I do."

"That's still us," she told him. "That's still who we are."

"It doesn't feel like it."

"So how do we fix this, then? How do we go back to how we were before?"

Her question hung between them, for a long time, and they were both silent, as the words drifted and settled, then he sighed.

"I don't know," he finally said. "Maybe we don't. Maybe that's a time that's come and gone, and will live again only in memory and that's just the way of things."

"You don't believe that."

"How do you know what I believe?"

She opened her mouth, but no words came, because for the first time, she realized he was right. She looked at him for another moment, then she turned and looked towards their house, in the clearing, and the two great trees that were next to it. She turned back and looked at him again, there in front of her.

She opened her mouth, but he spoke first.

"Maybe it's best if I leave," he said.

"*Leave?*" she asked. "To go where? And what will happen here?"

"You're better than I am with them. And Kain's old enough to tend the fields on his own now."

"We're a family."

"Yes, we were once, weren't we?"

She heard him, and swallowed heavily, as her breathing quickened.

So would that be it?

Would that be his final word?

She looked back at him as she took that in, what he'd just said, and a tear started to slip down her cheek as she shook her head softly.

"Don't go," she said to him.

He looked at her and then stuck his sword down into the loose dirt in the field that was under their feet, so the sword stood on its end, then he came closer to her. He reached up and gently took her face in his hands, and when he did, he looked into her eyes and into her soul.

"I can't change what's in my heart," he told her softly, shaking his head, as she looked behind him at the sword that was still standing upright in the dirt. "I can't change who I am," he said again.

"This isn't the way of things," she whispered to him. "We're meant to be one. That was our promise. That was our oath."

"I know it was. But promises sometimes aren't meant to be forever, and I don't think it's the first time an oath such as the one we made will be broken."

Tears started to come.

She didn't want them to, but she couldn't help it, and he gently brushed them from her cheek then kissed her softly on the forehead, letting his touch linger.

"The promises of others, maybe," she said to him. "But not ours."

"It'll be better this way," he told her as gently as he could.

It must be his voice, she thought.

It must be his voice inside that's telling him this.

Then in front of her, he turned before she could see the tears that were on his own cheek; he turned and then there weren't any more words as he walked away from where they stood and picked his sword back up from where he had stuck it into the dirt, fastening it to its place at his waist, then he went a few more paces to where Kain had dropped the smaller sword and let it slide and fall to the ground, and he picked that one up, too.

He turned back and looked at her.

He looked at her one more time.

They stood there, together, with the whole history of Creation and each other between them.

Then he turned and began to walk towards the forest.

She waited and watched as he went, as the very last of the light began to fade, then he was gone, and she still waited.

She stood there and prayed he would come back.

But he didn't.

The moon began to rise.

She stood planted to the same spot then wondered again about the future she would have, and what would now come. She wondered if she should have fought harder, or what she could or should have done differently. She knew what she felt, and what she'd seen, but should she have just ignored it?

No, she thought, she couldn't.

But if she had, they'd still be a family, wouldn't they?

She didn't know and fresh tears came to her cheek then she heard her children calling from back at their home, and she knew she needed to go to them, and she also knew she needed to be strong.

So she wiped the tears away, and she went.

They ate dinner together in silence.

Nobody spoke about their day; nobody laughed, nobody joked, then when their meal was over—when it would normally be time for them all to go to sleep—she instead stood and went outside, alone. She went to stand in front of the great tree again, the Tree of Knowledge. She'd done this many times before, stood in front of the tree with nothing but moonlight and her thoughts, but now everything seemed so much closer. It seemed so much more immediate, and suffocating. The fruit called to her. It called to her and told her that contained within it was everything she'd ever wanted to know—about her, him, them, the future—but even in this lowest of moments, even in this moment when the branches seemed so close and she wanted to know more than she had ever wanted to know before, she was also strong, so she would still honor that which she had promised; she would still not eat any of the fruit, as she'd sworn she wouldn't.

But she wanted to.

Oh, how she wanted to.

Because she knew the answers to all that she wondered was right there, at her fingertips, just in front of her, only inches and a moment away.

"Mom?"

Then her thoughts vanished when she heard the voice behind her, and she turned, expecting to see her youngest son.

But it wasn't him.

It was Kain, coming from the house.

And as he came from the house, he walked across the clearing to stand next to her, then they were there together, in the moonlight, in front of the great tree, and as she looked back at him, she realized for the first time he'd grown taller than her. He wasn't yet quite as tall as his father, but he'd surpassed her, she saw, and she hadn't even realized it.

"Where did he go?" Kain finally asked, very softly.

"I don't know," she told him.

He accepted that, with a small nod.

Then he went back to looking at the tree.

She watched her son, her oldest son, there in the night and with the shadows from the moon dancing in sharp contrasts across his face, highlighting his features.

"I thought you would have gone out into Creation tonight," she finally said to him. "Like you normally do."

"No," he said, then shook his head. "Not tonight."

She kept looking at her son and thinking of what his father had told her before he'd left, the words that were meant to hurt and be cruel, and the ones that were false, too, that she knew were so false and as she thought of that, Kain turned to her, and he saw the pain that was in her eyes.

And he knew it was more, she could tell.

He knew it was more than just his father leaving.

"What's wrong?" he asked her.

She hesitated for a moment, standing there, together with him.

Should she tell him? She wasn't sure.

But he was almost a man now, she could see, so she would treat him as one, she decided.

"Do you think I spend more time with your brother?" she asked him, this the thing that had been weighing on her more than all the others her husband had said. "Do you think I care more for him than I do for you?"

"You used to take me into Creation, too," he told her. "But it was my choice to stop that. It was my choice to stay behind in the fields with him."

"That doesn't answer my question."

"No," he said. "No, I don't think that."

She watched as he kept looking at her, both of them, there, illuminated by the moonlight above.

Then he turned his eyes from her.

He turned his eyes and went back to looking at the tree, in front of them.

The Tree of Knowledge.

"I can handle the work in the fields now, with him gone," Kain told her. "And I can protect us, too."

"Protect us from what?"

"From whatever might come," he said.

Then he waited for a moment, for one more moment before he turned and without anything further, he left.

She watched as he went, and he was almost back to the house, almost back inside, but she still had one question left.

"Kain . . ." she said.

He heard her say his name and he paused at the door.

"What?" he asked, as he turned back.

She thought she was going to ask him one thing, but then when she saw his eyes, and the moon in them, she decided against it, and decided to ask him another.

"Where do you go at night, when you go out into Creation?" she asked him.

"I go to search."

"For what?"

He paused again, then looked down at his feet.

She saw the color rise in his cheeks and she realized it was almost as if he was embarrassed, but what could he possibly be embarrassed about? What could cause his cheeks to flush in such a way, just at the mere thought of talking about it and discussing it with his mother?

There was one more moment, as he gathered himself, then he told her.

"I've seen the way you are with father," he finally said to her. "I've seen the way you're together, and how you lay with each other, by the river."

"So?"

"There's no one else with us here, in our clearing."

"No, there isn't."

"So I go out into Creation to look for someone who might lay with me in the same way," he told her, then swallowed heavily.

She looked back at him, and her mouth hung open, she knew.

That wasn't what she'd been expecting.

Should she have, though? Should she have expected it?

She probably should have, she realized.

And as she kept thinking of it, a great sadness came over her.

It was a great sadness for her son and this burden he'd carried that she didn't know about, this thing she'd had no idea of and that was clearly causing him so much pain.

"And what do you find?" she finally asked him, when she found her voice again. "What do you find out there, when you look?"

"That's just the thing," he told her, continuing. "I search, every night, every single night . . ."

Then he hesitated, paused, gathering himself again.

And he looked back at her, and he finally shrugged.

"I search, every night," he told her again. "But there's nothing there."

SHE SPENT THE NEXT DAYS praying and asking for guidance and help.

She prayed as much as she could and asked as often as possible, but no help came. She wondered how she could have known so little of her oldest son, and she wondered how their family could have been broken and torn apart so easily, when her husband left.

She spent her days searching for him when she wasn't praying.

She left Habel in the clearing with his brother and went out into Creation alone. She didn't forage or gather anymore, but instead spent all her time searching for him and any trace of where he might have gone. She wanted to tell him about his son. She wanted to tell him to come home and fix what he'd done, but she needed to find him first to be able to tell him that, or even anything at all. So she spent her hours and days looking but all she found was a footprint here, or an unnatural mark carved into the bark of a tree there. While she did this, Kain tended to the fields and took care of his brother, too—as he said he would—and never once complained, though after their conversation by the tree, he'd stopped wandering into Creation at night when his work was finished.

She never spoke with him about what he'd told her.

She knew he thought she would agree and tell him there were no others with them there in Creation, so there were no others for him to be with in the same way she'd been with his father, but as time passed, her heart didn't continue to break for him as she thought it would, because did they really know that? Did they really know they were alone, and that they would be for all time? So that was one of the things for which she now prayed, too; for someone to come and make her oldest son happy in the way she'd once been happy with his father.

She searched for him for many days.

And though she hadn't yet realized it, in this simple or plain of terms, she'd learned much from the hope of her oldest son.

But then, one day, she decided to stop.

After so much crossing and re-crossing the vastness of Creation, she realized her husband very clearly didn't want to be found, or wasn't ready, so she would give up trying. She never stopped loving him, even though he'd left, just as she'd sworn she would never do. She wouldn't ever stop, even if there were a million others that came to Creation, and she would always honor the promise she'd made to him because it was a promise made of her body, and it was also a promise made of her soul.

But things needed to change, she knew.

A great many things needed to change.

So they did.

She made a new routine, one where she continued to go into Creation alone and Habel stayed in the fields with his brother, and once they'd decided on that, everything went back to some semblance of normal, or as much as normal could be without a husband and father. And when she wasn't out in Creation gathering, she spent much of her time in the clearing watching her oldest and how he worked in the fields. She was worried because she saw the pleasure he previously seemed to have taken from his work was gone—that great and profound light that had been in his eyes—and it now seemed to her as if he was just going through motions and only doing what needed to be done for the family to survive and continue.

Was the change because he'd simply done the same thing, so many times before, over and over.

Or was it something else?

She didn't know.

But she was pleased when Kain seemed to find joy in other things.

She watched as he spent more and more time with his brother and taught him how to use the plow, even though Habel had no interest in metal or dirt and wasn't really strong enough to use it yet. But when they were done, Kain would take him so they could play in the river together. When his brother got hungry, Kain would feed him, and when Habel got tired, Kain would give him rides on his back so he didn't have to walk. Then when Habel had finally grown too big for the small bed he'd previously slept on, it was Kain that made him a new one, fashioning and carving it in the same way their father had done for him, when he'd outgrown his own first bed, too. She would watch them together, as often as she could, then one day when she returned from Creation, she saw them sitting next to each other under the Tree of Life. They were there in the shade from the branches and eating their lunches and she watched and listened as Habel looked up at the shining fruit above them and asked Kain about what it was.

Kain told his brother it was fruit, like all the others they knew, but it was also fruit that was forbidden, and not to be eaten.

"Why?" Habel asked him.

"I don't know," Kain told his brother, not used to such questions. "Because it's the Tree of Life, I guess."

"But what does that mean?" Habel asked.

She watched as Kain looked over at his brother, next to him, then not having the answer or knowing what else to do, he roughly ran his hands through Habel's hair, pushing it around and messing it up as brothers do to brothers.

Then Kain stood and went back to the fields, but when he did, Habel remained where he was.

He remained where he sat, under the tree, and as he sat there, he kept looking at the fruit that was on the branches above him; the Tree of Life was smaller than the Tree of Knowledge, much smaller, and its branches closer to the ground, within reach of even a child, even one as not-yet-grown as Habel. He sat there and cocked his head to the side as he kept looking at the tree, and fruit, and branches, with the light from the mid-day sun filtering down and through the leaves and creating patterns and jagged shadows that danced across the features of his young face.

He sat there alone, for one more moment.

Then he finally stood and left, too.

MORE TIME PASSED and both children grew.

Kain started to wake even earlier in the mornings—before the light of the day came, even—so he could finish his work earlier, too, and after their family meals, he began to go out into Creation again. She would prepare their meals with Habel at her side, then when Kain had finished his work and gone down to the river to wash the dirt from the day away, he'd return, they'd eat together, clean all the things from the meal and put them away, then he'd quietly slip out and into the night as she'd settle down on her bed with Habel to tell him a story before they went to sleep.

She didn't ask where he was going anymore, because they both knew now.

She saw the look in his eyes, and realized it had changed.

And she saw his eyes had changed, too.

He had more energy and more purpose, and there was a brightness and anticipation in his features as they finished their meal and it was almost time for him to leave. He hadn't yet discovered anything: not his father, or any other humans. But that's what the cycle of hours does to us, she knew. Expectation comes, then it goes, and the mornings cure all, so that even the pain of another wasted night is washed away when we wake and rise and are replenished by the sun and new day which we need to come and rejuvenate us as we prepare to be unmade all over again, and in the exact same way we had been before.

It's not logic, of course, that we listen to, in these instances, it's something else, and something stronger.

It's hope.

And hope . . .

That's the great gift she saw again in the eyes of her oldest.

But her youngest, that was a different story.

He didn't seem to grow as fast as his brother, and he didn't seem to grow as strong, either. While Kain had spent all his formative days in the field with his father, plowing the dirt and building his muscles, Habel spent his early days in Creation with her, his mother, so the muscles in his chest and arms stayed as they had been when he was a boy, even though his legs and thighs began to swell from the great distances they travelled and she knew his lungs had expanded, too, and his endurance increased. And while his brother had been interested in swords and strength and all the other things his father had been interested in, she saw that Habel was interested in other things. He was interested in life, and what it was, and how it came to be. He was interested in the texture of the bark on the trees, and what would cause the leaves on the branches to change color, and why. He was interested in how the river flowed towards them, and not the other way around.

He was interested in all Creation, and he was interested in why it was the way it was.

These were all questions she of course didn't have answers to, when he asked about them, so she just answered as best she could, as best as she herself knew. She told him of her own first hours in Creation, and how she met his father. She didn't tell him of the doubts she'd had but instead told him of something else; she told him of the feeling that would often come to her, and how it came more often in those early days.

She told him how it felt like it came from deep in her stomach, and how she taught herself to listen to it, and how she knew it was urging her forward and towards the plan and order that had been laid for them, the plan and order they all tried to follow as they led and lived good lives.

"Where do you think the voice comes from?" he asked as they walked together. They were picking berries from the bushes that were around them and putting them in their baskets that they'd fill before they returned to the clearing.

"I don't know," she told him. "But I'm telling you about it because you have it, too, the same power, within you."

"How do you know?"

"Because you're me, and you didn't come from the earth. You came from my flesh and my blood. So what I have and what I am, and what's inside of me . . . you have all that, too, and it's a part of you also."

She watched as he thought about this.

He took in what she'd told him, analyzing it in his mind, and he was clever, she knew, so she also knew he was now thinking about more than what she'd just told him, and she knew he was now thinking about blood and legacy and destiny and all that we carry and pass down through generations, and even young as he was, she knew that's all he was thinking about and what he was turning over in his thoughts.

He turned back to her again.

"How do I hear the voice, too?" he finally asked.

"You quiet your mind and thoughts," she told him. "Then when it's very quiet, and very still, that's when you can ask for help and guidance, and listen to what comes in response."

"It's that simple?" he asked.

"It's that simple," she smiled.

Then she saw as he thought about that, too.

He thought about all of that as they kept walking then very slowly a small smile came to his face. She could tell he didn't want it to, that he wanted to keep it hidden, and he wanted to remain stoic, but it did, and it came, and he couldn't hide it. They went a few more paces, and as they did, he reached out and took her hand in his, and held it, which is something he hadn't done in a very long time, not for many days, or for many years; not since he'd been much smaller, and very young.

THEY RETURNED to the clearing at mid-day but they found it was empty. It was unusual for them to come back and for Kain to not be there, hard at work in the fields, and as she scanned the orchards and fields, she saw the plow and other tools he always used sitting there.

But she didn't see her oldest son.

She went to the house.

She walked in and didn't find him there, either, so she went to the river.

It was calm and clear, and there wasn't anyone there, so she turned around.

She went to the Tree of Life, then the Tree of Knowledge.

She didn't find him anywhere, not in any of the places she went and looked, and that's when the panic started to rise in her throat.

"What do we do?" Habel asked from his place at her side.

She waited for a moment, then shook her head.

"I don't know," she answered.

She looked down at him next to her then turned back to the clearing and with nothing else left she could think of, she began to yell.

"Kain!" she called, as loudly as she could.

She waited but heard nothing in return.

So she yelled again.

"Kain!" she called, even louder.

Next to her, Habel began to yell for his brother, too.

They both spun around as they yelled, still looking in all corners of the clearing—all corners of where they could see—and that's when her mind began to wander. She thought of what had happened the day he'd been conceived, and the great battle they'd survived in the forest, then her thoughts began to go even further back, too.

She thought of the dream she'd had, the dream that wasn't a dream.

She thought again of the time when the dark angel had come and offered her the fruit, and how it had been so tempting. She thought of her son, and what she knew of him. She thought of what the dark one could offer: the knowledge of what he so desired, of another to come and become part of his flesh in the same way she'd been part of his father's, and to lay with him and have children and start their own family.

What if she'd been wrong, and it wasn't her husband who would be tempted next.

What if she'd been wrong, and it was really her son that would be tempted?

She ran as fast as she could back to the Tree of Knowledge and this time she looked up and checked its branches, for any sign of disturbance or missing fruit, but all the fruit that had been there before seemed to be accounted for, at least as far as she could tell.

So she strained her ears.

She was very quiet as she stood there and strained them as hard as she could to hear anything—the sounds of a distant battle, perhaps, that even if it was being fought at the furthest edges of Creation, she would surely be able to hear, or even a son calling for his mother, calling for help—she strained and tried to hear anything she possibly could, but she heard nothing.

There was just silence.

Then there was a voice, right next to her.

"It's alright, Mom," the voice said.

And she turned to look down at Habel, who was at her side again, and who she'd forgotten about and she saw he'd closed his eyes. Then she saw as he opened them, as he spoke the words he spoke, and she cocked her head to the side as she looked at him and wondered about the authority and certainty she heard in his voice. She wondered about it all, then it hit her, and she knew; she knew exactly what he'd done because he'd done precisely what she'd just told him about in the forest. He'd quieted his mind and his thoughts and he'd felt for that which came from deep inside him, and that's what his voice had told him.

It's alright, his voice had said.

She looked back at Habel, with a deep pride that came from her seeing her youngest and smallest child cut through the fear that had gripped her own heart, then she heard something else, too, and it was the same word, herself being called again, but by a different voice.

"Mom . . . ?" she heard.

She froze when she did.

Then she and Habel both turned at the same time to see Kain walking back towards them from the forest, and when she saw her oldest, everything that she'd been feeling instantly melted away into a heavy and beautiful relief that she felt in every corner of her body, every last and distant inch of her limbs.

But then she saw something else, too, and it startled her at first.

It made her breath catch in her throat in surprise, because she then saw there was someone else with him, as well; she saw that coming from the forest with his strong and familiar arm wrapped around his oldest's shoulder, and a wide smile on both their faces, she saw that there with Kain was a husband and father and man who had finally decided to stop wandering, and to return home.

<h1 style="text-align:center">18</h1>

FROM THE ISOLATED ROOM in the palace where he still remained, high above in Heaven, Michael watched all that happened in Creation. After Selaphiel had left and Michael had chosen solitude, Gabriel returned to the peaks of Aetlas, as he'd sworn to do, while Raphael stayed behind at the palace to train those that were still there in order to be ready for the war that was sure to come and continue. Michael, however, remained in isolation and did nothing but watch. He watched the humans very closely. He watched how they lived, then he watched as all that changed; he saw the moment when she returned and found her husband in the field with their oldest son, the swords in their hands, the weapons he'd made. He saw their fight that came, and he saw him leave, too. Michael watched as the man left the clearing and went into the forest and wandered throughout Creation on his own, and Michael could feel what was in his heart, because it was close to what was in Michael's own, he realized.

It was the same pain.

It was the same emptiness, and loneliness.

It was the same confusion and it was the same lack of direction, too, that they each then felt as Michael watched him walk everywhere he could think to walk in Creation and it still didn't do anything to ease what he felt, it still didn't heal any wounds, and while the man walked, Michael heard her prayers, from back in the clearing.

He was sure God had heard them, as well, and he waited, and waited.

But still God did nothing.

He thought of sending her husband back to her himself, but that wouldn't solve anything, he knew. If he'd sent him back prematurely there would have just been another fight, then a bigger one, and then a bigger one still after that, and the cumulative damage they each would have done would have been irrevocable.

So instead, he let the man wander.

And as he wandered, Michael continued to watch.

The man woke later, and stayed up later, too.

He did whatever he wanted, and at the exact moment it pleased him to do it, and in the beginning that was exciting for him because the man didn't yet know all she'd brought to his life and all he then didn't have without her there and in it—all the commitment, the meaning, the specific type of strength that was deeper than just physical strength, and most importantly, the love—so Michael let him experience not having any of that, which would make him ready to return one day, he knew. Michael had felt this loss in his life, too, the loss of a partner that gave him these things, so he knew the power of that loss, and how it changes us; he knew intimately the power that comes from the understanding that at any instant it could all be gone, taken away, everything that's important, everything that makes us who we are, never to return, not ever again.

Michael knew all that, and that's now what he watched as the man learned it, too.

And through all of this, their children still grew, and Michael watched as Kain took over for his father in the fields. It wasn't unnatural because children are meant to take up for their parents, but it was premature.

Kain and his mother grew closer, though, through it all, which Michael saw. And he saw Habel, too.

He saw as the younger of the two sons of the humans learned more and more about Creation, wandering to all corners of it with his mother, and Michael saw how he took in even more than she realized, also.

Michael's eyes travelled.

He saw in a distant place the man's resolve begin to weaken, as he wandered further, alone.

Then he saw as his resolve failed.

Pride, she'd seen in him.

Pride, and love.

There had been both before, but now during his solitude one had been stripped away, at least until it wasn't again, and without pride there was then only love, and that's the thing that would eventually lead him back home, Michael saw.

Michael saw and felt as the man's decision was made, but then something happened: a great cloud came over Michael and he could no longer see, and with that cloud that came, there also came a darkness, and a feeling, and he recognized it as the same one that he'd felt a long time ago before Phosphorus had been banished from Heaven and sent through space and time into darkness.

And though his vision to Creation was still clouded, a different fog was lifted.

Michael's limbs began to feel less heavy.

His mind began to become sharper, and more clear again.

He knew what the feeling was that had come, and what he had to do, also, so he finally stood and left his solitude and the room where he'd stayed and quickly went back out into the palace.

He rushed through the halls.

He ran around corners and across great spaces.

Then he finally came to the courtyard where Raphael was training the angels that were still with them, in Heaven, all the angels that hadn't left for darkness with Phosphorus, or for other, with Selaphiel, and as they turned and saw him again for the first time in so many years, he saw the doubt that was there in their eyes; the doubt about him, and his leadership.

He saw it all, as clear as he saw anything, but there was no time for that.

There was no time for doubt now.

"What is it?" Raphael finally asked him.

Michael paused and he waited for a moment.

He waited as the eyes of all the gathered angels turned and looked into his own, and once he knew they were there, he stood a little bit taller as he turned back to Raphael and as he did, and the color came back to his skin and strength came back to his great wings, all the angels were reminded why Michael was who he was and they all waited to hear what had finally brought their leader back from his solitude.

"Call for Gabriel," he told them.

"Why?" Raphael asked.

Michael waited for one more moment, all their eyes still on him, their minds racing, their breaths held.

Then he told them.

"He's come back," Michael said. "And he's coming to Heaven."

19

WHEN HER HUSBAND had returned to the clearing with Kain, she saw he'd left the weapons he'd created somewhere behind. She didn't ask where he'd put them, or anything else, she just waited as he came towards her, and she held her breath. He'd motioned for Kain to wait back so he would speak with her alone. When he reached her and stood in front of her, she looked up at him and noticed he looked different: his eyes were duller, the thin line of his lips and mouth seemed to turn down instead of the way it used to always seem to so quickly turn up into a smile, and his skin was more rough, and weathered. It was from time sleeping without a roof over his head, she realized.

Then he reached out and took her hands into his.

"Can I show you something?" he asked her.

"Show me what?"

"It's a secret."

She hesitated, for a moment, as she looked back into his more-aged eyes, trying to judge his intention.

"Please," he said.

And though he hadn't yet said anything to this affect, or anything similar, she could hear contrition in his voice and the importance of what he wanted to do, what he wanted to show her, and how he wanted to make right all that had turned so wrong.

She hesitated, for one more moment, then she finally nodded.

"Alright," she said.

When she did, he turned to their boys who were waiting behind them.

"Watch your brother," he said to their oldest son.

Kain nodded, once, to his father.

Then he began to lead her away from the clearing.

They went together, walking slowly, and as they did, he glanced behind her, just once, to see Kain picking Habel up and putting him high on his shoulders, like he used to do so often, when he was smaller.

They laughed as they went back towards the house.

They joked, playing with each other.

Then she turned from her children to what was in front of her, and she kept going, with him, as he'd asked of her.

They went through the forest, heading north.

Then they were through the forest and came to the great field, where she'd first woken.

But they didn't stop there.

He kept walking.

And she kept walking with him.

They went through the field then on and past it towards the mountains that were there, and when they got closer to them, she finally began to smile, because she knew where they were going. They began to climb the rocks of the mountains and up towards the waterfall, but this time it was him that went first, and she went after him. They didn't speak as they climbed, and as they did and she saw him above her and the fluidity and confidence of his movements, she realized he was no longer afraid of heights.

When had it happened?

She didn't know.

They kept climbing.

They soon came to the top, and as they did, he reached his hand down and helped her up the last few feet then they stood there together on the great piece of rock where they'd also once stood before when they were both much younger. He took her hand in his again and led her towards the edge, towards where they could look out together, at all Creation.

And they did, taking it in, breathing in and out.

Then she turned to him, next to her.

"What are we doing here?" she finally asked. "There's work to be done in the clearing. Kain always needs help in the fields, and Habel can't go into Creation on his own yet."

"I know," her husband answered, his words coming slow, and deliberate. "But this is important."

"What's important?"

She watched as he waited one more moment, looking out, gathering himself.

Then he turned back to her.

She watched as he looked down, deeply, into her eyes.

"I wanted to feel the same way we did when we first came here," he told her, and she took that in, both his words and what his eyes were telling her.

What had he learned, she wondered?

What had he learned, out there in Creation, on his own?

She found herself wondering that, then she smiled wryly because she realized the answer: she realized he'd learned that sometimes the greatest thing one can do is to leave, because when we leave, that's then when we can choose to come home again.

But he hurt her, and he hurt his children.

Was that part of it, too?

Was that part of the plan, and path?

She thought of it all, then her smile slowly faded.

It faded not because of what she'd just thought, as that was something that would be left to God, she knew, that was something that would always be left to God; instead, it faded because there was still something unresolved between them, one last thing that still needed to be made right.

"And what of the weapons you made?" she asked him.

"I didn't bring them back to the clearing," he told her. "But I didn't destroy them either."

"You put them in the hands of our son."

"I did."

"Why?"

"Because he's like me," he said, and she watched as he spoke, the words coming slowly. "I can see it when I look into his eyes, and I can feel what's in his heart. And I can feel it," he continued, "because it's what's in my heart, too. He's like me, so his hand will always reach for the sword. But not for the wrong reasons."

She thought about that.

Then she thought back to the feeling she had when she first saw the weapons, right after he'd made them, and what she felt when she saw the sword in Kain's hands for the first time; it had been a feeling as strong as anything that had ever come during her time in Creation, a feeling of warning and fear.

"Help me understand," she told him. "Because everything inside, everything that I've felt, it tells me the things you've made and brought into our lives will only bring pain and death for us and others, when before there was none of either."

She watched as he heard those words, taking them in, processing them. Then he spoke again.

"I have something inside of me, too, as you know," he told her, and his words were stronger now. "And what I have inside tells me to protect you, and to protect our family. It's the strongest thing I feel, and the weapons I made are the tools which I know I need to be able to do that," he said, then swallowed as he kept looking back at her. "Just the same as you look inside and receive guidance, I do, too, and this is what my voice has brought to me; this is the knowledge I was given, and what I was shown how to create, and do."

"When you were gone, we were fine. We didn't need to be protected."

"But for how long?"

"What do you mean?"

"They haven't returned yet, but one day they will. We both know that."

She took that in.

That was something they both could feel, as he'd said.

That was something they both undoubtedly knew.

"There are different types of strength," she finally said, "and the greatest types are greater than what a sword brings, they're much greater, as a sword gives strength to those who don't deserve it."

"I know," he nodded. "That's one of the things I learned when I was in Creation. That's why we were put together, you and I, not because we're the same, but because we're different. You're strong in the ways you're strong, and I'm strong in the ways I am, too, in the way that I was made. The weapons were brought here, against our will. But they were brought here."

She thought about this.

The solution was so very simple, that they needed to be gotten rid of, but why couldn't he see that?

Why couldn't he see what was so obvious and right in front of him?

"And the other thing?" she finally asked.

"What?"

"You said that was one of the things you learned. What's the other?"

"That I love you. And I don't ever want to be without you, not ever again, not for a year, a day, a minute, a second."

"Then why did you leave?"

He looked at her, straight into her eyes.

Then he shrugged and spoke truth.

"I don't know," he said.

And she saw he meant it, that he didn't know.

But she did.

Because she knew that sometimes what we do is beyond our own choices and our own control and is rather in service of something greater, and higher, and sometimes we don't understand what we do, we just feel, then we act, and are left to pick up the pieces that come from actions as best we can.

She saw that in him, and in what had happened.

And even though she didn't want what he said to be true, she recognized now that it was. Then a great cloud passed over her heart. She knew there was tragedy to come, and it was going to come soon, she couldn't help but feel it. But she also knew it was inevitable, and not to be stopped, and it was part of the ever-marching time and order and plan that wound its way through all that there was and would be.

"Thank you," she finally said to him, very softly.

"For what?"

"For being the other half of me. And for together helping us to be the whole that our family and our children need."

"No," he said.

"No?"

"It's you," he told her. "It's you that keeps us together, and it's you that they need . . . and so do I."

Then she saw the tears that came to his eyes again, and this time he didn't try to hide them from her as she reached up and gently brushed them away and realized for the first time that they perhaps understood each other; they really understood each other, and who they each were.

She thought of all it meant, then she smiled again.

"Are you ready?" she asked him.

"Ready for what?"

"To trust me."

He heard her words, the same they'd spoken together at this very same spot, so long ago, a lifetime ago.

Then he smiled, too.

"With all that I have," he told her. "With all that I have, and then even more than that, until I have nothing left."

She looked up at him, next to her, then took his hand.

The last time they'd been there and she'd jumped, she'd jumped by herself, but this time, instead of going alone, they would go together.

So they backed up.

They went to the edge of the rock and they paused.

There was one more look, deep into their eyes, a look of a love that had been renewed, strengthened, deepened.

Then they began to run.

They went together, holding hands, barreling towards the edge.

Then they were to it and they leaped.

They flew through the air and out over the outcropping of rock, still holding their hands, and for a moment they stayed there, in the air, in defiance of gravity and all laws of Creation, because this was a moment, they knew, and perhaps so did God, she thought, and nature, and it was their moment.

Then gravity finally came, and so did the wind, and they began to fall. *Down, down, down . . .*

. . .

. . .

. . .

They plunged towards the water and the pool below that raced to meet them and they held their breath as they crashed through the surface of the pool and into it and their momentum brought them to the very bottom. Their feet found the rocks that were there, at the bottom, but instead of pushing off them and shooting back to the surface, they waited.

They waited, just for a moment, just for them.

And as they did, she moved towards him and her lips found his and parted around them, and they kissed there in the pool, under the water, then they began to run out of oxygen so they finally bent their legs and pushed and kicked their way back to the surface which they broke, together, and treaded water.

They waited, for another moment, holding each other.

The feeling had come back, the one that had been there before.

"*Perfect*," he whispered, his lips near her ear.

"*Perfect*," she whispered, too.

And they said it because they knew that it was.

They also each knew what the other wanted, and what would come next.

They turned and swam back to shore.

They climbed out of the water and came closer together, their bodies touching, wet skin against wet skin.

He bent down and kissed her again, then they layed down.

She took his tunic off, up and over his head, the one that she'd made for him, and when she did, she saw there were even more scars that were covering his body now: his arms, his torso, his legs.

She gently reached out and touched them.

She asked him where they came from, but he didn't tell her, and she didn't ask again because she knew these scars were the price we pay for wisdom gained.

"I've missed you so much," he whispered instead.

"I never left," she told him. "Just like I said I wouldn't."

"I did, I know that I did. But I won't ever again."

She heard his words and knew they were truth.

And she also knew that truth was enough, that it would always be enough.

So once their oaths and vows to each other had been renewed and spoken again, that's when it then began. They had a rhythm and simple poetry they'd found to their love—both before their children came, and after—but that afternoon she decided to change that rhythm they'd grown used to. She didn't know why she did, it just seemed to her as if one version of who they'd been had faded and would be replaced by a new one. So she wanted their love to be new, too, and when he moved in the way he usually did, on top of her, she stopped him. She saw the surprise in his eyes, but he didn't protest as she changed places so he was on the ground, and it was her that then had more control.

"Okay?" she'd asked, once she'd done it.

"Okay," he nodded to her.

Their words were barely more than whispers.

And that's then when he'd given in, too.

She'd thought of this moment as often as he had, she knew, when he'd been gone, and now it was theirs, and it was theirs in a way it never had been before.

Time seemed to stand still to her.

There was no flowing river or pool next to them, or tall mountains above where they lay, or waterfall crashing down; there was no field of wild flowers and dandelions, or vast forest and clearing beyond.

There was just him.

And there was her.

There was all that they were, when they were together.

Then when their love ended, they just lay there and held each other and looked up at the sky and the sun and clouds and they stayed there like that for a long time. They stayed there for a very long time. Her head was on his chest, and she felt it moving as he breathed—up and down, up and down—then she felt him gather himself, his muscles tensing and constricting before he spoke.

"I guess we should be getting back," he finally said. "They'll be waiting for us."

"They'll be alright."

"What do you think they're doing?"

She stayed staring at the sky, above them.

She felt him take her hand and rub his thumb back and forth across it as she thought about his question, making small patterns with it there in her palm—marks and movements known to none other than him— then she smiled, as she gave her answer: "Kain will have Habel helping him in the field," she told him, speaking slowly. "He'll show him all the tools he has, and how they're used, and Habel won't be quite strong enough to use them, but his brother will help. They'll work together. Then they'll stop early, because we aren't there, and Kain will take him to the river."

Then she paused.

They both listened to her words and they could see the images, too, of their children: they could see the images exactly as she was describing them.

"And then what?" he asked her. "What will they do after that?"

"Kain likes to carry Habel on his back, when he can't keep up, and when they get to the river, Kain will teach him how to skip stones, just as you taught Kain. And they'll laugh. They'll play together in the water then Habel will notice the sun, how it's beginning to set in the sky, and he'll tell Kain it's time to go."

"Where will they go?"

"Back up to the house. Habel will show Kain everything he and I gathered yesterday, in Creation, then they'll prepare it together, on the table, ready to eat, and they'll wait for us to return."

"It sounds like a good life."

"It's a perfect life."

"So what do you think, should we go back to it?"

She waited, for a moment, one last moment.

Then she finally nodded, and they stood, and looked around them.

They looked back at the waterfall and the rock from where they'd jumped, then at the pool and river below. They looked at the wide field of dandelions and wild flowers, and the forest beyond, the path that led them back home.

They looked at all of it, together.

Then she took his hand in hers again and they began to walk.

THEY WERE DEEP IN THE FOREST when the clouds began to gather.

They'd seen storms before, but these clouds seemed to move faster than any others that had previously come to Creation, or that they'd seen. Then they heard the thunder, which was louder than any regular and normal thunder, and there was lightning, too, jumping back and forth in electrical charges between the fast-moving clouds, but there was no rain that came. The thunder continued to crash above them in the way they hadn't heard before, and the way they now in an instant recognized to be unnatural, and that's when they looked at each other and she couldn't help the feeling of panic and dread that came to her body, which started in her stomach, and ran up her spine and through every last inch of her.

"What's happening?" she whispered.

"I don't know," he said, shaking his head.

Then after he spoke she saw and watched as they then both thought the exact same thing, at the exact same time, and with it came more fear.

The children, they both thought.

So they began to run.

They dodged through the trees and past the branches whipping across their faces, and they ran as fast as they could, as above them the sky continued to turn dark and the electricity that came from the clouds continued to thunder and crash.

Then the trees began to thin and part, and they were back to the clearing.

They looked past the fields and orchard towards where Kain was standing next to Habel outside their house, Kain holding his brother's hand, and they both turned when they saw their parents. Habel left his brother as soon as he saw them and ran and hugged his father, first, who picked him up and carried him back towards their home and where Kain waited for them.

"What is that up there?" Kain asked.

"Let's go inside," she said.

"It's happening again, isn't it?" Kain said, still looking up at the clouds.

Then he looked back down and between them, all of them.

She saw Kain's eyes and hesitated, and as she did, she looked at her husband, next to her, still holding their youngest; she knew they wouldn't lie to their children, but she also knew it was their job to protect them, to make them feel safe, and she watched as her husband set Habel down and stepped forward.

"It doesn't matter what it is," he said from his place next to her now, then reached out and put his arm around her first, and his two boys after that, next to them, and they were finally a family again. "Because whatever it is," he continued, "whatever comes, we'll face it as a family, which means that we'll face it together."

She heard his words and nodded.

Then she echoed his words with her own.

"Together," she told them. "Always together now."

They each nodded, too, when they heard her, in turn, because they knew no matter what was above them, and no matter what else might come . . .

They knew that it would now and always be as she'd said.

20

$\mathcal{M}$ICHAEL HELD HIS BREATH as he stood in front of the high walls of the palace. Raphael stood next to him, and the rest of the host that remained stood there and were with them, too. They all watched with dark and troubled eyes as the great cloud that gathered in front of them drew closer, then Michael looked up as from a different direction there was something else that caught his eye: there were three fast moving specs that looked like bodies with great wings that were coming quickly towards them, from the distance, and then . . .

Thump.

Thump.

Thump.

Gabriel and the two other angels that flew with him descended from the sky in a blur, and the ground shook as they landed next to Michael and the others. These were the angels that had been guarding Creation, from their place atop the peaks of Aetlas, but they'd heard Michael's call and the word he'd sent and they'd now come back to help guard Heaven from those who would try to conquer it. When Gabriel landed, his eyes went to Raphael's, first, and he nodded to him, then they flicked to Michael's.

Gabriel looked him up and down, measuring him.

It was the first time Gabriel had seen Michael in many years, and he saw the change that had come to his friend, and he nodded when he saw it.

"Good," Gabriel said.

Then Michael nodded, too.

"So now that's settled," Raphael spoke. "But what do we do?"

Michael thought about that, as he stayed staring back at the dark cloud in front of them as it got closer.

"There will be too many of them," he spoke softly, almost to himself.

"We'll fight them no matter how many there are," Gabriel said.

"But we won't win," Michael said. "We need more angels."

"How?" Gabriel asked.

Michael turned to a young and swift angel next to him.

"Fly as fast as you can," he told the young angel. "Take two others and search for Selaphiel, and those that fly with him. They're our only chance."

The young angel nodded, once, resolutely.

Then he quickly walked away from where they were, spread his wings, and exploded into the sky with two others next to him.

Gabriel and Raphael watched this, then when he was gone, Gabriel shook his head.

"Selaphiel's a traitor," he said to Michael, "a traitor to the light. We don't need him and he doesn't deserve to be here to share in our victory. So why do you keep putting so much faith in him, and those that left with him?"

"This is the light, here in Heaven," Michael told Gabriel. "This is where the light is strongest."

"Yes, it is," Gabriel nodded, not understanding.

"Phosphorus knows that, too, and knows this is where his power is weakest. So that means if he's coming here, then he's bringing something else with him," Michael told them as his eyes flashed and darkness came closer, lightning bursting in front of them in great flashes and thunder crashing. "And faith is all that we have, Gabriel," Michael continued, his eyes never leaving the coming storm. "It's what built this kingdom, and it's what will save us and deliver this kingdom, too. It's all we've ever had, and it's all we'll ever need."

Gabriel looked at Michael for a moment, at his friend; he looked at the light that was back in his eyes and heard the fire that was back in his voice, the strength that had returned to his speech.

This was the Michael he'd known before.

"Welcome back," Gabriel said.

Then Michael drew his sword, from where he kept it fastened at his waist.

So did Gabriel, next to him, and Raphael, then all the other angels around them drew their swords, too, together.

For a moment, there was nothing.

Then there was a great thunderclap, and as soon as it hit, they were met by a wave of powerful wind that slammed against them and blew their hair and temporarily blinded them with the darkness it brought, then the wind departed and with it so too did the darkness. Then when it was gone, there was Phosphorus, flying in front of them, Michael saw, with Báal next to him, and the other dark angels, all dressed for battle, all arranged in their places behind their leader, though Mamanos was nowhere to be seen.

Michael stared at Phosphorus, across from him.

He stared at the angel who'd once been his friend, and more than that, too.

Then Phosphorus landed in Heaven and he stepped forward.

"Have you come to ask for God's forgiveness?" Michael asked as Phosphorus' feet touched ancient and sacred stone, and his voice was loud and clear and strong.

"I've come to give you one more chance," Phosphorus answered.

"No, you haven't," Michael shook his head. "You haven't come for anything other than what's now in your heart, the darkness that's come and taken you over."

"You always did know me, didn't you, Michael. You knew me in ways no other possibly could."

"I did," Michael nodded, as he looked back at Phosphorus, searching his eyes, looking for any bit of who he'd previously been that remained: the angel that had been called Light-Bringer, Morningstar, Shining One, and the angel that had been loved by God. "And I still do, Phosphorus. I still do know you, which is why I know it's also not too late."

"It is, though."

"Why?"

"Because here we are, and this is how it ends," Phosphorus told him. "This is now how it ends."

They waited, one more moment, looking at each other.

And then it began.

Phosphorus spread his great wings and in an instant sped across the distance between them—moving faster than light, faster than sound, faster than anything at all—and Michael held his ground, bracing himself, raising his sword.

Then their two weapons met, one more time.

And the great battle began, too.

Behind Michael all the other angels of light rushed forward and there was less of them than their opponents, but they quickly began to take the upper-hand against the darkness they faced, there in the light, where they had more power.

Michael went on the offensive.

He spread his great wings and flew after Phosphorus, who began to retreat after his initial attack.

Then Phosphorus turned and flew up.

Up, up, he went, and Michael followed after him.

"I know what you're thinking, Michael," Phosphorus called back as he flew, speaking over his shoulder.

"And what's that?" Michael answered.

"That we've been here before, in this exact same place, and we both know how it ended then, and that you're stronger than me, especially here in the light."

"Then why have you come back?"

"Because this time . . ." Phosphorus spoke, and after a moment, he smiled. "This time, it's going to be different."

They went higher, higher, higher.

Phosphorus flew, and Michael chased after him.

They soon were high enough where they could see the entire battle spread beneath them.

Michael looked back at Phosphorus, but then he paused.

He looked down at the battle, where his angels were winning, and he looked back to Phosphorus again, trying to make sense of it, because Phosphorus was smiling.

"What have you done?" Michael whispered, very quietly.

"What I had to," Phosphorus told him.

Then he nodded to Báal, below them, and when he did, Báal let out a call and there was a great rumbling in the distance.

Heaven was solid, but this power shook even the most solid of things.

And Michael watched as even the great, strong walls of the palace moved and shook where they stood, back and forth, back and forth.

"What evil is this?" Michael asked very slowly.

"One that's much older than you or me," Phosphorus told him.

Michael looked back at Phosphorus, not understanding, and then, over Phosphorus' left shoulder, he saw them.

First it was Mamanos that flew towards them, from the distance, leading the way and showing the path to Heaven.

Then behind him were the titans.

Okeanos came first, then all the others, and when Michael saw them, his heart sank, as he took in their presence, there in Heaven.

He turned back to Phosphorus.

There was horror in his eyes; horror at the evil that had been done.

"Do you remember nothing, Phosphorus?" Michael asked him. "Do you remember nothing of what we were told?"

"I remember everything! But the past doesn't interest me, Michael," Phosphorus said, then smiled in return. "Not anymore. The only thing that interests me now is the future, and that's what's here. That's what's now come to your door."

There was silence, for a split second, then a great noise as below them bodies slammed together.

Michael looked down.

Titans came and tossed angels aside as if they weighed nothing, as if they were nothing.

Gabriel saw this and rallied all the angels of light he could to face off against the titans, and the titans fought back against those that he rallied.

All, except for one.

Okeanos.

The leader broke from the rest of the group, and Michael watched from his place above as Okeanos came straight towards him.

Then Michael turned back to Phosphorus.

He watched as his friend began to slowly back away in the air, and when he did, Michael knew what was going to happen, and he knew then what Phosphorus had planned.

"You'll regret this," Michael said as he met his friend's now ash-dark eyes, one last time. "You'll regret all of this, and for all eternity."

"This was always what it was going to be, Michael."

"It didn't have to."

"Are you sure?"

Michael opened his mouth to respond but before any more words came, Okeanos was to him and Michael quickly raised his sword again and met the great blow of the titan.

The sound echoed through Heaven, then their battle began.

Michael was thrown backwards by the force of the blow, but he spread his wings to stop his momentum and help gather himself to re-engage as he saw Phosphorus fly into the distance, then below him he saw all the other dark angels leave with him, too, so he was left facing

Okeanos in single combat, and Gabriel and the other angels that were with him fought against the rest of the titans.

Michael saw Phosphorus' plan now, he saw it clearly, and knew there was nothing else he could do so he closed his eyes and quickly said a prayer, a prayer for strength—both for him and those that were below, in Creation—and for deliverance and victory. Everything around him had become explosions and bursts of bright light as he prayed, the sounds and sight of angels dying, being killed by the great titans, then he finished his prayer and opened his eyes because then Okeanos was on him again and there was no more time for anything else.

He raised his sword, one more time, with an already-weary arm, and defended himself.

The blows that came from Okeanos were stronger than any he'd ever yet endured, but he would, he knew, he would endure, because he had to, because this was the moment, the moment when it all mattered, so he fought with everything he had inside even though he was overmatched. His height only reached to the top of Okeanos' knee, but still Michael matched blows with the great titan, because in the distance Phosphorus had disappeared into the bright clouds with the other dark angels, and when he saw that, Michael knew they were fighting for everything then, for all those that were still left, and were still of the light, so they were fighting for *more* than everything.

Because he knew then where Phosphorus was going.

21

$\mathcal{S}$HE STOOD NEXT TO HER TWO SONS and together they watched the sky as the dark clouds gathered, then grew even larger.

Thunder pounded in their ears.

Flashes of lightning danced across the heavens.

She could feel Habel next to her as she watched the clouds, and as she did, she held him closer; she could feel Kain, too, there on her other side, and how his breath had then evened, and deepened, and how he steeled himself for whatever it was that might come and intrude once again on the Creation they'd made their home.

Kain had been told the stories, she knew.

And she saw in his eyes he was ready to take his own place in them, the same as his father had.

It was misguided, like all war and death was, but it was how her husband told her he'd been made, and it was how he told her that her oldest son had been made, too.

"Here," she heard her husband's voice.

And his voice came from behind her.

She turned and saw him coming from the woods and in his hands she saw he was carrying with him the two swords he'd made. He got closer to them, and as he did, he kept one for himself, then Kain stepped forward and away from her and joined his father as he took the other, the smaller of the two weapons.

She looked at them, with Habel next to her, then she met her husband's eyes.

It'll be alright, his eyes told her silently.

And they continued to speak with their eyes.

They spoke without words, so their children wouldn't hear, or anyone else.

But, against all odds, someone did.

She was about to open her mouth, to respond to her husband, and her oldest son, but then . . .

There was another response, another voice.

"Are you sure it will be alright?" they heard the words come from behind where they stood together, and she was still looking at her family when she heard them, at her husband's eyes, and she could see he was wondering if this voice was real because it was a voice that was more beautiful than any he'd ever yet heard or thought was possible.

But she knew that it was, because she'd already heard it.

Then she turned and that's when she saw him.

He was standing between the fields and the forest, where he'd landed, and she watched as he tucked his wings away before he began to walk towards them.

"What are you doing here?" she asked, the words catching in her throat.

"I came to speak with you again," he answered with his small, secret smile that she remembered, too.

Her husband and oldest son raised their swords, as he got closer.

He looked at their swords, at their weapons, but he did nothing.

He just smiled even wider as her husband stepped forward.

"Stay away," her husband told the dark angel.

Phosphorus looked at him, taking him in, from head to toe.

Then he shook his head.

"No," he told him. "I don't think I will."

"We'll fight you," Kain said, from his place next to his father.

"I know you will, young one," Phosphorus nodded. "But in case you hadn't heard, I can fight, too."

Then as he spoke, something happened.

A new darkness came and covered the sun for a moment, and when it did, everything went black. She looked up as this happened, expecting to see another cloud—like the one they'd just seen—but instead, it was something else, and it was something more.

It was wings.

Great, feathered, dark wings.

The sun was blotted out by all the many score of dark angels who had now come to Creation, and they descended from the sky in the same way their lord had come, and they landed in the clearing behind Phosphorus.

Then they started to walk.

They came forward as one; they came forward as a host.

"Stay away from us," her husband said again, with less confidence this time.

But Phosphorus smiled. He just smiled.

Then he nodded to his angels, as he spread his own wings, and she knew what would come an instant before it did.

Then it happened.

The dark angels spread their wings again, too, and flew at them in a great burst and rush as her husband and oldest son stepped even further forward.

It was to protect them, she knew.

But it was also misguided, and completely miscalculated.

"No!" she shouted.

But her words were no use against her husband's nature, or her son's.

They were hopelessly outnumbered, but they would still fight.

She watched as father and son stood shoulder-to-shoulder and raised their blades to meet the blades of their enemies, who had first brought those weapons to Creation.

Steel met steel.

The humans shouted and they were answered in turn by the angels.

Chaos erupted all around as the battle broke out, and as father and son fought, she searched with panic in her eyes for her youngest, then she saw him, and pulled him closer to her. She sheltered him against her body, then tried to use her muscled and powerful legs to run through all the chaos of battle, but as she did, she was grabbed roughly by the arm.

She was spun around and saw a dark angel, next to her.

He was holding onto her, his strong fingers bruising her skin, and he was just about to raise his hand, the one that held his great sword in it, when the arm was severed. Her husband had seen the dark angel come after her, too, as she'd run, and when the angel had reached his arm out and grabbed her, he'd forgotten everything else—everything that was in front of him, and behind him—and her husband had swung his sword with everything he had, swung it in a great, sweeping arc, swung it to save his wife. The steel blade that had been born of the river that was their river, caught the angel at the elbow and cut his arm completely in half, and the angel screamed in pain as he watched his torn appendage fall to the grass, but the attack had left her husband exposed; he was completely undefended, and as she turned to see what had happened, she saw this, too, and she yelled, she yelled as loudly as she could, but she was too late.

A dark sword was swung and it slashed her husband across the back.

He fell to the grass, crying out in pain, and as Kain saw his father fall, he came to stand over him, and tried to defend him.

But he couldn't.

He wasn't big enough. He wasn't strong enough.

And there were too many of them.

Habel was ripped from her, and she screamed again, and so did he, then soon Kain and her husband were surrounded, too, where he'd fallen, surrounded by steel and darkness and wings.

Then she tripped, where she was held, and fell heavily to the ground.

She quickly stood again, and when she did, she saw all that had happened.

She saw the dark angels that had disarmed her husband and picked him up and were holding his arms twisted behind him, and she saw the other dark ones that were holding her two sons with swords at their throats. She made quick calculations and knew that strength wouldn't work, not against the numbers they faced, so if strength was out of the question, then there was only one other way, she knew, and so that's what she'd try, she decided, as she slowly turned.

She saw Phosphorus, standing there, watching her, and she met his ash-dark eyes.

"Let them go," she said to him.

"You know the only way that will happen," he told her, still smiling.

She heard his words, and took in what he'd said, then she nodded, very small.

"You win," she told him, and he smiled even wider because he had what he wanted then, she knew. "You win, and so it will be."

She knew what came next, too.

He turned to the dark angels and gave them his command.

She watched as they started to take her family back towards their home, and they struggled against them.

"What's happening?" her husband called to her. "What did you say to him?"

"No!" her oldest son yelled.

But they were no match for the angels, for their strength.

Then Habel who was much smaller kicked out and slipped free of one that was holding him, showing them all strength they didn't know he had, and he ran as his mother had taught him—as he'd run with her, trying to match her long and powerful strides while gathering out in Creation—and he reached her. She could see in his eyes he would have fought Phosphorus, he would have fought the two dark angels who flew after him, and he would have fought all of them together, too, for her, but she reached down and put her hand on his cheek.

"It's alright, my little one," she told him. "Remember what I taught you. Always remember to search for what's inside."

"No, Mom," he said as tears came to his cheek.

"It's the only way," she told him, as gently as she could.

"It can't be!" he yelled. "Fight them!"

"I will," she told him, as she nodded, then leaned close and whispered. "I will, but in my way now."

Then the two dark angels who followed were to him, and they each took Habel by the arms again as he continued to struggle against them, and he yelled.

It was so very out of character for him, she thought.

"*Mom, Mom, Mom!*" he shouted at the top of his lungs.

But he was no match for their strength, either, and they pulled him away.

She watched as he went, tears in her eyes, helpless to do anything about it, she knew, and she watched as her family was then taken further away, back past the fields and towards their home, and finally pushed inside of it and out of sight.

When they were gone, it was quiet again in the clearing.

She reached up.

She wiped a single tear away, then looked above them, up towards the heavens.

She waited, looking, searching.

But she saw nothing.

"He's not coming," Phosphorus said from his place next to her, and she could feel his words were truth, so she nodded, accepting that, then turned to him and it was just them, then, just the two of them.

And she knew that they were alone, truly alone.

"After you," Phosphorus said.

She waited for a moment, knowing what he wanted.

Then she finally nodded, resigned to what would happen, and began to walk.

She went past the fields and orchard, and he followed after, all the way to the far side of the house where the two great trees stood and waited: the smaller Tree of Life and, of course, the larger Tree of Knowledge.

The Tree of Knowledge loomed tall, above her, and it cast a crooked shadow over everything as the sun descended behind it.

She waited for a moment, looking up at it.

She looked up at the bright fruit that was there, on the branches, and listened to the peaceful sound of the river that came from the distance. Then her thoughts drifted and she imagined again her boys playing in that water, playing in it in the way they had when they were younger, and she imagined again the nights she'd spent by its side, with her husband, next to her, nothing else between them but skin and moonlight and love.

She wondered about the look she'd seen in Habel's eyes.

She wondered about Michael, and the other angels, and where they were.

She wondered about a great many things—about her family, and future, and what would happen to them—and as she wondered all these things, he then spoke again.

"It calls to you even more now, doesn't it?" Phosphorus whispered from his place behind her.

She waited for a moment, taking in his new words.

She still stared at the fruit, and the tree, as she answered him.

"It's always called to me," she told him, very simply.

And they both knew it was truth.

"Of course it has," Phosphorus continued to whisper. "And why shouldn't you have what the fruit holds? Why should God take all the wisdom and knowledge that's inside of it, and keep every last bit of that for himself? Why should those things be only for him, and him alone, and for Michael?"

She waited, another moment, still looking up.

She studied the fruit on the branch that was closest to her, the shape of it, the size, the color.

"I just have one question, though," she said, still not taking her eyes from it.

"Yes?"

"Why in this way?" she asked.

"What do you mean?"

"You could have killed us," she said to him. "Or just me, if that was what you intended, and not just today, either, here in the clearing, but a great many other times, too, I'm sure. So why go through all this trouble to make me eat the fruit when you could've ended this so many times already and in so many different ways?"

"You really don't understand, do you?"

"I haven't eaten," she said as she turned back to him, and it was her turn to smile then, even in the face of what she knew was about to happen. "So no, I don't."

"God created you," Phosphorus told her. "He created you each, in his image, and he gave you your will."

"Yes," she nodded. "I know."

"So your death would be a blow to God," Phosphorus nodded. "But the bigger blow, the greatest one I could possibly strike against him, would be for you to use his greatest gift to betray his most sacred command. For you to betray him, and what he decreed . . . *of your own free will.*"

She took that in, turning it over, and realized she still had a question, one last question.

"But why me?" she asked him.

"I don't understand."

"You could have tempted any of the others: my husband, either of my sons, but you never did. It was me that you came to, every time . . . it was always me."

"Yes," he nodded. "It was."

"Why? Because they were men, and I wasn't, so you thought I would be weaker?"

"You really don't understand, do you?"

She stared back at him, and he saw she didn't understand, so he would tell her.

"Think about it," he said. "Then think about it further. You were born from dust, the same as the man who was born with you, that you call your husband. But your children weren't. Your children were born of flesh—of your flesh, and his, too—and that's the great gift and power God gave to you: the gift and the power of *life*. And he gave it to you, and to no other, you do realize that, right?"

"So what does that mean?"

"It means that I chose you, dear human, very dear, sweet, young soul . . . I chose you for all those reasons. I chose you because while your husband might be God's hand, here in Creation, you're God's heart, and so for you to eat will be a bigger blow to him," he said, then was silent for a moment, before he nodded, once, very slowly. "I chose you," he continued, "not because you were weaker, but because you were stronger, and because you were his favorite, like I was . . . and you were the one he created to show his ways to the world."

She took in his words and let them settle inside her, and she found she didn't know if they were lies or truth.

So she thought of him, her husband.

Then she thought of her children, the ones they'd made together.

She thought of everything that had happened in Creation—everything she'd felt, and everything that had already come—then there was no more time for thoughts or memories because Phosphorus began to walk towards her, then past her, and he reached up to take a single piece of fruit from the lowest branch of the tree. But when he did, she reached out and stopped him, then she spoke, and she didn't know why she did, or how, because the words that came weren't her words.

"No," she told him.

"No?"

"I will choose the fruit."

He hesitated, just for a moment, looking at her in front of him.

Then he nodded, and moved back, so she stood there alone.

She looked up at the tree, something she'd done so many times before, but now the moment she'd thought of so often was upon her, so it all seemed so much closer, so much more intimate, and immediate.

She looked at the piece of fruit he'd already touched.

Then she looked past it.

She saw the biggest piece that was there on the tree, which was a few inches higher than his piece, and that's what she reached for. She stood on her toes and her fingers just barely grazed against it, and as they did, she felt a great and powerful jolt spread through her entire body, and with even the faintest of touches, the fruit came loose from the stem which had attached it to the branch and it rolled off and into the palm of her hand.

She looked down and stared at it.

She slowly breathed: in and out, in and out.

And as she did, she kept staring at the brightness of the fruit, the strong, vivid, and unmistakable color, then she thought of all it contained inside, all the secrets of Creation and the Universe and perhaps even more, too, all the great secrets of time, and space, and of both the known and unknown.

She thought of all that, then turned from the fruit, and looked back at him.

One more time.

"What will happen if I don't eat?" she asked.

She was thinking of the oath she swore: the only thing she'd been asked by God and by Michael to obey.

Phosphorus thought of that, too, his head cocked up and to the side.

And while he didn't speak, he would show her what she asked.

He came forward, further, closer to her.

Then he was right next to her, and she watched as he reached out and took her arm with his hand, the arm that wasn't holding the fruit; he didn't ask her permission to do so, as Michael always had, and as soon as he touched her skin, images flashed in her mind.

She saw her husband, her oldest son, and her youngest.

They were standing in their house, next to the group of dark angels that had taken them, and she tried to yell, but she couldn't.

She could only watch.

And as she did, the dark angels who were standing behind them forced them to the ground, to their knees.

He tried to fight back, her husband, and so did Kain.

Habel yelled next to them, but it would be no use, she knew, as the dark angels were too many, and they were too strong.

They drew their swords.

They waited, just for a moment, as one of the dark angels turned and looked directly at her, where she watched.

Then he ran Habel through the chest, first, and she tried to scream again but nothing came, then the other dark angels drew their swords and stabbed metal into flesh, her husband, then Kain.

She kept screaming.

And as they all fell, together, dying . . .

She came rushing back.

Back to the clearing, and to him.

She looked around in panic, and saw the Tree of Knowledge in front of her, and the fruit that was in her hand.

Phosphorus was next to her, with the smile still there on his lips.

"What have you done . . ." she whispered.

"Nothing yet. What you saw hasn't come to pass, but it will, if you don't eat."

She was silent, taking that in, all she'd just learned.

"And if I do? What happens if I do eat?"

He reached out and touched her arm again, and the same thing happened, as once again everything changed and new and different images flashed in front of her.

She saw a different field, and different orchard, and she saw her husband.

Then she saw her two sons, too.

She was walking out of a different forest, with Habel next to her, and they were walking towards where Kain worked in the new fields with his father.

They were all older.

There were lines and wrinkles in her features, and her husband's, and there was hair that was starting to grey at their temples.

She saw the fields, and everything else that was around her . . .

She saw it all and didn't recognize it.

The sky was less blue; the dirt was harder for them to turn; the crops that grew were smaller, and more difficult to tend, and she coughed into her hand as she walked.

Then she looked down and saw brown grass at her feet.

And as she looked, she saw a dying flower, too, and as she looked at it, even closer, her eyes focusing . . .

She once again came rushing back to the clearing.

She thought again of what she'd just seen, and how she didn't recognize it, any of it.

"Where were we?" she asked.

"You know this place where you live as Creation," he told her, very slowly. "But it isn't. It's Paradise. And there's a whole other world out there where there's plague, and sickness, and drought. There's a whole other world where the colors aren't as bright, and the fruit is less sweet and plentiful. That's what lies beyond the mountains you haven't crossed: a world of pain, and a world of suffering. Because outside of Creation lies a world where all you now know will one day turn to dust, just the same as the dust you once came from."

She heard his words and took them in.

Then she closed her eyes.

She willed herself to go back to the vision he'd just given her, then she was surprised when she did.

She found herself right there, at the moment where it had ended before.

She looked down at the brown grass and dying flower at her feet.

She saw it again, but this time she looked further . . .

She looked past the dark and rotting petals, and down towards the stem, the root, and that's when she saw it.

A sliver of green.

It was there amongst the brown, there amongst the death.

And she knew what that meant.

New growth.

Then she looked up as her husband saw her and stopped his work in the field, to wave to her, and despite the lines and wrinkles and grey hair, there was still love.

There was so much love.

Then she looked at Kain, next to her husband, and she saw unhappiness in his eyes. She saw again the unhappiness he'd told her about, but there was still love there, too, and family, and even if there was nothing else, there was that, because unhappiness could be overcome, she knew, but before her memory went any further . . .

She returned again, back to the clearing, and back to the dark angel that stood in front of her.

She looked again at the fruit that was in her hand.

She looked at the perfect shape of it, and the bright and vivid color.

Then she looked up and met Phosphorus' eyes, one more time, and she held his eyes with her own. She watched as he just gazed impassively back at her, waiting for what she would choose, waiting for her to make the decision he'd given her.

There was only one thing left, she knew.

And she would use it, the greatest and most powerful gift she'd been given.

So she closed her eyes, one last time.

She closed her eyes and turned inwards and searched for the feeling and voice that was inside her, and once she found it, and felt it fill her and heard what it told her, that's when her prayer then began.

It was silent at first, no more than just a whisper.

But that didn't matter, because it existed, and that's what mattered; that's all that mattered.

She calmed her mind and spoke her words and truth and as she did, the prayer that she'd created came from her heart and left through her lips and it travelled up, up, up, high up and into the bright, clear sky, between and past the clouds, through space and time and across a very great distance, because that's the power that prayers have. She'd always thought her prayers went to Michael, or God, but the thing about prayers she didn't yet understand was that they went exactly where they needed to.

So her prayer kept going, on and on . . .

And this is where it went.

FAR AWAY AND AT THE VERY EDGE of eternity, Selaphiel stood with those that had left Heaven and Michael's dominion to fly with him. He'd searched far and wide when they'd left, looking in every corner and place he could think to search for that which he'd lost, but he hadn't found what he'd been looking for, not even a glimmer, not even the slightest bit of hope. So he stood amongst the great mountains that were at the furthest-most edge of eternity, and where he'd continued to search, then he felt something. It didn't come from Heaven, as he'd expected, and that he'd felt before. It had come from Creation, instead. He listened and heard the prayer that was brought to him—the prayer that was brought straight to his soul, and to his heart, and he felt the strength of it, too—then he turned and looked up at the sun above. He unconsciously stretched his great wings from where they'd been curled and folded against his back as he looked up at the bright rays and felt the warmth they brought to his skin.

He listened to her words, as they came, then he heard others, too.

He heard more voices, many more, crying out for help.

"What is it?" one of the young angels next to him asked.

Selaphiel waited for a moment, analyzing what had come.

He waited as he then thought again of all he'd lost, and all he'd been searching for.

He looked into his soul, and when he did . . . he then knew what they had to do.

So he finally turned to the young angel next to him, then all the others, as well.

"Are you ready to return?" he asked, very quietly.

"Why?" the young angel frowned. "Why would we go back?"

"Because something has been changed," Selaphiel said, then drew the sword he carried at his hip. He looked at it, the steel, the tip, as it glinted against the rays of the sun and he felt again the prayer as it passed through him: he felt the words, the love, the hope. He felt all of that, and recognized it, because it was all something he had once felt, too, then lost. "Something has changed," he continued, "and we've been called."

"By who? Michael?"

"No," Selaphiel shook his head.

And with no more words, he spread his great wings, then exploded up and towards the sun.

IN THE SKY OUTSIDE THE PALACE WALLS, Michael bled from the many deep and serious wounds that covered his body, but he still fought. Everywhere around him, the other angels that were still in the sky and that still flew fought also, but they gave up ground, and the titans came closer and closer to breaching the walls of Heaven. And what's worse was that Michael knew what was sure to be happening in Creation, too, yet he was powerless to do anything more than what he was doing. He was locked in a battle he couldn't win and he knew the only way he'd be able to match the strength of the great Okeanos was with the power that came from deep within him, the power that wasn't his—the great and sacred power that had come from God, and that he'd used to expel Phosphorus from Heaven, what seemed like a lifetime ago—but the problem was . . . he hadn't felt that power inside him in some time, not since the last time he'd used it, just before Creation had been made.

When had it left?

It had gone when Phosphorus had been banished, and was that the reason?

Did it leave because Phosphorus had left, too?

Michael didn't know.

All he knew was that it was what he needed to possibly be able to defeat Okeanos, and God hadn't saw fit to bring it back to him. Michael called and called upon it to return as he fought against Okeanos, and was losing, being pushed further and further back, and nothing happened.

But then, all of a sudden, something did.

There was a warmth that came to him, and it spread everywhere, all throughout his body.

Then as the warmth came, he listened and could hear human words, too, and could feel real and powerful hope, and that's the thing he didn't yet know about prayers, either; he didn't yet know they could go to more places than just one, but in that moment he realized they could, then he heard. He heard what she spoke and asked for, and it filled him. It filled him with strength and truth and light, which was exactly what he needed. He thought about what was happening, in Creation, then he saw a vision of her under the Tree, with the fruit in her hand, and he also saw in his vision that she hadn't eaten yet. She held the fruit but hadn't yet bitten into it, which meant she didn't yet have the knowledge the Tree contained—all the knowledge God had placed there, and had warned them against and that she'd been tempted with—and in the absence of that knowledge, there was still a place in her heart for one thing, the most important thing, the most powerful thing . . .

And that's what Michael now felt.

He breathed deeply and flexed the fingers that were wrapped around the hilt of his sword as Okeanos watched curiously from across the sky, not realizing it was the simple love and faith of a human that had just restored Michael's great power, that had just brought back everything Michael would now need.

"It's over, angel," Okeanos said.

Michael was silent for a moment, for one last moment.

Then he looked up and met Okeanos' eyes.

"Yes," he said. "It is."

And then it began.

His body started to glow again with the same bright cobalt aura, coming from deep inside him where the faith had gone and settled then spread, throughout his body, every inch of it, and Okeanos kept watching, very curiously, as the light kept growing, growing, growing, getting brighter, stronger, then finally . . .

The entire cobalt blue aura exploded.

It exploded into a great shower of light that was greater than anything that had yet been seen in Heaven, greater even than what had come and banished them before, and the light blinded both angel and titan, who each covered their eyes.

Gabriel and Raphael and the others tried to look . . .

But they couldn't.

All they could see was the outline of Michael through the great burst of light he'd brought back, the same light that then lifted the great titans from their feet—such was the strength and depth of this faith and power—and it hurled them through space and time in the same way it had previously done to Phosphorus.

The titans were all cast from Heaven, back into darkness, then the light began to fade.

It retreated, back into Michael, back into his body, into his soul.

Then finally, it was gone again.

He saw Gabriel, next to him now, and he saw Raphael.

He saw all the others, too.

He saw how they were looking at him: not how they once had, not very long ago, but with more than they had before. There would be much to discuss between them all, he knew, there would be much that would come next, there would be much, much more indeed . . .

But it wouldn't be yet.

"Quickly," he breathed.

Then he spread his great wings and exploded towards Creation.

"SO?" PHOSPHORUS ASKED HER. "What will it be?"

"It's time now, isn't it?"

"You've seen both paths and now the choice is yours."

She stared down at the fruit she still held as she heard his words, and this was the moment she'd dreaded: this was the moment she'd feared, but then it receded, almost to the point where it was completely gone.

A smile came to her face.

Phosphorus saw that smile, and when he did, he frowned, because it was something he didn't understand.

"What is it?" he asked. "Why do you smile?"

"Because of what you think you've offered me: either Paradise, or exile."

"That's right," he nodded. "That's exactly right."

There was one more moment for her, just one more moment.

And in it, she thought of his words, and realized that it was now time.

She raised the fruit to her lips, then she met his eyes, and as she did, hers flashed with brilliant strength and truth.

There was no more fear in them.

Then she ate.

She chewed slowly, deliberately, letting the sugars settle in her mouth as she swallowed the pulp and flesh. She waited for change to come, but nothing did. She felt the same. She was the same, she thought. She kept chewing then the bite was finally gone as Phosphorus stared back at her, reveling in this, his moment of triumph and greatest act of darkness.

"It's the end for you here in Paradise," he told her.

"This isn't Paradise."

"Then what is?"

She closed her eyes and a million images flashed quickly in front of her.

They came again without him touching her, and this is what they were:

The first moment she found her husband, in the forest, beside the river.

The house they built together, him working in the fields, her out gathering in Creation and the trip they took to the waterfall and their time together in the pool.

The first time her hand found his, and held it.

The end of the great battle in the forest, and what happened after.

The birth of their first child, and the look in his eyes as he held his son for the first time.

Then their second son coming, and what he would mean to his mother.

Their times together by the river as they grew older.

When he returned from Creation, and when they went back to the waterfall.

She saw again all the times that had been . . .

And then she saw more.

She saw times that hadn't been, but would now be, she knew.

She saw as they left Creation, as a family, and went into the World and made a new home in a new clearing.

She saw as they grew even older, faces lined and wrinkled, hair streaked with grey and she saw as they had more fights, more conflict, but they came back to each other every time, they always came back to each other.

She saw as their children grew and left, and had children of their own.

Then she saw their end.

She saw how they got sick, and how they passed, many years from then, holding each other, still holding each other, always holding each other, through everything.

Then the images slowly faded, and she was back again in Creation.

But the feeling that the images brought still lingered, and she smiled as she answered the question that Phosphorus had asked her, the one about Paradise, the one she knew he might not ever understand, and she also knew that what he didn't yet understand was his greatest weakness.

Then she thought about the fruit.

She thought about how she thought there'd been no change, when she'd eaten it, then she smiled.

Because of course there had been.

She'd just seen it.

He cocked his head to the side as she thought all of that, looking at her curiously, trying to make sense of why she'd smile after what had just happened, but he couldn't, so instead he shook his head and drew his sword as he began to walk forward, towards her, his own smile gone and a menacing look on his face and as he got closer to her, the ground shook and knocked her off-balance and she saw more wings, next to her, in front of her, all around.

"Go no further," she heard a strong voice say.

Then she saw Selaphiel.

He was standing between her and Phosphorus with his sword drawn.

He'd flown faster than all the other angels he'd been with, and he'd gone faster because of the strength and power the prayer she'd whispered had brought to him.

Would the others come?

He didn't know, but even if they did, it would still be some time, he knew, and it might be too late.

So he would fight alone.

"You don't want to do this, young one," Phosphorus told him. "You can't save her. She's already eaten."

Selaphiel looked down at the fruit in her hand and he saw the bite she'd taken from it.

Then she watched as he looked up, and at her, and she saw his eyes: she saw what was in them, then, and what he felt, and how it had changed him, how it had brought him home.

And it was her that had done that.

It was her that had helped him, had shown him the way back, had shown him how love couldn't be lost, because that which is eternal is never lost.

"Yes, she's eaten," Selaphiel spoke slowly, then turned back to the dark angel. "But yet you're still here, Light-Bringer, so there must be more."

Phosphorus paused at that as he stared at Selaphiel, across from him.

It was impossible for her to read the dark angel, to understand what he was thinking, or what he might be feeling.

Then Phosphorus opened his mouth and spoke again.

"Let it be known, Selaphiel, that I offered you your life," he said.

Selaphiel heard him, and she watched as he nodded, once, very simply.

"I understand," he said.

Then the clearing exploded.

She watched as everything around her erupted in a great flash of wings and steel as Phosphorus flew across the distance between them in a blur, sword raised high, and their battle began.

Phosphorus was bigger than Selaphiel, and stronger, and the blows that came pushed the younger angel further and further back, and as she watched their battle, she already knew how it would end: she'd seen the battle in the woods, and remembered it, so she knew Phosphorus was strong, and the only one that could match his strength was Michael.

But where was he?

She wanted to help the young angel, but didn't know how, then it came to her.

She wasn't any use with a sword, she knew, but there was a power she had that was greater than any metal or steel or any weapon that might be invented to inflict pain and death, so she closed her eyes and continued her prayer. She didn't know where her prayer went, or what it did, but she knew its power, so she still continued.

She didn't see her words, as they left her body.

She didn't see as they rose from her along with her thoughts, and she didn't see as they travelled across space and time and found Michael where he flew and gave him more strength, helped him fly even faster, and she didn't see as her words and thoughts then found the other angels, too, and did the same for them.

She didn't see any of that, or know that it happened, but she hoped.

And then she opened her eyes.

She saw Phosphorus and Selaphiel still fighting, and the dark angel was on top of the young and bright one now, bringing heavy blows with his great sword. Selaphiel would soon be overwhelmed, she knew, then she saw as the moment came, and he stumbled.

He spread his wings.

He tried to fly out from underneath Phosphorus, but the dark angel grabbed Selaphiel by the throat.

Phosphorus slammed him back to the ground and the whole earth shook.

Selaphiel struggled underneath him.

He fought back against Phosphorus with every bit of strength he had, but it wouldn't be enough, she knew; Phosphorus still held him by the neck with one hand, while he raised the other above, his sword held tightly in it, light flickering and shining off the blade.

"No!" she yelled.

She ran across the distance between them and threw her body against Phosphorus.

It didn't do anything.

She raised her hand, about to try to hit him or push him from his place on top of Selaphiel, but before she could, he grabbed her and threw her from him as easily as he would have thrown a small rock. She sailed through the air then crashed into the trunk of the Tree of Knowledge, where she fell heavily back to the ground.

The air was pushed from her lungs, and she struggled to breathe, but she still couldn't look away from the scene in front of her.

She looked back to where Phosphorus would deliver death to the young angel, and she was too far away to do anything further. She was too far away, she knew, to do anything else at all, so there was nothing else left but to watch as he raised his sword, one more time, then when they were mere moments away from the inevitable . . .

She saw Selaphiel swallow, accepting his fate.

She saw him understand that while his light would soon be overcome and extinguished, it had been extinguished in the cause of truth, so it would perhaps not ever really leave. She watched as his lips moved, a silent prayer, asking for his fractured soul to be returned and joined again with the one that had previously departed, and she wondered if his prayer would be answered—if faith worked the same way for angels as it did for her—then Phosphorus' blade came flashing down with all the force of darkness that was within him, and it came straight towards Selaphiel's neck, just as Creation rocked and shuddered. Then with movement that was quicker than her eyes could follow, a blade swung and met Phosphorus' blow with a mighty crack that was louder than thunder, then she saw it was Michael that was holding the sword. She looked even further and saw the force of his flight and arrival had created a giant crater in the earth where his feet had landed, and before any of them had time to speak, Michael then brought his blade back around in a mighty blow of his own.

Phosphorus parried.

But the great force of it took him unawares and knocked him backwards and away from Michael, as Michael turned and helped Selaphiel to his feet.

Then Michael froze, as he stood there, because he saw something else, on the grass next to him.

He saw the fruit, with the bite taken from it.

She watched as he stayed staring at it and she also watched as he processed what had happened, and what it would mean.

Then he turned and looked at her.

He met her eyes and she couldn't read what was in his own.

Was it anger?

Disappointment?

Fear?

She kept watching him and his expression didn't change except for the very slightest suggestion of a quiver that came to the left side of his mouth, his upper lip moving in the very smallest of fashions, the beginnings of what she swore might've been a smile, but then a voice came from behind him.

"You're too late, Michael," Phosphorus told him.

"Was I?" he asked, still looking at her.

"You've failed to protect them, failed in the most important task that was given to you."

Slowly, she watched as Michael turned, away from her, and he turned back to face Phosphorus.

She watched as Michael took him in, his head cocked curiously to the side as Selaphiel came to stand next to him, too, both their weapons still drawn and Michael still looked back at Phosphorus, then she watched as his lips finally turned further, all the way up, into a full and unmistakable smile.

"Yes, my friend," Michael nodded. "I have failed."

"So why do you smile?" Phosphorus asked, as he frowned.

"Because we all stumble, both in Heaven, like I have, and here in Creation, too. But we have will. So when we stumble . . . we do so that we can get back up again."

Phosphorus heard his words but he didn't understand.

He shook his head as he stared back at Michael.

"God will punish you for what you've done," he said. "He'll punish you for your failure, and for what you've let happen here."

"Maybe that's how darkness works," Michael told him, shaking his head. "Maybe your new God is one of spite and vengeance, but not the one who speaks to me."

"They'll still have to leave Creation. That was the rule, and it was iron."

"Yes," Michael nodded. "They will have to leave."

"So it's over."

"No. But it is time for you to go."

Phosphorus opened his mouth.

He was about to answer again, when—

BOOM.

Gabriel landed next to Michael and Selaphiel, then—

BOOM.

Raphael came and landed, too, as—

BOOM.

BOOM.

BOOM.

BOOM.

All the rest of the angels of light that had come from Heaven landed in the grass near Michael, then she watched as they all turned towards Phosphorus, who faced them.

He was alone.

But there was no fear in his eyes.

He took them in with a measured and calculating look, then he pursed his lips together into a tight line so the two lips looked like one. He let out a high-pitched whistle and she covered her ears at the sound she knew was surely heard in every corner of Creation and beyond, and that's then when they came, all of them, all the other angels of darkness that followed him.

They came from the sky.

They came from the forest, too.

Then she saw they also came from the house.

They all flew with their great wings pumping up and down—Báal, Mamanos, and the others—and they landed behind Phosphorus then spread into a great, wide circle, surrounding her, and Michael, and all the others that had come from light, so once more there were two great hosts that faced each other.

They weren't equal this time, though.

Their power was equal there in Creation, where it was neither light nor dark, but there weren't as many angels of light as there had been before: much of their host above had left with Selaphiel, when he'd departed, and of those who stayed, many hadn't survived the Battle of Heaven against the titans that Phosphorus had freed and brought through time and darkness to their walls.

She took all this in, then saw as Selaphiel turned to Michael.

He realized all this, too, and what he'd done.

"I'm sorry," Selaphiel said.

Michael heard him, and he knew it, as well, but shook his head.

"No," he told the younger angel. "You followed your heart."

Then Gabriel stepped forward, next to them.

"This still isn't over yet," he said, bleeding from a wound across his torso. "We might be destroyed, at the end of this, but we can still take them with us, too."

"Yes, we can," Raphael nodded.

And he limped forward, on an injured left leg, to stand next to his friends.

Michael heard them.

He heard each of them, from their places where they then were, at his right, and his left.

But instead of turning to them, he turned to her.

He met her eyes and she waited for what he would tell her.

"When it begins," he said quietly. "You need to run, as fast as you can."

"Where?" she asked him.

"Away," he said, speaking as softly as he could.

And then, before there were any more words . . .

The battle began.

Phosphorus spread his dark wings and with a great rush of displaced air that she felt suck against her, he once again exploded across the distance between them and headed straight for Michael.

Michael flew into the air, too.

He tried to once again reach inside and use the same great power within him that he'd used to expel Phosphorus from Heaven, as he rose into the air, but he'd just spent all the strength and light he had in his battle against Okeanos, and so as Phosphorus flew with his sword raised, Michael had no other choice but to bring his own weapon up, at the last moment, and their blades met with thunder. Then Phosphorus brought his fist around and struck a great blow to Michael's face that sent him spiraling from the sky and down to where he crashed to the ground in a shower of dirt, near her legs.

He painfully started to get to his feet.

Then he saw her still there, still standing there.

She was rooted to where she had been before.

"Run!" he said to her, and he yelled now.

She could hear the urgency in his voice, too.

Then Phosphorus was on him again.

She watched for another second, as the dark angel descended in a great blur, and as their duel continued, she turned and ran, as he'd told her, with once again another great battle between angels raging in the sky above her.

Her legs were strong and muscled.

She was glad she'd used them so much in Creation.

She turned them towards the house they'd built, as she ran across the entire distance of the clearing, then she was to the house and went inside.

Her eyes darted around, towards every corner, and there was relief.

She saw they were alive; her husband and her two sons.

They were still whole and in one piece, but their hands and legs were bound and mouths muffled so they couldn't talk or move, and she went to them and tried to remove the bindings, but she couldn't. They were too strong, tied too tight. She stared down at them for a moment, wondering what she could possibly do, and how she could possibly free them.

Her husband tried to get her attention.

Her eyes flicked to his then followed them towards what he wanted to show her, what he wanted her to see: the two swords he'd made, that had been such a cause of discord between them and that were on the ground in the corner.

She hesitated, just for a moment, as she looked at them.

But then she had to put her previous feelings aside, she knew.

So she ran over and picked up the larger of the two blades and quickly went back and used the sharpened edge of it to cut their bindings.

Then when they were all free, Habel ran to her and threw his arms around her waist.

"Are you alright?" she asked them.

She looked around, meeting each of their eyes.

"Yes," Kain nodded.

Then he went to the corner and picked up the other sword, the smaller one, his sword.

"Are *you* alright?" she heard.

She turned back to look at him, her husband.

Their eyes met, and he could tell that something had happened, she knew, something important: but could he tell exactly what?

She didn't know.

But there would be time for that later.

There would be time later for many things.

But only if there was going to be a later at all.

"We have to go," she said instead.

"Where?" he asked.

"Away," she told him, echoing what Michael had told her.

He took that in, then nodded and she saw they were all in agreement and understanding as they began to make their way through the house and towards the door, together.

But first, he went to her.

He took the larger of the two swords from her hand, his skin brushing against her skin, his hand holding hers, just for a second, as Kain still held onto the other.

She hesitated.

It was only a moment.

Then they went to the door and looked outside and she heard Habel next to her inhale sharply as he saw for the first time the sight that was there in front of them: all the angels, both those of light, and those of darkness, that flew in the sky and fought a great battle above Creation.

She saw the apprehension and fear that was in his eyes.

Then when she turned to her oldest son, she saw something else, as he took in the sight he'd heard and dreamed about and wondered for so long if it would ever come again.

And now there it was.

It was right there, above them, beside them, all around them.

Their clearing was bordered on the east by the river, and the main part of the battle was to the north and west, so there was only one way for them to go.

South.

"Stay next to me," she told Habel, as she squeezed his shoulders, and he nodded.

They each took a deep breath, then another: in and out, in and out.

They waited, together, for one more moment, then broke from their cover and began to run.

She went first, with Habel next to her, as they were the two strongest runners and would lead the way.

Then her husband and Kain came next, behind them.

They held their weapons at the ready, to guard against anything that might come, any of the dark angels that might break from the battle and fly after them.

They all put their heads down and ran as fast as they could.

They covered the distance of the clearing then came to the forest, and they dodged between trees, as they kept going.

She told Habel not to look back, just to run.

She told him to run, run, run.

They would keep going, they would all keep going, and they wouldn't stop until they were safe again.

BEHIND THEM, still in the sky above the clearing, Michael and Phosphorus twirled and twisted as they kept rising, locked in fierce combat against each other.

Metal struck against metal.

Feathers were ripped from wings.

Blood was shed and fell to the ground.

Michael was stronger than Phosphorus, they both knew, but Michael had been injured and had been weakened by his battle with Okeanos.

And that's what Phosphorus used to his advantage.

He began to get the upper-hand as he looked down below to where his dark angels also fought against Michael's host of light, outnumbering them greatly, and he saw that the darkness that was there was beginning to overwhelm the light.

The battle was finally beginning to turn, and Phosphorus smiled as he saw it.

"You didn't have to do this," Michael told him, through gritted teeth, his great blade locked against Phosphorus' great blade.

"I've done nothing," Phosphorus responded.

"You've spent your whole existence since you left trying to tempt them, trying to sow discord!" Michael yelled back over the deafening noise of the battle.

"I didn't sow anything," Phosphorus answered him. "I merely called upon and brought out that which was already there, which means that God did it, your precious God; all I did was water what he'd made, and the darkness he'd already put inside them, in each of them, and help it to grow."

"I loved you," Michael told him, his teeth still gritted, and tears on his cheeks. "We loved each other."

"It was nothing compared to the way he loved you."

"He loved you, too. You were his favorite."

"He gave you everything!" Phosphorus shouted now, his eyes flashing bright and his blows coming with more strength.

They kept swinging.

They flew higher, higher, together.

"He gave me nothing," Michael told him.

"He gave you a palace, and Heaven, and dominion over all his Creation. And so what was left for me? Chains and shackles and eternity spent in second place, and you'd try to convince me he's just, and fair? All I wanted was a piece of what he had, Michael, a piece of what *you* had."

"Then you should have looked inside yourself."

Their battle continued as there were suddenly bright explosions of light and color below them, then Michael looked down.

He saw that his angels were faltering, falling, dying.

He saw their souls as they departed from Creation.

Two of the dark angels flew away from the battle and began flying up, and towards them.

Michael parried a blow, then the two new angels were to them, and Michael was surrounded.

So he fought against three enemies now.

He spun and twisted and swung his great sword, and he blocked many of their blows that came.

Then he grimaced in pain as one broke through and pierced his side.

He grunted, fighting against what he felt.

He grabbed the dark angel who held the blade.

He pulled him closer, closer, then he unleashed a great blow before he threw him down through the air and towards the ground where the angel crashed into the dirt with a loud and sickening thud, then Michael turned to the other angel and unleashed another great blow that sent him spinning and far away, too.

So then the duel returned, back to how it began.

Just him and Phosphorus.

But Michael was wounded, and failing, losing too much blood.

"It's not too late, Phosphorus," Michael said through the pain, through his gritted and bloody teeth. "He's in everything, in all that there is . . . which means there's still a piece of him in you, too."

"No," Phosphorus shook his head. "Not me."

"Yes," Michael nodded. "You can still be forgiven; you can still be the Light-Bringer again."

Michael watched as Phosphorus heard those words, and he watched as Phosphorus paused, and waited.

"Forgiveness?" he asked, speaking very quietly, slowly, looking at the battle raging around them and for a moment, just a moment, Michael saw his soul again, too, the one he'd loved so much, the one he still loved.

"Yes," Michael nodded.

"Even after all I've done?"

"Even after everything," Michael told him. "Because God forgives, and there can still be grace, even for the very lowest and darkest among us. That's why he is who he is, and that's why he's God."

Phosphorus took that in for a moment, and as he did, Michael could see the doubt that was now in his eyes.

It caused him to hesitate.

"I wish it could be," Phosphorus finally said.

"It *can* be," Michael urged.

"No," Phosphorus shook his head. "I know myself."

"What does that mean?"

Phosphorus was silent for a moment, again, and looking down, still taking in the battle then the gathering darkness, too, so close to his dream being realized, so close to his goal and to everything he'd ever wanted.

So he shook his head free, clearing it of the doubt, then looked back up and met Michael's eyes.

"*Den tha ypiretiso*," he said, speaking the ancient words. "I cannot serve."

"Don't do this," Michael told him softly.

"I have to," he said, his voice cracking.

"No, you don't."

"Yes I do."

Then he did.

In less than an instant he flew across the distance between them and Phosphorus swung a great blow which Michael parried, then another, and another, and Michael tried to keep up with his friend who was now truly an adversary, he tried to keep up with his speed and strength but his own had failed him.

He fought as hard as he could.

He defended himself, as much as he was able to, then Phosphorus brought his blade around in a great blow that caught Michael in the back, just where the knuckle of his wings met his lower shoulder, and the blow cut straight through one of them, severing the right wing from the body.

The wing itself began to fall.

And then so did Michael.

He twisted and spun as he fell, past the battle around him.

Down, down.

Through space, through air.

…

…

…

Then—

He landed on the ground, and where his body hit earth, another small crater dug out in the dirt, then Phosphorus was there, too, on top of him, pinning him with a strong foot to the chest where he lay and keeping him there with a sword pointed at his throat.

This was the end, Michael knew.

But he wasn't scared.

He tried to look into the distance, to catch any glimpses of the humans he could, and to see if they'd made it …

But he saw nothing.

Just the clearing and the forest beyond.

"So this is how it ends," Phosphorus said.

Michael turned and looked above him.

He looked at Phosphorus, holding the sword at his neck.

"You were everything," he told Phosphorus, as the dark angel stood over him. "You were everything to me, and I want you to know you still will be, even after I'm gone."

"You thought he had a plan," Phosphorus said, then shook his head, the darkness returning to him. "You thought he was watching, and listening."

"He does have a plan."

"So what is this?"

"Part of it."

Phosphorus looked back and could see something in Michael's eyes.

His belief.

His unwavering belief.

And just as he took that in, there was a great noise above them.

Phosphorus turned his head to see what it was, and Michael grabbed a rock and knocked the sword away from his neck.

He rolled away to safety then painfully stood.

They looked at each other.

Their eyes met, one last time, and they both saw together what the noise was and what had come: the other angels of light, the ones who had flown from Heaven with Selaphiel, had finally arrived and come back to Creation.

They joined the battle.

They fought with the light, and against the darkness.

Then the tide of it all began to turn.

The angels of Heaven began to overwhelm those that had brought darkness to Creation, then so it was, and the battle shifted and the few remaining angels of darkness that were left were soon surrounded: Phosphorus, Mamanos, and the others, in the middle of a circle of light, with Baal on the ground next to them, dying.

Phosphorus looked over at Báal.

He watched his last moments.

Then he covered his eyes as Báal's body began to glow then explode into a great cloud of darkness, and when he was gone, Phosphorus slowly turned back to Michael, and the others, and looked at them.

They were all there, together, and arrayed against him.

As he saw them, he smiled, but this smile was different.

This smile was for what could have been, and what he'd now lost.

Michael watched him and he knew his friend, he knew the Light-Bringer, and so he knew what Phosphorus would do next.

"No," Michael whispered, softly.

"I told you," Phosphorus answered. "I know what I am, and so I have to."

"Resist."

"I can't."

"Fight against what's inside."

"I don't fight what's inside . . . I give in to it," he said.

Then he flew.

One last time.

He flew up into the sky then straight towards Michael with his sword raised and Michael couldn't fly himself, not with just one wing, but he raised his own sword, too, and so did all those other angels around him.

He parried Phosphorus' great blow.

And the battle was short.

Phosphorus was quickly overwhelmed by their numbers, by their strength, and by their light.

He was disarmed, knocked from the sky, and fell to the ground.

Then he slowly stood, in front of Michael, weaponless, powerless.

He stood one last time, in judgment, in front of the one who had been his greatest friend.

"Now it's time," he said, nodding. "Now it's the end."

Michael hesitated.

Next to him, Raphael leaned and whispered into his ear.

"It must be done," he said.

Phosphorus undid the straps of his armor and breastplate, and let it fall to the ground, so he stood there bare-chested.

He would make it easier for them.

Michael hesitated, for one more moment.

Then he took a deep breath and walked forward.

He held his sword in his hand as he stood in front of his friend.

"You're wrong," Michael told him. "And you know that you're wrong. It's not the end, and it never will be."

"Then what is it?"

"The beginning," Michael said.

Then he struck.

Michael turned his eyes away as he yelled and plunged his sword deep into Phosphorus' chest.

And as he did, Phosphorus' own eyes went wide.

At first, they went very wide.

Then they closed, and opened again.

He stared back at the angels in front of him as Michael let go of the sword, then he looked at Michael: he looked back at his face, at his body, the wounds covering it and the single wing that was now on his back.

He stood there and looked at his friend.

Phosphorus painfully went forward, and he kissed him, three times, once on each cheek, and then on the lips, the last moment their skin would touch.

Then he backed up again.

He stayed staring at Michael, and the others, then turned his head.

His eyes found Mamanos and the other dark angels that were still with him.

"When it happens," he spoke very softly, his words barely a whisper, meant only and just for them. "I want you to fly, and go after them."

They knew of who he spoke, but there was still one question.

"Which one?" Mamanos asked.

"*Her*," he whispered.

Then his voice failed him.

His body began to shake, and glow, the darkness coming out from the inside, from his heart, from his soul, from all that he was.

It kept growing, growing, inside his body, then his body began to change.

He became a bird.

A leaf.

A titan.

All disguises he'd used in Creation, or evil that he'd brought to it.

An insect.

A different angel.

A spider.

A rock.

Then he ended as a serpent, coiled on the ground.

Everyone was still for a moment, looking at it.

Then the serpent struck, it's body coiling and flexing and flying quickly through the air, in less than a blink, straight towards Michael, straight towards his throat.

And he didn't react.

He just stood there, resigned to what was about to come.

He spread his arms wide, in peace.

Then a sword flashed in front of Michael, travelling in a blinding and precise arc and it cut the serpent in half. The body fell to the ground in two pieces and Michael turned to see Gabriel next to him, holding the then-bloodied sword that had just saved his life.

Michael opened his mouth, about to speak.

But then there was a deep and thunderous explosion that knocked them all from their feet as the great cloud of darkness that had come from Phosphorus' soul burst then rose from what had once been a celestial body.

It rose, rose, higher and higher, until it finally departed Creation.

Michael and the others slowly began to stand again as the darkness started to blow away and disappear, and the noise from the explosion began to fade, too, as it was carried on the wind to all corners of Creation and beyond, though their ears still rang from it and what had come.

But then, as they saw the noise and darkness begin to fade . . .

They also saw what it had done.

It had given Mamanos and the others time to fly.

Michael saw them in the air and he knew where they were going, what they were going to do.

Panic rose in his throat.

"After them!" he yelled.

And all the angels that were left—all the angels still made of light, and of goodness—they spread their wings and rose and flew as fast as they could, trying to make it to where the humans ran, before the dark ones that flew in front of them got there to them first.

THEY'D MADE IT SOME DISTANCE from the clearing, and that's when she finally risked a glance behind her and saw them coming.

The dark angels, the last of them, speeding towards them.

The humans had run as fast as they could, as fast as their legs allowed, but since they didn't have wings, it would never be fast enough.

So when she saw the dark ones gaining on them, she paused and called to the others.

"Stop!" she yelled.

Her husband looked at her, and so did Kain, then they all skidded to a stop next to where she'd already slowed and grabbed hold of Habel next to her.

"What is it?" her husband asked.

Then he turned, and looked, and he saw, too.

He saw the dark angels flying faster even than the wind, and he saw that they would soon be to where the humans stood. She saw the other angels behind them, the angels of light and goodness that followed, but they were too far behind, and they would be too late.

"Go," she heard her husband whisper.

Then he turned and looked at her.

"No," she told him, shaking her head. "I won't leave you."

"Do it, Mom," Kain nodded as he came forward to stand next to his father. "Take Habel and run. We'll hold them. It's the only way."

"We're a family," she said. "That means we stay together."

Her husband opened his mouth, about to speak, one more time, but before any words came the dark angels were on them and the battle began. He raised his sword and parried the first blow, then yelled to his oldest son.

"One of us on each side of them!"

Kain heard and understood.

She watched as her husband went to stand in front of them, and Kain went behind them, so that she and Habel were protected between each.

The dark angels circled overhead.

Then they attacked again.

The angels didn't have much time for that which they'd come to do, they knew, not with the other angels in pursuit, so their attacks were fierce.

One of them came in, too reckless, and she watched as her husband swung his sword in a great arc and stabbed the angel through the chest.

But his sword stuck there.

It was stuck, as the angel fell, and he couldn't pull it out, which left him vulnerable.

He flexed his muscles and tried one more time to rip it free from the chest of the angel where it was held, but one of the other dark angels was on him too quickly, and he let go of the blade as he jumped out of the way of the new attack but the blow still caught him in the torso and he fell to the ground. The dark angel that had brought the blow came to stand over him, even as the other body on the ground next to them—the one with the sword still protruding from its chest—began to glow, and as the body began to glow and disintegrate, she watched as the sword began to come loose from flesh and she ran forward and grabbed and pulled it free.

Then the dark angel turned to look at her.

He smirked, when he saw her, then swung and the force of the blow sent the sword spinning from her hands.

But she still stood there and faced him.

If she was to die, at least she'd die on her feet.

"Run!" her husband shouted from the ground.

But she would do no such thing.

She was standing and looking back north towards where she saw the angels of light just about to reach them, to deliver them, and the dark angel raised and swung his sword, one last time.

Then Gabriel slammed into him from behind.

The force of it knocked the dark angel off-balance and Gabriel grabbed him with his great and strong arms and carried him as he flew higher, higher, and then Raphael came, too, and Gabriel ripped one of the dark angel's arms from his body and tossed it aside, then ran him through with his own sword.

Selaphiel joined the fight, too.

He flew to where Kain fought against the last of the dark angels, the human boy holding his own against them, and Selaphiel watched him for a moment, not realizing behind him the body that was still glowing, glowing, glowing.

And then the body exploded.

It knocked them all from their feet and threw them a great distance from where they'd stood.

The dust began to clear and settle, and as it did, she painfully got back up.

Her ears were still ringing and her eyes still blurry.

She rubbed her eyes, then looked around, trying to find her children.

And then she saw.

She saw that the final dark angel was standing right next to her, his sword raised in his hand, and there was nothing else.

Selaphiel was too far away.

So was Gabriel, and Raphael, and the others.

And where was Michael?

She'd searched the skies when the dark angels had first come, but she hadn't seen him, so she knew she was truly alone.

She was now and finally truly alone.

She looked at the dark angel and he smiled at her.

He smiled because he knew, even if it cost him his life, which it would, that he was going to be able to complete his master's work.

She closed her eyes.

She spread her arms, as Michael had done, too, hoping for time, for peace, for a final prayer . . .

Then he swung, and—

"Mom!"

The angels were too far from her, as she'd seen, but her oldest son wasn't, and he jumped in front of the blow and blocked it.

She opened her eyes.

She saw that even though he'd blocked it, the force with which it had come—from a grown angel against a boy still just on the verge of manhood—the force of it had knocked him off-balance, even with how much he'd changed, how much he'd grown, and he stood there and she saw what would happen next.

"No!" she yelled.

She reached out, tried to stop what would come.

But it was too late.

The dark angel swung once more, and Kain parried the blow, but the angel knocked the blade from his hand.

He was defenseless, vulnerable.

He was exactly as he'd been made.

The dark angel picked Kain's sword up, the one his father had created, then without anything else thrust and ran it straight through Kain's chest, and his eyes went wide. She saw the look, the terror, the life already beginning to slip from him and she reached out to grab him but his hand slid through hers, then he fell.

The dark angel turned back to her and raised the same sword.

By then Selaphiel was on him, with Gabriel, and Raphael, and when they ran him through, they gave his body to another to take far from there so when he exploded in darkness it wouldn't hurt them, and that's then when she fell to the ground, too, next to the body of her son.

She tried to take his hand, but it was slick with blood.

There was blood, blood, too much of it, everywhere.

Then her husband ran and joined her.

He bent down, also, as she rested Kain's head gently in her lap and she watched his life spill out and into the grass around them, and she was powerless to do anything to stop it.

Neither of them knew what they should do.

Neither of them knew how to help him.

So her husband looked up, to the angels, gathered all around them.

"How can we save him?" he asked, with panic in his voice.

The angels looked at them, and they opened their mouths, but they had no answers.

They didn't know either.

They had no notion of the rules of Creation or of mortal life or how death could be defeated or reversed, because that was a fate none could escape, they knew, not mortal or angel.

"... *father* ... *mother* ..." Kain spoke, and the words came softly, weakly.

These would be his final breaths in Creation, she knew, and so did he.

"We're here," she told him, through her tears.

She didn't bother to brush them away.

Then her husband took his hand, too.

"We're right here next to you," he said.

She stroked Kain's cheek and he tried to reach his hand out, to touch hers, to touch his father's, and he tried to tell them something, too, but then his strength failed him and no more words came, and he lay still.

His breathing had gotten shallower, shallower.

Then it stopped altogether.

She watched as his once-bright eyes slowly faded, then finally went empty and blank as they stared up, up at the bright sky above them, up at the heavens ...

And then he was gone.

Her oldest, her first-born.

She still held him in her arms, slick with the blood he'd spilled across her, across him, across them, and everywhere else, too. She held him tightly against her body, then he held her, her husband, their family together one last time.

But she realized there was one missing.

She reached for Habel, next to her.

She reached for him, but she didn't find him.

Where was he, and where had he been?

She turned and looked and saw him some paces from where they were, and he was sitting with his eyes closed and breathing in deep, measured intervals.

"Habel ..." she said.

He heard her voice.

He was silent for a moment, a moment longer.

Then he opened his eyes.

She looked at him, curiously, at the look she saw, then he spoke.

"Can you carry him?" Habel asked softly.

And she saw he wasn't looking back at her; he was looking at Gabriel, the largest and strongest among them, and Gabriel looked back at Habel and even as young as he was, especially as young as he seemed, speaking to an angel, there was something about the nature of his question, the tenor of his voice, the strength of conviction in his tone.

"Of course I can carry him," Gabriel said. "But where would you have me go?"

"Back to the clearing," Habel said. "As quickly as possible."

Gabriel hesitated for a moment, then he looked to her.

But she didn't move, she didn't speak, she didn't do anything.

So Gabriel nodded to Habel and slowly went towards where Kain's body was still in her lap, her tears wet and fresh on his cold cheek, and Gabriel gently picked the body up, and she didn't stop him. There was something about Habel's voice and his command that she didn't question, but her husband would, as they watched Gabriel rise into the sky with the body of their oldest in his arms.

"What's he doing?" her husband wondered aloud.

Then Habel went to Selaphiel.

She watched as he whispered into the angel's ear, then Selaphiel nodded and picked him up, too, and pumped his great wings and began to rise.

Then she knew . . . she knew what he'd done.

And what she knew made her chest fill and swell with pride because he'd done exactly what she'd taught him: he'd turned inside and asked the voice he found there, and now it was happening.

It was something she'd taught him, her son, her own flesh and blood, and it was something that had been such an important part of her life in Creation, but she'd lost it somewhere. Before her children came, before the trouble with her husband, and all the rest, she'd done it every day . . .

But when was the last time she now had?

She couldn't remember, she realized, as she shook her head, but her son had: her youngest, beautiful son.

And what had the voice told him?

There was only one way to find out, she knew, as she stood and watched as above her Gabriel flew into the distance with Selaphiel next to him and the others following behind.

"What's going on?" her husband asked again, from his place next to her.

"We have to go after them," she told him.

She raised her arms.

He saw what she did, and so he did, too.

Two of the angels came and lifted them from earth and carried them after the others, flying above the trees, flying above Creation and looking down at it in a way they hadn't ever done before, then soon they were back.

They landed in the clearing and before her feet even touched the ground, she started to run.

She was looking for Habel, for Kain, for the other angels, then she saw them.

They were there, together, by one of the great trees.

But not the one she expected to find them next to.

They weren't next to the larger of the two, where she'd just stood with Phosphorus, not so very long ago, and where she'd eaten the fruit she'd sworn she would never eat. That's not where they stood, not at the Tree of Knowledge; instead, they stood at the tree next to it, at the smaller one, with Kain's body on the ground beneath its branches.

The Tree of Life.

Of course, she thought.

Of course . . .

Her mind had been so occupied by the Tree of Knowledge and what it represented and what was contained within its fruit she never stopped to think about the tree next to it, and what might be in the fruit that was there on its branches, hanging lower to the ground . . . hanging where even a child could reach.

She thought of all the afternoons Habel had sat there.

Then she watched as he reached up and picked a piece of the fruit from the branches and looked down at it in his hand. It wasn't bright and vivid of color like the fruit of the tree next to it: it was softer, duller, muted in color and odd in shape, but it didn't matter.

He put the fruit to his own mouth.

She was about to call out, but then stopped herself, and she didn't.

Next to her, her husband came to where she stood and reached out and took her hand in his as they watched Habel put the fruit to his mouth and then bite.

He bit, and chewed . . .

But he didn't swallow.

Instead, he took from his mouth the small piece of fruit he'd made into the size of a bite and had crushed to a more pulpy and liquid state with his chewing, and he bent down next to his brother. She watched as he opened Kain's mouth and put the chewed fruit inside, and then closed it, and they all waited. She realized she was holding her breath as the fruit went down his throat, towards his stomach, where it would be digested and then spread throughout him.

They all stood there for another moment, angel and human alike.

They stood there and they waited.

And as they did, Habel bent his head and closed his eyes and began a prayer, and then soon the others did, too—following the lead of the boy, of the very youngest amongst them—and they waited for the fruit to break down and spread to every corner and inch of Kain's body: his stomach, his limbs, his lungs, his brain, and finally . . .

His heart.

A sharp inhale of breath.

They all opened their eyes and watched as Kain slowly sat upright underneath the tree, looking at the branches and fruit above him, then at his brother next to him. Then he looked past his brother, and at all the others, his parents, and the angels, too.

"What happened?" he asked.

For a long moment, no one answered, then Gabriel finally spoke, emotion choking his voice.

"You were delivered," he said.

"How?" Kain asked, still not understanding.

Gabriel looked from Kain, to Habel, next to him, then to her, and to him, too, her husband, and instead of answering he just nodded, once, then with the rest of the angels started to walk towards the edge of the clearing. They began to spread their great wings, just about to fly up and into the sky and leave the humans alone, once again, but before they left, she knew there was one last thing.

"Where is he?" she asked.

Gabriel paused, then turned, and looked at her.

He knew who she was asking about.

"He's gone before us," Gabriel told her, very simply.

"So what do we do?" she asked him. "What do we do now?"

Gabriel kept looking back at them, with Raphael, and Selaphiel next to him, and all the others, and he knew what she meant, what she was asking.

He kept looking back at them . . .

Then he heard Michael's words again, his words from just after Creation had first been made.

That will be up to them, he'd said.

So Gabriel didn't answer.

He just smiled and nodded again then turned and spread his wings once more. He took a few steps, then his wings began to pump—up and down, up and down—and he rose into the sky and so did all the others, around him, then they turned and started into the distance as the humans watched them. The humans all stood there, together, and watched as the angels disappeared over the peaks of the mountains and towards the then-setting sun, and they continued to watch in silence until the angels were all gone, then they were all that was left in Creation.

They stood there, together, and for a moment longer.

Then Kain turned to them again.

"What really happened?" he asked, the same question once more.

She waited another moment, staring, still at the sky.

Then she turned to him, too.

She looked into his eyes, into his heart, into his soul.

"Everything," she finally told him.

"How did I come back?" he asked. "What did you do?"

Kain was looking at her, and she looked back at him.

But she just smiled and shook her head.

"It wasn't me," she told him. "I couldn't save you. It was your brother."

She watched as Kain turned and looked at Habel standing there next to them, taking him in, and really taking him in: here was an older brother, twice the size and built with more than twice the strength, and he was looking down at a younger brother who had just performed the greatest miracle that could ever possibly be performed, and in that moment they all learned something true about power and love and hope, from what had just happened, and how it had happened.

"I love you," Kain told him simply.

"I know," Habel said.

Then Kain hugged him.

He held him, as closely as he could, Habel's head pressed against his chest, but she didn't look at Kain.

She looked at her youngest, who now looked back at her, too.

She looked at him and saw all she'd tried to teach him, because there it was, right there in his eyes: all the wisdom she'd ever had, and had now passed on, and then even more besides. She had one son who was his father, she knew, but she had another son, too, who was hers, who was only hers, and she saw all that reflected in his eyes and finally understood what it was to be a parent and to pass along the best of what and who she was.

She had never been more proud, she realized.

Her heart had never been more full.

"So what happens now?" her husband asked, from his place next to her.

She took that in for a moment, thinking about it.

"Now . . ." she said. "We prepare."

"For what?"

"I don't know."

"The fruit was eaten, so this is the end, right?" Kain asked, also looking at her, and she opened her mouth, about to answer both of them, and she knew what she was about to say, but then paused and hesitated: she reached back inside herself again, like her youngest had just done, and what she found there was different, and the exact opposite of what had just been said. She heard the words that were resonating inside, and she listened to them, then she smiled again before she spoke the words out loud.

"No," she said, shaking her head. "It's not the end."

"Then what is it that we prepare for?" her husband asked.

"The beginning," she told them.

Then she looked at each of them in turn: Habel first, then Kain, and finally her husband, next to her.

"Now . . . we prepare for the beginning," she told them again.

22

MORE TIME PASSED in Creation and nothing changed. No more angels came, light or dark, or anything else.

She didn't know what to do, or when their time in the clearing would end, as had been promised when she ate the fruit, so she decided they would simply carry on as if she hadn't eaten, as if they hadn't been banished. So her husband and Kain started working again, in the fields. Much of the crop and trees of the orchard had been destroyed during the second great battle between darkness and light, so they saved what trees and crops they could and replanted and started anew with the rest that couldn't be saved. She began to go back into Creation again, with Habel, to search and forage for fruits and nuts and other foods to subsidize what they'd lost in the fields, then soon after they had their stores replenished, she began to stay back at the clearing while Habel went alone, and she stayed because both her children were growing.

They were growing, seemingly even faster than they had before, and that meant they needed new tunics.

So she sat underneath the Tree of Life as she worked, weaving the fabric she'd made together, and sewing it into the shape they'd wear, and she would pray over her work, too. As she sewed the tunics and fashioned them into very precise body-shaped patterns, it was prayers of strength and prayers of protection that she prayed. Then when she wasn't praying, she watched her husband and oldest son in the fields. Since everything that had happened, they'd each returned to their roles in the clearing, the same as they had been before, and while Kain didn't talk much about what had happened to him, when he thought no one was watching, she would see him look down at his chest, at the scar that was still there, just below his heart: at the place where his life had been taken, and then given again.

They would continue to work, her husband and oldest, as the sun beat down on them . . .

Then Habel would return from the forest.

He would bring with him whatever he'd found that day.

She would watch as he would go to them, first, and they'd take from his basket a small piece of fruit or handful of nuts to help get them through the last of the work before dinner. And as she'd watch them from her place under the tree, she would think about his future, her youngest. He would never be as big, as tall, or as strong and broad of shoulder as his brother, or even his father. He would be a different type of man, she knew. He wouldn't ever be the type that would find pleasure in the fields. He would be one who gathered, one who collected and prayed, and one who found himself, and God, in silence and nature, rather than sweat and muscle. He would have strength, too, of course, but it wouldn't be the same as strength was for other men; it would be strength of his own type.

No, that's not right, she thought.

That's not right at all.

Because his strength . . . it was the same as her strength.

MORE TIME PASSED and still no change came as they continued their routine; she worked under the tree, her husband and Kain worked in the field, and Habel went out alone into Creation. She kept working on the new tunics, weaving and sewing and making even more fabric and thread each day, from her place in the shade, but soon the tunics were nearly complete and she began to become eager to return to Creation again, herself, and all the places she loved outside their clearing.

So one morning she woke early.

It was still dark and everyone was sleeping and she went by herself.

The sun was not yet up and there was still mist and dew on the grass that clung to her ankles as she walked through the clearing, then towards the forest, and further north. She followed the river and the same path she'd taken after she'd first woken up, so many years ago, and started to travel south, in the opposite direction she travelled now. Then when she got to it, she paused at the place near the river where she'd first seen him, and where she'd first seen Michael, too. She thought about how she'd felt then, when she'd first seen him, then she thought about how she felt when she thought of him now, and again, at that particular moment, so many years later.

Was it the same?

No, she realized.

There was less innate curiosity, less excitement, and more familiarity.

But that didn't mean she felt less for him.

It actually meant, she found, that when she stood there and once again looked inside herself, she felt even more for him: she felt more because of all they'd experienced and all they'd been through and how they'd fought and persevered and were still together. She also thought of the family they'd created, because the two were now so irrevocably linked and intertwined, and she thought of each of them and their children who were also small pieces of their parents and how it all came together to make a unique and irreplaceable whole.

She thought about all that, and she smiled.

Then she slowly kept walking.

She continued on through the rest of the forest and the trees began to thin and part, and she came out on the other side of them, and into the field where she'd woken up, the field of dandelions and wild flowers.

She went to the exact place where she began, then she sat down again.

She sat there and looked all around and as she did, her mind turned to what she'd thought the last time she was there, about the man that was in Creation with her, her husband, and how she hoped there'd never be any more secrets or questions or anything else like that between them. She realized now, again, so many years later, that it was perhaps more complicated than that, but she also realized it was perhaps better that way; she realized perhaps it was better in the way it was and not in the way she'd once wanted it to be. Because without secrets, she realized, where would there be discovery? Where would there be growth? Where would there be room for new truths to be found and uncovered?

She kept looking around.

She looked at the forest, the river, the flowers, the waterfall in the distance, and the mountains.

The sun was just beginning to crest over the peaks and she breathed deeply as a purple-orange glow came, one that was unlike anything she'd ever yet seen, and the brilliant light that came from it spread across all Creation, as far as she could see. She took it in as she sat there then felt on her cheeks the warmth it brought and as she felt it, she thought back to the last time she'd been there and the other thing she'd wondered that day and she wondered now how she could have ever thought what she'd thought then, about God, and how she didn't know him, and how he didn't speak to her, because there he was, she saw.

There he was, in all that was there, and all that she could see.

There he was in everything, in all Creation, in all the beauty that was in front of her.

She breathed deeply again, taking it all in.

And as she did, she slowly blinked against the tears that came to her eyes, unbidden, both at the beauty of it and the gift she knew she'd just been given, and the gift she would carry within her wherever she went and for all the rest of her days. Because it was a gift that had come directly from God, she knew, so it was also the very greatest of gifts.

"Thank you," she spoke, very quietly.

Then there was silence for a moment.

There was nothing but silence and brilliant light and the familiar scent of the dandelions and wild flowers, for one more moment, then she heard a voice, coming from behind her.

"I'm glad you decided to come back," the voice said.

She heard and recognized the familiar tone and pitch.

She slowly turned to see Michael standing there, in the field, watching her. She hadn't heard him land or walk towards her or anything else and when she took him in, she saw he walked with a slight limp still, and she also saw his shoulder. It was the one with the wing that Phosphorus had cut off during the battle, and where there had once been a wing, there was now only a small and new growth that was just a fraction of the size of the intact wing next to it. She walked closer to him, and before she reached him, before she touched him, she looked at him and she asked:

"May I?"

He nodded, so she reached further.

She reached out and touched it, very gently, running her hand softly over the new growth for a moment, and for a moment he let her.

"Will it return?" she asked.

"Eventually," he nodded.

Then he took her hand from his wing and turned to face her.

She looked into his eyes, deep into his eyes.

She knew what came next.

"You're here because it's the end, aren't you?" she asked him.

"Yes."

"When?"

"Not yet . . . but soon."

"And where are we to go?"

"You already know," he told her. "You've already seen it, where you will go, the way out from Creation."

She thought about that for a moment, then the images came rushing back to her. She remembered her time wandering through Creation and following the great river as it flowed south. She thought of what she'd seen, the river passing between and through the un-passable mountains, and shook her head.

"It's too dangerous," she said. "We can't swim it."

"No," he told her. "But there's another way."

"How?"

He stepped closer to her, and raised his hand, with his palm facing towards her forehead.

"May I?" he asked.

She knew what he wanted, what he was asking.

So she nodded.

He placed his palm on her forehead, and as soon as he did, everything went black. And then, once again, the same way as before, after a moment the darkness began to slowly lift. Then when it did, she could see, and this is what she saw:

She saw a structure, made of pieces of wood fashioned together, and she saw how the wood fit together to make it.

She saw the work it would take, and how it would have to be done.

Then she saw further.

She saw how it was able to float on the water, on the river, and how it sailed through the currents they wouldn't have been able to swim on their own, then how it continued on its way through the mountains, too, and towards whatever lay there on the other side of them.

She took it all in, then she heard a word, a single word.

Boat.

She repeated it, over and over in her mind . . .

Then the darkness lifted and she was back in the field.

She looked around and opened her mouth to speak, and though she opened her mouth, no words came, because she saw Michael was gone, and that she was alone again.

She looked around, once more, at everything.

But there was no trace of him, not anywhere that she looked.

WHEN SHE ARRIVED BACK IN THE CLEARING, everyone else had woken from their sleep, though they hadn't yet started their work for the day. They all watched from the house as she came back to the clearing from the path in the forest, their eyebrows raised in question, then when she came to them, she gave them the answers to that which she knew they wanted to ask.

She told them where she went, and why.

She told them she'd seen Michael, and spoken with him, then she told them how he'd shown her what would come next.

"What did you see?" her husband asked her. "What did he show you?"

And then she told them about her vision and what she'd heard.

She told them about the boat, and how it was made from wood that had been cut and fashioned together, and how it would float on the water of the river and carry them south and through and past the mountains that bordered Creation and then on to whatever else lay beyond.

And what else was it that was beyond?

She could see the question in each of their eyes, looking back at her.

No, that's not right, she thought.

She could see it in the eyes of her husband, and the eyes of Kain, his son, but in Habel's eyes?

In his eyes, she could see something else.

It was in his eyes she saw something that bordered on sadness, she thought, though she wouldn't know for many years just exactly what it was.

They gathered wood from the forest.

And they did it together, as a family.

They went back to the area where the battle had taken place, first, and there were broken and shattered trees that were at the edge of the clearing: some had been uprooted entirely, some had trunks that were hewn in half and only part-standing, and some just had branches that had snapped and fallen to the ground. Some of the pieces could be carried, but in order for them to be fashioned together and in order to be able to get the larger pieces back to the clearing, they would need something more than just their strength.

So her husband showed her what he would do.

He heated more of the rock he'd found in the bed of the river—the rock that wasn't grey, like all the rest, but the one that had the pink and orange hue mixed in—and he created a new mold, too, one that wasn't in the shape of a sword, or weapon, but something else. It was long and straight with handles on each side and a sharp and serrated edge on the bottom of it. He showed her how it would work—how he and Kain would each hold a side of it, and pull it back and forth, to cut the large trees into pieces of manageable sizes—and how they would then take the pieces of manageable sizes and use the tool to fashion the individual pieces into the exact shape they needed.

Saw, she heard him call what he'd made.

Where had the idea come from?

Inside, his eyes told her.

So she nodded and knew that it would be.

He used the saw in the forest with Kain and she carried the pieces they made back to the clearing with Habel, and as soon as they had enough pieces, they began to fashion them together. She called on every bit of memory she still had of the image she'd seen to give them the guidance they needed, and while the process was slow, steady progress was made.

The vessel began to take shape.

Then they tested it on the water.

They pushed what they had down to the river and found it could float, as she'd seen, so then from that moment on, the day they'd have to leave would soon be there, she knew. And she could see it in her family's eyes, in their movements, and interactions with each other, that they knew, too.

They knew that one life was about to end, and another would soon begin.

Then one morning, after she woke and they'd all started working, she heard a voice.

It's time, the voice said.

She'd been standing in the clearing and looked around to see if her husband had heard it, or either of her sons, and they hadn't.

No one had . . . except her.

But the voice was so clear, the words so firm, she knew what they were.

She knew exactly what they were, and where they were from.

So she gathered her family together and told them what she'd heard and where it had come from and now what they must do. It was a moment that had been a long time coming, they all knew, and now it had. They ate their last meal in silence. As they did, she looked down at the table where they sat, the one her husband had made for them—the first thing he'd made, in Creation—and she thought again, also, of the vision she'd had of exact moments like that one, and as she thought of it and saw it again, right there, in front of her, a tear then came to her eyes.

Her boys didn't notice.

But he did.

He reached out and took her hand in his, under the table.

Then when the meal ended, they each went separate ways.

Kain left to go back into Creation again like he had so many times before, and to her surprise, so did Habel, too, though they didn't go in the same direction. She let them leave, alone, not asking any questions of either of them, then when they were gone, she was alone with her husband. She turned to look at him, at his eyes, and his were already there, looking into hers, waiting for hers, then he took her by the hand again and led her in the opposite direction. He led her away from the house, and the clearing, and back towards the river, the one that was their river. It was the same one that had led them there, to their clearing, their home, and it was the same that would also take them from it. And they were there again, on the bank, and they didn't need words anymore, they just needed the moon that was rising in the distance over the mountains and the small bit of light it brought as they lay down next to each other. They weren't in a hurry. They had the whole night, they knew, so they took their time with their love. She felt his skin and the scars that now covered his body, and he felt hers, too, the places on her body that had changed since she'd had children, and in his touch, she could feel his thoughts and she was scared, at first, but all his thoughts told her, she found, was that he thought she was more beautiful than she'd ever been. She thought their love could have never been better than it had been that day after the pool, after the waterfall, after the first time, but it was. And it was better because it was different, she realized. It wasn't physical anymore. It was physical, of course, but it was more than that, too.

When it was finished, they lay there together, and she looked at him, next to her.

"What are you thinking?" he asked, his voice no more than a whisper.

They were leaving their home the next day; they were leaving their home, never to return again, and she thought back and remembered the first time they'd lay together, and what his eyes had said to her then.

You're my home, they'd said.

Then they said it again, she knew, as he looked at her.

And so it would be, she felt.

And it would be enough.

They rose together and went back to their house and when they went inside, they saw that Kain and Habel had already returned and were in their beds, with their eyes closed, sleeping, chests rising and falling, up and down. They kissed them each on the forehead then went to their own bed and lay down in it, together, one last time. He held her, his arms wrapped around her body, and they'd experienced so much, they knew. They'd already experienced so much and there would still be so much more to come, though it wouldn't be in Creation. She thought of it all, where they'd come from and where they were going, and she realized she still had one wish, and that was that she wanted to see Creation, one more time, and see it in the same way she'd seen it when the angels had picked her up and carried her back to the clearing and to the tree where Habel had returned his brother's life to him. Her wish was to be able to see it again from those heights, and in that way, the entirety of it, the vastness. But it was impossible, she knew. It was impossible, and could never happen. So she closed her eyes, for one last time, in Creation . . . and that's then when she flew.

23

$\mathscr{S}$HE ROSE FROM HER BODY, up towards the roof of the house, then she went further, and through the roof. She wasn't awake, she knew, but she also wasn't sleeping, either; it was the same feeling as when the dark angel had first come to tempt her, but this time, now, this wasn't temptation . . . it was freedom.

She rose above the house, and clearing, and took in all of Creation.

She saw the forest, the river, and the mountains in the distance.

She looked to the east, to the south, to the west, and the north, she looked at all of it, illuminated by moonlight, as she flew. She had no wings, but she soared over all that was below anyways, the same as the angels soared, and she saw the world in the way they saw the world, too, as she'd asked. She took it in, then her eyes went to the waterfall to the north, and the rock above it, and a great many memories came rushing back when she saw it.

Then she turned south, one more time.

She saw a different mountain there, a high peak and plateau—the highest in all Creation, she saw—and she didn't know why she was drawn to it, but she was, so she went. She flew south and eventually came to it and landed softly on the plateaued rock at the peak then looked back at everything. She saw all of Creation, from there, one more time. Then she turned her eyes south. She could see what was on the other side now, and from the vantage where she stood it didn't look much different than Creation to her, and all she knew and was used to.

"I know it looks the same," she heard the familiar voice again, behind her. "But it's not."

She looked back and up and saw Michael descending slowly from the clouds.

His injured wing had grown more since the last time she'd seen him, and though he flew unevenly because of it, he still flew, and when he landed on the plateau and took his first steps, she saw his limp was gone, too. He came closer to where she stood then stood there, also, taking her in, and this was the moment, she knew. This was the moment of anger, and wrath, and punishment, for what she'd done, all that had changed and been ruined because of her and her decision. That's what she was expecting to hear, and what she thought she deserved to hear.

But instead, the angel smiled.

"You did well," he told her.

She opened her mouth, about to speak, but then her words changed, after hearing his, and she shook her head.

"I ate the fruit," she said, not understanding. "I did the one thing you forbid me to do."

"No, not me," Michael told her. "God."

"Which makes it even greater."

"He gave you the gift of will so it could be used, and that was his greatest gift, the greatest one of all. You took his gift and chose to eat, even though it was forbidden. But why?"

She looked back at him, blinking.

Then she told him, very simply, what she'd known, what she'd always known, and felt in her heart. She saw her husband in front of her, before she ate, and her two sons, next to him, too, during a perfect afternoon together, laughing, and she'd seen a meal shared at the end of the day at a table that had been carved by hand and love for that exact purpose.

"Because if it's a choice between love and anything else, even Creation . . ." she spoke slowly, deliberately. "Then it's not really a choice at all, is it?"

"So you understand."

"All I understand is that's what's in my heart."

"And if you understand your heart, then what else is there?"

She took that in and processed it as she turned again to look out past Creation and towards what Michael had called World, and the place that would soon be their new home.

Her eyes settled, taking it in.

"What's it like?" she asked him.

"It's the same as here, but also different," he told her, and as he spoke, she found she could see what he described, even without him touching her forehead this time. "There will be more weather," he continued. "Snow, which you haven't yet seen. The soil will be harder to till and the crops more difficult to grow and keep alive. And there will be less food to go around because of it. There will be sickness. There will be age, and pain, and death. But there will also be new growth."

She flinched when she heard the word death and it was because of the future she'd seen glimpses of, with her sons, with both her sons, the future that had first come when her husband had put the sword in her oldest's hand; the sword he swore would protect them but had actually taken their child's life, only for another child to come and bring it back and erase what his father had done.

"I've seen something," she said. "Something in the future, with the two boys."

"Yes," Michael nodded, his face serious.

"What will happen to them?"

"Your oldest will continue to be a tiller of the soil, like his father, and your youngest . . . he will continue to be a gatherer, like his mother."

"Are there more of us?" she asked. "Will there be another out there in the World, like my oldest searches for here in Creation?"

"There will be," Michael nodded, then she saw that, too, another female the same age as Kain walking from the forest and coming towards the new home they would make in the World. "She will come, and it will change everything, and that's when it will happen. You'll bring a piece of the fruit with you from Creation; not from the Tree of Knowledge, but from the Tree of Life, and you'll try to use it in the same way your youngest did, with his brother, after all that comes. But the fruit doesn't work in the World the same way it does here in Creation."

She saw pieces of the future, of what he told her, and it brought tears to her eyes.

Michael watched as she wiped them.

"So that's it? That will be the end?"

"No," he told her. "Even if a soul should depart, their memory will always be eternal, and with that memory in your heart you'll have more children even after the first two. There will be another son that comes, and he'll be neither a tiller of the soil like his father, or a gatherer, like his mother, and after the ordeal and pain that comes to your family with the first and second, this third son . . . he's the one who will be the beginning, the beginning of everything, the father of all else that will come."

"How?"

"There will eventually be a flood," Michael told her. "There will be a very great flood," and then she saw as he told her—she saw the warring tribes of the World, all the humans who had forgotten God and stopped living in his image and all the different weapons they carried and used against each other, and she thought: why don't we ever learn? Why can't we ever learn? Then she saw the great waters continuing to rise and how they came to overtake the tribes and the land, then in this flood she saw something else: she saw glimpses of a small vessel bobbing amongst the waves. "And it's your third son's line," Michael continued, "the tenth generation, descended from him, that will save the world from the waters that will come and help both human and beast continue safely into the next generations." She saw all this then, too, and she saw the vessel more closely. She saw as it survived the rough and apocalyptic waters then came to land among the mountains of Ararat, and she saw the family that then came from it, and how they would spread from that point. "And the progeny that will rise from his family and line," Michael continued to tell her, "they will go forth after the flood and populate the world to ready it for the coming of the Son."

She took all that in, all the information she'd just been given, and just seen. Then she thought back to Creation. She thought back to Phosphorus and the other dark angels and the look in their eyes. She saw more families that would come after hers, so many more families that would come and not all of them looked like her, or them, but they were all still and truly made of God and so they were beautiful, also, and it's those families who were the ones that darkness tried to attack and erase and she didn't know why, just that it did, and that was the eternal battle that was being fought and always would be: between those who thought they had a monopoly on God, and in their ignorance, and pride, didn't realize that God is all, and in all, and so who are they to say who is, and who is not? And she also knew what all that meant.

"He's not gone, is he?" she asked Michael, very softly.

"No," Michael shook his head. "It's a battle that's been started between good and evil, between darkness and light, and he'll never be very far away, him and those who serve him, so it's a battle that will never truly end."

"Is there any hope for him?"

"Sometimes evil is just evil; sometimes there is no redemption."

"What can we do?"

She watched as Michael thought back to something, back to what Phosphorus had told him and were very nearly his last words in Heaven and as an angel of God:

I am only as he made me, Phosphorus had said.

Michael thought about it and knew those words had been truth.

They were truth for Phosphorus, for who there would be no redemption, and the words were truth for Michael, too, as well as all the other angels and humans and all else there was and would be.

"The only thing that we can do," Michael finally told her, "the only thing we ever can do, is love each other as much as we can and teach that love to as many as possible."

She heard his words and took them in, her eyes turned down as she thought about it, turning it over and over in her mind, a million different thoughts running through her; thoughts of the future, and them, and of everything she knew and had just learned.

Then she looked up and met his eyes again.

"How will we be remembered?" she finally asked him.

"Is that important to you?"

"Yes."

"Why?"

"Because it's our story; because it's who we were."

She saw the surprise in his eyes, at her question.

But she also saw he would answer.

"People will get it wrong, what happened here," he told her, seeing all else that would come. "People will get it wrong and they'll make up lies to suit their own needs. They'll build houses that they'll claim are God's houses, but are really theirs, and in these places they'll say you ate the fruit from weakness and created sin, that you came from him, that you were made second in Creation and thus should be second in all else, and people will believe those lies they're told, for many thousands of years. These same people will use your story and many others along with yours to try to fashion the world as they would have it fashioned, not God, and for their benefit, and people will listen to them. Too many people will listen."

"Why?"

"Because they'll want to; because it'll be easier."

"But why wouldn't they search for truth? Won't they know that it's there, inside of them, waiting to be found, if they only cared to quiet themselves and look?"

"Some will. They'll search for truth, and some will even find it, but for a long time they'll be silenced by those who see and feel only power when they look inside. They'll give you a name that's not your name, one that was not given by the wind, and they'll all be told that this is a story about how the first of their kind came to fall. They won't realize, until they take the time to look inside themselves again, that it's really in fact the opposite of that."

She heard these words from Michael and was silent again for a moment. And then she saw all this, too, the entire span of human history and the great noise that would come and push people further from God and from light and how her story would be used to discriminate, to repress, to persecute. She saw bits of dissent along the way: a priestess blessed with vision, speaking her truth to deaf ears behind the doomed walls of Troy; a merchant who had travelled to all corners of the world then returned to the ancient streets of Babylon; a golden conqueror from the West, setting off in search of the rising sun; a brave Roman soldier, crucified for speaking what was deemed heresy; a monk sitting in cold and damp darkness, with pen and paper in shaking hand, defying both order and vows; two farmers in Egypt, uncovering a long-preserved secret; a young man, returning home, armed only with vision and truth, alone, alone, always alone, until the story is finished, until the story is told, until she finally comes to him. She saw all this in quick bits and flashes the same as she'd seen before, then she saw a shift. Even with the great noise that was still there in the world, she saw it all start to lessen: she saw things begin to slowly change, to evolve, to progress, after her story is written and begins to spread.

She smiled to herself as she saw it, because while she saw all the darkness that would come in the next many, many thousands of years, she also saw that the darkness wouldn't be forever.

It wouldn't be forever at all.

"What do you see?" Michael whispered.

She waited for a moment, letting all that had just passed in front of her settle, and then letting it build.

"Eventually they will understand," she finally told Michael, sharing her vision with him. "It will take a long time, perhaps much too long of a time, but eventually someone will come and tell them what really happened, and the people will listen. And that's all that matters."

"So it's true then," he said. "It's true, and you see."

"Yes," she nodded, then turned to look at him. "And I understand my part in it all . . . but what about you?"

He was looking out, at all that was in front of them.

He was looking out at Creation and all God's work.

"We'll continue to guide, and to protect, whenever we're asked and called upon, but nothing more," he told her, then finally turned from Creation and back to meet her eyes. "This is your story," he said with strength, with power, with truth. "This is your story, as it always has been, from the very beginning . . . and as it always will be."

She stood there and faced him, on top of the highest mountain of Creation.

The great angel that was across from her had just laid the whole history of the world at their feet, all the greatness of eternity, and that was what was now between them.

She opened her mouth, about to speak . . .

But no more words came.

And he just smiled.

"I know," he said, nodding.

Then he paused.

"I know," he said again.

And that would be enough.

He walked closer and stood in front of her and there was one more look, one last smile, one final glimpse of great feathered wings and celestial light and perfect, pure beauty.

Then he raised his hand.

He moved it forward and placed it on her head where he used his palm to gently rest over and cover her eyes, and as soon as he did . . . everything again went dark.

24

$\mathcal{I}$T WAS THE END OF THE TIME for the humans in Creation, but it also wasn't the end. Michael returned to Heaven after he'd left her and the first thing he did was go to find Selaphiel. The reason why the first thing he did was to search for the young angel was because of something he'd seen, something he'd just seen in her eyes when they were speaking of Knowledge, and God, and Love. He'd first seen it then, there on the mountain at the edge of Creation, and it was a feeling that grew inside him as he left and returned and it grew so strong he knew it couldn't be ignored.

He found Selaphiel standing on top of the great walls.

The young angel was looking first one way, back at Heaven, behind him, then the other, into the distance, away from the palace and towards all that was there and beyond.

"What do you see?" Michael asked, as he climbed the steps and walked towards him.

Selaphiel turned and saw Michael there.

He waited for a moment and then shrugged.

"A choice," he said simply.

"You were right," Michael told him.

"About what?"

"Everything that you said before: you need to leave here again, and you need to go back."

"Go back where?" Selaphiel asked, his nose wrinkling with the question.

"To where you were when you heard her prayer. You need to go back to where you were, and keep going."

"What will I find?"

Michael looked back at him because he knew then what it was that Selaphiel would find, and it was the human in Creation that had shown it to him. She'd shown him what belief and trust can bring us, in whatever form it comes, and how it leads us on its path to the only thing worth searching for.

"Everything," he said. "That's what you'll find."

"I don't understand."

"Bodies die, of course they do," Michael told him. "But what is a body?"

Selaphiel waited for a moment, processing that, turning it over in his mind then finally understanding. Michael came forward as he saw the understanding come to the young angel and he kissed Selaphiel softly, on both cheeks, as Phosphorus had done to him, then backed up again and they looked at each other.

"I'll come back," Selaphiel said, nodding. "This time I leave for a reason, and it's so I can come back."

"I know," Michael smiled.

Then with one last look, Selaphiel turned and spread his great wings and exploded into the sky, up towards the clouds and all that was beyond. Michael knew what Selaphiel would find and it made him smile even wider. He knew how Selaphiel would return to the mountains where he was when her prayer had reached him, then how he would go even further. He would search amongst the distant peaks and valleys, then he would come to it, the moment, the moment his life would begin again. Angels die, as we all do, but then they're also born again, as we all are, because souls aren't bodies, souls are eternal, and that's what he would find: he would find a pair of new wings, and they would unwrap from where they covered a naked and perfectly unmarked body, then when the angel that was born turned to him, he would see bright green eyes looking back and his soul which had been torn and broken would then finally be whole again. She'd taught Michael something, with the choice she'd made, and how she'd lived during her time in Creation, and Selaphiel had taught him something, too, with his choices, and how he'd lived in Heaven, and when he'd left. If only Michael had learned these things earlier, he thought, then it all might have been different, it all might have been so very different—with Phosphorus, Heaven, Creation, everything—his friend might still be the Light-Bringer, the Morningstar, and God's favorite, and his, too, but no, he thought, no . . . he had to put it from his mind because there had been a plan, and there still was a plan. And he was a part of it, and so were the angels, both light and dark, and the humans, and every other thing that had been created, too, and the plan was greater than even the sum of all those souls and hearts and stories and words that had been seen and felt and said from the dawn of time until that very moment, and also all the time that would come after.

On and on, as he'd once said.

"Is it done?"

He heard a voice next to him and turned himself to see Gabriel climbing the stairs, with Raphael beside him, then when they reached the top of the wall, they came to stand next to him. The three angels stood there, together, at the same great height, on top of the same great wall, and they looked out at all that was there in front of them and beyond.

"Yes," Michael nodded. "It's done."

"It's all been written, hasn't it?" Raphael said. "From the very beginning."

"Yes, it has."

"So what do we do now?" Gabriel asked.

They waited for another moment, together, then they received their answer.

There had been a time, not very long before that moment, when all Michael had wanted and all that he'd prayed for was to hear the words of God again. He'd heard them before, soft and comforting, strong and powerful, but he longed to hear them once more, to guide him, to tell him he was still on the path and doing his work and carrying out his plan. Michael had prayed for that reassurance for many nights, and in that moment, it finally came, and he spoke to all three angels and they heard what he said. But the angels didn't hear his words in the way they each spoke to each other; rather, they each heard his words in their hearts, and they felt him in their souls. Then along with the words, something else miraculous happened. The walls and the palace and Heaven itself, even, faded away, faded away and into nothing then they looked out and around at where they were. They couldn't quite place it, couldn't quite figure out what had happened, but then they looked in front of them again, and they saw, and that's also when they knew.

They had been summoned.

Finally.

They stood and faced God, there in front of them.

He looked different to each of them.

But he also was the same.

And so were his words, when he spoke, and so was what he told them.

He spoke of the past, and of Creation, and he also spoke of the future, and of the World. And he'd come, he told them, to address what Gabriel had just asked:

What do we do now?

So he gave them his answer.

He told them how Michael with his truth would preside over the Angels of Presence, those angels that would remain closest to God and to Heaven and so would have the most power in their proximity to him and the light; Gabriel with his strength would preside over the Angels of Sanctification, and they would be of the second highest order, and they would reside between Heaven and the World as intermediaries between God and his humans as Gabriel had already done during his time on the peaks of

Aetlas watching over Creation and Heaven both; Raphael with his gifts of compassion and healing would preside over the Angels of Nature, those who would be responsible for all the plants and animals that were already there in the World, and those that would still come, too; and there was one more who had been summoned and stood in front of God, also, and heard his word, and it was me. You might be wondering who I am, as we spoke of in the beginning, and before the great Battles of Creation I was called something else entirely, something that's ancient and forgotten now, but after I stood with my brothers and looked upon him and received his glory, I was then called Phanuel—"the face of God"—and he'd seen how I'd fought in Creation, he told me, and he'd also seen how I'd loved the humans he'd made and so he created a fourth class of angels, the Angels of Guardian, and I would be charged to rule over those angels and protect the humans that were already in the World and also all those that were still yet to come.

So we all heard his word, together, then knew that it would be.

Once he'd told us each what we'd be and we'd received his knowledge, then everything faded again and we were back on the walls above the palace. We all looked at each other, finally knowing what our futures would be; finally knowing and seeing how the battle between dark and light, above and below, would continue, on and on and on, not ever stopping, not ever being won or lost, just fought.

It would be our eternity, as I've said.

But it was also, we then knew, why we'd been made.

"Let's go," Michael finally said, as God's presence faded from around us.

"Where?" Gabriel asked.

Michael smiled, feeling something come from Creation.

"To bear witness," he said. "Because it's almost time now."

Then he spread his wings and flew into the sky above and we followed after him. We followed him through the clouds and down towards the great mountains of Aetlas, where we landed again, all four of us, then together we looked below towards where the first rays of light broke over the jagged peaks in the distance, and shone down on Creation, one last time.

$$25$$

$\mathcal{S}$HE WOKE FROM HER DREAM and the darkness with a great start.

And as she woke, she looked up to see her husband standing over her, with concern in his eyes and a great many questions in them, too, but she just shook her head, anticipating his questions.

"I'm alright," she told him.

"What was it?" he asked, keeping his voice soft and low so their sons wouldn't hear.

She waited for a moment as she turned and looked over to where they each were just rising. She looked over to where they were each just getting up from their beds then getting dressed, getting themselves ready for the long and uncertain journey that was now ahead, and that they knew they were all now about to face. Then she thought about her family, all of them, together, and she thought again about her dream that wasn't a dream, she knew, and all she'd learned within it.

She kept looking at them, both of them, her sons.

Her eyes lingered on Kain and how he helped Habel get everything ready, how he helped his little brother.

She watched them, for one more moment, then put her hand to her stomach.

She couldn't feel anything that was there, at least not yet, but she'd been with her husband again the previous night—they'd been together, by the river, one last time—and she knew then what that would cause and what would come because of it. She knew there would be another son they would all soon be blessed with, as Michael had told her, and she knew then when and how he'd been conceived and that he was already growing inside her.

She thought about it all and how it had happened, then found that she was glad: she was glad their child had been made in Creation, even if once he was born, he wouldn't be born there in Creation, and would be a child of the World.

No, not a child of the World, she thought, remembering Michael's words.

The Father of the World.

The Father of All Else That Would Come.

"Nothing," she finally told her husband, in answer to his question, then smiled to reassure him her words were truth. "Nothing at all."

"Are you sure?" he asked, still next to her and looking at her hand and where it was placed. "Was it like before?"

She paused for a moment, thinking about that, then smiled again.

"No," she told him, and touched his hand with her own to make sure he felt what she felt, and he did.

Then she finally rose.

They began to make their last preparations.

They gathered as much food as they could—fruit and nuts and everything else they'd been saving—and she loaded it all onto the wooden boat she'd built with her husband and two sons. She'd also knit each of them a fresh tunic she'd bring, and she watched as her husband returned from the forest and field and carried with him the tools he'd created— the saw, as he'd called it—and the others he'd made before the saw, too, to help plow and turn the soil of the earth and that they would bring from Creation and into the World.

They pushed the boat together, as a family.

It was a difficult task and it took the combined strength of all four of them, but they moved it from where they'd built it, and pushed it across the grass and to the bank of the river then finally down into the water where it made a large splash when it entered. They were all about to climb into the river and up the ladder on the side onto the deck, where they'd be on the boat as it sailed, but then she stopped them.

"What is it?" her husband asked again.

"Look," she told them, and turned from the boat and the river to look at all that was behind them, all they were leaving. There was the clearing, and the fields, and the orchards, and their shelter. There was the Tree of Knowledge, and there was the Tree of Life. There was the great forest and the river flowing through it and the field with the wildflowers and dandelions beyond, she knew, and the mountains north of the field, with the waterfall and the pool that was their pool.

"It was our home," Habel said softly.

"You haven't asked me about it," she said to them, without taking her eyes from Creation.

"Asked you about what?" Kain asked.

"The fruit," she said. "And why I ate it."

"It's not your fault," her husband said quickly.

"But it's still why we're being banished from here, because of what I did. Because I ate the fruit."

"Mom . . ." Kain started, but she cut him off.

"No, it's alright," she told him. "I want to tell you what the dark angel told me, while we're still here, in Creation, because I've seen what lies beyond, too, in the World: he told me that this was Paradise, and if I ate the fruit then we would be cast out from Paradise. But that's not why I did it. I ate the fruit because I love you—*all of you*—more than anything else in Creation or the World or Heaven or Below. But this place where we've lived isn't what he said it was, and that's what I need you to remember. This isn't Paradise. And only one who knows nothing of love could ever think that, because Paradise is what's inside of us. It's the love we each feel for each other, and we've been cast out of Creation, but no matter where we go, no matter where this boat takes us, however far and however wide and however distant a place . . . as long as we're together, then we'll bring Paradise with us," she said, then finally turned from Creation and back to look at them. "Do you understand?" she asked.

They were silent for a moment, as tears came to their eyes, then Habel walked forward and hugged her before her husband did, too, then Kain, and they were all together, holding each other, the boat bobbing on the current in the river behind them.

They stayed like that for a moment, then she nodded.

"Alright," she told them. "It's time."

So they all then went to the river.

They all went together, all of them except her.

She watched as Kain went to the boat first, and helped Habel up onto the ladder, and she watched them together as they climbed and soon they were both up and onto the deck, and her husband went, too. He got to the ladder, but then before he climbed, he turned around to see she was still there on the bank.

"Are you coming?" he asked her.

"I'm going to go back, one more time, to make sure we didn't forget anything," she told him, and he nodded.

She left the river and walked back up towards the clearing.

She went slowly, knowing it was the last time she was going to be able to do so, then when she finally got there, she went to the house, first, and went inside and looked around at everything; she looked first at the bed he'd carved for them, the one they'd shared so many nights in together. Then she looked at the beds of each of her children, and the crib that was against the wall, waiting for another child to fill it that would not come and bless them there in Creation, but rather somewhere else, then she went past the crib and to the table. She thought back to all the meals they'd shared there together—first just two of them, then with one son, who had joined them, and then another—and she thought about how more than anywhere else, that's where they'd become a family. She paused for a moment, seeing it all again, feeling it all again, and as she did, she thought back to their beginning and remembered something else, something she'd almost forgotten.

She turned and went back to the bed she'd shared with her husband.

She stood there and looked down at it, then gently pushed it aside.

She bent down next to where it had been and saw there were marks there on the floor where dust had gathered and where the wood of the bed had worn against the wood of the floor. Then she saw that what she was looking for was still there, too. She saw the small hole that was still in the floor, the hole she'd made, and she reached into it and found the flower she'd put there so long ago. She took it from the place where it had rested through so much, through everything, and when she did, she brought it closer to her and looked at it. It was still pressed flat, and while it had aged, it was still very clearly what it was and as she looked at it, she felt it, too, which is to say she felt again all the same things she'd felt when she'd originally come and put the flower there, what she'd felt in those first moments of their true union, those very first moments of discovery, after he'd given it to her.

She thought of it all again, with great longing, as she looked at the flower.

Then the longing passed.

She looked at the flower for one more moment, then tucked it into her pocket, and stood again. She turned from the place where she'd knelt and she left the bed in the place where she'd moved it to, and where it would stay.

Then she began to walk.

She left the house and went outside.

She went through the orchard and then the fields, and saw the crops that they'd planted in both places still growing on either side of her. She looked at the forest, in the distance, one last time, then kept walking and went to where the two great trees stood. She stood in their shadows and looked up at the first one, the Tree of Knowledge, which once had fruit on its great branches that was bright and shining, but in the last few days, the leaves had begun to change color and the fruit had started to wither and fall to the ground, and decompose, returning again to the soil.

She saw all of that, then she turned to the second tree.

The Tree of Life.

The fruit that was on its branches had remained there, she saw, and she also saw the fruit had remained ripe and un-spoilt. The branches were closer to her than the branches of the taller Tree of Knowledge next to it; they were closer to the ground, easier to reach out and touch, easier to take its fruit and she stood there and looked at it. She looked at the fruit for a long time, hanging in front of her, and she thought back to her sons. She thought back again to what she'd felt, and she thought of the glimpses of what she'd seen, both in her own mind, and when she'd been with Michael, and she thought of the bright angel, too, and what he'd told her of the future, what he'd *shown* her of it, also, and what she would do. She thought of all that, as she stood there, then she thought of something else.

She thought of Destiny and God and Faith.

And that was it, she knew, that was what it would be.

It would be Faith.

Then with no more thoughts she put her hands in her pockets and felt the pressed flower that was there and without taking the fruit that was above and without a second glance or look behind her she turned and then went back down, back down towards where she knew they all stood and waited for her, back down towards the river and the boat and all that would then soon lay away and beyond.

Epilogue

T**HEY SAILED TOGETHER** for many days and nights, even after they'd gone past the mountains and left Creation. I watched them from my place on the peaks of Aetlas as they left the clearing and sailed down the river, towards the mountains in the south she'd seen so many years ago, and I also watched as they went through the narrow and dangerous rapids between the peaks that tossed their boat about in the great current, tossed it this way and that, and they lost much of their food in the swells that washed across the deck.

But they still continued.

I watched as they made it through the rapids, and between the mountains, and eventually came out on the other side.

Outside of Creation, finally.

Outside of Creation, and into the World.

Michael and Gabriel and Raphael had been with me until that point, also watching the beginning of the human's journey, but that's when they left to go back to Heaven and divide and recruit the other angels there into each of the new orders God had created, and to show them how to take their new places and start going about their new duties.

But I remained.

I watched as the humans passed through and on to the other side of the mountains, then I watched as they sailed further and further away from the mountains, and Creation, and everything they'd ever known. I watched as they kept sailing, looking for the exact right spot to begin again, and I still watched as they eventually found the new place they would make their own and when they saw it they ran their boat against the bank of the river and got out. They jumped over the side and splashed to the shore together and what they'd found was another clearing, on the banks of another river, and with a great forest next to it, not unlike all they'd just left.

This would be the place, I heard her say to the others, remembering.

Then I saw them nod because they knew it would be, too.

And so did I.

I watched as they unloaded their tools and weapons, and I watched as her husband began to build a new house for them, in the same way he'd built the previous one, while her oldest began to plough new fields and plant a new orchard. Kain chose the place where the fields and orchards would be planted very carefully, and without the supervision of his father, then when he'd chosen where they would be, he used the tools his father had made to start turning the dirt, as he knew how. But he found it was harder to turn the dirt there in the World than it had been in Creation, and it was harder for crops to grow, too. There were seasons, they soon discovered. There was frost, and snow. There was blight, disease, and famine. There was rain when they didn't want it, and none when they did.

And as Kain worked in his fields, and his father worked on their house, I watched her, too, and what she did.

She began by going out into the World, just as she'd done in Creation, and the first time she went, she went alone. She searched then found a spot that felt like it would be ancient and sacred, and in that spot, she bent down and with her hands moved some of the dirt that was there and created a small hole. Then she took the pressed flower she carried with her in her pocket—the flower she'd been given, and had been with her ever since her very first days in Creation—and she kissed it once, one last time, just the same as she had the first and as she kissed it, she bowed her head and softly whispered as she planted the flower and since the flower was love, as she planted it, she asked that as the tree that would come from it grew, that with every bit of new growth that would come so too would the prayer and words with which she'd planted it also grow.

She waited there, in the forest, for one more moment.

She looked down at the spot and the turned earth.

Then she started to walk again and went back to her family and that was the only time she left their clearing alone, in those first days; every other time she ventured away, she went with Habel at her side, and when they went from their new clearing into the World together, it was to forage and search for food to sustain them while Kain and her husband stayed behind to build and plant. At first, Habel stayed by her side and went everywhere with her, both of them together, but then they started to split up to cover more ground because it was harder to find fruit out there in the World, harder to find berries, harder to find nuts and flowers and vegetables and anything else that was edible.

Then after some months, her belly started to swell.

With each passing day it became harder and harder for her to walk, and she'd learned from her previous two births that she should stay closer to the clearing as the moment became more and more imminent, the further along that she got.

And so Habel started to go out alone.

His work of gathering took longer, there in the World, and it took longer for his brother in the fields, too. They all experienced sickness, fatigue, bouts of ill health. Her skin started to get leathery from the elements and sag, and so did his, and the hair on each of them began to show its first traces of grey. The house that her husband worked on eventually rose and was complete, then when it was, he joined Kain in the fields, joined with his oldest son in the tilling and planting and growing, and Habel kept foraging as she knit a blanket for the one that would soon arrive.

They would eat together in the evenings at a new table he'd carved, this time with the help of his oldest son, and as they sat there together and ate, she would think back to her first moments in Creation and the questions she'd first wondered when she was there.

Who are we?

Why are we here?

And what's our purpose?

As she thought of those questions again, she would smile, because it was so clear then, as she looked back at them—at her family, all around her, as they laughed, smiled, told stories—and she wondered how she could have ever once not known.

I watched all this, then I watched as it all changed, too.

After they'd come to the World, Kain had begun to wander from their house at night again. She knew what he was looking for, and so did I, but that's not how he found it. Instead, it happened on an ordinary day like any other, an ordinary day while he was working in the fields and then she simply just appeared and came from the forest. She came from the trees and walked towards him, fully formed and beautiful and seemingly the exact same age as he was, and he dropped his tools as he saw her there, standing, staring, looking back at him. Then Habel, who had grown, too, came back from his foraging and she turned and looked at him, and when I saw that look—that very first look between them—that would be it, I knew.

That would be the future.

I knew she'd seen pieces before, during her time in Creation, and with Michael, then she saw the whole. She heard her sons ask how this could possibly be, when this stranger came, so she told them again the story of how she'd been made, her and their father—how they'd both been born of nothing, and how their life had come from earth, and from light, and from God—and so if there were two of them who had been made in such a way, then why couldn't there be another?

But that was in Creation, I heard her sons say.

Yes, she nodded to them, *but there's still magic here in the World, too, and there's still God, and light.*

They knew that she knew of God, and of light.

So they accepted that and went back to their work.

Her belly continued to grow and grow, then her third son eventually came and after he was birthed and they were all there together, that's when she heard the wind come again and bring the child's name to her—*Seth*, the wind said, *this is Seth, the Father of all those that will come, the Father of all those that will endure*—and then just as quickly as the wind had come, it was gone again, and all that was left was them. She looked up from her birthing bed as her husband held their new child first, then her eyes turned and went to her. Not to her new son that had just been birthed, no, but to *her*: the new human that was now amongst them and that they'd taken in and she saw the way Kain looked back at her, but she had no eyes for her oldest son; she only had eyes for their middle child now, for her Habel, for the son that was her and not his father or his brothers or anyone else.

I watched as she felt Kain's thoughts, as he broke and hurt and wondered how God could have heard his prayers, heard everything he'd ever wanted or desired, then given it to his brother.

I watched as she felt all of this . . .

And I watched as she did nothing.

As I told you in the beginning, I'm here to tell you a story, and it's her story I'm here to tell.

And so this is where I'll end.

There are many who have lied about what happened, in Creation, during their first hours, and there are many that have lied about what happened after, too, when she brought her family into the World. Many will question why she chose what she chose, and why she did what she did—especially after what she saw of the future, and what she saw of her children—but such was the depth of her faith; such was the depth of what she'd learned in Creation, and the strength of that great gift she'd been given and brought from where it had been born and into the World. But those that lie won't care. They won't care it was her that gave them that gift. They'll have no time for faith or Creation or truth.

They won't care about any of those things, because they won't be able to quiet their minds and turn inwards and let their soul speak to them. They won't be able to sit in a field of dandelions and wild flowers and see in front of them the very face and nature of God, and so their lies will continue, on and on, because the lies will help them gain in some mortal and temporary way, though it will also keep them on a path towards a gathering darkness they won't even realize.

But really, such lies only do one thing.

They push us further from God, and from light, because eventually . . . there will be truth.

There will always be truth.

I was there, so I know all this, all that I've now told.

I watched over them in their first hours—her, and him, and Kain, and Habel, and Seth, too—and I watch over all those that have come from them, also, all those that have come after in so many different and unique and beautiful ways and are still here in this world: the ones that still fight, that still love, that still work, that still struggle, that still make homes, that still have families, and still carry Paradise within them, wherever they go. I was there with the first of them then, in the beginning, and I'm here with you now, too. And I always will be. So if you're lost, if you need help, if you need someone to come and walk beside you as you search for faith and order, as you look again for the path we all walk and sometimes stray from when darkness comes and is too much and clouds the way, then all you have to do is ask.

That's what you need to remember.

Look inside, look inside, and look for the light, because that's where I am . . . ready to guide, fight, protect, ready, always ready.

On and on.

Forever and ever.

Until there's nothing more, and it's all one.

Until there's nothing more, and it's all Light.